PRAISE FOR
THE SINS OF SUMMER DAUGHTERS

"*The Sins of Summer Daughters*, Lo Patrick's latest moody, propulsive mystery, will keep readers guessing and turning pages until the final shocking scene. A grisly murder in present-day Georgia causes narrator Meg Gregory to reckon with long-buried secrets from her own disturbing childhood in the 1970s. The story alternates between past and present, with Meg racing to protect those she loves most from ghosts—real or imagined—from the terrifying past."

—Lauren K. Denton, *USA Today* bestselling author of *The Hideaway* and *A Place to Land*

"A new Lo Patrick book is cause for celebration. In *The Sins of Summer Daughters*, four generations of women struggle with life in a small Southern town where the heat and lack of options are oppressive and snakes hide in the tall grass. Patrick's writing sparks with stunning observations and a flammable wit. I'm a huge fan."

—Joshua Moehling, *USA Today* bestselling author of *And There He Kept Her* and *A Long Time Gone*

"Joshilyn Jackson meets the Coen brothers in this searing, Southern, soul-cracking mystery. How a novel can be written with such gravity and humor at the same time is astounding and so rarely done well, but Patrick does it with the ease and grace of a Southern summer evening. *The Sins of Summer Daughters* is nothing short of a work of literary witchcraft."

—Emily Carpenter, author of Gothictown

PRAISE FOR *FAST BOYS AND PRETTY GIRLS*

"Past and present intermix in this riveting story that proves, no matter how much you might want it, you can't ever really leave your past behind. Lo Patrick does a masterful job setting the stage for the gripping suspense that had me turning the pages long into the night."

—Suzanne Redfearn, #1 Amazon
bestselling author of In an Instant

"*Fast Boys and Pretty Girls* is a haunting and atmospheric mystery with turns as sharp as a Georgia back road."

—Jennifer Moorhead, Amazon bestselling
author of Broken Bayou

"Lo Patrick's latest novel, *Fast Boys and Pretty Girls*, tackles the complex and emotional difficulties that often come with first love. Patrick's powerful writing makes this novel a standout, an absolutely riveting read."

—Donna Everhart, bestselling author
of When the Jessamine Grows

"*Fast Boys and Pretty Girls* is a character-driven mystery about the wounds of first love and the hunt for belonging. Lo Patrick is a compelling Southern storyteller, exploring the tension between obligation and desire."

—Audrey Ingram, author of *The Summer We Ran*

"Is there a woman alive who never, at least once, found herself obsessively drawn to a bad boy? Patrick's skillful writing will keep the reader turning the pages as Dani's past crashes head on into her present."

—Diane Chamberlain, *New York Times* bestselling author of *The Last House on the Street*

Praise for *The Night the River Wept*

"Haunting and unputdownable, *The Night the River Wept* is a gritty rendering of small-town tragedy and the far-reaching shadows it casts. Lo Patrick writes a stubbornly resilient heroine determined to untangle the secrets of a forgotten past and skillfully leads the reader along a twisty path to an unexpected yet satisfying ending!"

—Laura Barrow, author of *Call the Canaries Home*

"Lo Patrick introduces us to vivid characters populating an authentic small Georgia town, their lives tangled like kudzu vines. *The Night the River Wept* is an intriguing mystery that will have you turning pages until the wee hours of the morning."

—Beth Duke, bestselling author of *It All Comes Back to You*, *Tapestry*, and *Dark Enough to See the Stars*

"*The Night the River Wept* is a page-turning exploration of small-town secrets and the far-reaching effects of tragedy. With wit and wisdom, Lo Patrick weaves an unforgettable story of heartbreak, love, and second chances—and proves herself as a compelling new voice in Southern fiction."

—Kristy Woodson Harvey, *New York Times* bestselling author of *The Summer of Songbirds*

"This is a gripping portrayal of a small town where everyone has their secrets and the lines between guilty and innocent blur."

—Quinn Connor, author of *Cicadas Sing of Summer Graves*

"Smart, sassy, and utterly heartbreaking, this seductive Southern novel has to be my favorite mystery of the year. I rooted for Arlene as, struggling with her own loss, she becomes obsessed with the Broderick boys and their story. *The Night the River Wept* is a brave book that explores how difficult it can be to escape the past."

—Emily Critchley, author of *One Puzzling Afternoon*

"In *The Night the River Wept*, Arlene is a frustrated, lonely house-wife until she finds a job at the local police station bagging evidence. There she immerses herself in a decades-old murder, determined to solve the crime. Lo Patrick writes an original and moving tale brimming with mystery, heartache, and wit. Sure to be a Southern fiction favorite, Arlene's journey pulls the reader in and doesn't let go."

—Rochelle B. Weinstein, *USA Today* bestselling author
of *This Is Not How It Ends* and *What You Do to Me*

PRAISE FOR *THE FLOATING GIRLS*

"A compelling mystery… Kay is the smartest, funniest, most curious young narrator I have come across in some time. Her voice stuck with me long after I finished reading."

—Tiffany Quay Tyson, award-winning
author of *The Past Is Never*

"*The Floating Girls* is a powerhouse of a Southern novel… This lush and mesmerizing debut has a beating heart of its own. Lo Patrick is a standout new Southern voice."

—Andrea Bobotis, author of
The Last List of Miss Judith Kratt

"Fans of *Where the Crawdads Sing* will love this immersive mystery set against the salty air of Georgia's marshes. In Patrick's atmospheric prose, the water and its characters come to life."

—Lindsey Rogers Cook, author of
Learning to Speak Southern

"To read *The Floating Girls* is to feel a small-town slowness seep into your bones. The book's narrator, Kay Whitaker, is a stubborn young girl you'll never forget. A cracking story that unfolds in gorgeous prose in the stultifying heat of the American South."

—Hayley Scrivenor, author of
Dirt Creek

Also by Lo Patrick

The Floating Girls
The Night the River Wept
Fast Boys and Pretty Girls

the sins *of* summer daughters

a novel

LO PATRICK

For Mom and Dad

Published by Sourcebooks Landmark, an imprint of Sourcebooks
1935 Brookdale RD, Naperville, IL 60563-2773
(630) 961-3900
sourcebooks.com

Library of Congress Cataloging-in-Publication Data

Names: Patrick, Lo author
Title: The sins of summer daughters : a novel / Lo Patrick.
Description: Naperville, IL : Sourcebooks Landmark, [2026]
Identifiers: LCCN 2025052322 (print) | LCCN 2025052323
    (ebook) | trade paperback | ebook
Subjects: LCGFT: Detective and mystery fiction | Fiction | Novels
Classification: LCC PS3616.A8725 S56 2026 (print) | LCC PS3616.A8725 (ebook)
LC record available at https://lccn.loc.gov/2025052322
LC ebook record available at https://lccn.loc.gov/2025052323

Printed and bound in Canada.
MBP 10 9 8 7 6 5 4 3 2 1

1

2024

There were no knocks at the door with drawn faces, or somber police officers sitting on our couch with tea. It wouldn't have been my couch anyway; it would have belonged to Nina—my daughter. Instead, it was a woman at the grocery store who cornered me by the canned beans and asked if I'd heard about the murder.

"You hear about Josh McGill?" She leaned close to me in the manner of a falling domino.

I'd been going to get some garbanzos, but I pulled my hand back. "I know Josh." Josh was my granddaughter, Lucy's, boyfriend, though they hadn't been going together for all that long. It was a name I was just getting used to.

"Murdered," the woman said. I went limp, a thousand dormant vulnerabilities within me congratulating themselves on waiting it out; they finally had an opportunity to completely pull me under. I found I could hardly stand.

The woman watched me closely, clearly expecting me to say something. I thought I recognized her from the high school—Lucy's school and Nina's before her. I couldn't remember if she was a teacher or a parent or maybe even the PTA woman who went door-to-door with the wrapping-paper-sale flyer. Yes, it was her, the PTA woman—Darcy or Marcy, something like that.

"What?" I finally managed to say. "When did it happen?"

"Last night."

"That's awful," I answered vacantly, though I could only hear my voice out of one ear; the other was clogged with blood and bad memories. I'd been ambushed like this before; there is no preparing for it—the inconceivable. "Just awful."

"Police are at the house now."

"Right." I might have been trying to act like I'd already heard. This seemed like something I should know. I had not seen Lucy the night before. Nina had said she was spending the night with a friend—it was summer break, no school. June was my favorite month; I'd almost named Nina June. We talked every day, Nina and me. Lucy as well.

"How's Lucy holding up?" She continued to talk to me like we were old friends. I wanted to tell her that she didn't know me and that I'd never volunteered for the wrapping-paper sale. Not once.

"She's just fine," I said stupidly. "I mean…I haven't talked to her about it. I have to go." I pushed my cart forward. It rattled into the metal shelves. "I have to talk to Lucy," I said as I rushed past the shampoos and out into the parking lot.

"Lucy," I said to the fetid air bubbling off the hot asphalt of the parking lot. "I have to talk to Lucy."

My mind was filled with what little I knew of Josh McGill during the hurried drive back to the house—without my groceries, most of which I hadn't really needed. Going to the store was a way to pass the interminable time, restocking the peanut butter just something to do.

Josh was someone I had not previously spent a great deal of time considering. He was new, rather superfluous, I'd assumed. A rebound, as they call them. Lucy had had a boyfriend since the ninth grade named Daniel. I mostly liked Daniel, thinking him a harmless type of person with frizzy hair who doted on Lucy. They liked to laugh, although I could never really figure out at what, because neither of them had much of a personality. Lucy was a very nice girl but not very magnetic. I enjoyed that about her; she was quiet and careful, kind of a pale-yellow hue to her personality.

Daniel was much the same. They liked Chewy granola bars and Dave Matthews Band and throwing the Frisbee. There was a lot of giggling and hand-holding and suggesting different reruns to watch on television.

They were at my house a lot. Lucy said Nina didn't like them hanging around. Sometimes I thought Nina didn't like anything but her hand weights and her hair dryer; in retrospect, I think she was worried Lucy would make the same mistake she did and marry her high school sweetheart out of nothing more than reliance—a reliance she would come to loathe. And then, just like that, Lucy and Daniel broke up, and Josh entered the picture. He was far less likable than Daniel. Nina was relieved; she didn't see this lasting.

When I finally got home from the store, a journey that felt unfathomably stretched out by long traffic lights and slow-moving vehicles, I called Nina the instant I walked in the door. "What happened to Josh McGill?" I shouted into the phone.

"Stop shouting," she said in an urgent, frenzied way.

I waited. "Nina. What happened to Josh?" I was emphatic.

"Mom, I don't know. I really don't know."

"The wrapping-paper woman told me he got killed. Nina, she said he was murdered." I was talking as though this was somehow Nina's fault.

"I heard that too, but I don't know, Mom. Everyone is talking about it, but I don't know." She had that nervous click to her voice that she got when she didn't understand a question. "Lucy's been in her room all morning. I think someone told her, because she hasn't come out. I haven't talked to her yet."

"What do you mean, 'everyone'? What exactly did you hear? And you haven't talked to Lucy? Why haven't you talked to her?"

"Beverly. From next door. She said he was murdered." The word sizzled on her tongue. "I don't know what to believe. I want to let Lucy be for a while, I guess. I don't know if she knows or if she's sleeping or… I don't know anything. What am I supposed to say? 'Good morning, and hey, did Josh get murdered?'"

"Nina," I said. "You have to talk to her. She must be awake by now."

"Okay, okay." She said. "I'm just… I'm not sure what to do here." I could tell Nina was walking; I heard her feet on the floorboards and the swing of doors, then a faint knocking. "Lucy? Is everything okay?"

"Nina, open the door and ask her about Josh!" I was hissing; the receiver of the phone was damp.

"Honey…" Nina's voice was muffled. "Did you hear what happened to Josh?" Nina might have been talking about the neighbor's pet hamster. We really didn't know what had befallen us. There was really no way to know what was coming.

2

Meg Gregory. Margaret, if I'm honest, but Meg to anyone who's ever spoken to me. I came from a troubled family, dropped out of school, and have had bad knees my whole life; it's something with my hips and walking a little pigeon-toed. One doctor said my kneecaps were off alignment; he was dead certain of it, though he also admitted to being a heavy smoker. "Can't quit," he told me. "Hard to be a doctor now, with all we know about cigarettes. People won't listen to me." He seemed to feel he needed to apologize for my pain and his lack of trustworthiness as he staved off the emphysema. My knees ached and ached, but still I pressed on; bad knees and unruly gas were my cross to bear—that, and the troubled childhood and lack of education.

"You're not that old," Nina would say when I complained of chronic bodily discomforts, things she couldn't begin to fathom at her age. She never told me I was uneducated though; that was a battle she did not choose.

I should never have named her Nina. It ruined her personality to be called that—she needed softening, not force. I found I couldn't say her name without pursing my lips. She was snappy and insistent, much like my face when addressing her. Nina overexercised and had a gaunt, sinewy look to her that only further suggested she was a rubber band about to snap. Meanwhile, I did everything slowly now. At sixty-four, I suddenly felt exhausted—by all of it.

Nina's father had only briefly been in the picture. Sometimes I barely remembered him, though that was just my defenses acting up. Ferrol. What an asshole. He was a music industry executive who talked loudly on the phone and wore laminated backstage credentials to concerts for a living. But I'd been so certain of him, my love nonsensical. I even thought that when Nina came along, he would discover that he felt the same way about me. Oh well, it was a long time ago. He went and had another family; I have stayed alone.

We both live in Tuskin, Georgia, now, Nina and me. She's here but very busy trying to stay thin and pulling her hair with a barrel brush. She's divorced and very strident that it's the best thing that ever happened to her—not the marriage but the way it ended, with cops standing outside her and Michael's house while he shuttled his belongings to his Dodge. I figured Nina was imitating me, though Ferrol and I never did the whole screaming-with-police thing. It was rather a quiet unraveling of the crusted knot that had been holding us together. Nina had put on a show, their daughter, Lucy, watching on in horror. She was seven at the time.

Lucy has called me Tata since she's called me anything. "Meg" is hard for a toddler to pronounce, and I didn't want to be "Granny." I thought I was too young for all that; it would have been perfectly suitable, but I had designs on a longer youth—clingy and desperate. Now I wear suede to hide my gas and stumbling.

I hadn't told Lucy much about my life—my family, quitting school and running away from Tuskin, him, *her*. None of it. Nina either. I certainly didn't tell Ferrol, though I tried the hardest with him—to explain myself, my history, my nuances and hang-ups, their causes and repercussions. I thought maybe he would understand; this chain-smoking, hubris-drenched megalomaniac from San Francisco could surely appreciate a good story. But he'd always look at me funny when I explained what happened.

"That doesn't sound smart," he'd say, as if I was asking for his approval.

It was a few days after the wrapping-paper lady dropped the news of Josh's death at the grocery store. It was a well-known fact now in Tuskin that he had been killed—murdered—though details were sparse as to what exactly happened.

Conjecture about the murder spread like wildfire, but none of the rumors had been substantiated; the only thing we'd heard for certain was that Josh was indeed dead and where the memorial service would take place. Lucy begged to go. I couldn't decide if I thought that was an odd reaction. I'd been treading carefully around her, never knowing quite what to say. She was not herself, but of course she had a good reason for that.

The funeral was on a Tuesday. Everyone inside was wearing lacy black dresses. The room was filled with pale women in red lipstick, completely wiped of color save their mouths, where the agony and the oxygen came in and out. There was sniffling and an occasional gasp. He was so young. The fathers were there too, standing at odd angles, trying to deflect the blame for this lapse in safeguarding.

Josh's mother had long blond hair with sharp bangs. She was more hopeful than hysterical. She must have thought that he would return if she was just buoyant enough, that perhaps if she were wailing and gnashing, he'd think to hell with it and stay put. I watched her closely, wondering what kind of person she was and what kind of person she would become after Josh's death. Everyone was shaken—a teenager murdered in Tuskin. But it was something familiar for me, something long settled in my blood, like a small pebble in a stream, set to get caught in my heart and kill me with its puny blockage. It had been there for decades.

I watched Lucy as mourners moved to and fro, finding seats and avoiding the closed box containing sixteen-year-old remains, as if that is old enough for anything to remain. She was solemn, dignified, almost calculating in her plaid skirt and white blouse. I told myself she was holding it together for the sake of Josh's family. She caught me watching her and put her finger to her right eye, as if wiping a tear. Her cheeks were dry. It's the shock, I told myself. Always the shock. She doesn't know she's not crying.

A large photograph of Josh smiling in a polo shirt was propped up on an easel by the door. There was a guest book on an abutting table surrounded by floral arrangements. I looked at the picture, deciding that when young people die, all the photos of them while they were alive are suddenly sad. It was like they knew what was going to happen to them.

I had liked Josh immediately when I met him, even though he wouldn't look me in the eye when he spoke to me. It was in the same sort of way I'd liked Ferrol; I'd seen him as a gateway to something more interesting. Women like me often confuse bad behavior with excitement. It's not a cloak I wear proudly, this movement toward the fire. It was also not a personality trait I associated with Lucy. Josh had a swagger, a fast car, a knowing way about him, and a maturity that unsettled me. I didn't look at Josh head-on either. He kept his gaze averted, just a little to the left, while mine was slightly down.

Then he was gone. Now he was gone. And I remained. Haunted.

After the funeral, everything changed. I'd called Ferrol to tell him what happened, thinking he would be worried about Lucy. That he *should* be worried about Lucy. To tell him that *I* was worried about Lucy. He didn't answer. I left him a message in which I explained that Lucy's boyfriend, Josh, had been killed, that the police thought it was a homicide and were investigating it as such, and that Lucy was in a terrible state. I said that after the funeral, they questioned her for the first time. And then again. That the detective had seemed a little too focused on her. "He was watching her, Ferrol," I told his voicemail. "Wouldn't take his eyes off her at the memorial service." I didn't mention Lucy pretending to cry.

And she did appear to be of interest—I wasn't imagining that. There was suddenly a mist about her that would not clear. I'd never had this sensation with Lucy. It was an entirely new feeling to think there was something about her I did not understand.

"The kid with the sister?" Ferrol asked when he called me back two days after the funeral—he was on an at-least-forty-eight-hours response time when it came to anyone but himself.

"I don't know if Josh has a sister," I said.

"That's too bad," Ferrol said.

"It's awful, Ferrol." I was very uneasy, as it seemed to me the police were inordinately interested in Lucy. I couldn't make sense of how many times they'd already questioned her. Nina kept calling to say that the detective had come to the house again.

"The police showed up here," she'd say.

"Again?"

"Yes. They ask to speak to Lucy. They act like she's…I don't know, a troublemaker or something."

"Are you supervising their conversations?" I'd asked her.

"Should I be?"

"Nina. Yes."

I'd also asked Nina if Lucy had an alibi. Nina only said, "Does she need one, Mom? Stop talking like a TV show." Nina just didn't know. It was my fault; I'd never told her how bad things can get.

Josh's case was still on the front page of the local paper, the primary subject of every news broadcast and the water that turns the rumor mill. Though the talk of it had changed from disbelief to fearful conjecture: Who was next? What demons had we failed to restrain? Nina said that she was scared to be alone in the house and that several neighbors were doing a watch where they walked the streets in pairs all hours of the night, looking for misfits and marauders. She spoke of this as though none of it had anything to do with Lucy. I'll admit I did a good bit of peeking through the curtains in the evening, but I was more concerned with what I was hearing about the police and Lucy than I was about being attacked in my own home. No one would come for me; I had been irrelevant for years. And anyway, Josh was killed in his car.

The lead detective was a young man named Adam. He had come to the funeral; his presence there had been stifling. I felt watched and assessed while grieving someone I barely knew. I had also noticed him watching and assessing Lucy. His glance grazed several of the other mourners, but I caught him looking at her more often than the rest.

The town had been in a quiet flurry, like watching a tornado form from a distant location. It was terrible, but what happened? No one knew, and the young detective was this kind of elusive character who hadn't been in Tuskin long and who had a very innocent face that didn't speak of wisdom, experience, or even puberty in some light.

"So this kid died in Tuskin?" Ferrol asked.

"Yes. So Lucy is very upset," I repeated. I couldn't tell if he was clear on what was going on. "He was murdered, Ferrol."

"Well, do you want me to come out there?" he asked like I was requesting he shine my shoes with a toothbrush. "Was this guy that important?"

"Stop sounding so apathetic," I said. "And it's not 'out there.' We're not even two hours away. Lucy's very concerned, is all. I don't know what you should do. There's a detective kid who's talked to her a few times already. I don't love that. Has Nina not called you?"

"She called last night, but she didn't say anything about Lucy talking to the police. I mean—that's not totally weird if she was this kid's girlfriend, but if it keeps happening…I don't know."

I shook my head. Nina kept Ferrol on the periphery of life—to a fault. She admired him, his success and gravitas. She felt silly living in Tuskin because of it. Silly and common and very unlike him. It was for this reason that she was always sparse on details when talking to him. Leave it to Nina to think a homicide was an extravagance Ferrol didn't have time to acknowledge. I could hear gurgling noises in the background—that, and the sound of a woman singing something about wheat. It had to be his wife, Martha. She didn't look like a Martha. She looked like a Bobbi, very specifically with an *i*.

"I guess I'm assuming this was a drugs thing," I said loudly. "But the police keep talking to Lucy, and she's not a part of that crowd." Most of the crime in Tuskin centered on drugs and stealing NyQuil to make labs in bathtubs—that sort of thing. It was dangerous, but we were usually about to shrug something off by saying, "Well, meth'll do that to you."

"That you know of," Ferrol said.

"No, she's not."

"I don't really know what you want me to do, Meg. I know some good lawyers, but they're all industry people. I can ask around though."

It was always Ferrol's answer to make some calls. And he didn't do it; his assistant did. A man-child named Argus who had to be at least fifty but dressed as though he'd asked his parents' permission to ride his BMX at the skate park.

"Fine. I don't know," I said angrily. "Yes, get her a lawyer. I haven't even… Well, why would she need a lawyer?"

"I don't know. I just think it's always good to lawyer up, and you're telling me she's talking to the police. You can't talk to the police without a lawyer. Ever."

"She's not the one… Well, I don't really know what they think happened. They found him in his car."

"How'd he die?"

"Someone slit his throat." Even saying it made me wince. And anyway, I wasn't sure that was true. It was the rumor. I kept asking myself if it had to be his throat, again with the familiarity.

"Goddamn."

"Yes. Goddamn is right."

"What does Lucy say?"

"She hasn't said much." The way that came out had me wincing further, more puckered and squeezed. Because it was true. I thought Lucy was acting strange, and not the appropriate kind of strange. "She's upset," I said, correcting myself. "Very upset. Hasn't been back to school, lots of staring off into the distance. I don't know— they weren't together for very long. It's not like this is Daniel...the one with the sisters. I can't tell what she's thinking."

"This was a different boyfriend though? Not the little clingy guy—Jordy? Or...what was his name?"

"Jordy? His name was Daniel, Ferrol." And he was small and clingy—there was no way around that; at least Ferrol had that one right. "Daniel's been out of the picture for a while." That wasn't true. It had been only about six months.

"Well, it's okay," Ferrol said. His attention was clearly focused elsewhere.

"It's horrible, is what it is."

Ferrol and I got off the phone as we usually did, in a kind of huffing, exacerbated way. He was not particularly annoyed with me, but rather was reacting to how frustrated I was with him—always.

The phone rang almost immediately after I'd replaced it in its aging cradle. "Yes," I said into the receiver.

"It's Nina."

"Oh, thank God," I said. "I was just about to call you."

"So, Mom…Lucy's at the police station." She sounded confused, as though the preposterousness of all this was just now dawning on her.

"She is? Shouldn't you be with her?" I stood up from the table.

"Should I?"

"She's fifteen, Nina."

"They told me they were getting her a lawyer."

"What?" I slammed my hand on the table. "I was just on the phone with your dad. Nina—he can get her a lawyer. You need to tell him what's going on!"

"Oh." She sounded disappointed. "I was hoping to keep him out of this."

"Why? He might know a good defense attorney. Lord knows, with the crowd he runs in…"

"Can you call him back for me?"

"Yes!" I was shouting. "But you need to get over to the police station, Nina. Now!"

"Okay! Okay. I didn't know that I should… Whatever. I'll meet you there."

I high-tailed it to the garage, where my ancient Mercedes sat. It was a relic from the days when I thought I needed to drive a

Mercedes. Ferrol liked his wife to have a nice car, and I sort of collected that from him. I collapsed into the front seat, finding the fit of my pants a hindrance. It was June, but late spring was hanging on like grim death, a mercurial time in middle Georgia, a period of enduring terrible allergies and tying sweatshirts around your waist by noon to cover the back sweat.

It was *him* who I thought of on the way to the station—my car serving as a waiting room for all my ruminations. Not Josh. Not Lucy. Him. Tyler. My poor Tyler. I usually kept him out of my head with half a dozen deadbolts, but goddamn, he could pick a lock, couldn't he? Whenever there was an errant sadness, mine or someone else's, I would see Tyler as though he were standing next to me, reminding me of all that had become of us. I noticed I was frowning. I frowned the most deeply when I thought of that time. Sometimes I really couldn't get my head out of the past. I lingered there, among the breezes and crackling of my history. I was watching myself from the other side of the hour.

3

Lucy was in a holding cell when I got there, bars and everything. "What the hell?" I said upon seeing her. I'd walked straight to the back of the station, and there she was, like some prime rib on display at the meat counter.

"Can I help you?" It was the detective. Adam Rinaldi. He was suddenly in front of me, reminding me of someone. His face was serene, almost lost or intentionally clouded. I could tell he didn't know what to do, about any of it. He was as bothered as I was. It had been a long time since I'd thought someone could understand me. I turned away, uncomfortable with the presumptions I was making.

"I'm Meg Gregory. I'm Lucy's grandmother."

"I'm not sure who let you back here, but this area is off-limits." He stared at me in the same way he had stared at me before, at the funeral, as though I was familiar but he wasn't sure what to make of that.

"What's she doing in there?" I pointed at Lucy, who had clearly been crying. "Is this about Josh?"

He dipped his head. "Miss…I'm sorry I didn't catch your name, but can you please…"

"Gregory," I said, thinking that he knew exactly who I was. "Why is she here?" I turned to face where I'd come in. No one had tried to stop me. When you reach a certain age, you start projecting utter harmlessness. I'd stolen a candy bar from the grocery store not three weeks earlier just to see if I could get away with it. No one was even looking at me when I shoved the Butterfinger in my coat pocket. I felt bad about it later and went and taped a one-dollar bill to the sliding glass door after the store was closed. I could see I got picked up on camera, so I stuck my tongue out. Sometimes I really don't know what I'm doing anymore.

"We have information that your daughter was at the victim's house the night of his death."

"Nina?" I turned around, my long, unnecessary sweater swirling behind me like a paper airplane.

"Oh, sorry. Your granddaughter."

"Since when do you have this 'information'?" I asked, imitating the way he'd said it. "Does information just appear out of thin air? How did you get the *'information'*?" I could tell that I was out of control. I had to bite my tongue to keep from continuing to mock him.

"We have a witness who says she was she was at the McGills' house."

"Josh was her boyfriend. Would it have been so strange for her to be at his house?"

"Well." He paused. "I'm not at liberty to disclose more information at this time, but please…" He motioned to the front of the station again.

"She should have a lawyer with her," I said.

"She does not need a lawyer present today. We are only asking her some questions."

"That's how it starts, my friend," I said. "And you know it."

He frowned but said nothing. I couldn't place this feeling of having swum in the same small pond, the same dirt under our nails, the same mud in our underwear. He was too young to know. I would have to keep telling myself that.

I finally moved in the direction of the lobby and took a seat in one of the plastic chairs at the front of the station. I was alone there, alone and fidgeting. I'd gotten up several times to see if Lucy was still in the cell—she was. I'd used the bathroom, mostly out of boredom, and then sat back down, trying to get a glimpse around the corner and into the back area, hoping to catch sight of Lucy.

Just when I thought I wouldn't be able to adjust myself on the chair even one more time, a young woman came through the door in a high-end-looking navy suit. She glanced at me and, finding me superfluous, continued walking.

I stood up. "Excuse me," I said.

She turned. "Yes. Are you Lucy DeWitt's grandmother, by chance?"

"Meg Gregory," I said without extending my hand.

"I'm Deirdre Mansell. I'm a criminal defense attorney in Atlanta. My father is one of Ferrol Highfield's friends. He called me."

"Well, I won't hold that against you," I said. She smiled but didn't respond. "I'm not sure what's going on," I said to her silence. "Lucy's boyfriend was murdered. It's really awful, but I barely knew the kid, so I suppose…right now my concern is that they've pulled Lucy in for questioning and are holding her in this cell thing. I can't believe anyone would think she had something to do with this. My daughter, Nina should be here any minute. She'll be the one you want to talk to."

"Yes." Deirdre nodded. "I'm going to speak with the detective, but I do need to talk to Lucy first."

"I'll show you where she is. The detective told me to stay here and wait for a receptionist or something, but there's been no one here at all. Place is run like a discount shoe store." Deirdre had clearly never shopped in a discount shoe store. Her expression remained blank and almost pained. "I used to live in Atlanta too," I said as I walked her back to the holding cell. This was an entirely irrelevant detail, especially given the circumstances. I suppose I was trying to prove myself.

"Oh." Deirdre didn't care about Atlanta or me living there. It had been my one distinguishing characteristic in Tuskin. She used to live in Atlanta. She was married to this music guy. People didn't say it as much anymore.

"You got here quick," I said.

"I was told it was an emergency." She did not look at me.

I made like I was going to walk to the back with her, but Deirdre stopped me. "You shouldn't come with me," she said. "You're not her legal guardian, are you?"

"No, but Nina's… I know more about this kind of thing than Nina. That's my daughter."

"Yes, but the only person who'll be allowed back there is a legal guardian. I'd rather talk to Lucy alone anyway. At least at first."

I wasn't sure what she was saying…that I couldn't go with her or that she didn't want me to. "I've practically raised her," I said stupidly.

"Well…" She was dismissive. I realized that this Deirdre person thought Lucy had done something wrong. I shouldn't be claiming to have raised her, is what her expression implied.

"You don't think she killed her boyfriend, do you? She's like a little church mouse."

"No." She said nothing more. My discomfort was paralyzing.

I waited in the lobby for another hour. Nina showed up during that time; she said she'd called Ferrol before she left the house. We sat together in communal disbelief, saying very little. Apparently Ferrol had told Nina to keep quiet around the police and to let the attorney do the talking. She instructed me upon arrival. "Dad says mum's the word."

It had been an agonizing morning and brought back so many helpless memories. Finally, Deirdre came out of the back of the station, this time with Lucy. "We've talked," she said as Lucy stared at me and Nina a little defiantly. "They are not holding her, and I think it's best if we don't say anything more to the police. Not now." Deirdre held up an index finger. I assumed it was meant to silence me; I had opened my mouth to speak. I closed it while Nina sat next to me like an upright corpse.

I stood up, thinking that Lucy would approach me, throw herself into my arms, but she didn't. She hadn't even done that when we got the news about Josh. Or at the funeral. I remembered her pretending to wipe away tears. It had not been a convincing performance.

"Lucy, I would not go to school, nor would I talk to any of your friends," Deirdre said. They were clearly having a conversation that I was not a part of. "I would not use your phone or your computer."

"Why? She hasn't done anything wrong." I'd condensed my voice into a slippery whine.

Lucy looked at me and then at Deirdre. "Please, Tata," she said. It was all I could remember. *Please.*

4

It was just me and Mom for the longest time. We were on our own for two grades at least. I had an older sister, Rainy, but she was living with her boyfriend, Tripp, up in Cashiers, North Carolina. It sounded nicer than it was. They had to stay with his uncle, who was a trucker. He was gone all the time; that's why Rainy said they'd stay there. "Part-time roommate." She came to visit us in Tuskin every once in a while. Too much, said my mom. Rainy took food when she came, food and toilet paper. Rainy said she thought family was important; that's why she moved away with Tripp and only came around when she needed money and shit wipes.

It had almost always been just Mom. My daddy came and went for a while; when he came, he was real weepy and sorry about himself. Mom would take him back and let him give us money and good times, but then she'd throw him out again. I never really knew why he left or why he came back. My mom never let on whether she knew either, but she seemed just fine with not knowing. She was one of those people who think it's better to be in the dark. I wanted the lights on; I figured that out early.

Then Lon moved in with us when I was thirteen. He was my mother's boyfriend. Lonnie was his real name, but he didn't like that. "S'a girl's name," he told me. I wasn't afraid of him even though he acted like the kind of person you ought to be afraid of, real quiet and sullen and pissed off. My dad tried to come back a couple of times when Lon was there. Lon would go out to the front of the house and stand like a bulldog by the front door with his shoulders all hunched. My mother would pretend she didn't know what was going on and get the mayonnaise out of the refrigerator or pretend she had to wipe something off the table. "What's this mess?" she'd ask, as if the dishcloth was the most important thing in the world. I'd go to the window and watch. All they did was stare at each other. No one knew what to say; it wasn't a thing worth fighting over, not this life.

I was only eleven the first time I ran away. I told the guy who picked me up that I was going to Cashiers. "You're goin' wherever I'm takin' ya," he said. He was drinking a Bud right there in the car. I stayed with him for seventy miles—believe you me, I watched the ticker. Georgia's long, though, so I didn't make it out of the state. He got pulled over for speeding, and the do-gooder cop asked who the hell I was.

"I'm the hell Meg," I said. The officer squinted, and by the afternoon I was home again. My mom wasn't mad, but she made me read about perverts and how they abduct young girls. We went to the library, and she pulled out the *P* encyclopedia and made me sit. I didn't care. I liked to practice reading even if it was about bad stuff. That was the only time she ever took me to the library.

It was different then. Kids were always out walking around on their own and standing next to highways. We were from Tuskin in the middle of Georgia, not a sight to see, but a place anyway. I remember Rainy saying, before she actually did it, that she was going to move to the mountains so she couldn't see straight anymore. "I don't want to be able to see for miles." My mom said she was a doper now. Tripp was a doper all along.

"He came outa the hatch smokin' reefer," my mom told her friend Johnna Martin. They both laughed. Johnna was around all the time, trying to get my mother's life right for her. She worked at Burger Heaven and had to take the stand when someone died of food poisoning. She was a straight talker.

Johnna gave me a few lectures about running away and all the dangers in it; she'd tried not to laugh when I said the guy was drinking a Budweiser, because that was her beer too, but she said I had to promise I'd never do it again. I was just getting started, but they didn't know it. And I still cared what Johnna thought. If she said I should cut it out, then I was gonna at least pretend to try. Johnna kept an eye on me in this kind of menacing, all-knowing way. I'd stare right back at her. She'd tell my mom I was hell-bent and that was why she loved me. My mom would nod. She loved me too, but I don't think in the same way. Regardless, I had no plans of staying put in Tuskin; it just didn't seem like a good option.

Lon wasn't altogether bad. He showed me how to do things when he was in the mood. Other times, he was real quiet and watched TV for three days straight. He was tired, is what my mom said. She would know; sometimes she'd lie there with him all hours while I wandered around the house and then out the door, searching for someone to say something to.

"You're a regular chatterbox," Johnna would say when she came over and I talked her ear off. My mother and Lon would go comatose in the summer, and who could blame them. It was hot as hell up on the hill where we lived—and calling it a hill was being generous. But our street did go up, and then the land went back down at the end of the cul-de-sac, so it was at least something in all that flat. Lon would take a month off so he could go to the beach, only he didn't. He just lay on our couch with my mom. They drank Dr Pepper and watched TV. It didn't beat the beach, as far as I was concerned.

"Everyone here's asleep," I said. Johnna came over to check on us.

"We can go to the lake if you want." Johnna would take me places just to hang out. Sometimes she'd tell me about Ray, my mom's brother, who Johnna had gone out with for half her life before he died. And sometimes she'd just be quiet or ask me questions so I could talk. I guess she figured I needed to get some things off my chest, because I was living up on the barely hill with Mom and Lon. Tuskin had a lot of barelys.

"Ray wasn't like your mom at all. We were going to live on the Great Lakes. Did she ever tell you that?" Johnna had a truck with a white stripe around the middle. It rattled down the road, making a real racket because of some loose part inside that Johnna wouldn't fix.

"No. I don't think Mom likes to remember Ray," I said. It was true. My mom always made a shaking motion with her head if you said anything about Ray. He'd been a good brother, the kind you didn't want to lose to sadness the way she did. He killed himself when I was a baby. "I wanna see the Great Lakes too."

We pulled up to Lake Bally, which wasn't a great lake or even a very good one, but it was cool and wet, and Johnna did know how to have a good time on the water. She always brought a cooler and blew up inner tubes for us. She liked to swim. My mother stayed dry no matter where she was. Lon was always bragging that he was going to take her to Miami, but I couldn't imagine her there. She'd sit on the sand and sizzle.

"Is the Great Lakes bigger than this?" I asked after we'd gotten set up. Johnna had an umbrella and two chairs. She got Cheez Doodles and some pudding in a container. She said she forgot spoons, so we'd have to lick.

We waded out into the water, pulling the tubes behind us; they weren't too full, because Johnna got winded. The bottom of the lake was fluffy-feeling; for every step, a whole ball of it would explode underfoot. It took Johnna a few tries to get up on her tube from one side, but I could pull up from the middle and put my feet out. We just floated there for a long time.

"Yes," she finally said. I'd forgotten I asked about the Great Lakes. "They look like the ocean."

I'd seen pictures of the ocean and of course on TV, but I couldn't really imagine a lake having waves like that or going on forever, stretched out and endless. That was the thing with Tuskin—everything had an end. I thought it would be nice to stand on the end of the land, where it dropped off and disappeared.

"Why did you go there?" I asked. "Can you see the other side?"

"Ray got a job in Michigan. On the Upper Peninsula. I thought it was so pretty there. We went and I never wanted to come back. And no, you can't see it. The water goes on forever."

"Too bad you couldn't stay," I said.

"Don't squint, Meg. It'll give you lines."

"I like lines," I said, squinting harder.

"Yeah, he was sad all the time there in the winter, so we had to come back."

"I get sad in the winter a little," I said, trying to make her feel better about Ray.

"Well. That'll do it." She flicked some water at me and tilted her head back. She had lines around her eyes; they were like ridges. I put my fingers to my face—still smooth, but I did try to pull my cheeks down.

"I don't want to live anywhere," I said.

Johnna shot her head at me. "Don't say that, Meg." I guess she was thinking about Ray, who also hadn't wanted to live anywhere.

"I just mean it don't seem like there's any good place to live, is all."

"Plenty of good places. And don't go running off again. You nearly gave your mama a heart attack." She'd already told me this five times; maybe if she'd said it six, it would have changed things. I don't know what the lucky number was, but we didn't get there.

"All anyone does is complain," I said.

"Just grown-ups being grown-ups." Johnna laid her head back. "It was funny; I didn't mind working none or any of it when I had Ray, but alone it really does seem like a drag, huh? But anyway, you shouldn't be thinking like that. You're a kid. World is your oyster, Meggy."

"I never ate an oyster," I said. Johnna laughed because she hadn't either. I liked those days with Johnna. I figured I was replacing Ray and she was replacing my mom, who preferred Lon.

When we got home, Lon was outside doing something to his truck. He had his shirt off and was wet all over—sweat, not swimming. I thought he gave Johnna a funny look when she got out of the car. We were both in our bathing suits still. We'd ridden with the windows down, sitting on towels. I was near dry by the time we got back. It was dusk but still bright. The sun was behind a thick sky; it was hazy and orange along the edges.

"That woman," Lon said after Johnna drove away.

"What about her?" I said. Sometimes I talked like a mad grown-up to Lon. He seemed to like it. I could tell him to shut up and all that without getting read the riot act.

"She's something," he said.

"Yeah," I said, not sure what he meant. "Something."

"Pain in the ass, if you ask me." He laughed a little. I looked up at him and laughed too. He fixed his pants from the sweat and asked me to hand him a wrench. I liked helping him with things. He knew how everything worked, at least on a car or a truck. I would think later that maybe Lon was the first weirdo I sidled up to; that was where it started—me picking the wrong people. It was like I felt sorry for him, maybe in the same way I felt sorry for myself. I never did give him the judgment he deserved. He wasn't the last. I could convince myself of anything.

5

"Lucy." I continued to say her name over and over again during the ride home from the police station, much like how I said my cat's name every time I saw him. "Bingo." "Bingo." "Bingo," I repeated throughout the day. He didn't know his name, nor did he care that I was saying it. Lucy was much the same on this afternoon. I had no memory of her ever being despondent, apathetic, rude.

"What, Tata?" she said after the third series of Lucys. "What is it?"

"Did something happen?" I'd told Nina I would take Lucy. Nina had been completely beside herself at the station. She kept grabbing my arm, tugging like a small child who wanted to show me something. She spoke in a hissing, frantic whisper, asking over and over again if Lucy needed a sweater because of the air-conditioning.

"She has goose bumps!" she wheezed in my ear.

"Yes, well, I'm sure she'll be fine."

When they said we could go, I thought it best if Lucy came with me. By the end, Nina seemed to have lost the will to live. I almost put my hand in front of her mouth to make sure she was still breathing.

"Josh got killed." Lucy barely moved when she said it, as though it had no effect.

"Right, but, Lucy, what are the police saying? What did the lawyer girl say?"

"Deirdre?" She turned to me, clearly pleased with Deirdre and not so much me. I was distantly aware of having lost ground.

"Yes. What was that about? Is everything okay?"

"Other than Josh being murdered?"

A gust of wind hit the side of the car. I gripped the wheel tighter. It had been balmy and mild all morning. "Where is this wind coming from?" I offered.

"The sky."

"I know, right?" I sounded too willing. I was. I looked at Lucy's hands; they were a child's hands, fumbling and tiny. She did not yet make womanly gestures or have any frailty to her the way I did. It sets in in the forties, though it remains largely undetectable for another decade. But it's been there, creeping like ivy up a slender tree, ready to choke out the life under a heavy blanket of gnarling, clenching teeth. Time is an invasive species; by the time you notice it, it has already taken over. "But do you know what happened to Josh? That's what I'm asking."

She sighed.

I tried to ignore how it sounded. "Lucy," I said.

"No," she answered. "No. I don't know what happened."

I took her to my house. I'd always enjoyed fussing over her, doing things in an old-fashioned, careful sort of way. I would put Chips Ahoy! cookies on fine china and serve her milk in a stemmed wineglass. She was getting too old to be entertained by any of this, had been for a long time, but I pressed on, fearing I had nothing more to offer. It was either cute pleasantries for a child or the cold, hard truths about life. I had no in-between. I wasn't sure anyone did. With Lucy, all the growing up was about the boyfriends. I could remember Nina saying she was too young when Daniel came around.

"Way too young."

"But it seems more like a best-friend thing, Nina," I told her. "I wouldn't worry."

I hadn't felt the same about Josh. That was different; he was different, more like a man, with man thoughts on the brain. Lucy hadn't appeared to change at all—not at first. She still wore T-shirts and running shorts every day. Her hair was always in a ponytail with the loose strands tucked behind her ears. She looked the same as she always had. As I look back, there were probably subtle shifts in her personality that had gone largely unnoticed. Josh was a real departure from Daniel though—there was no denying it. She had always let people lead the way with her. Daniel had been gentle, kind, a soft sort of person. Josh was all angles and points on which Lucy could scrape herself. But I would decide all this later. During the most crucial time, I was busy with my canned beans and suede, ignoring all warnings.

Lucy sighed again, heavily, before getting out of the car. "I'm so tired," she said. She was moving as though tethered to the ground. To combat this feeling of weariness, I was bouncy and ebullient. I stumbled over the heel of my boot and tried to do a side kick to make it look like all this flailing about was intentional.

"Would you like a snack?" I asked. We were standing on the front porch, stalling before going inside—everything had a stalled, lingering feeling to it, like we couldn't move on to the next moment. Ever. There was a layer of pollen on every surface. When the wind kicked up, or even a slight breeze, the pollen lifted and scattered, like a yellow plume of smoke from a cigarette. Lucy ran her finger through a pile of it, leaving a swirl on the plastic case holding my rarely used garden hose. When I had moved back to Tuskin from the city and purchased the house, I didn't know a thing about plants or hoses. I was happy to buy a tidy ranch with three small bedrooms and two bathrooms and a compact yard with a weather vane, not that I knew what a weather vane was for, but there it was, regardless. Ferrol's and my divorce settlement had been generous, even though I'd signed a prenup not even knowing what that was at the time. Ferrol also played dumb and said something about having to sign twenty contracts a day. "I'll sign anything!" He winked at me—this from the guy who had three attorneys on retainer, always. He had no problem lying, none at all. I heard the hymn "It Is Well with My Soul" the one time I tried to go to church upon coming back to Tuskin and wondered if Ferrol wrote it. I scoured the hymnal looking for his name, credit given. Nothing.

I sent Ferrol an email with a picture of the house—still trying to win him over even after we'd split. "Its a house!" was his response. He'd left off the apostrophe. If I was honest, I'm not sure he knew one belonged there.

"Where's my mom?" Lucy asked once we were inside. I noticed she'd rubbed her finger on her pants. There was a small trace of yellow.

"I'm not sure." I paused. "Did you want to go home?"

"Sort of."

"Okay. I'll take you." I frowned but tried to hide it by turning my head. I hadn't put my bag down yet.

"I could walk," she said quietly.

"Home?" I was incredulous. It wasn't far, but she'd never made this suggestion before. "Why?"

"I don't know, Tata!" She raised her voice. "I just want to be alone."

"Okay, then. You're a teenager." I tried to sound like I was joking, but it fell flat. We were both frowning now, slopes of irritation in place of our lips.

"I just need to think. I'll be fine…It's not that far."

"Yes, of course," I said, though I couldn't recall a single other time in her fifteen years that Lucy had told me she needed to think. She didn't appear to be able to answer a simple question either. *What happened to Josh? Why are the police talking to you? What the hell is going on?* The Lucy I knew did not have to think, alone, on long walks. I was at a loss. And so I let her go. "Please have your mother call me when you get home. I'll be worried." I didn't say about what, but it was everything. I would be worried about the walk, the thinking, the need to do so, and this change. This revolution in her was so subtle, but isn't that how it always starts?

Lucy went out the front door without another word. "Bye, Lucy," I called, but she was already at the end of the driveway, walking quickly with her head down. I watched from the front steps, scowling at my lack of control. At the familiarity.

Tuskin is laid out like a pile of rulers tossed on a table, all straight roads placed at angles with sharp corners and tight turns. It made me wonder if the people who did all the building wanted to slow everyone down. You couldn't make a right without a hard brake. Maybe Lucy was right: It was easier to walk. Because of the unceasing flatness of my street—all Tuskin streets, for that matter—I could see Lucy walking for a long time, with her head down. When she finally disappeared at the end of the road, I was still standing there. I didn't move for a long time. When I turned to go inside, I thought I saw someone by the window in my kitchen, the one over the sink that was in constant need of cleaning. Dark hair; knobby knees; a sly, cracked grin. *No. No.* I couldn't make sense of why I was thinking of her now.

The phone was ringing; I couldn't tell for how long, but when I finally noticed it, it pulled me out of my memory.

"Hello?" I said, hoping it was Lucy, but she didn't have a cell phone with her, and of course she wasn't home yet.

"Hi, Meg?"

"Yes?"

"This is Andrea Farmer."

"Oh." It was Daniel's mother.

"Lucy is standing outside our house. I can't get in touch with Nina."

My breath caught in my chest, a most peculiar constriction—an uncontrollable coughing fit of realities I was trying to expel. "Well, she must have run there," I said after a long pause of repressed reflection. "She only just left here." Had she? How long had it been? Daniel lived just a short distance away—between my house and Nina's.

"I don't know, but she's standing in the front yard. It's…it's… Something's wrong. Daniel doesn't want to go out there and talk to her. I've tried, but she's not responding. I'd say she's almost catatonic. I tried Nina too, but she didn't answer."

"Oh my God," I said. "I'll be right there. Is she having a seizure or something?" I hung up the phone before Andrea could respond. It was all so familiar, this worry, this uselessness. I could never forgive myself. It seemed my guilt had come home to roost, a tumor of my own making, dense and rubbery. I couldn't cut it out with a knife.

6

Summer was over—time for eight grade. I didn't really feel one way or another about eighth grade. A lot of kids were making a big deal out of it because it was the last year before high school, but high school seemed like more of the same to me. August was what it was—hotter than hell, with homework.

I tried running away again after Lon asked Rainy to bend over that first week she was back. She'd moved in right after school started up again. Tripp couldn't keep a job, and the uncle said they couldn't live in his house anymore without paying rent, so she was home. Lon threw a spoon on the ground and asked her to pick it up. She was in her pajamas, which was just a long T-shirt. She did it like she knew what she was doing, real slow with her eyes in the upper corner of her sockets. I threw my spoon on the ground too, so I could be more like Lon, who I'd already decided I liked better than any of them. Rainy ignored the clatter.

My mom came to get me after realizing I took off again. I wasn't in a stranger's car this time but just walking along Minton Road. "Get in!" she shouted. It was raining, and there I was.

"No!" I said back. I kept on with my arms folded across my chest.

"You're gonna get kidnapped by a pervert!" She raised her voice and was tapping her foot on the gas so the car would go forward just a little. Ever since my mom had heard about perverts, she was throwing the word around like rice at a wedding. She called the cop who gave her a ticket for an illegal turn a pervert, and the girl at the checkout who overcharged her for Wonder Bread too.

"I wanna live with Johnna!"

"You can't."

"Bullshit!" I actually didn't know if I was allowed to live with Johnna. I'd asked her a few times if she could take me in. She always just laughed, but then she'd show up the next day to do something fun.

"You don't even know Johnna," my mom said, chuckling to herself.

"I do!"

"Get in, Meg. I have to go to work." Now she sounded tired. We both flinched a little at a close crack of thunder.

"You're always so tired!" I picked up the pace and the volume.

"Working nights'll do that to you. I hope you'll never understand."

Rainy said Mom was a stripper. I didn't know it, but it made sense with how Lon acted, like he got the jackpot with her. All the men at the dancing club would be jealous, is what his attitude said when he walked through the door. No one ever said that's what she was doing, but I started to figure it out with how she was always working on her tan and looking at her butt in the mirror.

"It's no fun at home," I said.

"Who said it was supposed to be fun?" She meant it. "I'm not havin' fun neither, but we gotta keep on."

I stopped walking, which made the rain in my face worse. I ran my hand over my forehead to keep the wet out of my eyes.

"I don't like Lon," I said. It was the first time I'd used him as an excuse. But I think everyone knew that I *did* like him. He was the only one in the house who had anything interesting to say. Sure, it was about lawn mowers and stuff, but at least he could tell me about things. My mom just made macaroni and looked at herself in the mirror before sighing and saying it was going to be a long day.

My mom closed her eyes. "I don't know what to tell you, Meg. I need someone home at night. I gotta keep him…" She stopped herself. "Gotta keep him around."

"What about Dad? Where the hell is he?"

"Haven't a clue. And anyway, he was never around at night. Get in."

I complied but rode in the back just to get my way a little. "I'mma move away as soon as I can," I told her.

"I hope you do." I don't think she realized that within a year I'd be gone, but she sure sounded like she meant what she said.

7

Lucy didn't move at all when I pulled up to the Farmers' house and parked at an angle across their driveway. My car made a screeching, lurching sound as I slammed on the brakes. Lucy didn't seem to notice anything. She stood stock-still with her arms down by her sides, little toothpicks dangling from her shoulder girdle, and her hands open. Her lips were slightly parted on her otherwise blank face. She reminded me of Nina—an upright corpse. I assured myself she couldn't stand up if she were dead.

I got out of the car and approached her very slowly. Again, she did not seem to notice anything going on around her.

I'd called the pediatrician—Dr. Lucas, who wore very tight pants for a pediatrician and had a light-colored mustache that didn't appear fully grown in—before I left and asked that he come too. Andrea Farmer hadn't been all that clear about what was going on other than saying that "Lucy is in some sort state over here."

Dr. Lucas had sent one of the nurses from the office and said he would come after his last appointment. I'd met the nurse several times; her name was Mindy. She'd made a comment to Nina once that she thought I was overbearing. Nina laughed when she told me. "Says you're all up in our business!" I suppose she thought I would enjoy hearing that. I did take Lucy to a lot of her appointments when Nina was busy, and I suppose I asked a lot of questions while there. I just hadn't wanted Lucy to feel neglected. I fought neglect tooth and nail for her, having experienced so much of it myself. Nina always did say I made everything about me.

Nurse Mindy was known for performing dance moves while checking blood pressure and other vitals; the office even had a framed photo of her on the wall doing the Electric Slide with a thermometer in her hand. She'd had this schtick for as long as I could remember. Lucy still pretended to laugh when we went in, but her visits now included talk of her periods and sex ed. Mindy continued to do a jump switch with her legs when she pulled out the ear light for an exam but wasn't quite as eager about it.

Mindy arrived shortly after I did. "What's going on, Lucy?" she asked. She did a small shoulder shimmy but kept it conservative. "I think she's in shock," she said after she'd tried carefully but unsuccessfully to talk to Lucy. As bizarre as Lucy's behavior was, I was most alarmed by Daniel, who refused to come out of the house at all.

"Is he afraid or something?" I asked his mother. Andrea just looked at me like how could I not know? "What?" I said. She didn't answer.

Nina had arrived quietly and was now standing at the edge of the yard. She looked so much like Ferrol sometimes. She had a rectangular face and wide nose with light blue eyes, all things she shared with Ferrol, though she made them beautiful, softer—no five-o'clock shadow or cigarette-stained teeth to go with them. Lucy looked more like her father, with birdlike features and a small, pointed chin. Nina's hair was aggressively straightened, as it had been at the station and every other time I'd seen her in the last decade. It stopped like a cliff at the edge of her collarbone, the strands like small razors set to cut her.

Nina wasn't the only one to have shown up in the ten or so minutes since I'd arrived. Other neighbors had emerged from their homes with worried expressions, looking over hedges, peeking around corners, or congregating at the end of driveways with their hands over their eyes, blocking the midday sun to get a better look at the mayhem, which was really just Lucy catatonic in front of the Farmers' house. I rolled my eyes at each of them. "Gooseneckers," I said under my breath. No one would get close; a fungus was spreading—first the news of a murdered teenager and now some girl standing in the Tuskin streets like a zombie. A girl who had just been questioned by the police, no less. People wanted to see what was happening but not necessarily touch anything.

"Lucy," Nina said meekly as she approached. Lucy turned toward the sound of her voice. I was briefly jealous—I had not garnered a response at all. "Lucy, what's wrong?" I saw a curtain move at the corner window. I figured it must be Daniel's room. Mrs. Farmer was looking in that direction too.

"We're going to kill him," Lucy said. It was the first time she'd spoken. Nurse Mindy took a step backward. "I know it." Lucy continued to stare at the house.

"Lucy," I said, but more to myself. She wasn't listening. I looked around, wondering what the reaction to such a statement would be, but no one other than the nurse seemed to have heard what she said, even though by this point many of the stragglers had moved closer. I'd noticed people walking up and then away, talking in hushed voices, looking more self-important than concerned, which is usually the way when a tragedy happens. There'd been one woman who'd crept into my periphery but escaped before I was able to give her a closer look. Dark hair lying like a blanket over her head and back, a sheet of heavy-lying black. I saw the edge of her, and then she was gone. I had to catch my breath.

There were suggestions to call the police, but Nurse Mindy— bless her—said that shock was normal and we should wait until Lucy came to.

"But she said something—" someone started to say, but Nina

jumped in, aggressively moving everyone back and away. "Give her space!" I wondered if Nina had heard what she said too. People started dispersing then, grumbling and shooting suspicious looks. In the end, it was only me, Andrea Farmer, Mindy, and Nina. And, of course, Lucy.

"Lucy," Nina said calmly. "Lucy—is everything okay?" I sighed. We'd already asked her that a hundred times in the course of twenty minutes.

Finally, Lucy appeared to deflate and said she had a headache. Those were the first words spoken: "I have a headache." I pretended she hadn't said anything else, this reference to killing Josh stricken from the record.

Dr. Lucas had arrived but stayed back, allowing Nurse Mindy to finish what she'd started. He wore his scrubs skintight, with the pants stopping at the calf. He approached, putting his hand on Lucy's shoulder, speaking softly. She looked at him, but I could tell there was now something missing in her. I began a slow slide into despair, recognizing all that she had begun to lack. *At least we know Josh is dead*, I thought foolishly. I could remember not being sure; that had to have been the worst of it. Him lying in the field and me wondering if he was still breathing. Josh *was* dead. Lucy could depend on the finality. She was not fated to live with the tumor of an unvoiced suspicion, left alone to grow somewhere out of sight and hidden from consciousness.

But then again, it is no longer a suspicion when someone says

"We were going to kill him." That sounded like a confession. I pushed it into the hollows along with all the other things I was too afraid to know, my willful ignorance a remnant leftover from believing that people don't die in fields or get murdered in their cars. The letdown is the weight of the world.

8

1973

If August was hell, September was August's armpit. Johnna said I could come and stay with her for a week as a treat. Sometimes I thought Johnna could read my mind; she knew when things were getting just bad enough. "But I have work, so you're gonna be a latchkey kid after school," she said when she came to pick me up at the house. As far as I knew, I'd always been a latchkey kid. There was nobody waiting at the door for me at any time of day. "Heather said she'd give me a week, but not a day more." Johnna only called my mom by her name every once in a while. It was such a pretty name, very feathery and soft. Johnna was named after her dad, and I was named after no one.

"That's funny," I answered, because my mom didn't know I was around half the time anyway. I guess she needed me home where I'd be easier to forget. I knew I helped Johnna too. She was lonely like I was—different because of being a grown-up, but the same. Loneliness has mostly the same flavor no matter what you sprinkle it on.

"But we gotta do something with that hair if you're gonna stay with me," Johnna said.

I put my hand on top of my head. "It's always been like this," I said. "It's like I got electrocuted." It stood up off my head like it too was trying to escape. I couldn't calm the frizz no matter what I tried; even covering my head in butter didn't do any good. That had been Rainy's suggestion, but she was messing with me. It took a month to get the butter completely out. My hair looked like sewer water.

Johnna laughed and went over to my closet. The doors had come off and then been removed. Johnna said landlords didn't care about their properties. I wrote that on one of my school assignments. The vocabulary word was *property*. *Landlords don't care about there propertys.* I got a minus one.

"You need some new clothes too, Meggy."

"I guess." I mostly wore Rainy's hand-me-downs. She was real short for her age and could have worn kids' sizes right up to sixteen.

"This underwear's gotta be from kindergarten!" Johnna was appalled. It had pink polka dots on it and a hole in the butt. I wore them all the time.

"Still fit," I said.

"Good grief." Johnna packed my bag for me and didn't ask for any input. It was all terry-cloth shorts and tank tops with ties on the shoulders anyway. "We'll get you some bras too. It's time."

I put my arm over my chest. "Well. Whatever," I said. It did sound fun to go shopping.

"And a haircut." She sounded real serious when she said that.

Johnna had set up a bedroom for me in her spare. There was a double bed in there and towels. Her house was neat as a pin and very quiet. She rented too, but it didn't have the same feeling, like she was begging to live there and would take anything.

"I think we should get pizza for dinner," Johnna said after I'd put my things around the room. I felt a little silly because I was only staying for a week, but it was fun to pretend like this was my new place. I patted the bedspread—light pink with flowers. It was stiff and cold. The AC was blowing right on it from a vent in the wall.

"Should I call my mom?" I asked.

"Naw, she's good." Johnna glanced at the clock. Mom would be getting ready for work. She left the house at seven.

Pizza Hut was my favorite; Johnna knew that because she and my mom took me there when I graduated from fourth grade. I'd actually been held back a year in second because of dyslexia. My mom said she didn't have health insurance, but the woman at the school said it wasn't like that. I had to take special classes so I'd stop writing everything in the wrong order. It got better in fourth because I went to see Mrs. Davidson. I got pizza for the effort.

"I'm not going to have a husband or live with anybody when I'm older. Not even one person." I was using a fork for the cheese.

"Your hair's the color of cheese," Johnna said. She had a Coke. "Or butter."

"The butter came out," I said. "And I like that color." I was smiling big.

"You'll change your mind about a lot of things when you get older, Meggy. I'm sure."

"No way. It's all just bad luck," I said, thinking of the men always coming and going.

"Well…not so much."

"What about Uncle Ray?" I said. "He was bad luck."

"Naw. He was just sad, and then the bad weather."

"The weather'll do it." I ran my hand through my hair and left a trail of grease. "Oh, shit," I said.

"It's okay. You can take a bath."

"Yeah." I nodded. "Why don't you find another man, then?" I asked. "Mom never misses the chance to have a man around."

"That's not really true, but maybe Lon's a good thing."

"No. He looks at your ass." I took another bite of my food. "Real hard-lookin'. I know how to look at something hard." I opened my eyes wide and stared at the table. "He's trying to stare your pants right offa you."

Johnna closed her eyes. I thought maybe she was smiling. I was sure it felt good to have a man looking at you. That was what the twist of her mouth said. "No, he doesn't. He loves Heather." She had a twinkle about her the rest of the night. I almost wished I hadn't said anything, because even though he wasn't trying to stare my pants off, Lon paid the most attention to me. She was still smiling when she helped me get the pizza grease out of my hair. I smiled too. Lon liked both of us; I could share him with Johnna since she was my favorite.

It was a good week—the last one I can remember. I met Tyler shortly after that, and all the dice got turned to different numbers. Nothing ever added up right again. Johnna never looked at me the same neither. I still swear she could read my mind.

9

I was home again. Alone. Nina had been almost affronted that I had thought Lucy should come back with me. "Both of you," I said to correct what had clearly been a mistake. "You should both come back with me. Both of you."

But they had gone home, to Nina's house after a third vitals check. Dr. Lucas and Mindy high-fived and got in their respective cars, feeling that because Lucy's blood pressure was in the zone, there was nothing more to worry about. I could hardly swallow; the impenetrable mass of despair lodged in my throat was set to choke me.

I noticed that I had a message on my answering machine. It had been an unnerving few days—I couldn't imagine who would be calling or who wouldn't be. I was sure everyone had heard by now that Lucy's boyfriend had been murdered and that she'd just had a catatonic episode in the Farmers' front yard. And that she'd said something.

"You didn't hear her right, Meg," I said to myself. "You didn't."
I'd watched Nurse Mindy like a hawk as she was leaving. She didn't
seem the slightest bit rattled and didn't even look over her shoulder at Lucy as she left. "That's because you misheard her." I nodded
determinedly. I had misheard her. That, or Lucy was in such a state
that we shouldn't take anything she said seriously. It was probably
that. Yes, that was why Mindy didn't seem to care.

I honestly couldn't say I knew who anyone was around the
Farmers' lawn, save a few vaguely familiar faces, not that I knew
all that many people in Tuskin anymore anyway. I'd been back for
almost twenty years but seemed to have only dipped my toe in the
place. I had my reasons—this thistle from the past stuck to my
pant leg, catching on every present moment the burr of what I had
allowed to happen. I'd been less aware of this specific discomfort
in Atlanta but had developed new unpleasantries to contend with
there. I didn't want to belong in Tuskin or anywhere.

And it surprised me, as Tuskin had become softer in the time
I was away, a place where a person lived a quiet life that you took
pictures of—photos you looked at fondly, where children grew up
with memories of quaint gatherings and family traditions. That was
not the Tuskin where I had lived, and I don't think it was that way
for anyone I knew. Not then. When I came back and asked about
kids I'd grown up with, their stories were all sad, incomplete, dis-
jointed. Someone had gotten sick and died, someone else was in
jail, oh, she ended up a bad drunk—you never would have thought

it. I'm sure there were kids who made it out or made it better; we had Students of the Month and star player this or honor roll that, but I didn't hear about them, what became of their legacy.

Nina couldn't understand why we were moving back. I remember arguing with her about it. She was thirteen and vulnerable to such shifts. The divorce had been difficult, and then we were moving out of Atlanta. I remember her telling me she thought that her middle school years had a lot to do with her own divorce.

"It was very destabilizing," she said over and over. I think she was waiting for an apology.

"What a luxury to be able to think like that," I'd said instead. "I didn't have time to try and figure out why I was so messed up. All we've given you is time, and all you use it on is worrying about yourselves."

I pressed the button on the answering machine absentmindedly. My thoughts had been wandering more since the murder. It was an escape to chew on all these old concepts, ancient history, things that no longer mattered and couldn't be changed. I found I could ruminate for hours on the irrelevant details of years gone by.

The robotic sound of the message pulled me out of the memory, startling me back into my kitchen, into my skin. "This is Deirdre Mansell, Lucy's attorney. She asked that I contact you regarding her case. I need to speak with you immediately. I might suggest—if you are to remain her point of contact—that you get a cell phone so you are easier to reach. Please return my call as soon as possible." She left her number, which I had on the business card she'd given me.

I picked up the phone to call her back but wondered if I should call Nina first. "No," I said out loud. "No, that will disturb Lucy." Nina had said they were going to go home and take a nap. Nina talked about Lucy like that—it was always a "we" with her.

"We're going to try cheer!" Lucy hated cheerleading. I thought Nina should be able to clearly see that Lucy did not have the personality of a cheerleader. Lucy cried her way through the first practice and refused to go the following week. That was followed by lacrosse, which Nina also claimed "they" would love. "We're giving it a shot!" Lucy got a concussion during the second game and had to ride the pine for the rest of the season. "We're going to take an art class!" The list went on and on.

My hands were shaking, something fairly new but exacerbated by the day. I dialed Deirdre's number and waited. She answered on the third ring. "Hello." She was matter-of-fact.

"Yes, this is Lucy DeWitt's grandmother—Meg."

"Ms. Gregory," she said heavily.

"Yes."

She took a breath. "So I've spoken with the detective, and he says they're preparing to charge Lucy."

"With what?" There was a thin stream of bile rising in my throat. It had a sharp, metallic taste and quality, almost as if I'd swallowed barbs from a fence, and though I had thoroughly chewed them, I couldn't keep them down, not with all that was happening. I coughed; it sounded like a fork on metal.

"With murder."

"This is impossible," I said loudly. I thought maybe I'd meant to say "ridiculous." I didn't know what I'd meant to say, but it was impossible, and it was ridiculous. "How can this be? Have you met Lucy?" I was screeching, a chain saw of indignation.

"Yes. I met her today…as you know. There's—" She stopped talking. "I'm afraid it's going to be Lucy and a few other kids. You said she has a boyfriend, Daniel Farmer? He's being charged as well."

"Daniel?" Something suddenly made sense. "No, Josh was her boyfriend," I said. "Not Daniel anymore. That's her ex." I paused. This was such a stupid thing to be talking about. "Does Andrea know?"

"I'm… I don't know who Andrea is."

"Daniel's mother."

"I don't know what she knows. There were four of them."

"Four of what?" I asked. It was too warm now for my outfit. I pulled at the neckline of my shirt—a turtleneck. If you'd told me at any point in my young life that I would own and wear turtlenecks, I would have called you a damn fool, and yet here I was.

"Four kids are now implicated."

"This is impossible," I said again. "Who?"

"Daniel Farmer is one of them. That's all I've been told."

"But why? Why would they be charged?"

"Because the police are saying they killed him." She sounded annoyed that I wanted this unspeakable detail clarified.

I shook my head. "This is Lucy we're talking about. You don't know her, but this isn't… Listen, she's a little church mouse. I can't… There's no way for me to make you understand, because you don't know her, but this is just plain wrong." My accent was slipping. So refined I'd become in my later years. Ferrol hadn't liked the Southern thing. He was originally from California and held his origins in high regard. The longer I was in Atlanta, in Ferrol's life, the less and less I was able to slip into the old Meg, the one I'd brought with me from Tuskin. Most of her had already disappeared with Tyler. I think I'd hoped to find her again by returning. But I'd had a hard time conjuring her spirit. It was why I didn't bother with having friends or proving my existence. I had been half a person for so long I didn't see the point in forcing such a small ration on anyone.

"Ms. Gregory, I don't think you understand. The police cannot charge and hold your granddaughter without evidence."

"What evidence could they have? This detective guy just walks around staring at everyone with his mouth open. Adam or whatever his name is."

"Apparently they've found a hideout."

I almost dropped the phone. "A hideout?" I gagged the word into the telephone receiver.

"That's what I'm being told. The police have found a hideout, and in it is a bunch of incriminating evidence."

"What? This is insanity." I kept blinking and shaking my head; my brain was like a penny banging up the walls of a can. *We're going to kill him.* Had someone told the detective Lucy said that?

"They swabbed Lucy today, and her DNA is all over the inside of Josh's car, his bedroom, and this cabin over off Pirkle where the kids are said to have been meeting."

"Pirkle," I said. It was a question but not said like one. She had no right to have that word in her mouth when she was talking to me. "There's no cabin on Pirkle."

"I'm telling you what they told me," she said.

"That ain't right," I said, finding myself for a second. "That can't be right."

"Oh." She sounded surprised. "I need to go, but please arrange to have a cell phone if you don't think you will be home all of the time. I need to be able to get in touch with you. They are not going to arrest them yet, but within the next couple of days. It sounds like they are trying to make sure they have enough to keep them. I would prepare bail money if you can."

"Oh," I said. "Oh—I'll have to ask Ferrol for that." I spoke quietly, subdued and humiliated by this consistent reliance on him. "Nina and I don't have… I don't even know how much it is…" I trailed off. "Have you told Nina that we need money or…"

"Lucy would like for you to handle things. She made that clear."

"Okay," I said. I had to make it through this for Lucy; I had to calm the simmer. She was snared in the net. It's always the same net; in different water, but the same. It drags the bottom for the subtle treasures usually missed or overlooked. People like Lucy, Tyler—not me though. I'd slithered through a tear. I was the type to find a hole.

I hung up with Deirdre, feeling annoyed at how she'd said "Pirkle" like it didn't mean anything.

10

It was getting colder, without much to look forward to. I was too old to trick-or-treat and didn't have anyone to go with anyway. Our street was kind of a wasteland when it came to kids my age, and Mom worked at night. There was no one to drive me anywhere. We were on Platts, which made a *T* with Pirkle—we called it the T-bone. Pirkle was the main road, the one that took us anywhere and then back home after it. I'd have to go down Pirkle to get to heaven or hell.

I didn't know it yet, but my mom had sort of lost her job. She was still going in but working behind the bar. Some kids—mainly Robin, my friend at school—said something about my mom being too saggy for the stage anymore. I told Robin she didn't want to do table dance anymore because of her morals, but Robin shook her head adamantly.

"She's too old now," she said. I guess she'd heard her dad

talking, or somebody else who went to the club. Shakers. I really hated the name when I turned eleven and suddenly knew what it meant.

"Okay." I tried not to sneer. Robin's mom was real nice, with hair that she did with curlers and pink lipstick. It was different at their house. Robin's mom seemed happy all the time, with those cookies that look like little flowers and pillows on the couch that had ruffles around the edges. Robin had two brothers who were older like Rainy, but then nothing like Rainy. I remember going over there one day after school and Mrs. Goode telling one of Robin's brothers that I was Rainy's little sister.

"The girl who went off with Tripp Forrester?" the brother asked. He looked at me like he was trying not to look at me.

"Yeah," I said, feeling defensive. "What gives?"

"Oh, man." That was all he said.

"You sure don't," I answered. Robin and Mrs. Goode were watching me. Mrs. Goode said something about turning the sprinkler on in the yard.

"It's so hot!" She was excited to have something else to say. "You'll need towels." She didn't have to work at Shakers or anywhere else. Everyone knew it; it was like the highest compliment.

It was kind of a good thing that Mom was down at the Shakers bar though, because she was bringing home all the cherries and lemons and limes at the end of the night. Rainy and I were putting them in everything. I had maraschinos in my cereal most mornings.

Rainy said she was going to get a job at Shakers too, now that my mom was behind the bar. Mom was wary but got her a gig slinging drinks. I was no longer one of them now that Rainy was just like my mom. They laughed all the time about the people at Shakers and talked about how they scammed the till and the owner was such a sleaze and all sorts of things I didn't understand. I was there, but on the outside. I guess they thought I admired them for being grown up and wearing cutoff shirts at night. She and my mom dressed almost the same for work. I think my mom was proud or ashamed. It was one or the other, but not in the middle.

Lon told my mom that Rainy would end up dancing, but my mom said no chance. Lon just sucked his lip in his mouth instead of getting into a fight with her about it. Lon didn't like to fight; he was a quiet person, hushed and seething. He had a style all his own when it came to disagreement.

Even though Lon was looking at Rainy the wrong way and I thought maybe he was talking to Johnna the wrong way too, he was better with me than jam on toast. I started to spend a lot more time with him that fall because he was working at an auto mechanic's instead of whatever he did before. He'd take me with him to the shop, where I could have endless Cokes from the gas station connected to it.

The holidays came and went, and then the new year and spring break. My mom had slept through that, leaving a fiver on the counter at night when she came home from work in case I needed something during the day. I squirreled away the money and had twenty-five by the end of the week. It was a nice start for when I would finally run away for good. Lon wasn't letting me come to the shop as much, because I guess there had been some complaints about my age and me hanging around there. It was a whole new kind of boredom at the house. I couldn't wait for the school year to end, though I didn't know why. At least school gave me somewhere to go. It seemed like the older I got, the more alone I felt.

Rainy turned twenty in April and had a big party at the house. I didn't know she had so many friends. They were mostly from school when she'd been in it, and then the people from the bar and their friends too, and then just some of the local riffraff. My mom and Lon sat outside all night. Lon made a fire in a big tub that was left over from a dryer. They just sat quietly and drank beer, watching the crackle. I stayed in my room but wandered out now and then. It didn't really seem like all that much fun; everyone was walking around drinking beer and listening to Grateful Dead. All the guys had their caps pulled low over their faces, and the girls were in tops that tied around the neck. It wasn't even summer yet but already hot.

I'd think back in time, over and over, and try to figure out if I ever saw Tyler before that night. He didn't look a bit familiar, not in the moment that I saw him standing by the door. He was talking to someone, that cheerful type of talk that people do at parties when they're not really saying anything but want to look like they're having a good time. He leaned against the doorframe, which was coming off in splinters. The only thing I thought was that he was going to get a wood shard in his hair. I don't really know why I noticed him, maybe because he looked a little younger than the other people there. I thought he was maybe sixteen, older than me but not like Rainy and her crew. I watched him for a while without caring that I was watching him. He hadn't noticed me; he had that way about him—happy to be watched, happy to be ignored. I liked the way he seemed tough to bother. My mom and Rainy and everyone else I knew were nothing but bothered. Life was all about getting pissed and looking like it. I just sat at the kitchen table there, staring myself silly until I decided to go out and talk to my mom and Lon.

"Whatcha doin', Meg?" my mom asked as I came outside and sat next to them by their fire in the bucket. Lon said lint was good for the spark. They had folding lawn chairs, but I took a seat on the ground.

"I don't know," I said.

"Probably gonna be loud all night. You can sleep in our room if you want." She was pulling on a cigarette. Lon had his arm around her. They looked younger in the red light from the flames. My mom had a dreamy face, like this was all she'd ever wanted. Lon was close to her and clearly had his mind on her with the way he kept giving her soft smiles. I kept thinking about Johnna and how she wasn't there and about how I knew Lon gave Johnna those looks too sometimes.

"Where's Johnna?" I asked. "Can I sleep at her place?"

My mom turned toward Lon with just a little bit of fear on her face. "She's visiting her mama in Sheldon." Both my mother and I watched Lon, but he didn't seem to notice that we were looking at him or that we were talking about Johnna. He looked like a pond on a hot day with no breeze and no flies, just flat and thick, the scum coming up.

I tried to think of something else to say. My mom wasn't a big talker; Lon didn't usually say much either, if he wasn't teaching me about cars and motorcycles. I'd helped him fix somebody's golf cart one of my last days at the shop. He let me take it for a test spin a couple of times while we were working on the steering.

"Wish I had that go-kart," I said after a long while of looking at the fire.

"That was a nice one too," Lon said. "A real burner."

"Why is Rainy so happy to be twenty and working at a table-dancer bar?" I asked. I didn't say it to be mean, but it was a real wonder. When she'd moved off to Cashiers with Tripp, she said he was going to college so she could teach elementary school.

"Just happy to be alive," my mom said, not feeling the sting at all.

I was bothered, because the fire was hot and unnecessary with all the tank tops people were wearing and the way some of the girls already had sunburns on their shoulders. I guess I wanted my mom to take the bait, and she didn't, so I stood up and said I was going back inside. She didn't really care about that either. She kind of flicked her hand at me, still with the dreamy smile. She had Lon; that was all she needed.

When I went back in the house, Tyler was waiting by the door, not for me but just biding time. It was a different door; this one didn't have splinters in the frame. I could tell he didn't really want to be at the party either.

"Hey," Tyler said. It was because I was standing on his foot. I actually don't know if he would have talked to me otherwise.

"Oh, sorry." I smiled. He had his hair pushed behind his ears, brown and straight and longer than a lot of the other boys' hair. It was shiny like in a commercial. His face was wide, with high cheekbones.

"S'all right. How's the fire?" He nodded in the direction of the tub.

"Hot."

"Yeah." His voice was low, like a man's. He put a cigarette in his mouth. "Oh," he said, probably realizing I was thirteen. "Kinda cool your house is, like, the party house," he said. It was also not something a thirteen-year-old could appreciate, at least not this thirteen-year-old. I didn't want to be anything like the people partying in my house—or the other people who lived there, for that matter.

"I don't like parties," I said.

"You might one day," he said.

"Well, maybe, but not with any of them." I pointed vaguely into the house. "I've already run away twice. Probably do it again soon. I turn fourteen in the summer."

He laughed while lighting his Marlboro. "Why you running away? Because you don't like Rainy?"

"Rainy's all right," I said. I wasn't sure what else I could add.

"I'm Tyler," he said to fill the void. "My brother knows Rainy and Lon." He nodded in the direction of the dryer fire.

Sometimes it seemed to me everyone knew Lon, though I couldn't figure out where he came from. There were a lot of Lons in Tuskin—everybody's friend who just appeared out of thin air one day. "Lon lives with us," I said. I was about to tell him more about it when a girl walked up to us. She had long, black hair that was hiding her face. She kept her chin down and didn't look at me; she slid up to Tyler like a cat and turned her eyes to his face. She said something to him and then walked away. She, too, had looked younger, like something that did not belong.

"I run away to see if anybody comes after me," I said a little too loudly. I was trying to get Tyler's attention back from the dark-haired girl. He seemed much more interested in her and was watching her walk back into the party, my stories about running away having gone by the wayside. "And I'm gonna do it again until I get far enough that I don't come back." It surprised me to say it; I guess I was showing off. "I went off with a guy. He picked me up on the side of the road. No funny business or anything but just gave me a ride."

"He mighta killed you," Tyler said. "I wouldn't go off with some guy in a car, not if I was your age."

"I was hitchin'," I said proudly. "Anyway, how old are you?"

"Seventeen," he answered. "Don't do that anymore—getting into cars with strangers or anything. If you wanna go somewhere, I'll take you. No funny business." He smiled from the side of his mouth.

"Yeah, okay." I stood there in appreciative silence, again not sure what to say or really why I was appreciative. It kind of didn't seem to me that I should go off in the car with him either.

"Lotta bad people out there looking for trouble," he said more to himself. I saw the girl with the dark hair on the other side of the room inside. She was watching us. She looked like a crow—dark and pointed, from a murder. She looked right at me and smiled. Her teeth were busted and cracked inside her twisted lips, which looked like a knot coming unraveled. I smiled back but didn't know why.

"Who's that?" I asked, but Tyler didn't hear me. A guy who looked an awful lot like him, but older and more beat up, came over to us. Tyler told me that was his brother, Parker.

"You can call him Rich though," Tyler said. They both thought that was funny. "Got a sweet ride; cost a bundle and then some."

They joshed each other around, leaving me out entirely. I had no idea what they were talking about.

I went to bed in my own room. I didn't like my mom's bed and wasn't going to sleep there no matter how rowdy things got; it was sunken in in the middle and smelled like cigarettes. The party got louder, then quieter, then a little bit louder again and then finally died out. When I got up in the morning, I went over to my window to see how many cars were still at the house. It looked like a handful, from my angle. I saw Tyler's brother walking toward a Nissan with a cigarette in his mouth and then Tyler behind him. I pulled myself back from the glass real quick, thinking they would see me. I didn't want to be caught looking, but I also didn't want Tyler to leave without talking to him again. I walked out into the house; there were people sleeping everywhere, all tangled up in their clothes, with ashtrays on the tables next to their heads. I opened the front door because I thought it smelled like piss and beer in the house. I told myself the real reason I was in a hurry to go outside was because I needed to get some air to keep my eyes from watering.

"Hey," I said when I got outside. Tyler was getting into his car. His brother was already in the passenger seat, leaning out the window with his smoke.

"Hey," he said, and he ducked his head down, then back up; he had one leg in the car and his hand on the door.

"I'm Meg," I said. I didn't think I'd told him my name the night before.

"Right. Rainy's sister. Listen, Meg—don't go running off with nobody. I'll take you anywhere you wanna go, but no funny business, okay?"

"Yeah, all right," I said. Tyler and his brother got all the way in and drove off. There was always a big burst of dirt when a person did a U-ie and headed down to Platts.

I smiled and stood there awhile. Tyler was the best-looking guy at the party, I told myself. And he'd talked to me; he almost seemed like he'd been waiting for me there by the door—almost. Maybe he would take me somewhere, far away and forever. I liked a Nissan as much as anything. I knew it wouldn't be the last I saw of him, or maybe that was the prayer I said to myself. That, and *no funny business.*

1 1

I called Nina, who sounded far away, like she was sinking into her exhaustion, a quicksand of fatigue and desperation to end it all. "Hello?" she exhaled.

"I'm going to buy a cell phone," I said.

"Okay."

"The lawyer says I need it. Nina, they're going to charge Lucy."

"Wait—what?" Now she sounded awake.

"Is she there? In the room?"

"No. She went to lay down."

"Murder, Nina."

"No. No! No, no." She kept saying it. "God, no!" I could see her strained face, folding like paper around her mouth. She wasn't keeping enough padding on her body to help absorb the blows. Life required that a person be able to fall without shattering. She was all sinew and clenched effort. Her hair would be frayed at the ends by this time of day, having lost its sheen and now looking like clumps of pine straw hanging over her exposed clavicle.

"I said the same thing, but they had a hideout or something. Do you know about this?"

"No, I don't think so."

"You don't think so, Nina?"

"I don't know where she is every second of the day, Mom. You're one to talk."

"What's that supposed to mean? I knew where you were when you were a kid."

"But you're from here and…"

"What? Has someone said something to you? Did someone say something about me?"

"What do you mean? And…I mean…yes, they're saying stuff. Everyone is saying—"

"No, I mean about me being from here. I don't know the McGills. They weren't here when I was young. I don't know these people." My mouth was dry as I tried to defend myself from these burning fragments of the past. "He was eighteen," I said, losing control for a moment. "He was eighteen."

"Josh was sixteen," Nina corrected me.

"I know. I just mean that I only know the people who were here when I was a kid. I was only a kid, Nina."

"I'm just saying," she exhaled with irritation, not understanding where I'd left her—that I was gone now, back on the field by the Boxy. She couldn't have known. "I'm saying," she repeated, "that kids from here are a lot looser or something. It's different than—"

"Nina, *you* are from here." I pulled myself together with a breath and an accusation. I did always use Nina to get myself in order. Finding her frustrating had always calmed my mood. It was the same with Ferrol.

"No, I'm not. I'm from Atlanta."

"Why are we arguing about this right now? Lucy is in trouble!" Another gust of wind bellowed against the window frame. I saw the knotted head of a dead hydrangea roll down the street in front of the house. It looked like a tumbleweed, or the husk of a wasp's nest. "She's in real bad trouble, Nina. I don't think you understand."

"Well, she didn't kill anyone, so I guess no—I don't understand. I'm sure there's been some kind of mistake and she'll be acquitted or however it works."

"That's not how it works," I said. "You can't understand what's going on here, because—"

"You don't understand either," she said quickly. "Don't lecture me on the police or—whatever you're doing. Stop being a know-it-all, Mom."

I sighed. I couldn't tell her. I'd never been able to tell her. "Nina, I need to talk to her. Where is this hideout?"

"I don't know, Mom! I told you, I have no idea what you're talking about. That's why I know there's been a mistake or something. I have no idea what this hideout thing is. Lucy goes to youth group at church and plays Ultimate Frisbee. That's it."

I heard noise in the background. It was Lucy; Nina was talking to her and then less audibly, as I could tell Nina had moved her hand over the mouthpiece. She was speaking softly, coaxing and gentle. That was the kind of mother Nina had always been. I credited her with Lucy's good humor, her docile nature, her rather bland pleasantness. I had been very harsh with Nina, abrupt and impatient. She hadn't needed me to be, but I always felt she required toughening up.

"Lucy says she doesn't know what you're talking about." Nina was back to her snappish, clucking voice—the one she used with me.

"Can I talk to her, please?"

Nina's phone was passed with a great deal of sighing and fumbling. "Hi, Tata."

I squeezed my eyes shut at the sound of her voice. "Oh, Lucy. What in the world is going on?"

"I don't know." There was a retreating quality to the way she was talking, like a child walking away from me.

"What could the detective be talking about, Lucy? He said something about Pirkle Road." I heard a change. It was as though a second had skidded on the clock, not stopping but stumbling over a small speck of time.

"Can I come over, Tata?"

"Yes." I wiped my face, which was hot and slimy with tears. "Yes, of course. I can come get you."

"No, I'll just walk." I heard Nina's voice. She was argumentative but still pampering. "Okay. Mom says she'll bring me. See you soon."

Apparently Lucy had climbed out her bedroom window while Nina walked to the car. She never came out to get in. Nina called me seven minutes later and said Lucy was gone.

"She just took off?" I asked.

"Yes!" Nina was hysterical.

"Okay, calm down, please." I blinked several times, bug-eyed and frantic, trying to figure out what to do. "I'll go out and look for her. You stay put in case she comes back."

"But what if she shows up at your house?" Nina was still screaming. "Mom! Where would she go?"

"I don't know, Nina. I don't know. I'll wait here a few minutes, but it sounds to me like she wants to be alone. Maybe if I'm not here, she'll stick around. Who knows."

"But where'd she go? She's never run off before. Never."

"There's a first time for everything," I said, my voice lilting with my Platts Road twang. "All kids get the urge to take off sooner or later." I wasn't sure if I was defending Lucy or myself.

It took me at least fifteen minutes of arguing with her to get her to promise she wouldn't call the police. "And anyway, she's only been gone a few minutes, Nina. The police wouldn't do anything yet."

"She ran away!" Nina kept on yelling. "Or, oh my God, she was abducted!"

That had crossed my mind too, but I knew I was being ridiculous. "She's gone to cool off," I said. "She's okay. We're going to go look for her. We'll find her."

We decided that I wouldn't leave the house while Nina raced around Tuskin in her purple Volkswagen. She would die on the hill that it was not purple, but it most certainly was—like the skin of an eggplant, or a My Little Pony's hair. The point of me staying put was that Lucy might show up.

"You need to get a stupid phone, Mom!" Nina hollered at me. She called the house every three seconds and then hung up on me mid-sentence. I kept thinking she'd found Lucy or had fallen in a well, the way she kept abruptly dropping the call. Then she'd call right back and carry on as though she hadn't just hung up.

"I don't know where she is!" she continued to remind me.

"I know, Nina. I know you don't." Now I was talking to her in the coaxing manner she used with Lucy. "Just try and catch your breath."

I did need a phone though. I didn't even have call waiting, so that was another thing to contend with. I didn't know if maybe Deirdre Mansell was trying to get in touch or the detective.

I looked out my back window, hoping to see Lucy on the swing set. It was empty, as it had been for many years at this point. The green swings shifted on a faint breeze, hanging from their rubber-coated chains, done like that so she wouldn't pinch her fingers. All the care I'd taken with her. I hadn't treated Nina that way. I'd been consumed. Ferrol had been like a plank in my eye, so wide and dense that I could see nothing else. Nina grew up in a town house, and the only playground she ever went to was the one at school. We would pass them sometimes in the car when she was small. She would make a comment about it looking like fun, which Ferrol would acknowledge while I watched the side of his face to see if he still found me attractive.

Nina and I decided, after what felt like hours and hours but was really only about half of one, that Nina would now come to my house with her cell phone in hand; she was holding it when she walked in, as though by grasping it tightly there was a better chance it would ring. She had her neighbor sitting at her house. Beverly from across the street had come out when she saw Nina running from door to door. Nina told her what happened, against my better judgment, because Beverly liked to talk. Beverly was going to stay there and call Nina if she saw Lucy.

"I didn't say anything about the police," Nina assured me when she arrived. "I told her Lucy had gone out and didn't say where she was going."

"Well, she knew about Josh. I saw her at the funeral." I liked Beverly just fine, but I was covering all the angles.

"Right. So Lucy is grieving." Nina was shaking. Her hands looked like mine, the skin so thin and the veins and tendons so pronounced. "This is about grief." She put her phone on the counter, then snatched it back up. "Yes." She was assuring herself.

"Yes, Lucy is grieving," I agreed with Nina. She had been through multiple rounds of therapy and used therapeutic terms in casual conversation, mostly with me. I'd heard her talk to her friends a hundred times; she never said things like "Let's unpack that" or "distant trauma" when with them.

"But, Nina, this hideout thing…" I pressed.

"I suppose." It was all she said, a very final thought.

"You suppose what?"

"Josh drives, so…I suppose they couldn't have been going somewhere."

"I'm going to his house." I'd been indecisive up 'til now. "I want to talk to his parents. They might know. Someone has to know."

"Okay," Nina said. "I'll wait here. Maybe she'll come here." She kept saying that—that, and checking her phone for messages.

I got in my car and did a loop around my neighborhood, going slowly while peeking between houses and around hedges, trying not to drive off the road or hit anyone. I didn't want to ask any of the people I saw in their yards or driveways if they'd seen Lucy. I didn't want to sound the alarm yet. There were too many alarms to contend with at the moment. I wasn't even sure what I'd say— my granddaughter ran away because she's going to be charged with murder. I didn't think anyone would offer to help.

Josh lived on Oleander. It was a well-known house because it was one of the only ones on Oleander, a very straight, flat road named for a plant that didn't grow there. The McGills' house was very far back off the road with a No Trespassing sign stapled to the fence at the start of the property. I ignored it and went up the dirt road with its strip of pressed rock down the middle.

I found I was nervous going up the drive, imagining what it had been like to find him there, in his car. He'd driven some sort of hot-rod thing that was old and refurbished and then old again and again refurbished. He was clearly proud of it and the noise it made, a low growl, as it came down any road. All Josh's details had been incongruous with Lucy, with Daniel, who I'd come to associate with her so closely it was hard to distinguish them. Even when they broke up, it seemed like Daniel was still there; it sounded like he was. He had something to do with all this, another unexpected detail.

The car was still in front of the house, parked at an angle. The police tape remained, though it was shredded and had fallen around the tires, caked in dirt or buried under leaf crumbs long dead—brown and papery. I'd more or less ignored the details of the tragedy—at least those that were being tossed around casually, as nothing had yet been confirmed by the police. Everything in the papers had been qualified with phrases like "alleged" and "presumed," sparsely detailed and indefinite at best. The evening news also discussed the incident—Josh's murder—with guarded care. They were uncommitted to any single theory as to what had happened. I had decided that it was easier to concentrate on Lucy, what with everything that had happened. It had only been about a week since they'd found him. It was one of those periods that are both drawn out and gone in a snap.

I found that part of me didn't really want to know how Josh had been killed. Nina told me that people were saying someone in the back seat, a right-handed person, had pulled a knife across his neck and then left him in the car to die. How she could have conversations like that with her neighbors was beyond me, but then again, Nina needed conversations with neighbors—extraneous relationships, endless chatter and mindless sharing. I did not. I avoided it.

But as for this theory, I remember thinking that Lucy wouldn't be sitting in the back seat of his car. She rode up front with him. But rather than argue with Nina about what she did or did not hear, I left it alone. I also hadn't yet mentioned what I thought Lucy had said in front of Daniel's house; I didn't plan to.

I didn't know the McGill family. I'd heard of them but couldn't pinpoint why or where. They weren't from back in the day. No one lived on Oleander when I was growing up.

There were two other cars in front of the house. It was a prefab with a wooden deck built on the front, common for Tuskin. There was a pot of flowers on one of the steps, recently watered and healthy. I remembered Josh's mother from the funeral. She lived here, with his car sitting out front. They'd found him in the morning. He came and went as he pleased, and they'd thought he was in his room. I read all these things and heard them from the checkout girl at the grocery store or the man who came to do my pest service. I hadn't talked to many people since it happened, but it was all anyone could talk about—the murder.

I saw movement at the front window; I'd been detected. I knew Josh had brothers. I'd seen them at the funeral too, dressed nicely in oversize suits with ties.

The front door opened. It was Josh's father, his face mostly obscured by a full beard and mustache—dark in color, more like a mask for his round, defeated face.

"Can I help you?" he said, standing on the small porch.

I got out of my car as quickly as possible, battling with the door, my seat belt, my age when climbing in or out of anything, rising from a chair after sitting for too long. "I'm sorry," I said. "I'm Lucy's grandmother. We're looking for her."

His face changed. I immediately thought it had been a mistake to come here. I wasn't welcome. "She's not here," he said.

"I really don't know what's going on," I replied. "I am so sorry about Josh." I put my hand to my heart. It was a hollow gesture; I'd been full of them.

"Yeah," he said.

"She's run off, so I thought…"

"She wouldn't come here. Josh isn't here anymore."

I swallowed. "Yes. I don't know… Did they hang out anywhere else?" I was having to raise my voice to feel heard. The birds were loud, challenging one another in volume and sincerity. I, on the other hand, sounded squeaky and desperate.

He closed his eyes halfway, something I figured was a tic, something he did when thinking or unsure. "They're saying she had something to do with this." He too sounded desperate, but it was not a desperation we shared, rather a competing one. Our despair trying to outwit the other's, who would be triumphant in their anguish.

"I can't believe it," I said.

"Well…" He was very still.

"But was there a hideout or a—" I stopped talking at the sight of his wife. Her name was Shelly; I knew that. Her face as blotchy, inflamed. She'd come up from behind him. She was frowning at the sight of me. The day had gotten on and was losing light slowly.

"They were asking me that too," Shelly McGill said. "About some place the kids went to…" She trailed off. "I don't believe it," she said. "About Lucy. I don't."

"Thank you."

Her shoulders were drawn in front as though closing her doors forever. I recalled her buoyancy at the funeral. "She's a nice girl," Shelly said. "I thought they were all nice girls."

"Yes, they are all—" I stopped. "All the… Who is that now?" I tried not to sound too eager.

"Wynn Lattimer has a place on the river. I know he lets the kids go there and drink and all. That's the only thing I can come up with. I told the police." She sighed, uninterested in revisiting all the nice girls.

"Off Pirkle?" I asked, flinching. I was hoping maybe they would think it was about the kids drinking.

"Yeah, down that way. Back end of town," Mr. McGill said. He couldn't have known how this news was throwing me.

No one said anything for a minute. I tried to figure out how to leave. "These things are so hard," I said. "You mentioned some… some other girls."

"Right." Mr. McGill was already turning to go. I had now been dismissed.

"We'll never be the same," Mrs. McGill said.

I accidentally let my eyes wander to the car. "I'm sorry," I said again. "Please let me know if you see Lucy. I…I don't have a cell phone, but I can leave you my number." I reached for my purse. "I can write it down."

"We won't see Lucy," Josh's father said. He'd almost gone but turned back toward me. "There were three girls," he said. "Three of 'em, but I don't know who they were. Only Lucy."

1 2

1973

The first time Tyler showed up at the house, it was Rainy who answered the door.

"Hey, fool," I heard her say. It was Saturday, midafternoon. Rainy had only just woken up.

"Is Meg here?"

I was in my room, looking at Rainy's old magazines on my bed. I recognized Tyler's voice immediately. I jumped up and ran to the door. "Hey!" I said. Rainy looked me up and down, smirking. I was wearing her old gym shorts and a blue tank top; my hair looked like a yellow mushroom on top of my head. I'm sure I'd seen better days in the beauty department, but I was too excited to care. I couldn't remember the last time someone other than Johnna had shown up at the house to see me.

"There she is!" Tyler said in his soft, enthusiastic way. "What's goin' on, Meg?"

"Nothin'," I said, shrugging. I was smiling, thinking there was a chance I wasn't going to have to spend the day following Rainy around or sitting in my room alone trying to think of something interesting to do.

"I came to take you for a ride in my car so you don't feel like you have to run away anymore."

Rainy let out a snort. "Yeah, she's gotta quit running off, or Mom's gonna send her to the military school." That was always the threat, even though the military school was for boys. Everyone in Tuskin told their kids if they didn't stop doing this or that, they'd have to go to the military school. Rainy and Tyler talked for a second with me standing next to them. I could tell Tyler was just being polite—Rainy too—and then she said she had to take a shower and went off toward the bathroom. My mom was still asleep, or she wouldn't have let me leave. I thanked God for her tiredness and went out the front door with Tyler like I'd been doing that every day of my life. We went for a drive in the Nissan all around Tuskin. All we talked about was what foods we hated and how people in middle school have bad BO. It was raining and so humid there was steam coming off the asphalt. It felt like we were trapped in a wet diaper, but I swear it was the best day I'd ever had. I was on the move.

Tyler started to come around all the time, even if Rainy wasn't there. Rainy said she barely knew him anyway. "He's not coming here for me," she said when my mom told her to stop inviting him over. "He's Meg's friend," Rainy said, correcting her.

My mom said he was making her nervous. "What does he want with a thirteen-year-old? And why does he just show up? Did you ask him to come, Meg? I'd never just show up at some kid's house." She was talking about him like he was a grown-up.

"He's seventeen," I said, as if that would set them straight. "He's hanging around; it's what kids do."

"He's not a kid," my mother said, more to herself.

Rainy seemed to agree. "He's weird. He's always been weird. Rich says he wants to be an actor or something like that." There were no actors in Tuskin.

"I'm weird too," I replied cheerfully. They couldn't understand how alone I felt in a house with strippers, bartenders, and auto mechanics, though if I was honest, the auto mechanic was probably my favorite. "And I could be an actress."

"Weird for a little kid is different than weird for a man," my mother said. "And there aren't actresses in Tuskin, Meg. Come on."

"He's only seventeen. He's not a man." I must have known I would need to believe this.

"Oh, but he is."

Tripp had come to visit and told Rainy he wanted to marry her. My mom said it was because she was raking in the money at Shakers and Tripp needed a place to stay. My mom also said it was because Tyler was coming around so much. Rainy talked to Tripp on the phone a lot and told him all about our lives—not that there was much to tell, as far as I was concerned. Rainy kept telling Tripp that I had an older boyfriend, even though I'd scream at her every time she said it, "He's not my boyfriend! You and Mom can't live without a stupid boyfriend, but I can!" My mom said Tripp was worried Rainy was going to get scooped up and that his broke ass would be replaced.

My mom had moments when she was real keen to explain life to us, like she would know. But she did sound smart every once in a while, even when she was putting on her eightieth layer of mascara. I figured a person did get to know about life even if they seemed to be having a hard time with it; maybe they knew more about it because it was so hard. I had to guess people who rented places with shitty carpet could tell all those millionaires a thing or two. But for the most part, I wouldn't give it to her. I figured out early that having no respect for other people is the best armor against hating yourself.

I told Johnna about Tripp coming down. She said, "God, how sad. What? Is he going to live with Heather and Rainy?" She rolled her eyes, but it was like she had a secret.

My mom and Johnna couldn't have been more different—at least as far as outward appearances go. Johnna kept her manager's job at the restaurant and wore this tight little button-down shirt, black pants, and a baseball cap every day, walking around with a clipboard and putting papers up in the bathroom so the staff could mark who and when someone had cleaned the toilets. She had to do inventory spreadsheets and help out at the window or the counter when it got too hectic. My mother lounged all day, trying to regain her strength for the evening shift. She hid cash in her underwear because she didn't want to share all her tips with the barbacks.

Johnna talked to my mom like one would to an idiot child. My mother appeared to appreciate it. She even held herself different when Johnna was around. She seemed to be trying to get her to say, "Good job, Heather! That's the way!" I wondered what she would have done if Johnna had come in to Shakers when she was dancing. But it wasn't a secret between them. I also thought the stripping might have been the reason my mom acted so small with Johnna. It told me that no matter what she said, she was embarrassed to get money thrown at her by the people who were fixing our power lines, even if she put up a hard shell about it.

Every time Tyler showed up, my mom was giving him the side-eye and Rainy was saying he was Chester the Molester, but he let it slide—if he even noticed or cared what they thought. At least there was someone with me, even if no one could figure out why. Mom had gone to Cherokee with Lon for a couple of nights to celebrate turning forty. They just left me there by myself. When she came back and realized I'd been on my own, she said she thought Rainy would be home.

"Nope," I told her.

"Oh." That was all she said. Tyler was over when they got back, and she gave him a sneer upon seeing him on the couch. "What's he doing here?"

"Just keeping an eye on Meg," he said.

I don't think he meant it as an insult to her fine parenting, but she said something under her breath anyway.

"Yeah, well, I got your number."

"No funny business," both Tyler and I said at the same time. We laughed. My mom hated when people laughed and she didn't know why. She made her pissed-but-embarrassed face. A lot of people in Tuskin spent their whole lives pissed and embarrassed.

She had to work that night and wasn't home again, so Tyler just stayed over on the couch. He was old enough to come and go as he pleased. His house wasn't like mine—laced a little tighter but not much. His parents thought kids were grown up at sixteen and that parents shouldn't meddle. Tyler talked about them like a person would talk about grandparents they didn't see much but liked just fine. I didn't see my grandparents; I wasn't really sure I had any left. Last we'd heard, my dad's dad was in jail for something about a car.

The next day we both got up and went to school. Tyler drove himself, but I took the bus; the high school started a lot earlier. He came right back to our house after school and waited for me to get home. He had a bag of chips and some Cokes. We had finished up eating everything at the table when my mom came out of her room, angry and scowling. I hadn't seen Lon since they went to Cherokee.

"Y'all woke me up," she said when she saw us. For a second,

I thought I'd finally figured out where I got my hair from. My mom's was standing up off her head like she'd touched a live wire.

"Sorry," I said. I pressed my Coke can down real hard and let it crumple. I did it again, but this time it slipped on to its side and knocked the empty chip bag on the ground. Tyler leaned over to pick it up.

"Why're y'all making so much noise?"

"I don't know," I said. "Just got back from school."

I could tell she was confused. It must have been a lot later than she thought. "Right," she said. "Well, quiet down. I have to work tonight. Weirdo." That last part was definitely for Tyler. My mom walked back to her bedroom. She mumbled something else about getting a job. I figured she was talking to me. All the Gregory women worked at Shakers—maybe she thought my time had come.

Tyler and I decided to paint some rocks. "That'll be quiet," I said, like I gave a lick. I kind of couldn't tell whether I did or not. Just like when I was going to the mechanic shop with Lon, I now had something else. I think in the end, all I really wanted was my own thing, just some uncrowded edge of life that was mine, where I could sit without worrying about falling off.

Tyler'd found my old paint set from second grade—school issued—and said we should use it before it rotted to dust. We went outside and started scrounging for good, smooth rocks. I felt like a little kid, but then I'd look at Tyler and see the shadow of hair on his face and hear him clear his throat. When we were done painting, we went looking for places to hide the rocks around the house.

"I wanna go to California, live in Hollywood," Tyler said when we'd finished our last rock. One of them looked like a boob with a nipple; it had been an accident. Neither of us meant to do all the circles in a pinkish-beige color. "Oops," he said. He didn't like being inappropriate. Some boys lived for it, but not Tyler. His mom was churchly, he said. "A real God-fearing lady."

"We're not afraid of God here," I'd said back. "Mom's a stripper."

Tyler laughed. "No, not like that. I just mean she cares about Jesus. She's no stick-in-the-mud, though; just cares, is all."

"I don't know what Jesus thinks of strippers," I said. "Probably doesn't like 'em."

"He probably just thinks they need money." Tyler patted my back. He liked to make me feel better about my lot in life.

We took the rocks outside to lay them around the house. "We can ward off evil spirits," Tyler said. Sometimes he would talk like that, about spirits and getting rid of omens and other things I didn't understand and never heard anyone else say. He told me it was his friend Larisa who knew all about it. He said she had the second sight and could tell fortunes and a bunch of other stuff that most people thought was crazy.

"She's a gypsy," he said like he'd just learned what the word was.

"For Halloween?" I asked.

"No. For real." Tyler gave up searching for perfect places for the rocks and plopped all his in one spot, like going to the bathroom.

"No, you gotta spread 'em around," I said. "And how come I never meet Larisa?"

"You can meet her. She'll tell your fortune for you; she can do it from looking at your hand."

"Oh, man—I don't want to know. That's for sure." I was scouting good locations and hid one of my rocks behind a tree stump. I tilted it at an angle so a worm could make a home there, undisturbed by outside forces.

"Naw, she knows what she's doing. She can see things."

"What does she see?"

Tyler was acting dreamy again. He was like this when he was talking about Larisa and moving to California to be a movie star. "She said I could be an actor, but whatever." He laughed to himself the way I'd laughed to myself when I told a kid from school they called it Shakers because of the salt and pepper. I thought he winced a little—that, or it was a tiny frown hiding in the corner of his mouth. I figured it was because he needed encouragement.

"I believe it." I smiled. I could believe it. Tyler was the best-looking kid I'd ever met, probably because of his personality, but still. He had the kind of face that I could imagine in a business suit or a hockey uniform or wearing a cowboy hat. When I looked at myself in the mirror, I usually thought I looked like everybody else in Tuskin. I couldn't see another story for me; even if I was in a ball gown, I'd look like I was selling cars at the Chevy dealership on Lantern Road. Sometimes they had a gal out there waving like she won Miss America and trying to get people to buy a truck. I fantasized about leaving too, going to California with Tyler and being an actor's friend. I wasn't sure what I'd do out there other than follow him around and hang out at the beach while he was doing his acting jobs. I thought maybe he could be on a show like *Mister Ed*, something that came on TV all the time. He had a nice enough way about him.

"She lives down the street. Her aunt taught her to find evil spirits and trap 'em." Tyler was still talking about Larisa. All this about the evil spirits didn't really match with my idea of him being on a nice TV show. "She wants to come to California too, because more people out there believe in that stuff and also have powers."

"Have you ever seen *Mister Ed*?" I asked. "The show about the horse?"

"Huh?" He looked at me. "Yeah, I guess." It obviously hadn't crossed his mind. He was too busy thinking about Larisa in California with him. Sometimes the way he talked about her bothered me. I thought maybe she was his girlfriend or that he was in love with her. I didn't know what I would do if suddenly they were going to get married and run off to Cashiers the way Rainy and Tripp had.

The sky started to spit, which worried me, but Tyler said the paint was dry and that the rocks would be fine. "Let's go back inside," I said. It was September and still white hot in the afternoons. "We can play Monopoly."

"Okay." Tyler looked up at the tree line. We kept the garbage cans at the edge of the drive. It was dense beyond. There'd been a way cleared for the house but not much else.

"What is it?" I asked. "Nothing up there but trees and garbage that flew outa the cans. We're too lazy to go pick it up."

"I thought I saw Larisa," he said.

"Why?" I couldn't think of anything else to say; it was such a strange thing for him to be thinking.

"I don't know. Sometimes I see her."

I squinted, not wanting to think Tyler was a weirdo. Everyone kept telling me, but I swore other than Johnna he was the only nice person I'd ever met. Maybe it was weird to be nice. If that was the case, then my mom let me hang out with weirdos all the time. Johanna had always been the nice one. No one ever called her weird.

But things had been a little funny with Johnna lately. She was more in and out than normal. She'd be around or calling, then would totally disappear. She'd used to ask to speak to me every time she called, but not as much recently. My mom would take the phone in the bathroom and come out already having hung up. I knew it was Johnna. I complained to my mom that Johnna didn't like me anymore, hoping she'd tell her to talk to me the next time she called, but we went at least a week without hearing from her. I felt a little like the roll after all the toilet paper is gone—no use anymore.

I guess my complaining paid off, because all of a sudden I was going to stay with Johnna for three days. My mom told me to get packed for my visit after Tyler left that afternoon.

"You need to get away from here for a minute," she said.

"Damn straight," I agreed, but I don't think we were talking about the same thing.

Johnna was even going to take and pick me up from school in her truck, a real treat. Hardly any of the kids ever had anyone pick them up. There was a day care called the Rocking Horse Ranch that sent a brown bus. Even some middle schoolers had to go. They'd turn their heads and try not to be seen sitting in the back.

"Thanks," I said when I got in the car with Johnna.

"Anytime," she said. She had a cigarette out the window. She didn't smoke much, but I'd been noticing it more. Even if she wasn't always pulling on a smoke, she had brown on her teeth like some people who do. Her bottom teeth were stained the worst; I could tell she tried to hide them when she was talking straight to you. She'd keep her lips real close and only smile with the top, like a beaver.

"But what if you're working?" I asked.

"Well, yeah, then I guess I can't, but I'm off for a few days." She blew a stream of smoke out the side of her mouth. Her skin was the color of peanut butter; she was tanned like a horsehide and had light streaks in her hair to make it look even more like permanent summer. Even in the winter, my mom and Johnna kept up with their tans. They had commitment.

Johnna said we should go to the park to feed the ducks. She brought a bag of old cereal, all kinds mixed up. "Was stale," she said.

We sat on the bench for what felt like a few hours. It was so hot, and our legs were in the sun. Johnna was wearing shorts and flip-flops; she kept stretching her legs out and squeezing her feet. "It feels so good to be outa that restaurant," she said. She had her head back.

"Yeah," I agreed. I didn't work in a restaurant. "It's hard."

Johnna laughed a little. "So," she said like she was going to tell me something important.

"What?" I was sweating bullets out there. I didn't really enjoy the sun the way Johnna did, because I wasn't trapped over fry grease all day and counting stacks of napkins the way she had to. "Is it about Lon?" I asked.

She turned to me. I could see she was surprised. "Why's that?" she said.

"I can tell something's going on."

"No, you can't, Meggers." She put her hand on my back. "But I do think your mom's gonna throw him out soon enough. Might as well get used to it."

"Get used to what?"

"He's not gonna be there for a whole lot longer."

"Where's he going? To live with Dave?" I was talking about the half-mute who worked at the auto mechanic's.

"Who's Dave?"

"The guy who he does all the repairs with."

"Oh," Johnna said dismissively. "No. Not with him."

"With you?"

She looked at me. "Meggers."

"Well, where's he gonna go?"

"He's goin' to jail, Meg. Your mama wanted me to talk to you about it, but I don't know what you're gettin' at here."

"Jail?" I remembered something funny I'd heard. Rainy said Lon was on the take. I didn't know what it meant, and when I asked, she said hush and stop eavesdropping. "Why's he going to jail?"

"I don't really know. He's robbed a few places…" She trailed off. She was disappointed; maybe she'd thought Lon was going to leave Mom for her, and now this. "He robbed the restaurant." She dangled her feet, letting the flops fall to the ground.

"Oh." I dangled my feet too, but I was wearing sneakers.

"Yeah, so I might be in trouble too." She shrugged to herself, accepting her fate.

It was quiet around us. The park was empty on account of the heat. I could smell cut grass and hear a buzz. There was nothing but a trickle of air moving. The ducks had come over a few times for the cereal, but even they were bored from the sun. It'll do that—a hot frying pan over your head all day will really slow you down.

"Do you think they know it's stale?" I asked when a few of

the ducks went to look at a Cheerio but then swam away without eating it.

"Naw, they're full." Johnna was looking far away from us like she was trying to fall asleep. "So, I don't work at the restaurant anymore. Gonna have to find something else."

"Okay." I put my hand on her leg. "That's okay, Johnna. I'm going to move away, so you won't have to take me around anymore…while you're working at your new job."

She looked at me with her brows drawn together. "You're not going away, kiddo."

"I am. Tyler wants to move to Hollywood. We don't fit in around here." Tyler had said that, though he said it more about him and Larisa. I decided that I didn't fit in either.

"Well." She pursed her lips. "Who wants to fit in around here?" A duck had been swimming in our direction but abruptly turned around and went the other way.

"Even the ducks," I said.

Johnna laughed. "Yes, even the ducks are over Tuskin, aren't they? But, Meg…"

"Yeah?"

"Be careful with that kid. Tyler." She said his name with a little punch.

"Aw, he's fine," I said.

"Well, we'll see."

We went back to Johnna's place to eat sandwiches. She kept

looking around at her good housekeeping and nice things and sighing. I suppose she thought that without her job she'd have to move or that she wasn't worthy of them anymore.

The sheets smelled like detergent, and the pillowcases looked like they had been ironed. I didn't sleep well, thinking that if I'd been waiting for a sign that it was time to leave, this was it. Johnna'd come off the rails, and God knows, maybe she'd start working at the strip club too. And then there was my mom, who didn't like Tyler just because he was nice to me. It was like she wanted me to sit around the house all day by myself, doing nothing and waiting for my turn at Shakers. She didn't even care about school or my grades or any of that. She went to my school conference and said she didn't think the teacher knew who I was.

"She kept talking about a Meghan, but that's not your name."

"Did she tell you I have all B's?" I asked. "My report card is all matching."

"Yeah," my mom said absently. I'm not sure she knew whether a B was good or not.

I stayed with Johnna another night, but she was very down in the dumps and didn't even cook the spaghetti right. It was hard on the ends. I just cut those parts off with my fork and told her the butter was really good.

"It's all about butter," she said. "You with your butter hair, Meggy."

I tried to smile, but butter hair's not much to smile about. I decided I would leave with Tyler the next day. I didn't want to be at home with Lon in jail and my mom sad over it and Johnna fired and in her head all the time now. I'd heard Johnna on the phone when she thought I was asleep. I could tell she was talking to my mom; she was making sure they'd already taken Lon away. Nobody wanted me to see that. It was like nobody was left now. A void always follows a change; something snaps off and leaves a big bunch of emptiness. There's a lot of bullshit about changes being good, but I've never seen that yet.

13

I decided I would go to Pirkle and try to find this hideout thing. Maybe that was where Lucy went, even though it would have been a few miles away—a long walk from my house. I'd walked to Pirkle a few times in my life; I knew the way no matter where I started.

Pirkle Road was long and wavy, like a strand of hair plucked out and laid on a lake of green. It was one of the few areas that weren't covered in trees. There'd been a farm there a long time ago, and it still looked like it if you didn't get too close, but everyone knew it was weeds and scrub. Somebody owned it and cut it short, but nothing grew. It had been a real dig to hear Deirdre Mansell say the names of these streets like she owned the place. She had no idea.

I drove up and down Pirkle and didn't see a damn thing. People didn't have a damn thing to do off this road, or Platts, or any of the others on this side of Tuskin anymore.

Josh's mother had said the meeting place was way back off the main drag, but there wasn't anything off the main drag. There wasn't a main drag. I tapped on my steering wheel to the beat of a song I wasn't listening to. I'd never cared much for music. Ferrol said it was a disgrace, given his profession, but he had terrible taste and only listened to it to impress people. When he was alone, he played *Tetris* on his computer. In silence.

After my third run, I did spot a dilapidated cabin-type structure down by the river; we called it the Boxy River because its real name was something like Boccifallous or another word no Tuskin person could pronounce. When I was a kid, we went fishing at the Boxy a few times, right near this spot, and then there was Tyler and Larisa. Larisa's house was long gone; it had used to sit at an angle about a hundred yards from the river a little farther down. They'd torn it down while I was living in Atlanta. The last time I'd set foot on this land, I'd been with Tyler. I refused to go near it since. No one ever asked me to, but I had a silent agreement with myself that it was forsaken, that I would never return.

The Boxy had a curse on it; it was said it was sick. People said dead fish would pop up when they were on the banks, with gills and bloated stomachs turned to the light. There was a chicken plant in Harper a few miles up the road, and the rumor was, the runoff had ruined the Boxy. People in Tuskin blamed a lot of things on the chicken plant. I think most people were jealous that Harper was chosen for it; apparently there were hundreds of good jobs at the plant and people all had medical insurance. All Tuskin had was a cursed river.

Other than Lucy mouthing off in Daniel's yard, there was this thing about the witness who said Lucy was at Josh's house the night he was killed that was eating at me. I hadn't had the nerve to ask anyone about that; the only people I could have asked were Nina and the lawyer, and I didn't want to bring it to their attention. I couldn't figure out who would have seen Lucy out on Oleander in the middle of the night; it had to have been one of the other kids involved. I knew a thing or two about rolling on somebody. All chickens come home to roost.

Even though I was pretty sure I'd found it, I hadn't turned off the road yet. I was squinting and leaning into the dashboard, trying to get a better look. Sure enough, there was a small building on the water's edge. It was nothing but a shed sitting there, tiny and insignificant looking—almost like a Porta Potty. I wondered if I'd seen it before. It had been there for a long time, by the look of it. It also appeared to have been neglected for a long time. Their hideout. Lucy with a hideout; it was unfathomable.

And here, of all places.

The radio was playing in the car, but it was as though all sound evaporated and went out the vents. I could see reminders of reality, time, and place slip through the plastic lines; my awareness went with them, in a thin stream. I was thirteen, and Tyler was in the field next to the river. No funny business—then why was he screaming? I'd slowed almost to a stop, my foot still on the gas but barely pressing. There were no other cars around, no one to honk at me or swerve around my Mercedes. "Go on, now," I said to myself. "They're not here anymore."

I turned the car off the road onto what looked like a path. The way I was rocking and rolling over every nook and cranny in the dirt made me think I'd misjudged whether this was a good spot to drive. I made it within a few dozen feet of the lean-to and got out, leaving the heavy car door swung open, shredding the grass. I heard the caw of a bird and the shutter of wings overhead. I'd been detected.

"Goddammit," I said as I started walking toward the shed. The ground was wet; I was wearing heeled boots, an unfortunate choice. With every step, I slid down and tilted backward. I was shuffling the whole way to the cabin, trying to figure out if I was alone. I could hear the snap of twigs and rustling in the long grass; the water's trickle was sad, slow, and faint. I kept turning around, but to nothing.

The cabin wasn't as small as I'd originally thought but was rather short; it had a low ceiling and a sloped roof. On the front was a porch. I could see empty beer bottles and cans, like Rolling Rock and the other good stuff the kids like. I knew none of that belonged to Lucy. She wasn't interested in drinking. Nina wasn't particularly strict about it, having read a French parenting book that she swore by, and I'd even offered to let her have a sip of one thing or another. Lucy never partook. She said she didn't like it. Josh had smelled like booze a couple of times when they'd been at my house. I remembered catching a whiff as he walked past me and being surprised. It was another thing that was so unlike Lucy.

The door was bolted shut with a giant lock dangling from a metal hook. It was curious because the place was such a dump, nowhere you'd want to rob; it hardly looked like it could stand. I knocked on the door, feeling foolish. There was clearly no one there. I looked at the thin river and remembered one time Lon had taken me fishing there. We caught three trout and talked about growing up. We never did it again; Lon said my mom didn't like him running off with me. She was a jealous person, is what he said. I'd been maybe eleven at the time and didn't understand what he meant.

I went over the edge of the porch and took the giant step down to the weedy grass. The water was clear, with small bubbles where it hit the rocks in the way. Apparently we could drink out of it when we were kids, but now no one dared. There was a grand row of trees on the other side of the water, so thick a person couldn't walk back there. I shuddered from a warm breeze that seemed to blow the past out of the dirt right there on the bank. I could see her face, staring at me from the copse—Larisa, with her pointed beak of mangled teeth hidden by a split lip that had never healed right. And Tyler, with his lenient smile and warm eyes, brown and swimming in understanding. No, it's not the same, I kept telling myself. No, it's not the same. They're both gone. Gone. She's not here anymore.

There was a line of police tape on some markers on the side of the shack facing the river, not visible from the road, but the location had not been given much significance, as far as I could tell. I couldn't imagine Lucy here; this and everything else I'd been told was incongruous with any idea I had of her.

I had been thinking, after leaving the McGills', that of course I'd noticed more than just small changes in Lucy recently—I'd been reluctant to notice them, but they were there. Lucy's relationship with Daniel, though rather uninspired, had made sense. When they broke up, she told me it was because Daniel was going to get a job. I'd responded that a person could have a job and a girlfriend, but she'd said that he wouldn't have time anymore.

Then suddenly Josh appeared, and although she looked the same, she was more coquettish and pleading in her manner. I thought, for the first time, that Lucy was trying to be sexy. She dressed as she always had; it was what the girls wore—everyone looked ready for a jog at any moment. But she got a little more deliberate with herself, tilting her chin, letting her T-shirts drop from her shoulder, cocking her hip to the side. I'd thought maybe she was becoming more womanly and would like to dress more feminine, so I bought her some dresses and sweater/jeans ensembles, but she either said it wasn't the right weather for them or she was saving them for special occasions that never came.

At one point I had the impression—which I similarly ignored or, more likely, misinterpreted—that someone was telling her how to act. She sometimes appeared to be trying to imitate someone, tilting her head awkwardly and running a finger through her hair or raising her eyebrows so as to appear innocent and willing, like she'd been instructed to do these things. It was unnatural but evocative. I'd see it and then not see it again, thinking I might have imagined it. Lucy was metamorphosing and had been for some time, longer than I wanted to admit.

Michael, Lucy's father, was a committed but rather ineffectual person. The fact that Nina could have had some scathing battle with him was hard to imagine, as he didn't have a lot of yang to his yin. I knew he tried to make his visits with Lucy count by planning excursions, but I think the two of them were so quiet together that the time felt long and uneventful. I'd asked Lucy what she and Michael talked about. "We don't really have anything to say" had been her response. She talked to Daniel though. I would hear them when they came to my house, lolling, silly conversations that neither startled nor interested me, but I'd been satisfied by them. Satisfied that Lucy knew how to have friends and that she felt appreciated, because other than Daniel, there hadn't been a lot of connections for her over the years. Nina would fuss and worry that she didn't have friends.

"She's invited to the birthday parties, but she doesn't talk to anyone when we get there." Nina would detail how she would try to get the ball rolling with one group of kids or another but that Lucy would stand idly by, as though none of it had anything to do with her. "She's sooooooo quiet."

But she wasn't quiet with Daniel and their group at church. She talked to me plenty; Nina would grunt in disapproval when I told her that. "Yes, Mom. She talks to me too, but we're her…relatives. I want her to have friends."

"I don't have any friends," I said in reply. "Did away with them years ago." It was true; the divorce and the move and the way I felt about myself just didn't allow for it. It is impossible to explain to someone who is much younger than you that you do not feel you have anything to give anyone else and that you are largely okay with it. The only person I wanted to fret over was Lucy. And now this.

Josh's father had said there were two other girls, three in total. I couldn't think of a single female friend I'd ever seen Lucy with. I had no idea who he could be talking about or who would have met her at this cabin where I was sitting. And then there was that moment at the Farmers' house and the fact that Daniel was going to be charged too. What could Daniel have had to do with any of this? Nina had been remiss on that detail, shrugging it off like I misheard or, on the other hand, of course he was going to be charged too!

I was also convinced that Andrea Farmer knew something. She'd been especially uneasy with us earlier at the house, anxious for the moment to pass so she could continue not saying anything, eager to have me and Nina gone and Lucy expelled from their property. Andrea had also been absent from the funeral, which was not a peculiar detail at the time, though I'd noticed it, but now that Daniel and Josh had apparently been hanging out with these other mystery girls, it seemed odd. Andrea did have a little bit of a side-eye for anyone and everyone. I had not thought we—as in Lucy's family—were included in that. But there'd been a shift. Always this shift.

I looked to my car; there were definite impressions in the grass around it, not made only by me. People had driven here before today, frequently. It was while staring at the trampled earth off Pirkle Road that I remembered something. Lucy told me that she'd had her cards read. She was at my house one afternoon after school, watching some show on television about making cakes look like other inanimate objects, and during one of the commercial breaks, she turned around on the couch and told me that she had bad cards. I was standing in the kitchen, cutting the crusts off her peanut butter and honey sandwich.

"What?" I thought I'd misheard her.

"I had a few really bad cards. I can't remember what they were, but I don't know..." She trailed off and let her attention go back to the screen. "Just weird," she said under her breath.

I'd assumed she meant tarot, because that was the only kind of cards I could think of. I didn't ask her about it, having a profound distaste for that sort of thing—tethered with knots and locks was this concept for me, forever connected to a crow girl who I'd never told Lucy about. I'd changed the subject—like a coward—asking her about math class and if she wanted chocolate milk. She might have been trying to tell me something, and I'd pretended she was seven and cared about the crusts on her bread.

But it was odd and very out of place on the map of Lucy's life. They weren't reading cards at Mount Calvary Christian Church. They didn't even let the girls wear nail polish there. I remembered thinking it was reminiscent, an irritating facsimile of something else I'd not wanted her to see, like a distorted photocopy of me smoking cigarettes in tenth grade. I'd have to explain that smoking was wrong even though I'd done it, and where did this come from? She'd had her cards read. Larisa used to do that sort of thing. We were meant to find all that so amusing, and then it just wasn't.

I told myself it was time to leave, having passed more minutes on the Boxy than I should have, more time next to the grass, the rancid field. The wickedness was a bile that burned my throat. Lucy was not here, and I was glad for it. I didn't want to picture her here, next to this grave. The dirt was still full of his screaming. Death is an indelible stain; it doesn't come out. Bad dirt makes bad seeds.

14

1973

It was winter break and there was a lot of thunder—a lot of thunder but no rain. "I only like storms in the summer," I told Tyler. We made hammocks out of my mom's old purses and skirts. She'd dressed like an old-lady office worker for a while, I guessed, because there was a whole stash of grown-up clothes in a box in her closet.

"She'd never wear this," I said, pulling a dress with puffy sleeves out first. I'd found everything a week earlier and asked her if I could have it.

"Burn it," she said. She was joking, but in a mean way.

Tyler was the one who said we could make hammocks. "Just sling 'em up between the trees out there."

"S'cold though," I said. I wasn't really arguing. Tyler was full of ideas. For every second of the day, he had an idea about something we could do to have some fun with our dire lives. I figured we were biding time 'til we ditched and ran off to California. Might as well make some hammocks and lie in them, even in the bad weather.

"We can get blankets," he said.

We set to work, cutting and sewing. Tyler said Larisa was the one who taught him how sew like that. He was giving himself a compliment, because I thought his stitches were a mess and way too far apart. There were gaps everywhere between the pieces, but I supposed it would hold. We were going to use these rope purses as security so our asses wouldn't fall through.

"So she's a psychic and a sewer?" I asked. I was getting a little tired of hearing about Larisa. She was everywhere but nowhere, as far as I was concerned. She'd never blessed our door with her holy presence; all I did was hear about her. I knew she had that long, black hair though. I could see it in my dreams at night; one reason I thought maybe she was a gypsy devil woman or something, sending parts of herself to me in my sleep. I'd asked Rainy if she knew her, but she said Larisa moved away.

"Only Larisa I ever knew don't live here anymore."

"She has black hair," I said.

"Yeah, that's the one." Rainy wasn't interested.

But according to Tyler, she did live here, and she was all he wanted to talk about. It made me more and more worried that I was going to get ditched. Before Tyler, it was Johnna who looked out for me, tried to make things fun and made life feel special. She still did it, but she was sad too. Tyler was the only person I knew who wasn't a downer or always trying to tell me how hard it was going to be. They'd all decided that I was grown up and had to face the facts. Tyler, the closest to me in age, thought I was still a kid. He let me think it too.

"She's not a sewer; that's where you dump water!" Tyler said about Larisa and her sewing. He never said anything like he was mad. He was glad to have something to say, even if we were disagreeing. I found I wasn't as happy talking to him about Larisa as I was about other things, and goddamn, did she keep coming up. "She just knows how to sew."

"Is she invisible?" I asked.

"No, but she's careful about who she meets. She doesn't want to get found out." Tyler would say she was around all the time, but I never saw her.

"Found out about what?" I snapped a strap into place. Tyler had carabiners for the hooks—those, and ropes. He had hammocks at home too. He said he and Rich laid in them and talked about life. I was like another brother, only younger and a girl.

"She's living with her aunt and it ain't legal, so she doesn't want anybody to know. She's kind of in hiding." He raised his eyebrows. The day was blustery, with heavy clouds that hung low and mean. It was a wet wool-blanket day; it looked like one and had that same sodden quality.

"Hiding and sewing," I said. "Sounds exciting." I felt like someone had to be honest about things.

"Well, her dad used to beat her up. She ran away. She's like us—she's not afraid to leave."

"I'm not afraid to leave," I said angrily, feeling accused. "Where did my mom get these clothes anyway? They're huge. She's never worn anything that wasn't skintight in her whole life."

"I don't know," Tyler said. He didn't care about my mom's strange clothing. "Maybe she was different before."

"Before what?"

"Life, I guess."

I heard footsteps in the leaves. Sometimes even a squirrel could sound like a truck on the ground cover when it was bulky enough. I turned, not because of the noise but because of the way Tyler perked up. "She's here. She's watching us," he said. He looked at me. "She must like you."

15

Not a soul had come over the humps in the grass to investigate a Mercedes parked in the weeds off Pirkle the whole time I'd been there. Tuskin people are busy pressing on. They don't have time for a displaced woman on the porch. The stories about the South are lies; people mind their own. They know you can pick up problems just by saying hi.

I stumbled up to my feet, having to first kneel and balance with my hand. I usually blamed my clothes for all this fumbling movement; the waist of the pants was too high and tight, the suede skirt hindered my maneuvers, my boots were a size too big and I couldn't get a good grip while sliding around inside them. The list of excuses went on and on. I finally got to my feet and wiped under my eye one last time. I'd pulled myself together, assured myself that Larisa wasn't here, that this had nothing to do with her, with Tyler, with me. "You're sixty-four years old, Meg." I often reminded myself of that.

I'd been crying, the eeriness faded and in its place, common sadness. My most uninteresting state of mind was that of being forlorn. Everything else had a bit of a whip crack to it, like the thing with the Butterfinger and the way I'd mouth off to the pest control service for doing a half-assed job with the wasp's nest. But when I was sad, it was plain—not bitter, not salty, not cloying, but plain.

There were so many things I should have asked Josh's parents but had been too embarrassed to, too unprepared upon seeing their stricken faces. I'd been completely absorbed in our trouble. Now I sounded like Nina—*Lucy's trouble*. Then they came to the door and I realized that they had trouble too. The victim is the first forgotten; I'd learned that a long time ago.

It was getting later, the slow decline of the day. I was increasingly alone with every dot of light that disappeared from the sky. My shoes made knocking sounds on the wood beams; I was like a clopping horse going to the side with the less steep drop-down. I heard noise from the road after it was suggested by a moving dot in the corner of my eye. The car appeared and then I heard it. It seemed to be slowing too. I'd been noticed. It was a black sedan, or maybe a station wagon. I couldn't tell and didn't have my glasses. I thought the driver was looking at me, and me at her. I thought I saw someone else in the car too, in the passenger seat. I saw a blond ponytail; I was sure of it. I waved, but both people turned to the front as the car sped up. It was a woman driving, a woman with long, black hair. More than one person in the world had long, black hair; I had to keep reminding myself.

"Lucy!" I yelled. I tried to run, but the heels on my boots slid into the ground with every step. I'd always walked hard on my heels. "Lucy!" The car was gone.

I was crossing strings, a tangle of kites not flying in the same sky. Lucy and I were not the same. I had not passed something on. I needed to get my head out of the past, where it liked to sit, on a post, removed from my neck so that it could defy all logic.

I thought I could go up to the old house on Platts. Maybe it would settle me. I never went over there, refusing to acknowledge what had been. I told myself I wasn't looking for Lucy there, wasn't going to find her anywhere near it. It would be something to do, keep me moving, salve the waiting. I could call Nina from a pay phone; I hadn't been gone all that long anyway.

I drove up the incline, having gone from the T-bone onto the hill. It looked the same as it always did, my old house—abandoned, left, a place where people don't matter. The Pawleys' house was still painted yellow, with a cinder block front porch. There was still an old tractor in front of where the Graysons had lived; that thing had been there for a hundred years at this point. It had one of those sloped noses painted an army-green color. I could tell a couple of the houses were empty now, having been given up on. They were leaning and caving in, places where someone had once fixed dinner. It was mostly forgotten, all the dinners and the people who ate them.

I still had dreams about the house, though I think I was dreaming about the person who'd lived there. A different Meg who got tangled up. I'd been so young, but there were no excuses anymore and no need for them. All the answering had been done. Tyler didn't live on Platts. I would not see his house today. I would not see Larisa's either.

I turned the car around in the circle at the end—not a cul-de-sac, but a dead end big enough to hold a long Mercedes. My mother had moved out before I came back. There was nothing of her here, though she'd given a good twenty years of her life to this place and the upkeep of everything in it. I thought of her as always letting things fall apart and away, like owning possessions on only windy days, but really she'd kept it mostly together. I went to school, Rainy graduated, we ate meals and had holidays. She did try; I had barely noticed at the time.

"I gotta get back," I said to myself. I looked at the clock on the dash; I'd been gone well over an hour now. A little panicked, I drove at a breakneck pace, jutting down Platts like the kids used to do when they left parties at our house, drunk and reckless with power.

I was unused to moving at such a clip on the road. I usually meandered slowly, veering this way and that, righting the direction of my car over and over as I crossed one line after another, but not today. Today I was like a bullet. I was honked at three times between Pirkle and home, but instead of it being for going so slowly, this time it was for blowing through stop signs and pulling out in front of oncoming traffic—twice.

My car ended up partly in my yard because I'd tried to miss a squirrel. I could see Nina through the front window. She was on the phone and pacing. I tore through the front door, tracking grime from the creek into my precious foyer. "What?" I yelled at Nina, who had not said anything to me.

She held up her hand and continued to talk. It was her cell phone. I looked at the answering machine on my kitchen counter; the light was not flashing.

"I have no idea," Nina kept saying, increasingly animated with each syllable. "I don't know, Dad!"

I exhaled. It was Ferrol. Of course it was. I waited with my hands crossed over my chest, feeling that if I removed my shoes, I would somehow insult the importance of what was going on. I could mop later. I could not mop at all. What difference did mopping make? Most things that I could think to do with myself had about as much significance as dust collected on a forgotten shelf.

The phone call was interminable. Nina seemed to be trying to convince Ferrol to come to Tuskin or get another lawyer or become a lawyer himself. "She's not even fighting it," Nina said. "She's just going to let them charge her. I have no idea. I could get my degree and do this myself a lot better than she is!"

I assumed she meant that Deirdre Mansell had not thrown her body in front of a speeding police car to thwart a criminal investigation.

"Can we get another lawyer though? We can keep Deedee, but I think we should have another one too. Someone who's a mother."

Now I rolled my eyes. "Nina," I said, "I need to talk to you."

"Hold on. Mom's here now." She turned to me. "No one called except the lawyer—Deedee or whatever her name is. She says you need a cell phone. No one has seen Lucy." Her mouth puckered, then fell at the edges into a trench on her lower face. "She hasn't come back. Beverly's still at the house."

"I found their hideout, or whatever it is," I said. "There's police tape, but it didn't look like anyone thought it was a big deal. I walked right up to it. I mean…at least, I'm assuming that was it. Maybe the police were there for some other reason. I really don't know." My shoulders dropped from my ears as I let out a breath.

"You found it?" Nina had heard only half of what I'd said.

"Can you get off the phone?"

"It's Dad."

"I know! But I don't… Can you please just get off the phone?"

"Dad!" Nina yelled. "I'll call you back."

She checked the screen for a couple of seconds before looking at me. She had dark, hollow spots under her eyes where the joy had left. I'd known people my whole life who had those spaces. I had thought I'd spared Nina of such cancers.

"Beverly hasn't seen her. She's texting me every three minutes, but it's always the same—nothing."

"Has Lucy said anything to you about a woman?" I could hear the bend in my voice, a twist in my delivery. I sounded like a politician.

"A woman? I don't—what? Like one of her teachers?"

"No, not a teacher." I shook my head ruefully, as though she should have known. "Has she befriended someone…someone my age or…"

"Mom." Sometimes Nina had Ferrol's accent, a northeastern, nasal quality to her voice that reminded me of him. "No. I don't know. Obviously I don't know what is going on, because I didn't know she was hiding out somewhere either. But no, I don't know if she's made any sixty-year-old friends. Where would she meet someone your age?"

"I don't know, Lucy. I'm just wondering." I couldn't say it, not even to myself. "I thought I saw someone, is all. And Josh's dad said there were three girls. Lucy was hanging out in a group of girls."

"You're hardly a girl," she snapped.

"I know that. I'm talking about two different things… Anyway, it's on the Lattimers' land." I said that last part more to myself. I'd been contemplating this detail but had yet to make any sense of it.

"The Lattimers? Who are they?"

"I knew Wynn way back. I guess there's a son, and the kids would go over there to party—or maybe it's not his son. I have no idea; I barely remember him. And maybe Lucy has never set foot there a day in her life. Everyone is just guessing, but Mr. McGill did say there were three girls."

"Lucy doesn't party." Nina was as certain as I was that this detail was incorrect. "And three girls *including* Lucy or in addition to Lucy?" Nina's eyes were bulging, along with a vein in her neck.

"I don't know. But did she ever tell you she was hanging out with a group of girls? And Daniel? What does he have to do with Josh?"

"Maybe she misses Daniel," Nina said. "She's sad. Maybe she just needs a friend." She was the one being reasonable at this point.

"Yes, of course," I said. "Of course. I'm…getting screwed up here. Just worried, is all." I paused, considering telling her that I thought I'd seen Lucy, and maybe Larisa, but Nina didn't know who Larisa was. And Larisa wasn't back in Tuskin; it was silly that I was making this connection. Every time something bad happened, I was in the room with Tyler and Larisa and she was laughing at me. It was so long ago. "It has nothing to do with Lucy," I said absently. "I'm just saying that the McGills told me there was a place all the kids were going to hang out off Pirkle, and sure enough, I found one. It had a lock on the door, a real serious deadbolt that didn't look old. I don't know what to think."

"I don't know what you're talking about, Mom. And no. I don't think Lucy met anyone or partied anywhere. You're the only old woman Lucy hangs out with."

I thought of the car I'd seen on Pirkle, the woman with the dark hair, Larisa's hair. Larisa's face pressed against the window.

"He's dead," I said.

"Who?" Nina asked. I didn't answer. I wasn't sure who I was thinking about.

16

1973

Mom did Christmas with a lot of heart. She said it was her favorite and why shouldn't we do things right for once in our lives? We always got a tree and decorated it with cheap ornaments from Walmart. She got more every year, so we had to really dig to find spots for them, and then one year she said if we wanted, we could decorate a tree in the yard too. These were the tinsel years, and we had it everywhere. She made sugar cookies from a mix, and Rainy and I both got presents. I made my mom a gift at school in art class. She said it was "real nice" and put it on the mantel. Rainy had said we should go to church to celebrate the birth of the savior, but my mom said she'd tried church on and it didn't fit.

It was a lot like old times for a while over the school break. Thanksgiving had been quiet, but we did it. My uncle Marvin came over with his wife and one kid named Dana, who took her shoes off before she came in the house, I think because she didn't want to get them dirty. Aunt Mary was a decent cook and brought three dishes covered in plastic wrap. My mom served wine that she brought home from the bar, and I thought it was just fine, as it always was. Tyler had a huge family, and they all had turkey in a barn somewhere like Tennessee or Alabama and wore flannel clothes, patting each other on the back and drinking his grandfather's homemade beer. It sounded fun, but I hadn't been unhappy at home. Johnna had come to Thanksgiving and Christmas before, but didn't this year.

"No Johnna?" I asked my mom the day after Christmas when we were eating crescent rolls and watching movies on TV.

"She's busy," she said. She was letting her hair grow a little longer. It softened her up. She'd also been in a good mood, since she had three days off work in a row. She said she'd never felt so rested.

"What's with all those clothes in your closet?" I asked her. It was Bugs Bunny on the television now. Before, we'd been watching a movie about King Henry the Second that neither my mom nor I could understand. The people talked with posh accents and made dramatic faces in white lighting right next to the camera. It was cold out, and it felt good to be lazy. I hadn't seen as much of Tyler because of his huge family and all their get-togethers. He said his face hurt from smiling so much. I told him, "Get used to it, if you're going to be an actor."

"What clothes?" my mom said.

"The ones we used for the hammocks."

"Oh, those weren't mine."

"Where'd you get 'em?"

She took a breath like she was pulling herself back to reality. "My mom got 'em from a friend for me. She wanted me to try to go to secretary school."

"Oh," I said, surprised. My mother never really talked about her family—that, or secretary school.

"Yeah, but I didn't finish high school. It probably wouldn't have mattered, but I didn't go to secretary school." She sounded like she thought that was funny, a funny shame. She adjusted herself on the couch. Her feet were by my shoulder and my feet by hers. We had an afghan over us with a few snares that our toes kept getting caught in.

"Do you wish you had?" I asked.

She turned her head to look at me. "No," she said. "I don't know what I wish I'd done."

"Hmm," I said. "Where's Rainy?"

"Beats me."

The following day, they both had to work. It was back to just me and the house, all by our lonesome. Tyler showed up in the middle of the day. He said his aunt was having a banger for New Year's. "Do you wanna come? Larisa's coming too," he said.

"Yeah, I'll come," I said, a little annoyed that Larisa had already been asked. "It's not in Tennessee, is it?"

"Naw, they're all coming here."

I usually did something with Rainy on New Year's, but we weren't really hanging out all that much anymore. I decided it was because her voice was always raspy from yelling in the bar, and her hair looked greasy no matter what she did with it. Her face was red and ruddy from being up so late, drinking cheap vodka. She always stayed after and hung out. My mom did sometimes, but I could tell she had some judgment that Rainy just couldn't let it go.

"We're in there half our lives already," I heard my mom tell Johnna on the phone. It had gone back to feeling like Johnna didn't want to talk to me when she called. My mom told her I had a boyfriend, so I guess she thought I'd outgrown her. Tyler wasn't my boyfriend, and I hadn't outgrown anything. My mom did always think men made all the difference.

Johnna had gotten another job at a dry cleaner's. She ran the register and took the clothes through the window. She had a stool and didn't have to wear black pants anymore; it was a step in the right direction. She'd told my mom about her new circumstances, and my mom shared it with me. "She gets to sit down at work. That'll be the day," my mom said, sounding a little jealous.

"I'm going to a New Year's party," I told Rainy on the thirtieth. It was all I could think about.

Rainy didn't sleep as late as my mom. She'd get up and make herself a sandwich or sometimes chili from a can—heated, of course. She liked to watch TV and look at magazines. She bought a few from the store every week and tore through them like memo-rizing their tips and tricks was the key to her survival. I'd notice her doing some of the makeup ideas or putting egg yolks in her hair. She always got *Cosmopolitan*, with all its sex advice. I didn't ask if she'd tried any of that.

"That's cool," she said. "I gotta work."

"What should I wear?"

"Oh!" She smiled at me, happy to be useful. I'd now outgrown her by a couple of inches. Our frames couldn't have been more dif-ferent—me long and loose, and her tight like a fresh pack of ciga-rettes all crammed in there together, no room to breathe. "You could probably borrow something from Mom."

We waited another hour before going into my mom's room. She'd put all Lon's things in a box that sat by the bedroom door. I assumed she thought he would be coming back; either way, he didn't have much.

"Meg's got a party," Rainy said. My mother was sleeping on her stomach and didn't move even when Rainy pulled the curtain back a little so we could see the closet.

"What time is it?" my mom asked. Her hair looked like school paste on the side of her head.

"Three," Rainy answered. "Here, Meg." She'd pulled out a long, red dress with a square neckline and puffed sleeves at the shoulder. "This is pretty."

I walked over to where she was standing. I'd never seen my

mom wear anything like it in her life. "This is nice." I ran my fingers over it.

My mom had rolled to the side and was looking. "Oh," she said flatly.

"Why don't you ever wear it, Mom?" I asked.

"Where?" she said, then flopped on her back. "I don't have any-where to go in nice things."

"Where'd you even get this?" Rainy was in awe of the finery.

"Your dad. He always did know how to waste money."

"It's so nice," I said.

"Well. He did try, didn't he?" My mom was back on her stom-ach. She never seemed very sad that he'd walked out that final time. Lon had kind of come in and taken all the air, sauntering around like he'd just gotten off a large horse and his crotch needed airing.

"What was he like?" I asked, surprising myself.

"You've met him a hundred times, Meggers," Rainy said like she was defending my mother. I suppose she knew better why things didn't work out between them. She could remember when he still lived with us without one foot out the door.

"I don't really remember," I said. "All I remember is Lon telling him to leave all the time."

"Yeah, well…Lon didn't know his ass from his elbow, did he?" My mom laughed and Rainy joined in, once again in her defense.

Rainy and I left my mom trying to wake up and brought the dress to my room. When Rainy pulled it off the hanger, we saw it still had a price tag, gone yellow on one edge from time and rubbing. It was from JCPenney. There'd been a shopping center in Hopewell for a while, with just a few stores, but it closed when they made a new freeway exit. It was hard to imagine anyone buying her a dress with puffed sleeves; she just wasn't the type. In every memory I have of her, she's wearing jeans shorts and a cutoff shirt. She'd always been proud of her navel.

"But what was it like with Dad?" I asked as I slipped the dress over my head. I could hear the trash truck at the end of the road. They usually just walked down to our house to grab the bins, then brought them back. It was too hard to turn around in the circle. One time, a truck had gotten stuck down there and had to have a manager come to help the driver get out. Everyone on Platts was standing in the street, making remarks about box trucks and which angle the guy should pull the wheel. It had been a sunny day and almost felt like we were becoming friends with our neighbors, about to put some hot dogs on the grill, but then the truck was gone and everyone went inside.

"You're getting boobs," Rainy said. "Maybe that's why Tyler wants you at the party." She smiled hopefully.

"No way." I put my hand across my chest. Johnna made comments about me needing better bras all the time. Being a teenager was proving to be a real embarrassment.

We messed with the neckline of the dress for a little bit with Rainy making noises in her throat; she sounded both like she was approving and trying not to vomit. "It looks nice," she said.

"Yeah, but what about Dad?"

"He was okay, I guess," Rainy said. "Mom said he did drugs and that was why he had so many problems. I guess he was a good guy before."

"What kind of drugs?" I asked.

"I don't really know. Some people are just depressed, Meg. He was like that, always moping around and making Mom do all the work. I don't even know what was wrong with him. He was nice, though. He thought you were cute as a button. He fussed over you all the time; he was good at that—hanging out with babies and little kids, but he didn't have a lot of energy or, I don't know. He just wasn't a man, couldn't take care of anything."

I thought maybe I was a lot like my dad, because I didn't have a ton of energy. It didn't really seem like anyone in our house did—except Rainy. "Mom's tired all the time too," I said.

"Naw, just during the day 'cause she's catching up. She's a worker bee; so am I." Rainy was proud.

"Do you know Larisa?" I asked.

"You asked me about her before." Rainy scrunched her face. "You should wear black shoes."

"I don't have black shoes," I said.

"Well!" She threw up her hands. "No, I didn't know Larisa, but she went kind of crazy with her sister and all that. Who knows with them."

"She has a sister?"

"She did, but her sister died."

17

I was home and waiting by the back door. Nina said she would go and get me a phone; she wanted to drive around anyway. "I'm restless as all get-out!" She pounded the kitchen counter. Every once in a while I could see Tuskin in her. I'd buried it in myself when she was young and then taken her back to it, trying to make up for all the lost time.

We'd confirmed that Beverly was still at Nina's house and that she was raiding the pantry. "She's eating every time I talk to her. Does she need a snack every five minutes?" Nina was incredulous.

Every night around this time, my neighbor would go out and sit on his back porch with a beer. His name was Gary; it was both comforting to see him so committed to his routine but also a little sad, in some way I couldn't define. I'd never worked—not like Gary. Ferrol didn't even work like Gary. Ferrol was in charge of everything, slamming around, barking at people, laughing at a two-martini lunch that he left for in his Jaguar. Gary worked at the roofing company, called Trager Roofing, doing something that required him to wear a button-down and a tie. Occasionally I'd go outside and say hi to him while he was sipping. I could hear his wife in the kitchen, calling something out to him while he stared at the sun. "Hiya, Gary!" I'd say. He didn't know what to make of me; he knew I was from Tuskin and yet not from Tuskin the way he was. I'd gone and come back with a different skin on my bones. He was friendly, but his expression told me he just couldn't relate—or rather, that he knew I couldn't.

I went outside while Nina slammed herself into her car. She wouldn't calm down. I was panic-stricken too, but it wasn't doing anybody any good. Nina said the detective had told her to "just wait."

"Just wait? What the hell is he talking about, 'just wait'?!"

Gary was on the porch already when I got outside. He held his hand up in salute but kept his focus on the hedges by the back fence.

"Have you seen Lucy?" I called over to him. "My granddaughter." Men never knew anyone's name.

"No." He had turned to face me but clearly didn't want to talk. "I haven't seen her. Just got home." Gary's wife, Anne, came outside. She normally didn't join us, choosing to remain in the kitchen or elsewhere in the house no matter how long Gary and I talked. She wasn't unfriendly, just polite.

"She was here earlier," she said. "I saw her at the end of the street. Was strange. She was just standing there. I thought to tell you, but your daughter was over."

"What do you mean, she was at the end of the street?" I walked quickly over to the chain link that separated our identical flat, rectangular yards. I could remember being so pleased to see the yard when I toured the house with my Realtor, a woman named Charlotte, who was unnecessarily intrigued with the Atlanta aspect of my life though I made it clear I did not want to discuss it.

"Did you ever see any celebrities?" There were dozens of questions like this over the two-week period that she showed me houses. "I guess I don't know why you'd want to move here. Tuskin's not that cool; there's no celebrities or anything here."

"I'm from here," I'd said coldly. "And there are hardly any celebrities in Atlanta. I'm not sure where you got that idea…"

"*The Real Housewives*," she said expectantly. I'd turned away from her to roll my eyes.

"She was…just standing down there," Anne said of Lucy. She wiped her hands on the front of her pants and shook her head as if trying to explain why vegetables tasted so awful and Twinkies so good. "It was odd, Meg. I have to say."

"When was this?" I tried to hide my frustration that she had not come to tell me my granddaughter was standing in the street in a clearly disturbed state.

"An hour ago, maybe? She wasn't there long, but I passed her on my way home from the store. She looked at me but didn't smile or wave or anything."

I thought maybe Lucy had run to my place when she went

out the window. "Did she come here?" I asked Anne, pointing to my house.

"No. She stayed up there by the Pollards'. I walked out after I'd put the groceries away and she was still there, but then about five minutes later, when I went out again to get the mail, she was gone."

"The Pollards'?" I asked. I didn't know that name.

"Yeah. The family on the end."

"I don't know them," I said.

"They haven't been here long. About two years, give or take."

"Oh." I tried not to appear embarrassed. "I guess I'm getting old."

"Yes," Anne said. "Maybe that's it." She was not convinced.

"I'll walk down there and introduce myself. Listen, Anne? Nina's gone to buy me a cell phone so I'll be easier to reach, but if you see Lucy, can you please tell me right away? I don't know if you heard what happened…"

"I heard." She nodded, then let her eyes wander to Gary, who seemed to be refusing to look at me. They'd clearly discussed the murder. "I swear, kids now deal with so much. Must be so hard to be young in this world," she said.

The veins in my neck popped; even my blood was angry to hear her say this. "Oh, it's always been hard," I said, trying to quell the urge to explain everything to her—Anne, with her Gary and her envelope-shaped yard and their dinner and TV routine. She had no idea how I grew up. I cleared my throat to get the moment to pass.

"Well, I'm sorry I didn't come say something to you. I thought maybe she was hanging out with the Pollard girl again and maybe it was some game or something. You know—statues in the garden, something like that."

"Hanging out with the Pollard girl? Who is this Pollard girl?" I sounded angry, like I was accusing Anne of withholding information, which I kind of was. How could she not have told me that Lucy was hanging out with people in the neighborhood I clearly didn't know? She could see that I hardly left the house, and when I did, I didn't talk to anyone—maybe Gary, if I was feeling particularly generous.

"Melanie Pollard."

"I don't know Melanie Pollard." My intensity was increasing.

"Oh. Well." Anne was tired of passing judgment on my unneighborliness. "She's Lucy's age. Give or take—so hard to tell sometimes. But they were friends. I saw Lucy down there a lot."

"Thank you," I said, turning away from her. "Thank you very much." I started walking back to my house with my hands shaking. "Have a good night!" I sounded like a balloon losing air, something silly dying, its empty latex shell left on the ground, ready and willing to choke a bird. "Bye now!"

I went immediately into the house, straight through the kitchen and hall to my front door, opened it and walked down the street. Anne had said the Pollards' house was on the corner. I had a clinging layer of moisture in my armpits, the kind you get when you're nervous, not hot. I was wearing a green sweat suit and brown boots with red laces. I looked like an olive.

I knew the house on the corner but didn't know it had recently changed hands. I'd never paid attention to who lived there. I paused when I got closer. The front porch was much larger than mine, a giant concrete structure with a lean-to roof. It was covered in plants—hundreds, hanging from hooks drilled into the wooden framing. There were pots everywhere, with only a narrow path to the door, strewn with refuse. It was familiar, so much so that I had a shifting at my rib cage that made me feel as though the top half of my body had slipped into another time and place. I was by the river again. Larisa's aunt's house. With all the plants on the porch. I looked at the front door and saw a woman standing behind the screen. She was familiar in the way of an illness. I always know when I'm coming down with something; I've been there before.

18

1973

Larisa was already at Tyler's when I showed up. We were going to his aunt and uncle's house for the party in Tyler's car. He said we could crawl home if we had too much to drink. I'd never taken a sip of alcohol in my life, finding its effects on the people I knew very unappealing.

Larisa was sitting on Tyler's bed with her legs crossed under her. She had a long strand of beads in her hand; it looked like she was making a cat's cradle. I quickly realized she was the girl from the party. I'd asked Tyler before if she was with him the night of Rainy's birthday. He said yeah but she had left because of the bad vibes.

I walked into Tyler's room not really knowing what to do with myself; this was my first time hanging out with both of them. I felt out of place and younger than I did with just Tyler. I certainly didn't sit on his bed whenever I was over; I sat on the floor. It seemed presumptuous, like Larisa thought she was the Queen of Tyler or something. I couldn't help but frown in my red dress.

Larisa's hair was long and dark, but not as dark as I'd remembered it; she had honey strands around her face and freckles. She had light skin, a wide mouth, and wandering eyes like a fox.

"Hey," she said, extending her hand to me. "I'm Larisa." She dropped the strand of beads on Tyler's mattress.

"Hey," I said, leaning forward to reach her. I didn't normally shake hands with people. That was something I saw in the movies or when men were having beers at a restaurant. "I'm Meg."

"Yeah!" She smiled and pulled at the hem of her dress—a pale-blue apron-style number, over which she wore a gray sweater. "You're fancy," she said. I got a better look at her mouth. Her teeth were crooked and all busted up. And she hadn't shaken my hand but rather held it, using the tips of her fingers to feel around. "Real fancy," she said again, but more to herself.

"Oh, thanks," I said. I wasn't sure anyone had ever called me fancy before. It wasn't a word that got thrown around our house much.

"I'll do your cards before we go. I can feel an omen on you—a bad omen. But then I feel riches too. Lots of riches."

"What's an omen?" I was wearing tennis shoes with my dress and hoping no one would notice. My hair was in a barrette over my right ear; Rainy had helped me. We'd found two good pairs of church-type shoes in the back of my mom's closet, but they were too big, even if I wore a puffy pair of socks with them.

"You get them from other people," Larisa said. "Like—someone can put one on you."

"Who did it?" I asked, surprised but not convinced.

"I don't know. I can't tell that much; might be a ghost or something."

"Larisa knows all about this stuff," Tyler said, suddenly chiming in. He'd been quiet up to this point, letting me and Larisa talk. I'd almost forgotten he was there, which was odd. I never forgot about Tyler, even when he wasn't around. "She's an expert," he said when I didn't respond. He was clearly impressed.

Tyler was wearing a flannel shirt and a bow tie as a joke. His hair was longer and even more turned behind his ears than normal. He was letting his beard grow in a little too. He looked so much older standing there with Larisa; I was like their daughter, or a toddler they were supposed to babysit.

We took Tyler's car to the party, which was near the lake. It was his aunt and uncle's house, but the way he explained it they were more like his cousins. I couldn't understand it. Tyler's family went on and on. My family stopped at Mom and Rainy; what a difference. Tyler said their parties went 'til all hours and that they were "cool as hell."

It was a free-for-all the second we walked in the door. There were Crock-Pots on the counter with ladles stuffed in them and crackers and meat all over a giant folding table in the middle of the room. The house had high ceilings with colorful light fixtures hanging down and what looked like bricks for floors. It was a bright, loud house where everyone was smiling and sloshing about, all grown-ups save a few patches of kids who were huddled together like they were cold, but it was more young awkwardness.

"Wow, is this all your family?" I asked.

"A lot of 'em are," Tyler said. Someone handed him a beer and patted him on the back. It was another man, but not his dad. Everyone there was wearing flannel; they were lumberjack people. Tyler had called them that once, saying they were from Wisconsin a long time ago. I looked out of place in my dress, but no one seemed to notice me at all. Larisa immediately wandered away from us, seeming comfortable. She was taking it all in, leaning over people's shoulders and tilting her head to listen. I stuck with Tyler, not sure what to do with my hands or how to stand. Tyler kept introducing me to people, but it was a fake interest that I got back. I was too young to be of consequence, or I looked ridiculous in a long, red dress at this wild party in the woods.

Tyler gave me a beer, which I sipped on, finding the taste was like sucking on coins. Larisa had made friends fast and was lecturing a group of younger women about something. They listened hard, leaning forward and nodding. I could tell she tried to cover her teeth when she talked, pulling her lips down and over them, just like Johnna did. Tyler had said she had a rough life. *Join the club*, I'd thought, but at least my teeth didn't look like that. I didn't have a lot to be proud of, but no one had ever hit me. I knew like a fish knows it's in water that someone had popped Larisa real hard in the face. She had a scar on her bottom lip too.

"Where's her sister?" I asked Tyler as we made our way through a loud crowd, yelling about something.

"Who?" he asked.

"Larisa's sister."

"Naw," he said, shaking his head. "She died."

I didn't like the beer and thought that everyone at the party was acting the same age, not old or young but somewhere in the middle—stuck in a time warp and pretending to be the age they liked best. I put my index finger in the mouth of the beer and carried it like that, worried my finger might really get caught in there and that we'd have to break the bottle to get me out.

It was the biggest party I'd ever been to, hands down. I thought Rainy would have been jealous because there were three times as many people there as at her big party. Tyler let me stick with him and almost seemed to like having me as a pet and having to explain everyone and everything.

"She's a hairdresser, but she got mad at her ex-boyfriend and shaved his head in his sleep, so she almost lost her beauty license."

"My dad doesn't like that guy anymore. He won't say why. My mom thinks maybe he stole from my dad."

It was story after story, mostly pleasant stuff or Tyler trying to be funny. "He has the worst breath this side of the Mississippi River," he said of his cousin. "You can't stand within ten feet of him."

"Where's Larisa?" I asked after a while.

"Probably drawing a crowd." Tyler laughed.

She wasn't though. We found her halfway between the house and the lake. Tyler's aunt had set up tiki torches out by the water. People were joking about jumping in and going for a swim. Someone had put on a life jacket as a joke and was standing around drinking a Long Island. He kept saying, "Gotta life jacket to go with my Long Island!" People stopped laughing after the fourth time he repeated himself.

"What's a Long Island?" I asked.

"A drink," Tyler said. He stuck to beer and had his cap turned around backward. His eyes were a faded blue, like jeans washed too many times. I caught myself staring too long and turned away, embarrassed. I didn't have a crush on Tyler. It wasn't like that.

Larisa was sitting on the ground a few yards away from the guy who was so proud of his life jacket joke. She had her eyes closed and was humming. "I feel something," she said when we got closer. I figured she felt us, or she wouldn't have known who was walking toward her.

"There's badness in the lake here," she said. "A snake."

"It's too cold for snakes," Tyler said.

"Not this one." She continued to hum. I looked at Tyler; he was smiling. He'd told me at least a hundred times that Larisa had all these sights and gifts and visions, but I'd never been able to picture what that was. Now she was singing to herself in the dirt at a party. I had to guess that was what it was like to be a clairvoyant, or whatever they were called. It wasn't as glamorous as I'd thought it would be.

"What happened to her sister?" I whispered to him, but I don't think he heard me. That, or he didn't answer.

19

I was up on the Pollards' front porch, having waded my way through the plants, trying not to step on a stem or a blossom or trip over a pot. I banged on the wood next to the screen door a few times, but no one came. I even pulled on the thin metal handle, but the screen door was locked. It budged just a little, its bottom corner scraping the frame but not moving more than a half inch. I'd passed another neighbor on my way up the street, a gentleman out for an evening stroll. I saw him often. I'd asked him if he knew the Pollards, and he said yes and pointed at the end of the block where I was headed.

"She's got a couple of kids—girls." He was sweating in the thick dusk air. It was warmer than it had been; the humidity was digging its way up from the ground, ready to lay its heavy hand upon us for the next six months, pressing and leaking with profound commitment.

"Melanie?" I said to the door, repeating the name my neighbor had said. "Melanie Pollard?"

The tremors were building again, a quake from the sea cracking its way through the coastal plain to Tuskin. Georgia's made like a bowl for a reason—to hold all the displaced sand. Its soil is full of shards from the ocean, small crystals of what's already been broken down. Resolve is fragmented away one millennia at a time. I placed my hand on the brick wall and waited for my blood to stop sloshing.

There was a bird calling from a nearby tree; it had a harassing, electric sound to its voice. My nerves were bouncing under my skin. The bird was increasingly annoying, and then I thought I could hear a clock inside the house or the low sound of a television with clicking buttons. I steeled myself against toppling over, feeling like I was sitting in Larisa's house again, the plants all over the porch, and the wind chimes clanging, hundreds of wind chimes. Larisa with her cracked teeth leaning over my shoulder, whispering that we had to get out of there. And Tyler. Tyler in the field.

"Tata." It was Lucy.

"Oh my God, Lucy!" I was still bracing myself against the wall. "Oh my God. Where have you been?" I sounded angry. "And who the hell lives here?" I sounded angrier.

"Tata," Lucy said. "I have to talk to you."

"Lucy—please talk to me." I started to walk down the stairs. She was in a multicolored rag dress, homemade, nothing like she normally wore. It was something Larisa would have had on. I blinked very quickly and shook my head, and then she was in shorts and a T-shirt again. I rubbed my forehead and found I was sweating; my skin was almost foamy.

"Can we go home?" Lucy had been walking in the direction of my house. "What are you even doing here?" she asked as I came down the stairs and over the corrupted stones that led to the street. She acted as though nothing out of the ordinary had happened, that I was the one who was behaving strangely.

I wasn't sure how to react, so I followed Lucy's lead and pretended I wasn't the least bit flustered. "Yes. Yes, let's please go home. Your mom is in a state like I've never seen. You can't just leave like that."

"I came back." Her voice was flat and low. I turned to look at her because it was such a surprise to hear her speak that way.

"Well…" I stared at her, waiting for her expression to change. I thought for a second her hair was darker and her nose more upturned. *It was a long time ago, Meg*, I told myself. *She's gone.* I looked back at the Pollards' house. I'd heard that Larisa had died. I had heard that, hadn't I? "I made a lot of mistakes when I was younger." I wasn't sure what I was talking about.

"And anyway, I didn't run off," Lucy interrupted. She sounded like herself again, light and buoyant. "I really did just go for a walk. Mom's a mess, and I'm…you know. Josh got killed." She was insistent.

"Yes, of course," I said. "I know you're upset. I… Lucy, the lawyer called and said they're going to charge you. We have to talk about this." It was now finally dark, a very decisive dark that had come over us in a hurry after lingering for hours on the edge of the horizon. "You're going to have to tell me what happened." We continued to walk.

"I don't know what happened," she said sharply. "I don't know."

"But, Lucy, you have to know something. What about this place on the river? The Lattimers'? Do you know them? Were you hanging out there?" I sounded more accusing than I had before. She put her hand to her mouth, her eyes turning away from me. I had fought such similar shame. I reached out to touch her but brought my hand back, realizing that I had nothing to offer.

We'd stopped and were standing in front of Gary's house, so close to the sanctuary of home and yet trapped beyond it. I wanted to keep moving, but Lucy took a breath like she might actually confide in me. "Josh was a bad guy," she said. "Melanie can see things. We had to do something."

I closed my eyes, telling myself I hadn't heard her right.

"Who is Melanie?" I said, refusing to ask what she meant. "Who are you talking about?" I'd started speaking more quickly. I didn't want to sound angry, but I was having a hard time controlling myself.

"She lives down there." She pointed at the house where we'd just been.

"Pollard?" I said. "I've never seen her, never met her, never heard her name." I was banging the blade edge of one hand into another. "Never, not once." I was fighting a building rage at not knowing who this person could be, this person directing Lucy who lived so close and was yet a mystery. And I had wanted to know, to care about, who she was spending time with. I had been diligent. I was not like my mother, just happy to have me out of the house. I shook my head again, the loose parts inside rattling, then falling into the wrong places. "Lucy, people are not always what they seem. I know what she said… She can't… Larisa…" My voice sounded as though it were going backward, away from me, like falling and reaching for the part of the sentence that made sense. I could not grasp it. "I mean Melanie."

"She can see things," Lucy said again. "And we had to do something."

20

Larisa didn't go to school, didn't work, and didn't seem to have anything else to do other than get vibes and fight omens—and hang out with Tyler, of course. I sort of wished he hadn't introduced me to her, because I'd had him to myself before. Now it was always the three of us. Tyler brought her with him every time he came over and acted like I wanted it that way. She was always at his house too, not that I could show up there without him picking me up, but for all the time I was spending with him, she got double. It started to feel like I was never alone with him; I couldn't remember the last time she hadn't been around.

She was nice enough to me. I think she bothered me more than I bothered her, or rather if I bothered her, I couldn't tell. She talked to me plenty, usually about my future, and made me all kinds of things. She had an endless supply of little baubles that she could turn into all manner of jewelry, necklaces, whatever. I found out later she was a real good pickpocket and that she just lifted whatever she wanted from any store she went into. She had a rule—had to be smaller than your thumb to take it. Tyler told me that. Larisa never told me anything about herself; it was always about me and what she could see.

She made me a bracelet with an evil eye on it to ward off people who might be jealous of me. "I don't know who'd be jealous of me," I said, but I liked the bracelet and even liked some of the stuff she talked about. No matter what we were doing or where we went, she could feel the vibrations around us. We had to leave the DQ because Larisa said there was a cruel wind in the store that was following us. She wouldn't let Tyler drive on Sharpes Pass because of the road demons who would move the line and make him crash. It made us feel important, like why did all the bad spirits care about us so much?

Spring came early with all the trees exploding, their buds in a frenzy to release. Tyler sneezed sixteen times an hour, and Larisa said the spring would be bad this year. "Sometimes spring has bad intentions." I figured she would know.

We went to Larisa's house only once—at first. There were all kinds of plants everywhere; the whole front porch was covered. "It's a forest," Larisa told me. She said her aunt planted everything to keep the bad spirits away. The inside of the house was dark and grimy, like all the surfaces had been wiped with a dirty cloth. That first visit had been a memorable one. I always wanted to go back to get a better look around, but Larisa said her aunt was wary of visitors. Larisa said she was too sensitive to have a lot of people around. "She soaks up their histories…*shhhhheeeeuuuup*." She made a sucking noise. Tyler's face was always serene when she talked about being a witch or whatever it was she was trying to be. It was like he'd known a dozen people like Larisa. I'd never met a soul like her my whole life. I couldn't have made her up if I'd tried.

Larisa talked about her aunt a lot, Aunt Kim. She hadn't been at the house when we went. There were signs that another person lived there, but few. The refrigerator was mostly empty, and the only things I ever saw on the clothesline were Larisa's clothes, the rag dresses she wore that tied around her neck. She cut up perfectly good clothes to make them. Someone had bought her a whole bundle of nice things, but she had her own style. She said she needed to get the vibes out of the clothes before wearing them. "I don't want to absorb."

Tyler said Larisa and her aunt got donations from the church because of their poverty and the way Larisa's dad had gone to jail. I asked my mom if we could get donations from the church, mostly because the clothes seemed really nice. "We don't go to church," she snapped back at me. I didn't think Larisa went, either, but they still got the clothes.

My mom had never liked Tyler coming around so much, but now he seemed like the better choice compared to Larisa. As soon as my mom met her, she said she didn't want her at the house anymore; she waited until Larisa wasn't there, but she made a point of it just the same.

"I don't want her over here, Meg." My mom came into my room to tell me. Tyler was there, helping me put a rod under my bed because it was sinking in the middle. He said he'd had to do the same for his cousin George, who loved Velveeta.

"What are you doing?" my mom asked Tyler.

"The mattress is all sunk in the middle," he said. "I'm puttin' a post under here, just so it doesn't sink down to the floor."

"Then she'll be sleeping on the wood." My mom put her hands on her hips. "And I don't want that girl here anymore."

"Larisa?" I asked, even though I knew exactly who she was talking about. I'd actually gotten used to her, almost preferring when she was around. I liked feeling like someone I knew had a handle on all aspects of life. Larisa lectured me and Tyler constantly. We were happy to be her students, feeling we had the upper hand in all situations because of her second sight.

"Yeah. I don't want tarot cards and Bagleys in my house." My mother's face was steely like a knife.

"Okay," I said. Larisa had only just started reading tarot cards, or at least she said she was in training for it. She said her aunt was a master reader. But she was a Bagley; there was no arguing with that.

"It's no harm," Tyler said, smiling. "She don't mean nothing by it, just for fun."

"That's devil worship," my mom said.

I watched Tyler, confused that he was saying it was only for fun. Usually we took everything Larisa said so seriously and listened to her warnings. "She's all right," Tyler said.

My mom shook her head. "You don't know," she said a little more loudly.

"I've known—" Tyler started to say before stopping. "Yes, ma'am."

We finished messing around with my bed, with my mom in the next room talking to Rainy. I heard my mom say Larisa's name and saw Rainy make a face like she had a stomachache. I'd never heard them talk about Larisa before. It used to be Tyler who they'd murmur over, calling him a creep.

"She better not show up here again. I know *alllll* about it." My mom was talking to herself again.

"He shouldn't be in her bedroom all the time," Rainy said. I don't know if my mother heard her.

Tyler went home to help his mom clean. She didn't like to do anything alone, so she had Tyler and Rich around as much as possible, helping and keeping her company. My mom went out, not to work but to meet a guy. His name was Terrence. She wore a tight shirt and a bandanna in her hair, like she was going to work on a farm.

"What's Mom's problem with Larisa?" I asked. Rainy and I were watching *The Mary Tyler Moore Show* and laughing through our teeth. It was an odd moment to ask about it, but Rainy had her guard down. She kept running her hands through her hair and pulling on her bra straps.

"Who?" Rainy asked.

"Larisa."

"Oh." She sounded disappointed. "Naw, it's her family. Crazies."

"Who's her family?" I asked. Tyler always made it sound like Larisa didn't have any family, or that her aunt had saved her from them. "Other than her dead sister."

"In jail now. Even her mama. Killer types."

"Okay," I said, rolling my eyes. There weren't a lot of killer types in Tuskin, not that I knew about. The guy who owned the gas station had gotten shot a while back, and there were some murders that people blamed on people driving through on Highway 7. It was a shortcut to Macon or somewhere bigger.

"Grifters," Rainy said, though I hadn't asked her to clarify, and anyway, I didn't know what that meant.

"But she lives with her aunt now," I said, defending her.

"Same shit, different toilet," Rainy said. "I don't even really know though. Just Mom not wanting Bagleys in the house. They were always doing voodoo and stuff, so Mom thinks she's rotten. They taught all their kids to do spells and curses and weird stuff."

"Okay." I looked down. Larisa had bragged a few times that she cursed someone. She didn't say it like a warning, more just telling us that she'd had to. People who wouldn't leave her or her aunt alone.

"And Tyler's a dork for wanting to hang out with you." She pushed me a little. "At least, I hope he's just a dork…" She gave me another friendly shove. I fell more than I normally would have; my balance was off because my thoughts were so heavy.

2 1

"Listen," I said to Lucy. "Is there anything you want to tell me before your mom gets back? Anything. She's gone batshit crazy over this…not even what happened with Josh, but you going out the window. It's code red, and I need to know what's going on. I promise I'll be calm. I'll help you. Whatever you need, but you have to tell me."

"Tata," Lucy said. "Josh got the Ten of Swords. He wasn't going to stop, ever. So we had to go ahead. It was that and the Hanged Man. It was going to happen to him whether we did it or not."

"What are you talking about, Lucy?" I pressed the tips of my fingers to my temples. I kept telling myself that she wasn't really saying all this.

"Melanie did his reading, and we all knew." Lucy spoke as though nothing even remotely out of the ordinary had transpired. She sounded like a computer.

"Melanie Pollard?" I was leaning over her like I'd done when explaining that she couldn't run in a parking lot or that she needed to chew her grapes for at least fifteen seconds before swallowing.

"Josh couldn't keep doing that," she said calmly. She didn't seem to notice that I was upset with her. And I couldn't think of another time when I'd actually been upset with Lucy—not one. When she'd been very small, I always closed our time together by saying, "Olive Lucy!" She'd taken my play on words to heart and told Nina "Olive you" one night before she went to bed. We had such a laugh over that, me and Nina. It was almost as though nothing bad had ever happened in my whole life. It's remarkable how things can fade into oblivion, even if for just a moment. They wait, hidden, but for a passing moment, they are not with us. The worst of times have momentarily disappeared.

"What are you talking about?" I repeated. I heard a car coming behind me and said a prayer it wasn't Nina. Nina would surely add a hurricane-like hysteria, even if she tried talking in her calming parent voice.

"I'm just saying it's not our fault, Tata." Lucy looked away, a stranger having overtaken her body. "We had to."

"Lucy, I really can't understand what's going on here. Are you on drugs? Drugs were a big thing when I was younger, and I can't recommend them." I stopped, composed myself, and restarted. "I, personally, have never done drugs, but I've seen a lot of people on drugs. People who went to jail. I just mean that if you are having trouble with drugs, I want to take you to see someone. There are programs for this."

"I'm not on drugs, Grandma."

"Tata," I corrected her.

"Lucy!" It was Nina in the car. She was screaming, her head-lights veering left and right, blinding us, then turning away to the other side of the street.

"Maybe Mom's on drugs," Lucy said, laughing.

"Lucy, none of this is funny." I grabbed her arm at the bicep, and shook her straight, forcing her to look directly at me.

"Stop it." She pulled away, frowning.

"Mom!" Nina had parked her car in the middle of the street, taking the time to put the hazards on but not to pull even the slight-est bit to the side. "Mom!"

"Sorry," I said, dropping my hand to my side, surprised by my own behavior. "Sorry," I said again. "But you're scaring me."

"Are you okay?" Nina grabbed Lucy as though protecting her from me. "Lucy, are you okay?"

"I'm fine, Mom. I just went for a walk." She shrugged.

The shrug unsettled me; it was almost disrespectful. "She was at the Pollards' house," I said. "Do you know them, Nina?"

"No, I don't think so," Nina said absently. She had her hand on Lucy's face and was smiling gently. It was dark enough for me to be unsure of Lucy's reaction. I thought she might be smirking. "I'm just so glad you're okay."

I was waiting for Nina to scold Lucy or at least tell her she'd scared us, but all she did was smile weakly, as though trying not to fall asleep. "I'm going back there," I said. "Right now."

"No, Mom. Let's just go home, or to your house so we can relax. I got you your phone, and… Are you cold, Luce?"

"It's almost eighty degrees," I said. I had no idea what the temperature was, but it wasn't cold. This was a ridiculous concern, given everything that was going on. "I'm going to the Pollards'. Nina, did you know she was hanging out with this Pollard girl?"

"There's no one there," Lucy said.

"Are they your friends?" Nina spoke as though addressing a preschooler.

"Yeah." Lucy nodded.

"I didn't know you knew them," I said.

"Well, I do. Come on, Tata. Let's go home."

"I'll meet you there," I said, turning toward the end of the street where the Pollards' house sat.

"Mom!" Nina was emphatic, having been awoken from her euphoric slumber, and was now bordering on shrill. "We just need to sit down and relax for a minute. It's been a terrible day."

"Yes, and it's about to get worse. They'll probably come to arrest her tomorrow. I'm trying to help you, both of you. These things don't just go away, and—" I was losing track again. "Are these girls involved? Do they know Daniel too?"

Nina shook her head. "I don't know, Mom."

"I'm asking Lucy," I snapped before she could continue talking. Another car came around the corner, heading in our direction.

"I have to move my car," Nina said. "Come on, Lucy." She took Lucy's hand, making it clear that I was being excluded, even if only momentarily. "Mom, I have your phone."

"I'll be right there."

Lucy kept looking at me over her shoulder as she got into Nina's car. She was concerned; gone were the arrogance, the strange mockery that had accompanied her down my street. Something rotten coming up from the sidewalk in the night. Now I sounded like Larisa. I told myself to stop it and walked briskly back to the Pollards'.

There was no one there; Lucy had not been lying. No one answered the door again, though it was, again, only the screen in place, the larger door still swung open. I didn't hear any sound coming from the house, which was entirely dark. I had the same sensation as before, that I'd stepped back in time, slid into another moment, a different person in my feet, placed there by confusion and survival. I could almost hear the sound of the river. There was a movement at the window, a lock of hair and an arm sliding away from view.

22

1974

I'd never been alone with Larisa. It was always me and Tyler, and then she'd come and go. Tyler came from a long line of people who got their kicks from having friends around. It only made my own house feel more desolate. We didn't have friends. We didn't have big parties with all our family and everyone we knew. There were always people at Tyler's house, being jovial and drinking something with his mom or helping his dad with a gutter or a drain in the yard.

"Some people are just like that," my mom said when I told her that we didn't have a lot of friends like the Crosses did. "Got people around all the damn time. House is like a hotel."

"Why are we loners?" I was helping her make tortillas. She had some odd talents, and making tortillas was one of them. Every once in a while she'd make a big batch and freeze some. It was so unlike her, but I was used to it, and all the other things she did that were unlike her.

"I don't have time for all that," she answered before dropping a blob of lard in the pan. "Time's all I got. I don't want to fill it with other people."

"Yeah," I said.

She glanced up at me. "You like having people around, don't you, Meg? Johnna's like that too."

I hadn't actually seen Johnna a lot recently, and whenever I had, she was alone. My mother said she was busy with her dry cleaning job, but I had a bad feeling that I'd done something wrong, or that because I was getting older, I wasn't as appealing. No one wanted to pretend they had a teenager. My mom had said that Johnna always wanted kids and that she was loaning me out to be nice.

"You can have friends over," my mom said. "Rainy always does."

"Yeah, but we don't have a big family or anything. And you don't like Larisa."

"Of all the people you could have met and become friends with, you had to hook up with a Bagley."

"What's wrong with a Bagley?" I moved some of the cooked tortillas around on the plate where they were resting.

"Don't mess with 'em, now." My mom pulled at her shirt to make it cover her belly button—self-conscious, I suppose, but only in front of me. Everyone else in Tuskin had seen every inch of her, as far as I knew. "The Bagleys are all crazy. They're all criminals, and that girl's as messed up as the rest of her family. The apple don't fall far from the tree," she said, plopping a tortilla down on the stack.

"How do you know them?" I asked. I was feeling curious and a little powerful. I finally knew someone or something of interest to my mom. Normally whatever I was doing or talking about was a nuisance, just something she had to listen to so she could get to the next thing.

"I don't know the little girl, or I guess she's not so little now, but that whole family was in and out of jail for a decade. I'm telling you, the women too. And anyway, they say that kid, Larisa—or whoever she is—they say, and I don't know, but they say she shot her sister in the face or something like that…" Another tortilla hit the stack.

"What?" I'd opened a bag of chocolate chips and was eating them three at a time. I stopped chewing, thinking they suddenly tasted like chalk.

"Yeah, she shot her. Didn't get jail time because of her age, or somebody said it was an accident or whatever, but Dena Bagley is dead, and, well—"

"She lives with her aunt though," I said. "And what does that have to do with tarot cards?" My mom had been so torn up over her having the cards out in my room.

"I guess she told the police officer who questioned her that her sister had the Death card or whatever it was, so she was just doing the prophecy. It's nonsense, all of it, but that family wrote the book on nonsense. I don't know, and I don't want to know. It's bad stock. Some people come from bad stock. She's not the first Bagley to get accused of killing somebody—not even close. They were all anybody could talk about for years and years." She sighed. "Old Tuskin trash, is all, but bad people. Real bad."

23

We went to bed—or rather, I went to bed. Nina and Lucy had gone home. We'd all sat around the table for a while discussing unimportant matters, with Nina making a slicing motion with her hand every time I tried to say something about the murder investigation.

"I don't know if I prefer white cheddar popcorn or regular popcorn with butter—they both have salt. I really don't know," Nina said sharply. The pace of the conversation was blistering. "And I've discovered that I absolutely hate umbrellas. I hate them." She was cheerful in her admonishment. "I end up more wet than I started. Haven't you noticed that?"

Lucy agreed wholeheartedly but was clearly as disinterested as I was. "Yeah," she said. "Umbrellas are the worst."

"So tomorrow," I interjected. "Tomorrow is... We need to be prepared if they bring you in, Lucy."

"Tomorrow is another day!" Nina sang. It was clearly meant to be an ode to *Annie*, but she had both the melody and the words wrong. "Tomorrow! I mean it! Tomorrow!" The moment was insufferable. Nina had never been able to carry a tune.

"Yes," I agreed, "but we need to be prepared. Do we know if the lawyer has tried to contact you?" I was looking at Lucy.

"Nope! I guess that means they're going to drop the whole thing," Nina chimed in. "Haven't heard a word. Beverly's still at the house, and she said the only person who called was Misty… you know, from Jazzercise." Nina had done Jazzercise for approximately six months and made ten lifelong friends while attending class once a week. Her group stayed at the back of the room and called themselves the Jigglers, which was absurd because Nina was terrified of jiggling—any type—and would refuse to eat the skin on an apple, claiming that was where the sugar calories were. They laughed and laughed over it, often while on the phone with each other when I was at Nina's house for one reason or another. The Jigglers. It wasn't even all that funny. "Deedee hasn't called. I think we're in the clear." Nina smiled expectantly.

"What happens if she does arrest me?" Lucy asked with benign curiosity.

"*She* won't arrest you, Lucy. The police will arrest you. It will be this Adam person with his strange last name." I pounded the table, mostly because I couldn't remember his name and he bothered me so much, with his vague familiarity and the itch-I-can't-scratch way he had of looking at me, like he was just about to explain his significance.

"She's not going to get arrested," Nina said stupidly.

And so they left, with Nina planning her weekly dinner menu, loudly and with forced bravado. "I'll do pork chops! I love them with a pepper jelly!"

I lay in bed for hours, tossing and turning, thinking I heard something or someone in the yard, waiting for the phone to ring, thinking Bingo had died because I didn't hear him moving around the house like I normally did. The quiet anxiousness of the night was like a fog inside, something unusual and unwelcome, a layer of mist hovering. I felt pressed to the bed because of it but also unable to rest. It was like lying under an anvil.

I even tried praying, something I'd always been terrible at—no training. I asked God to get Lucy out of this mess, to protect her from all this badness and return her to his fold and the church youth group, to the Daniels of the world, with her Frisbees and her Rice Krispie treats—where'd she been so safe, so contented. I found, in the midst of asking for help, that I was suddenly angry at God— furious, rather.

"I just don't understand," I said as my tone changed. "What with everything that's already happened, Lord, with Tyler gone like that. Did you have to do this to Lucy too? Why does she have to get messed up in this same shit? I never let her do the cards or the readings or any of that. I was a good grandmother—not entirely pious, I'll admit, but I didn't lead her down a bad path. I didn't even talk about bad paths with her! I kept her away from all of this, God! Is it Tuskin? Are bad omens and dead teenage boys a Tuskin thing? Should I have stayed in Atlanta? I find that hard to believe, given what's going on there day in and day out!" I stopped to take a breath and felt a stream of warm liquid roll from the corner of my eye and down my face onto the pillow. "I'm sorry for yelling," I said with a sniffle. "I'm sorry for yelling."

When morning came, I was relieved to find that I had fallen asleep. There was a papery, rancid taste in my mouth. I hadn't eaten dinner. Nina had made Lucy popcorn at my house, announcing that they would have pasta when they got home. I'd had but a few pieces before going to bed to scream at the Creator.

I poured some cereal into a bowl—Lucky Charms—and sat down at the table. Bingo was at the front window, scouting rodents. I'd named him that as a joke; it was a joke no one ever laughed at and that I was never asked to explain. I barely knew anyone, and no one I knew thought I was the least bit funny.

The phone rang, causing me to drop my spoon on the table. "Goddammit, I'm going to need some Valium," I said, having never taken Valium in my life.

"Yes?" I said, answering. The phone Nina had purchased for me sat on the counter. It was charged, with a welcome message on the screen. I immediately felt like a teenager, which was who I associated with cell phones, and in an aggressively negative light.

"The police are here." It was Nina.

"Oh, so you didn't get to make your pork chops?" I asked.

"What?"

"Sorry. I'm just not surprised, and I was so frustrated last night with you and this Pollyanna bullshit when there is clearly something very wrong, Nina!"

"The detective guy says he's not going to handcuff her, but they're heading to the station. What am I supposed to do?" she said, hushed and conspiratorial.

"Go to the police station. Call the lawyer. I'm going there now." I rose from the table, dumped the remaining milk and few bits of cereal in the sink, and headed to my car, still in my nightgown and bathrobe. I stuffed my feet in my yard boots on the way out and left the front door open.

Deirdre Mansell intercepted me in the small square of grass in front of the precinct. She was standing there on her cell phone, wearing sunglasses and looking entirely dignified.

"What's going on?" I shouted, hurling myself toward her, my pink fleece robe wrapped tightly around my waist in an attempt to cover my sagging breasts.

Deirdre held up a finger to indicate she needed a moment, and in an instant of regrettable impulsivity, I slapped her hand. "Don't you give me a wait-a-minute finger, bitch! I'm old enough to be your mother!" I tightened the belt of my robe as though putting punctuation on my remarks. "I'm a senior citizen," I announced even more officiously.

"Mrs. Gregory," Deirdre Mansell said, shocked but purposeful, "you are standing in front of a police station. I would recommend you not assault your granddaughter's lawyer. I am trying to help you."

"Yes, well, you're certainly taking your time." I didn't really know what I meant, but I thought if she was really giving her best effort, Lucy wouldn't have been escorted from her home by the police at eight o'clock on a Thursday morning.

"I need to get inside so I can sit with Lucy during questioning. Please do not touch anyone else—and I would dare say, you have plenty of time to go home and get changed. Lucy is not going any-where, at least not today."

"Oh my God," I said. I sounded bitterly angry, but it was dismay, something entirely different.

I refused to leave the station, and stood rather authoritatively in front of it while several people walked in and out. Some of them were in uniform, while others were in plain clothes. I had not seen Nina yet.

After about an hour of standing outside, I had to go to the bath-room and was becoming uncomfortable. My feet were sweating in my boots, and because I wasn't wearing underwear, I had the sensa-tion of tropical weather between my legs. I was not embarrassed—or rather, I kept assuring myself that I was not, instead thinking that a woman my age had every right to slap a lawyer and pee on the sidewalk.

I did not urinate in front of the police station but instead in one of its bathrooms, where I also started crying. It took me a while to compose myself. Every time I was certain that I was no longer weeping or just about to, I'd splash cold water on my face to calm my skin's fury only to start sputtering again. My little Lucy.

When I came out of the bathroom, Andrea Farmer was sitting in one of the chairs in the lobby. She was fully clothed and even wearing mascara. I judged her immediately.

"Is Daniel here too?" I asked.

"Yes." She nodded, looking around secretively. "They're bringing the other girls in too. Everyone in a different room."

"Who are the other girls?" I asked. "I went to this hideout thing, by the way. Over off Pirkle." The word curdled in my mouth.

"Yes," Andrea said, again letting her eyes dart. "Apparently the police were there for hours last night. They had to bust down the door."

"Place is a dump," I said, as if that mattered at all.

"It's this Pollard girl and her friend, Gracie. But that's all I know. I didn't know Daniel even knew these girls. I really don't understand what's going on, but I'm pissed." Andrea's face was oddly serene, yet guarded. "They've been hanging out. All four of them. I didn't know Lucy and Daniel were still seeing one another, but…well…" Andrea trailed off, I thought as a defense against saying something nasty.

"Lucy hasn't done anything wrong," I said. "It's this Pollard girl. I think she might be related to someone I knew when I was a kid who was from a bad family. I just have this feeling that—" There. I'd said it. It had been lingering, hovering like a nosy neighbor. "I know these people." I finished my sentence, and with its completion, my decision had been made. I did think this had something to do with Larisa.

"I don't think you know any of these people, Meg. The Pollards are from Texas." Andrea Farmer had no idea the gravity of what I had just said.

"Did Daniel tell you what happened?" I was trying to swallow but couldn't make the muscles work.

She glanced around us, appearing to make a decision. "Yes. Well, sort of. He didn't do it; I know that much. I don't really want to say… Has Lucy not told you what happened to her?"

"What do you mean, 'what happened to her'?"

She was quiet, pensive. "I guess Josh McGill did something to Lucy, and they all thought he was going to do it again, so they made this plan, but not Daniel. He says he knew the girls were going to do it, but he wasn't there. He wasn't there." She repeated herself while nodding and looking at the exit.

"What did he do to Lucy? What do you mean, Josh did something to Lucy?"

"I guess he… I don't know, Meg. I guess he violated her or something. Daniel didn't give me details."

"I need to go home and put on some underwear," I said. "And some deodorant." I stood up, my robe falling open, and walked to the exit, the cloth of my nightgown trapped in my butt crack. Before I could fully leave the building, I turned around to face Andrea with the door halfway open and my legs covered in goose bumps. "I don't believe a word of it," I said. But I did believe it. I believed it so much I threw up right there in front of the police station. There were little bits of pastel marshmallows all over the grass.

24

1974

It started getting warmer, and we always mistook this as a good sign. Tired of the gray and the leafless trees, we thought the lingering sun and the baking heat were welcome. They were not, but we couldn't be told otherwise. Not in February.

Tyler was set to graduate from high school in May. As far as I could tell, he didn't have one single plan of what he was going to do with himself when he finished school, and he didn't seem worried about it. Rainy had been a lot like that, just drifting, like everything she'd said she was going to do was done and now the next part was there to be filled, but with no assignments. We hated all the assignments at school, and then one day there weren't any more, just time.

"I'm thinking I'm gonna go to California," Tyler said. "Try my hand at being an actor finally." He'd told me this a hundred times but always said it like it was the first mention. I think maybe he wanted me to argue with him so he could explain why it was such a good idea.

"I'll come with you," I said. I didn't have a plan for after Tyler graduated either. I'd gone from having no basket to having all my eggs in one—Tyler. Him and Larisa, which was kind of a surprise. I was finding I actually wanted to be around her now, a lot of the time, even. Larisa never said anything about leaving, so I thought maybe I could hang out with her as long as my mom didn't know about it.

My mom, in trying to get me to be scared of Larisa by telling me about her family like they were devil spawn, had actually made me want to be around Larisa more. I kept quiet about it, but I liked Larisa. I thought she was probably aware of this effect on people; she seemed to get a kick out of being the forbidden fruit. I saw the way she looked back at folks who were looking at her. A reputation seemed both a bad thing but also like a superpower. I certainly felt about two feet taller when she got going with her prophecies and her otherworldly knowledge. It made Johnna at the dry cleaner's seem like a total dud. So what if she had a clean house? She had to wear these button-down shirts and think about bills and her sore feet all the time.

Larisa didn't care about anything but getting rid of omens and cursing people who'd wronged her; it was a hell of a lot more exciting, even if people thought she'd shot her sister. I didn't want to shoot Rainy, though. Thinking about that made me sad, and I kind of didn't want to know the real story anymore. Sometimes when I'd catch Larisa looking at me, I'd get a little bit of a shiver up my spine, wondering if it was true, and if she did do something like that, did I want to hang out with her?

I would later realize that it was this secrecy about her that made me believe everything she said. I understood that, by withholding any and all truth, she'd made herself unquestionable. No one had the nerve to make her explain herself, least of all me.

When the three of us would go for our walks—which was our new thing because Larisa was gathering roots to make teas that would clear bad auras—Tyler would talk about how he was going to take acting lessons in Hollywood, and Larisa would say that she didn't see that in his plan.

"You don't have that in your cards," she said. "There is a great darkness." I liked when she talked like this. It was so different from how anyone else talked, and the fact that she was talking to me made it all feel so special.

"Maybe that's because I'll be doing really gritty roles," he said.

"No." She eyed him suspiciously. "I'm going to make you a tea." She grabbed another wad of earth and sifted through it, looking for tiny tendrils.

She told me that I was going to be a wife because I was subservient. When I asked my mom what that meant, she said, "Beats me, but it doesn't sound good."

Larisa had a whole collection of roots and seeds and small

twigs and stems that she'd picked up when we'd head out for the afternoon. We'd be gone for hours, just trudging along. Cars would whiz by and honk at us or slow down to ask if we needed a ride.

"I'll bet Meg wants a ride," Larisa would say to whoever pulled over. "She's a hitchhiker." I'd bragged to her a few times about how I hopped in some cars, off like a dirty shirt.

We were back a ways off Downs Road; there was a side street that we set out on. I figured we were a few miles from home—mine, not Tyler's or Larisa's. He'd come over in his car with Larisa riding in the back seat. She wouldn't sit in the front of a car; she said demons could see you too easily if you were in the front. I rode up there with Tyler instead but did start to cover my face after a while, thinking a body is a lot harder to identify without a face. They couldn't follow me home if they couldn't see me very well, whoever "they" were.

It was only a gravel path on Downs, so the truck made a lot of noise coming toward us. There was dust leading the way, with me and Tyler coughing.

"Oh, here he comes," Larisa said, like she knew.

The guy said his name was Derek and that he was a known hustler. I looked at Tyler when he said it because it seemed like a strange thing to call yourself. "Where you going?" he asked us. The sun was bright, though the day was cool. All the trees were half in bloom, releasing just a little bit, corsets off and breathing with their ribs.

"Wanna go for a ride?" Derek asked mostly Larisa. He had shaggy light hair and two days' stubble on his face. Some of it was gray.

"She does." She pointed at me.

"Naw," Tyler said, confused. I could tell Tyler felt like a kid in a room with adults. It was how I usually felt; I wondered if he knew that.

"She's like a bug on your windshield," Larisa said, still talking about me. "You're going places, and she's coming with you." I thought maybe she was saying she didn't want me around. I moved closer to Tyler, trying to take cover.

"Well, she can come with me too," Derek said.

"She's Rainy's sister," Larisa said, and for a second she seemed different, like someone who went to school with Rainy and twirled her hair in front of boys, like a regular person who went to the bathroom and got canker sores.

"Rainy?" Derek asked, his eyes lighting up a little, not from affection but because he had an opinion. "Damn. I know Rainy and your mama."

"See?" Larisa said. Tyler was watching her with a funny expression.

I was ready for Derek to go away, but it seemed like Larisa was keeping him around. We had to talk loud over the sound of the truck's engine, and I was getting woozy from the exhaust, a burn in my nose, and my skin felt dirty. I grabbed Tyler's hand, something I'd never done, and started to pull him away. "Let's go," I said, not including Larisa.

She noticed us move and cut her eyes at me. I felt something slide down my spine like a spider in my shirt. I twitched to make it go away. "Don't walk away from me," Larisa said. The birds were arguing above our heads; what had been pleasant calls and soft twittering became louder and more urgent. I was nervous.

"Damn it!" Tyler jerked backward, pulling his hand out of mine. There was a snake at our ankles, turning between us in the shape of the number eight. I reached out my foot to stomp on it, which was what we did if we found a snake at home—that, or slam it with a shovel—but Tyler said, "No! Don't taunt it. It's a diamondback. Just be still."

"What's that?" I asked. Derek had moved back in his seat and mumbled something about hating snakes.

"They're monsters," Larisa said. She leaned over to get a closer look. The snake was as long as my leg and thick. Its back was black and shiny; it looked like black plastic in small chips, glued on in a diamond pattern. I was trying not to move too much, following Tyler's lead. He stood still as a rock. The snake was laid out long now, not a curl to its body. "It's fine," Larisa said. "Because it knows I'm here. When they're in a coil, you're in trouble."

Derek revved his engine, which caused the snake to lurch and slither away, zigging and zagging over the gray rocks like the letter S going down a slide. I twitched again, sure there was a snake in my clothes.

"I'm outa here," Derek said, putting the truck in gear and driving off. Larisa watched him as her legs got swallowed in his dirt.

She appeared to be floating on road dust. I hadn't noticed that she'd been barefoot.

"It's snake season," Larisa said, turning to us. "You don't need to be afraid of them. They have to be here." She was talking in her dreamy voice again, the one she used to describe how love and evil were always fighting through the trees and making the leaves fall and the other stuff she said about the Death card and Tyler's moons.

"I don't like 'em," Tyler said, giving himself a wiggle.

The birds were at it again, their voices slamming into one another, causing an echo effect that made me think we wouldn't know if someone was about to drop a bomb on us. It was so loud back off the road, even more so now that Derek and his truck were gone and the dust had settled. It was a swirling, round, all-around-my-head kind of loud. The snake had moved in the same way, encircling us in a curl.

"Drinking snake venom gives you powers," Larisa said. "You get the sight."

"Have you done it?" I asked, still looking around on the ground for the snake or one of its friends.

"Yes, Meg." She spoke efficiently. "We all do."

"The Bagleys?" I said.

"That's not Larisa's name no more," Tyler said like he wanted Larisa to appreciate him defending her. "She got ridda that." He was clearly pleased to be telling me this; correcting people on Larisa's name was a duty he performed proudly.

"Yes." She pulled her hair behind her ears, something she never did, preferring it to lie like a curtain over her face. Her appearance changed when her skin was exposed. Her hair no longer looked like ink or a charcoal-colored wave about to take her under. She was softer, with small freckles over the bridge of her nose and a pouting mouth that seemed careful and kind, mostly because it was so torn up. She lost her usual hazy gloss that always seemed like a cover for something sad, or even angry. Anytime I felt sorry for her, it passed real quick and I was back to thinking she could kill me if she wanted to. "It's not my name," she said. "I don't go by Bagley anymore."

"Changed it with the courts," Tyler said. It seemed they'd talked about this plenty; I had not been included.

"What is it now?" I asked, but neither of them answered. We were walking back to the house so Tyler could get his car. There was a bad feeling between us. I thought it was because I was hungry; all I'd had all day was saltines and a glass of grape juice. It was a favorite combination. I'd tried to tell Tyler about it when he first got to the house, but he was distracted because Larisa was with him and gave me kind of a funny look, like I was a real little kid talking about juice and crackers when he was a grown man.

It was because I was feeling strange about the thing with the snake and the way Larisa had acted with Derek that I thought I needed to get right with everyone. "Do y'all want to come over and make puzzles again?" I asked. No one had said anything for a long stretch. I'd been racking my brain for an offering. We'd made puzzles a few weeks back. We glued newspapers to a piece of cardboard from a box and then cut shapes out of it. Larisa had been the best with the penknife. Her puzzle pieces were the most elaborate. She'd put glue over the top of her paper too, so her pieces were shiny when they dried.

"Naw," Tyler said. He patted my back. "I don't want to do that again."

"Okay." I figured I'd been entertained.

When we finally got back to the house, I was shaky with hunger. I was also tired of them both. I couldn't think of another time when Tyler had gotten on my nerves, but his personality was becoming like a Band-Aid that got wet. I still wanted him there to protect me, but he was irritating and turning cold and slimy.

"Well," I said, "my mom's home, so…" There'd been some talk about how Larisa wasn't allowed at the house because of my mom and the way she had faulty vision. Larisa said my mother couldn't see auras clearly. She said strippers rarely could. They were jaded from a life of being taunted. "I guess that's it."

"I want you to drink poison," Larisa said to both me and Tyler. She acted as though she was doing us a favor by even suggesting it. "Snake venom is the gateway. You're both ready. Most people really lose it when they have a diamondback between their legs, but you didn't. I called the snake to us. He came to see what you would do, and you let him be. It's time."

Tyler chuckled, finding this funny for some reason. I was too hungry to care. "Yeah," I said. "I've heard about that."

"But can't that kill you?" Tyler asked. He had his hands in his pockets with his shoulders by his ears. He wasn't comfortable the way he normally was. That had been the thing with Tyler, this constant comfort. He looked like he was cold, but it was a mild and sunny day, the kind a person dreams about every time it's not that way outside.

"No." Larisa shook her head. "No way. Not if you know what you're doing."

It didn't feel like we agreed on anything, but they went and got in the car, with Larisa in the back seat behind Tyler where she always rode. They took off, and I saw a patch of gray moving in—with them gone, the sky could finally stop pretending everything was okay.

25

2024

Nina was at the station when I came back. I'd had a shower and was in a suit, the only thing that seemed appropriate to wear. It was riding high in my crotch; I felt like I was being violated. I also couldn't stop crying. I'd never been much of a crier, having decided that the worst had passed and there was nothing left to cry about. I was wrong.

"What's going on?" I asked as I walked in. It had started to rain outside, a pitiful, slow drizzle that there was no good windshield-wiper setting for.

"Nothing. They're still back there. The lawyer hasn't come out. Are you okay?" Nina asked.

"No, I'm not okay," I answered. "They can't have been talking for this long,"

"I brought snacks," Nina told me, showing me a cloth grocery bag filled to the brim with prepackaged crackers and nuts and other things made of what looked like crackers and nuts.

"Good thinking, Nina," I said, trying not to sound annoyed. "I wore a suit and bought a legal dictionary." I held up my bag from Hagman's Bookstore.

"I don't think you can just read the dictionary and defeat the police, Mom," Nina said. "Do you want some trail mix?"

We sat in strained silence for a moment, glaring at the industrial flooring. I was just about to relent and ask for a granola bar—that, or tell Nina what Andrea Farmer had told me, which I'd decided to keep a secret until this story about Josh hurting Lucy could either be satisfactorily confirmed or denied—when the door to the back area opened. It was Deirdre Mansell. Her hair was in a ponytail, her eyeliner smudged. I moved the bag from Hagman's under my butt, suddenly embarrassed that I'd bought a law dictionary. I'd asked the gentleman stacking the shelves at the store where I could buy a book about criminal law. He guided me to *The Complete Idiot's Guide to the Criminal Justice System*, which I immediately set on a nearby table covered in cookbooks for diabetics. "Thank you for that," I said, but he didn't seem to understand that I'd been insulted. I grabbed the dictionary in a moment of ego-driven impulse. It had looked like the most difficult to read. Because it was a dictionary.

"What happened?" Nina said, standing up. "Where's Lucy?"

"Lucy is not leaving," Deirdre said. I heard the door open again. It was a police officer escorting Daniel from the back. He walked briskly to his mother. I was reminded of all the mothers who never thought their child did anything wrong at all the playgrounds where I never took Nina. But I had taken Lucy. There would be some child tearing through the equipment, pushing or slapping the other kids, with their vapid mother standing idly by, saying something like "Oh, she's just being silly." And then there was what Andrea had told me about Lucy. I couldn't face her. It was unfathomable to think she might have known that and not told us, not tried to help, had done nothing.

But it appeared that maybe the police also didn't think Daniel had done anything wrong, as he was being released. I watched him for a second too long and saw that Andrea had noticed. She wrapped her arm more tightly around him.

"Woulda been nice to have a heads-up…" I said a little too loudly. "I would have told you."

"Mom," Nina scolded. "What are you even talking about?"

"Nothing." I didn't want to tell Nina what Andrea had said about Lucy being assaulted. I wasn't sure I would even be able to say it.

"Mrs. Gregory. Ms.…." It was Deirdre.

"Highfield," Nina said. "I'm divorced." Her statement explained nothing.

"Right. Is there somewhere we can go to talk? I could use some lunch." She looked around, eager to leave the building. It was either what was going on with Lucy or the fact that I was clearly in a disturbed emotional state.

"I have a cell phone!" I held up the device in front of her, proud and angry. It was how I had been conducting myself all day. I wiped my face again, the tears still aggressively sliding down my face. Nina was staring at me too, confused and angry. She had never had much time for proud.

"Excellent. You're going to need it," Deirdre repeated.

"I brought snacks," Nina said. "Can I see Lucy? She's probably hungry too. Can I at least leave her some snacks?"

"They'll feed her," Deirdre said. "You cannot go back there or give her anything. She's been arrested."

A silence passed over us like a large predatory bird blocking the sun and forcing us to seriously contemplate what talons would feel like on the shoulder girdle.

"I can't believe it," I said because there was nothing else to say.

We went to Grider's, a deli-style restaurant that also made vegan sandwiches out of nut cheese and fake mayonnaise. Deirdre ordered from the vegan menu, something called seitan that had the bile in my throat rising when I saw it sitting under a bed of fake bacon on a bun that appeared to have been made from Styrofoam.

"Since when did they start serving that kind of stuff here?" I asked Nina, who'd ordered a container of potato salad—three pounds of it that she planned to eat with her nut medley.

"The owner's wife became a vegetarian," Nina said. She knew a lot more about what was going on in Tuskin than I did.

"When I was a kid here, you couldn't even find celery at the grocery store," I said. "No one'd ever even heard of it."

"That's something," Deirdre said. "I don't really like celery. Not on its own, at least."

"No taste," Nina agreed. I could tell she was trying not to cry too. She was eating the potato salad with a spoon.

"My understanding, at this point, is that Daniel Farmer has more or less rolled on Lucy and said that she was the one who lured Josh McGill into the car, where Melanie…" She paused. "Melanie…" She paused again, reaching into her bag for a folder. "Melanie Pollard was hiding and slit his throat."

"Melanie Pollard?" I said. Unlike everything else I'd said that day, it came out quieter than I'd meant it to.

"Yes," Deirdre said. "She was apparently the one who actually attacked him."

"Did you talk to her?"

"No," Deirdre said sharply. "I don't talk to other people's clients."

"Down the street all this time," I said to myself, putting my sandwich down. They'd used too much mustard anyway; I wasn't enjoying it.

"Maybe it was an accident," Nina said stupidly.

"So," Deirdre interrupted, "being that they now have testimony from a witness saying that Lucy was complicit in getting Josh

McGill into that car so that he could be killed, we are going to have to either discredit Daniel Farmer and his account or perhaps do a plea, being that Lucy did not actually commit the murder—at least according to Daniel Farmer. I'm not sure yet what Gracie Bagley is saying."

I could suddenly hear Tyler screaming my name on the grass next to the Boxy. "Gracie Bagley?" I managed to ask, but no one noticed. My teeth were clenched so tightly together I thought I might have cracked an incisor. I tried to ask if she'd said Bagley again, but I couldn't talk.

"Yes, Daniel Farmer has been adamant that it was Lucy and Gracie who got Josh McGill into the car. Gracie's the other girl."

Nina was crying, but I had stopped.

"Bagley? I mean…why?" I asked. "Why did they attack him?"

"They killed him," Deirdre corrected me. "Lucy has not denied that."

"But *why*?" I exaggerated the word.

"Lucy just said Melanie told them he was going to hurt someone; they're all claiming that he was this awful guy and they were trying to be helpful—that's come up a bunch. Anyway, this is the story and no one is really saying anything different. The only one who's been pushy about anything is Daniel, and it's just that he only drove the car; he didn't go up to the McGills' house or Josh's car or anything. Lucy and Josh had spent the evening together, and then Josh took Lucy home. The other girls were waiting there and rode back to Josh's house, or near it, in Daniel Farmer's car. Lucy went around to the back of the house to knock on his window. I guess he'd been trying to get her to have sex with him, but up to this point, she'd refused—I'm not very clear on that part. She's very tight-lipped about their relationship. No one has been able to get a very clear answer from her about…where they were at, if you know what I mean."

"I don't know what you mean," Nina said.

"Nina, quiet." I placed my hand firmly on the table. I was tight-lipped too, having a hard time moving my jaw after all the grinding.

"So," Deirdre continued, "Lucy said she snuck to his house and went to his window."

I felt the room shift, a carriage on a typewriter sliding, with me untethered and wobbly. "The window?"

"Yes." Deirdre clearly did not think this was a significant detail. "So Josh came outside, and they went and got in his car. Melanie was waiting in the back seat, and that was that. They ran back to where Daniel was parked up the road, and no one inside the McGills' house was the wiser."

"Did you say Gracie Bagley?" I asked again.

"Yes," Deirdre responded absently. "Gracie."

"But…" I paused, casting a glance at Nina, who was wiping her eyes and nose with insufficiently sized deli napkins. "Daniel's mother told me that Josh…did something to Lucy?"

"What do you mean?" Nina asked. She held the damp napkin in her fist, cutting her eyes at me, daring me to give her worse news.

"Andrea Farmer said that Josh did something to Lucy," I repeated.

Deirdre was quiet, allowing Nina and me to talk. "Yes," she said faintly. "There was some mention of that."

"Some mention?" I said. "Did you not think it was important?"

"Well, Lucy is not answering any questions about it."

"What do you mean, he 'did something to her'?" Nina squeezed the napkin tighter.

"It sounds like there was an assault of some sort." Deirdre appeared to steel herself for a response. "But she won't say."

"I can't believe this." Nina's head was in her hands. It was all heavy sighing and stifled whimpering. "I need to talk to her. Why wouldn't she tell me this?"

"I'm not sure she's told anyone," Deirdre said. "It sounds to me like Melanie Pollard got this thing going after she heard something had happened to Lucy. I don't know if they were friends before, and I'm not sure Lucy has told anyone explicitly. Melanie knew Josh and apparently knew that he'd done this sort of thing to other girls…but I don't know. I'm speculating here." She picked up her sandwich, pieces of it falling back on to the parchment. Crumbs of fake bread and bad news lay all over the table.

"Andrea Farmer told me the same thing," I said.

"Why didn't you tell me this?" Nina was incredulous. "And how would Melanie hear about this if Lucy isn't telling anyone?"

"Because I don't know if it's true. It's Andrea Farmer, for God's sake." I don't know what I meant by that. We'd never had any issue with the Farmers. It was something to say. The constricted feeling in my throat and jaw was combated only by talking, which was becoming even more of a battle. "I didn't know if—"

"Yes, so let's not jump to any conclusions, but we should consider that there is more to this and that we might be facing some other very troubling revelations," Deirdre said. "They're all saying that Melanie did some sort of trippy psychic thing and knew that Lucy had been hurt. It's murky."

I looked at Nina to make sure she was still breathing. The halting silence at the table suggested collapse, suffocation, complete surrender. "Oh dear," I said. "I'm so sorry." I'm sure Nina didn't think I was talking to her. One aspect of our relationship that she had uncovered in therapy was that I never apologized. "I'm so sorry for Lucy," I said, needlessly clarifying.

"What kind of mother doesn't know this?" Nina said quietly. I could think of all kinds of mothers, but I didn't say anything. None of the mothers in question had known what was going on.

"Kids keep secrets," I said. It was the only bit of wisdom I had to offer.

But I was angry at Andrea Farmer for knowing more than we did. And for feeling so entitled to tell me. The morning felt like a different dimension, some other time and place during which people had told me important things while I sweat in my bathrobe.

It had already happened. It was happening again. Tyler. I didn't say his name out loud, but I parted my lips as though about to.

"So what's the plan?" Nina asked. She had stopped crying, with some visible effort. She picked up her plastic spoon as though she was going to resume eating her potato salad. Her shoulders continued to tremble, but she kept her face flat and composed. Her lips disappeared into a fleshy wad on her face, an overstuffed wallet of anguish currency, to be spent at the gates of hell.

Deirdre remained stoic—aloof, almost. I hadn't really taken the time to fully look at her since we met. She was always wearing these sharp-cut suits and stomping around authoritatively so as to be fully appreciated but not really noticed. She had long, curly hair and a round figure, much like Rainy with her barrel chest. She was shorter than both Nina and me but presented herself like a lumbering giant of a person, her expertise and education causing her to tower over us in both intellect and officiousness. I decided that I didn't much like her. She didn't seem to like us, either, me and Nina. She was a busy person, making time for people who needed her but not really noticing them. She'd not asked us once how we were doing, hadn't expressed concern about Lucy's delicate age, remarked on what these allegations were doing to our family—nothing.

"You're all business," I said to Deirdre. "You must not have kids."

"I have three children," she said flatly. "And yes, I am all business. I'm Lucy's lawyer." She took another bite of her ridiculous sandwich and shuffled some papers. I noticed a smear of fake mayonnaise on the corner of an important-looking document and felt mildly vindicated.

"So what do we do?" Nina asked again. "What do we do?" She'd put the top back on her potato salad and held the container close to her chest like she was protecting it.

"Well, that's what I need to figure out. It might be best for Lucy to make a plea deal and go into juvenile detention for a while to avoid a more severe punishment. If she can confirm that it was Melanie Pollard who killed him, then it will help her."

"But it sounds like she was defending herself," Nina said. "He did something to her; it was self-defense."

"Self-defense doesn't work like that," Deirdre said. "This wasn't self-defense, but if we find out that there were severe extenuating circumstances, it will certainly help Lucy's case." She folded her sandwich wrapper and used her hand to shuffle lettuce and other detritus off the table and into a waiting napkin. "I need to get back to the office. Can I get your cell phone number?" she asked me.

"I don't even know what it is," I said.

"Call me." She gave me her number very impatiently while I tried to find the phone in my purse and struggled to press the right buttons to make the screen light up. "It's not working," I said.

"You have to unlock it, Mom," Nina said. "The code is Lucy's birthday."

I spent a few minutes fumbling with numbers and misdialing, then hanging up, then misdialing again before allowing Deirdre to call herself from my phone. "Just give it to me," she said, reaching out her hand.

"What should we do now?" I asked Nina after we'd left the restaurant. Deirdre took off in her BMW after toppling an orange traffic cone sitting purposelessly in the middle of the parking lot. It folded, then bounced back. Deirdre looked in her rearview mirror and drove away.

"I don't like her," Nina said. "She doesn't care about Lucy."

"Or that cone." I pointed. "Why is that there? What's with all the fucking cones everywhere? It's like Mickey with the mops… They just keep coming and coming. No one's doing work in this parking lot. Are they messing with us?" I was livid.

"Mom." Nina wiped her face, pulling heartily at the skin under her eye. "Please be serious."

"I am serious! Everywhere I turn, someone's put an orange cone around which I'm supposed to drive. Why? Why can't I drive straight?" I paused just long enough to notice the wind kicking up again. It felt like a push in a crowd, the sensation of being lifted and then put back down, unsteady and fearful. Perhaps it was the wind that was toying with me—carrying all sorts of mania that I thought had long been laid to rest—firmly and furiously pressing the side of my face until I acknowledged that other things might have happened, until I dared to cast my eyes in its direction.

"Mom?"

"No, it's fine," I said. I didn't know what I was talking about.

"Did you hear me?"

"No." I looked at Nina, trying to pull myself back to her, the parking lot, Lucy.

"Don't cry, Mom," Nina said.

"I'm not crying," I said bitterly.

26

You ever drink snake venom?" I asked Rainy. For some reason, as of late, I'd felt closer to her. She softened up and now seemed like she wanted to take care of me. I even told her I thought she'd be a good mother one day, though I wasn't sure I could see it. I was starting to think like Larisa.

"Uh—hell no," she said about venom. "Why on God's green earth would I do something like that? How do you even get the venom? Like, suck on their teeth or something?"

"I don't know," I said. "I just heard you could get the sights or a good omen or whatever."

"Maybe stick to school," Rainy said. She was folding laundry. She did a lot to help my mom around the house. I was not as eager to lend a hand. I stuck to my bedroom, arranging and tidying in there. Rainy would comment that I cleaned around things. She said you had to move stuff to get deep. I'd overheard her and my mother talking about opening a cleaning business. It sounded like a real dream to clean, only there were just a few people in Tuskin who could have a maid. Rainy even said they could wear matching out-fits. My mom agreed that would be nice.

I only heard them talking about it once, but after that Rainy took a little more pride in how she wiped the counters and put the shirts on hangers. I think she was practicing. It would have been an improvement; Rainy worked all hours at the bar and talked about the people there like they were gods. She was real taken with the crowd at Shakers. I figured she was one of those people who make whatever they're doing the center of the world.

"I just heard someone talking about it, is all," I said.

"People talk about all sorts of things." She folded a pair of jeans, pressing down on them to secure the crease. "But drinking snake poison? I don't know. Too weird for me."

Tripp had come and gone, then come and gone again. My mom said Gregory women were attracted to "men like that." I thought Rainy squirmed a bit when she said it. Some days Rainy was happy to get roped in with my mom; other days I think she was looking for another way. Tripp had been a good student; that came up a lot. So had Rainy, for that matter. Sometimes she needed reminding that she wasn't my mom.

I left Rainy with the underwear and went off with Johnna for the afternoon. It felt like a different world when she was my only friend. I would sometimes tell myself I needed to keep my hands on the old Meg, not lose my grip entirely. I found throughout my whole life that every time I got close to someone, I felt like I was losing a little of me, like the only way to be true to myself was to be alone.

Tyler had never made me uneasy, even though everyone said he should, but something about the way Larisa controlled everything with him—with both of us—made me think I didn't have a mind of my own anymore. I told myself before Johnna picked me up that I wasn't going to think about Tyler or Larisa the whole time I was with her, just to see if I could do it.

"How's it hangin', Meggy?" she asked as I got in her car. I'd worn the red dress I had on for New Year's Eve. I'd received so many compliments, and Johnna liked nice things.

"Oh, now that's a dress!" she said.

"Thanks." I was pretty sure it was a compliment.

Johnna had her hair slicked back in a low ponytail and was wearing cat-eye sunglasses. She looked skinny and a little more spruced up than normal. "You look nice too," I said.

"Thanks." She hit the blinker and waited for a truck to pass. "I thought we'd go to Burger Heaven," she said.

"Oh." I didn't think that sounded like fun at all. Lon was still in the clink for robbing the place, and Johnna had been fired from there, and anyway, the food wasn't so great. They always burned the fries. They cut them shoe-string; they were too thin to fry like that.

"Yeah, I miss it," she said. I noticed her nails were done too, both sets. She was wearing platform sandals and white pants that looked expensive; they were stiff and pressed.

"I think I'm a little dressed up for it," I said.

"No." She was sure.

We walked in the restaurant, Johnna with her purse in the crook of her elbow and her sunglasses still on even though the day was a little cloudy. She stood in the middle of the restaurant for a second before taking a table in the back corner, a semicircle booth.

The menus were grimy and the table had little streaks from being wiped. Burger Heaven was one of those places where they waited on you.

"Hey, Johnna," a man said as he walked up with a pad in his hand. He wore a bow tie and a white shirt that was covered in faded stains.

"Craig," she said. She removed her sunglasses, and I could see she was wearing a vat of eye makeup. I looked up at Craig, trying to figure out if this was who she wanted to impress. He was older and thin, with knobby wrists. His hand shook a little while holding his pen.

"What would you like?" His face had deep wrinkles, like time capsules for all that he'd been through. You would have to dig to get to the bottom of them.

"I'll have a cheeseburger and fries. With a Tab."

"Yes, ma'am," he said.

"I'll have the same." I hadn't even looked at the menu.

"I just want them to see that I don't need this place," she said when Craig walked away. "I don't need them."

"Well, it's just Burger Heaven," I said.

"Right, but they're so high and mighty because of what happened, and I'm doing better than I ever did." Not a single person in there looked high and mighty. I think it was in this moment that I decided it would be a good idea to drink snake venom; I broke the promise with myself and thought about Tyler and Larisa. It was almost like God was telling me that this was the alternative. Maybe I could get second sight and figure out a way to never have to wear my best clothes to Burger Heaven to show everyone I was good enough.

I spent the night at Johnna's. I still loved it there because everything felt new even if she had a real sad quality to her—worse than when she talked about Uncle Ray. I guess maybe she'd been counting on something that didn't work out, but at least she still had her nice place. She was spick-and-span, even deep in the corners; Rainy could probably have taken a class from her on how to make it shine.

In the morning Johnna was back to her normal self, in her jeans and sweatshirt and not as mopey or desperate. "I'll drop you at home before I go to work," she said. Saturday was the busiest day at the cleaner's.

"Okay then," I said. We were eating pancakes. "Thanks for always taking care of me, Johnna," I said, feeling like she was looking for recognition. There's no real worth in being a grown-up a lot of the time; I could tell that.

"I enjoy it, Meggy. You're going to be in high school next year. You won't want to hang out with me anymore."

"Not a chance," I said. I poured extra syrup on my plate. It was cold and thick from being in the refrigerator.

When I got home, my mom was out in the driveway washing her car. "It's so nice out!" she said. Johnna pulled up and waved.

"You're up early," I said back.

"I quit!" She smiled brightly. "Terrence says he can take care of us. He's making a killing."

"Who's Terrence" I asked, even though I knew. Mom had been out with him a few times. She always came home drunk and laughing herself to the bedroom with him not far behind. Otherwise, she wasn't much of a drinker. She'd seen enough of that to last a lifetime, was what she said.

"So it's a whole new me!" She was excited enough for both of us.

"Where'd you go with Johnna?" she asked me. Johnna had hung my dress on a hanger and had me carry it like a person would coming from the cleaner's. "You get all fancy?"

"Burger Heaven," I said.

"Oh." My mom turned up her lip. She was in a bikini top and terry-cloth shorts. It wasn't warm enough for that, and I could see goose bumps down her legs. "Why'd she wanna go hang out there?"

"I really don't know." I went inside and saw a pile of things next to the couch—man things. I didn't hear anyone in the house; the door to Rainy's room was shut. I walked back to the front door. "Is he moving in?" I yelled to my mom, who was spraying her fender.

"Yes!" She tilted the hose straight up and let the water come down over her. It reflected the light and made small mirrors in the air.

"I'm going to Tyler's," I said. I couldn't stand to be home.

27

I'd pulled away from the gas pump with the nozzle still in my tank and ripped it right out of its socket. I was halfway down the road before I even noticed the noise.

"You've got the pump in your car!" a man yelled at me; he'd pulled up on the curb. "I've been trying to get your attention." He was clearly exasperated with me. "You've got the pump hanging!"

"Well, that's just great," I said to myself, looking in the side-view. I'd more or less left Nina in the parking lot of the deli. She was going back to the station to see if Lucy needed a snack. She said she'd spend the night there if they'd let her.

When I got home, I was wobbly. Gone were the tremors from earlier; now it was disorientation and loss of balance. I looked up the number for the gas station in the phone book and called from the landline.

"Hi. I'm the one who drove off with the pump. What would you like me to do? It's still in my car," I said wearily into the receiver. "I didn't mean to."

The attendant who answered the phone said it happened more than I knew and to keep the pump. I thanked him for his generosity. I thought it might be Pat Waverly. He'd always worked up at the Citgo, at least since I'd been back in Tuskin.

I had a strange urge to call my mother. She didn't live in Tuskin anymore; I was the only one who'd remained—or rather, come back. We didn't talk at all, not necessarily estranged but disinterested, satisfied by what we had shared and unwilling to expend any more effort. I'd had a hard time explaining Mom to Nina. It was also like she didn't really want to know.

Ferrol acted like he was concerned about this, but he was more than likely relieved. "She should know her grandparents," he'd say, right before announcing he'd be gone all weekend and it was better if Nina and I didn't accompany him. "Gonna be hectic. I won't have a lot of time. You should take Nina to see your parents!" He'd been concerned with Nina in only very specific ways.

Both of my parents had come to my wedding. My father was barely recognizable, mostly because I would barely recognize him anywhere, being that I'd seen so little of him during my life. He arrived with his sister, a woman I'd never met but who I thought I looked an awful lot like. My mother said hello to him, but their exchange was unremarkable. Ferrol asked him where the bathroom was before I explained that he was my father.

"Oh!" Ferrol hadn't known what to say. I'd talked to him dozens of times about my family and how my upbringing had lacked any real foundation, but he said I sounded like a self-help book and that his dad was an alcoholic. "People have to get over that stuff," he explained. "My dad was never home, and when he was, he was drinking gin martinis and listening to classical music." Ferrol threw his hands up in the air. "We couldn't disturb him unless we wanted to hear about Bach or some shit."

"My mom was a stripper," I'd said back.

"Oh, hell yeah!" Ferrol raised his fist in solidarity.

Now, instead of calling my mother, I called Ferrol. I understood from Nina's vague responses that she hadn't been honest with him about what was going on. I did think he needed to know. It was early afternoon, so I'm not sure why I didn't call the office, being that he lived there.

"Y'ello," he answered.

"Oh," I said. "It's Meg."

"Okay."

"I guess I thought Martha would answer." I don't know why I was admitting this. There'd been a period when I called and hung up when Martha answered. I'd call back just to do the same. They had caller ID. He'd asked me what I was doing, and I said there was something wrong with my phone.

"Have you talked to Nina?" I asked impatiently. He hadn't said anything, but I was reacting as though we were in an argument.

"No, but I talked to the lawyer. Doesn't sound good."

"No. It's not. Lucy is in a lot of trouble, Ferrol." I was standing in the kitchen, where I did all my talking on the phone. Nina had explained that if I had a cell phone, I could talk to people anywhere I pleased.

"I hardly talk to anyone," I'd said back. "I hate talking on the phone." Isolation and friendlessness were my most laudable virtues, it seemed.

"What's going on?" He sounded genuinely concerned.

"I really don't know. It's all so unlike her."

"Well, maybe not. Kids are always hiding stuff…"

"Not like this," I said. We both cleared our throats. The distress was meaty enough to choke on.

"Deirdre's a good lawyer," Ferrol said. "Really. She's done some work for a couple clients."

"This is murder, Ferrol."

"I know."

"Of a sixteen-year-old boy."

"Meg, what do you want me to do? I'm doing all I can. Where's her dad when all this is going on?"

"I don't know. Nina said he's been calling, and I guess he came over the other night. You know Michael. He's around but he's not around. He just doesn't want to deal with Nina, but apparently he has been trying to help Lucy."

"You deal with me," Ferrol said.

"Yes, well." Sometimes I thought maybe Ferrol knew that I'd never given up hope. No matter how angry I sounded when I talked to him, or how put out I pretended our relationship made me, I had never, not once, stopped wanting him to see me the way I'd pretended he saw me in the beginning.

When Ferrol and I first met, all he did was laugh, as though I was a clown sent to relieve his angst over the dissolution of his second marriage. He made what I now see as wildly inappropriate comments about my clothing, figure, the way I walked, even my wrists. "So tiny!"

I became completely dependent on this view of myself, a lovely bauble to be pondered, amused by and not at all considered in any important decision. I was to lie on the table and look special. I suppose that was what I wanted—to feel special; I was so young and so grateful to have been chosen. Ferrol was unclear about which attributes made me special; in the end, it seemed my accent and the fact that I'd never been on an airplane and would thus find him doubly attractive because of how much time he spent on them. When I dissected the relationship, I was left with very little to examine, like the owl pellet we cut open in the fifth grade.

"Meg?"

"Yes. I don't know." He'd asked me something about where Lucy was being held. "She's at the police station here. Will they move her?"

"They'll definitely move her. They can't house a person for

any length of time at the precinct." When Ferrol wasn't flirting or trying to get someone who didn't like him to change their mind, he could sound quite sincere, but I never completely believed anything he said.

"I don't know what to do. I want to talk to the other girls, you know—the ones who came up with this whole thing. It was their idea, Ferrol."

"We don't know that," he said.

"I do."

"Okay, Meg." There was the tone, the one that always, without fail, ruined the moment.

"Ferrol—I don't want to be a jerk here, but I see her a lot more than you do, and this is not Lucy. She's gotten wrapped up in something. I know how this goes…" It didn't seem anyone had, as of yet, told him about the rape. I hadn't let myself say the word. People were stumbling around it, calling it all manner of things, but I could tell. If it had been anything else, they would have said it.

"You should talk to the detective."

"I don't like him," I said abruptly. "I don't like him at all."

"I'm not sure you're supposed to like him, Meg."

"Listen, I have to go. You're not being helpful. Why don't you talk to him?"

"Because Lucy made you her contact with the attorney."

"Well, the detective is not the attorney, so that's a lame excuse, if you ask me."

"I'm full of lame excuses, if someone asks you." Ferrol sighed, revealing that he still sometimes thought about me like I mattered.

"I'll talk to him," I said.

"Just don't be a jerk about it. That won't help Lucy." And there it was. His deflection. "Lose the tone."

"Okay, that's enough." I almost slammed the phone down, but I would have found that embarrassing. People who don't give a shit about one another don't get mad enough to slam a phone down.

For lack of anything else to do, I thought I would walk to the mailbox and try to get a peek at the Pollards' place, though I was probably a couple of houses too far. I put on my yard boots and went out the front. I hadn't bothered with putting on makeup or with doing anything to my hair at all that day. I felt it was enough that I didn't remain in my bathrobe and had applied deodorant.

I saw a police car in the Pollards' driveway; that much, I could make out from my end. I wondered if it belonged to Detective Adam with the strange last name that everyone kept mispronouncing. "Aw, hell," I said and shoved the mail back in the box, heading toward the Pollards' house. What did I have to lose?

As I got closer, I could see Detective Rinaldi was in the car. The house, again, looked deserted. Romaine Drive was a quiet street anyway, but I had noticed the end of the block had a lilting stillness to it that made me think something was missing, like a photograph you've seen a hundred times and then you look at it again and a person who's always been in it is no longer there.

He saw me coming and opened the door of the cruiser, struggling some to get out. He had his cell phone in one hand and a small notebook in the other. "Mrs. Gregory," he said. He must have just arrived.

"It's not *Mrs.* anything," I answered, making my way over the grass separating the Pollards' from the house next door, another family I'd never bothered to notice. The dad drove a minivan; at least I knew that. "How's Lucy?" I asked, a taint to my voice.

"She's at Yeldon," he said. That was the detention center in McIntosh, about a half hour from Tuskin.

"She's fifteen," I reminded him.

"Yes, she's with a counselor. It's very nice there. They've redone the commons area."

"Do you send a lot of kids to juvenile hall?"

"If I have to." He was standing fully now, having adjusted his pants and everything he was holding.

"She hasn't done anything," I said. "Just mixed up with the wrong crowd, and…and she got hurt, you know."

He let his eyes wander. "Well."

"Well, what?" I put my hands on my hips, like I was going to intimidate him with my outrage.

"A sixteen-year-old boy was murdered, Ms. Gregory."

"But Lucy didn't murder anyone," I said. "She's caught up with this girl; her behavior has completely changed. I know how a friend can really turn your head. I've seen it." I stopped myself. "And…I know they're saying it's not technically self-defense, but she was… she was defending herself, was she not?"

He exhaled, seemingly unable to do or say anything else. Obviously, this wasn't the conclusion the police were coming to.

"Are they home?" I pointed at the house.

"No." He was curt.

The afternoon was soaked in light; sun dripped off every surface, bright and airy. It was a perfect day. It is the worst injustice to feel so embittered on a perfect day. "I don't know the daughter. Melanie," I said. "I don't know her."

"Lucy knew her." Again with this familiar tone. I was old enough to want to feel respected simply for being so much older than him, but he did not appear to see the age gap the same way. He had a restless urgency with me that I associated with an exhausted family member.

"I doubt she knew her very well," I said. "Listen—speaking of that, do I know you? Where are you from?"

"No," he said. "Is there anything else I can help you with? I'm about to take off."

"Where is she? Melanie."

"She's at Yeldon with the others."

"What about the Bagley girl?"

"Who? Gracie? She's there too."

"They're not with Lucy, are they?"

"Ms. Gregory." He again sounded like a young man having to

explain something tedious to his grandmother, like it was considered in poor taste to write a check at the grocery store. *Here, just put that away, Nana.* "I suggest you prepare yourself for the worst. We have extensive evidence taken from several locations that implicate your granddaughter in this crime. I would expect her to face consequences. I understand that she might have had reason to want to harm Josh McGill, but this was first degree murder."

"Yes, but what I think is going on is that no one cares about her, and someone is definitely fucking with me." I was on the verge of tears. There, I'd finally said it. "I think this has something to do with me. I've seen this house before."

"This is your street, is it not?"

"Yes—that's not what I mean. Lucy said this girl did the cards and that's why they killed him. It was the cards. There was a girl… I grew up around here, and I'm just telling you that this is the same as that. It's not, but… Do you understand what I'm telling you?"

"I do not. And now I need to go." He sat back down in the car and pulled the door shut. The engine started with him refusing to look at me again.

"I know the Bagleys!" I shouted. "They're coming after Lucy! I know it!"

He backed out of the driveway, keeping his eyes on the rearview. The car lurched forward once out in the street; I thought he was going to gun it, which would have really pissed me off. I was about to call out that this was a residential street when he stopped and rolled down the passenger-side window. "I would worry about your granddaughter and not yourself." I kicked his tire with my boot in response; they were good for more than just keeping snakes off my ankles. All I was lately was one big bottled-up reaction leaking out at everyone who dared provoke me.

When I got home, I called Nina to ask her if she could look up on the computer whether or not it was against the law to kick a cop car. "I've got a bad feeling," I said.

"Did you kick a cop car?" I could hear her fingers tapping at keys. Nina loved to look things up on the internet. It was a hobby, or perhaps an addiction. She would tell her doctors that her findings online didn't agree with their assessment and then go find a new doctor who also didn't agree before claiming the computer had lied to her. Nevertheless, I had foregone any real device and still had a large box-shaped computer that required a phone line. It was mostly worthless and only worked about 10 percent of the time.

"It says it's punishable by up to five years in jail," Nina said.

"That's not good news." I paused. "Nina, there's something… I should tell you something."

"About what?" She was still clicking away.

"I need you to listen to me."

"I am listening."

"Something happened when I was a kid. Something really bad. I was younger than Lucy, but still, I think there's… I'm concerned that because this Gracie Bagley girl might be related to someone else I know, that there's a reason to be concerned about that, because my concern is that there's—"

"Mom," Nina barked. "I'm really in a state here, and now you're probably going to jail, too, for kicking a cop car. Can you please?" Her voice was like pots and pans clanging—loud, irregular, and tumultuous.

"Stop yelling at me. What I'm trying to say is that I think this might have something to do with me."

She was silent. I knew I shouldn't have said anything. There were pages of my life that had been stuck together, missed, overlooked, secreted away in a large volume of mundane details. I wasn't purposeful in keeping them from her, but I didn't want her to know either. The only person I'd ever tried to talk to about it was Ferrol. I could remember telling him, crying and gesticulating wildly, trying desperately to explain while he glared at me as though I was wasting his time.

"That's sad," he'd said finally, when he was sure I was done with my story.

"It is," I'd agreed, waiting for him to tell me what to do. I'd been waiting my entire life for someone to tell me what to do about it.

"Nina?"

"I can't decide if I'm angry at you for making this about yourself, because that's something my therapist says you do, or if I'm angry that there's something really significant that you haven't told me that could have somehow affected Lucy, which is also something my therapist says you do. You withhold to make yourself feel more powerful."

"No, I don't want to feel powerful. I'm trying to tell you that maybe I can…help. I don't know. Do you know Gracie Bagley?"

"No." She spoke softly. "I don't know any of these people. How many times do I have to tell you that?"

"She hid them from us."

"I'm her mother," Nina said. "I know you two are very close—Deedee told me that she chose you as her contact, so there, you won. But I'm her mom. I should have known what she was doing. Now I think she was lying to me all the time, with all this youth group and church stuff. I don't think any of it was true. Andrea Farmer said the kids haven't been over to her house in close to a year. So this all started well before she started dating Josh or whatever she was doing. And then…well, what they're saying happened, and she just dealt with that on her own?"

"Maybe she blocked it out," I said of the rape. I still couldn't say the word out loud. I'd never been able to.

"But she didn't, because what he did to her was the reason they killed him. I talked to Deirdre this afternoon, and she said Melanie had also had a run-in with Josh. He forced himself on her, and she didn't tell anyone. She heard that happened to Lucy when he took Lucy to the fishing cabin, so Melanie contacted her and said they should meet and get revenge. How Daniel or the other girl got mixed up in it, I have no idea."

"That is so twisted it makes me sick," I said.

"Yeah. It's so twisted and so unlike anything Lucy's ever done in her whole life."

"Yes." I was half listening. "But sometimes when we meet the wrong people, we do things that we would never have done on our own. And she made a bad choice to date this Josh guy, which led to her being hurt, so…she got screwed up." My voice sounded like I was talking into a bell; it bounced off the receiver, coming back hollow and swallowed. I noticed I was squinting. Excruciating pain had overtaken the front of my face.

"Like a band," Nina said.

"What?"

"I don't know—Dad used to say that sometimes it's the right combination, and people write great music together and just have that special something."

"It's not like a band." I tried not to sound angry. "I do understand what you're saying, but it's the opposite of that. There are bad influences, Nina."

"Mom, I know that." We could have been arguing about her haircut in the ninth grade. It was the only even remotely rebellious thing she'd ever done, shaving one side of her head—that, and marrying Michael against my protests. Or rather, my pleading.

"Sometimes these things get out of hand. They do." I wanted to tell her.

"This is more than 'getting out of hand,' Mom."

"I know that. I know that this isn't a small error in judgment, but I can't believe—I refuse to believe that a clearheaded Lucy would go along with this, and also that she would keep all of this from us. Something's gotten her off track. I just—" I stopped myself.

"Either way, it doesn't have anything to do with you. You didn't murder anyone."

"Nina…" I said, preparing myself to tell her. She'd already hung up.

<h1 style="text-align:center">28</h1>

1974

I was thinking about Rainy on my way over to Tyler's. When we were little—or me real little and Rainy about eleven or so— she decided she would only eat waffles. All day every day, it was just freezer waffles, toasted with butter and syrup. My dad had been around more then; he'd help her with the toaster and act like he was cooking homemade for us.

I usually felt most sorry for myself when I thought about Dad leaving or how Mom worked at night and always had to have a replacement man around. I think I should have been more worried about Rainy. She'd taken the biggest hit because she was at a more crucial age when things really started going south. I was little and didn't know what Shakers was or why a dad would leave a lot. Rainy had to get through fractions while trying to make my mom feel better about her life. Even when we were older, Rainy had the bigger share of my mom. I'd made it clear somehow that

I wasn't on that line. I'd pick a different person to hold on to—it was Tyler.

"Hey," he said when he opened the door. I rarely showed up at his place, having only done it a couple of times. It had to be three miles to his house, and it wasn't kind turf for walking. "Larisa's here," he said. "We've got a snake." My heart hit my rib cage like a hot hammer. I felt a river of heat go through me.

"You do?" I guess I hadn't believed we were really going to do it. I know I went white, because Tyler did too. He was always worried by proximity. Some people feel other people's vibes so hard they absorb all their troubles. Tyler and Rainy would have been better friends.

"Yeah. It's a rattler."

"Is it dead?" We were still standing at the front door. I looked around Tyler, trying to see inside. I could hear the TV and his dad talking. There was a second when I thought I would run back home, away, anywhere but here. But I stayed. It was the one time I didn't run. I never did know how to pick 'em.

"No, but shhhh." He put his finger over his mouth.

"'K."

We walked back to his room together. His dad greeted me, saying something about the weather or how it was going to rain. I looked out the front window and nodded.

Larisa had a shoebox on her lap. It was taped up, secured on all sides with thick, shiny black tape, like the kind people use on pipes.

There were some small holes haphazardly poked in the top. I could see pink behind the holes; it was the tongue, and it made my skin crawl. "Quiet," she said. "It's mad as hell."

"Where'd you get it?" I asked as Tyler shut the door. There was an empty terrarium on the floor, along with a piece of a screen door and two bricks.

"I know him," Larisa said, putting her face down next to the box. "He found me. He says he'll do it."

"Do what?"

"Give us his venom so we can have the sight."

"I thought you already had sight," I said.

"It's different with every snake." She frowned at me. Tyler's room wasn't much bigger than the snake's shoebox home. I didn't think anyone at his house did laundry, because there was a strong sweat smell in every room, and I swear the sheets had the same stains on them since the day we met. Tyler's mom was a fine lady but kind of a slacker when it came to their house.

"But he has to get used to it here, so we're making him a home. He won't give us good sights if he's scared."

For the next hour, we took turns going outside as discreetly as possible and grabbing fistfuls of new grass, mounds of moss, small sticks, and weedy dirt and putting it in the terrarium. Tyler said he got it from his cousin, Ronnie. I'd met Ronnie a dozen times. He had dark hair like Tyler, but a cartoon-type face with large features.

"I like Ronnie," I said, a small act of defiance.

"Ronnie's going to die by the time he's thirty. He has sickness all over him," Larisa said.

I was about to tell her that he was a real stand-up guy and was always trying to make everyone laugh and that seemed a lot better than putting curses on people, but I didn't say anything. It was a real monkey-see, monkey-do kind of time for me. I guess I didn't think I had an alternative.

"I'll bless the cage." Larisa waved her hands over the terrarium. Tyler was smiling, first at Larisa, then at me. I smiled back—not a real smile, but an empty movement of my facial muscles so he couldn't tell how scared I was.

After we were satisfied with how the enclosure looked and had put a small plastic bowl of water in the corner, Larisa put him in, not appearing to care one bit if he might bite her. She held his head in a funny way, with her thumb under his chin. It seemed she had been trained. I certainly wasn't laughing anymore and sat in awe of her fearlessness and how mechanical she was, like Lon when he worked on an engine. Once the snake was inside the glass, Larisa put the screen over the top, and she and Tyler laid three bricks on it, a few inches apart.

"He can't get out," Tyler said, pushing the screen with his finger. "S'too heavy."

"He doesn't want to get out," Larisa said. "This is his home now."

We walked down to the river off Pirkle. It wasn't really a place to go. People thought a river was so much fun, but it was shallow and cold. The Boxy River—it even had a stupid name. There wasn't much to do there but look at it and fish, if that was your thing.

"Are we immature or something?" I asked as the three of us sat down on the bank. It was mud and rocks. I could tell my entire backside was covered in wet dirt. Larisa had pulled her dress up and sat down with just her underwear on the ground. Tyler grabbed a cigarette and lit it with his Bic.

"What do you mean?" Tyler asked. He chuckled when he talked, especially if he wasn't sure he agreed with what somebody was saying.

"Just playing and stuff, you know—with snakes." I took a stick and stirred the water at the edge. It was still, having found a small place with no current. The bubbles and swirls from the passing water went around it, carrying with them a light foam. I put a leaf in and watched it find a rivulet of its own, sliding over a fold and down toward where the Lattimers lived. They had a couple of boys who rode four-wheelers and knew how to cast. Other than them and Larisa's aunt, I didn't know a soul who lived on the Boxy. No houses, no souls, no nothing.

"I'm not playing," Larisa said. Tyler didn't comment. It was Rainy and my mom who'd put the idea in my head. Rainy wasn't that much older than Tyler, and she said he acted like he was my age.

"Why's he got so much time on his hands?"

"Some people like to have time on their hands," I'd answered.

My mom said the same. She thought he needed to get a job, even though Larisa wouldn't be able to.

"Not with that last name," she'd sneered. "She's killing time 'cause there's nothing left to kill."

"I don't know," I said to Tyler, even though I was answering Larisa. "Y'all hang out with me, and I'm pretty young. And anyway, even the kids I know are up to no good. We seem on the straight and narrow. Maybe that's not immature, but everyone else is getting busy and drunk all the time…" I trailed off. I actually didn't know if Tyler and Larisa got busy. I couldn't figure their relationship out. "It's strange," I said to no one in particular.

"I don't want to be like the people in your middle school," Larisa said. She put her legs out in front of her, straightening them so they became submerged in the water. She had cuts and bruises up and down her whole body. It was because she was pale, she said. She told me that everyone has small scrapes, but most of the time we can't see them because of suntans. Larisa said she didn't absorb sun; people with clouds in their aura never did. "Just regular assholes trying to grow up and pretending their body parts are interesting and that getting loose in the head is going to save them from the rest of their boring lives. It's not about maturity, Meg. It's about knowing more."

"Yeah," I agreed. I suppose I did think we were superior. All it took was Larisa reminding me. "No one really talks about anything except their grades or wanting to get high or trying to sneak out."

Tyler let out a heavy breath. "Yeah, I don't know what to say to anybody anymore. I want to get lost, like totally out of here, and live a different way than just the scraping by and waiting to get drunk at somebody's house again and all that. I don't want to be like Rainy." Tyler said her name like it was some kind of wart you got from sitting on dirty toilet seats.

"I…" I started to say. "What's wrong with Rainy? She's actually really smart."

"I know," Tyler said. "I know she is. She's just a townie type. I don't wanna stick around her, is all."

"She moved to North Carolina," I said. I was feeling like someone had to defend her. "Cashiers."

"She's nothing like us," Larisa said. I wondered if that included me. Sometimes I really couldn't tell whether or not I was part of their team. I got the sense that Larisa had big plans for Tyler, but I wasn't sure if she had them for me. And anyway, he was the one who wanted to be an actor in Hollywood. Larisa wasn't going to have any control over that.

The afternoon had the feeling of a waste. I was in a bad mood because of Terrence moving in and Tyler making that comment about Rainy, who couldn't help it if she had to look out for my mom and be a townie. I found I was in a bad mood a lot lately. My mother told me I should expect my personality to change as I got older because of hormones. I figured that was part of the reason why everyone was getting on my last nerve, or maybe I knew what was coming and was mad that I wasn't going to be able to stop it. I couldn't do much then—ever, really. I've always been a sidekick and never the force to be reckoned with. I always did the reckoning.

Larisa said we should meet the next day, Sunday, and that the snake would be ready. It could absorb Tyler all night and become one with his house. We agreed with her, having no real reason not to. We certainly didn't sound like Rainy when we were talking like that. We didn't sound like anyone I'd ever met before.

I went home still solemn and grumpy. Terrence was in my room when I got there. He said he was fixing my mattress for me. "Your mom said you put some wood under it, but I think it would be better if we just did another long board." He'd lifted the mattress off the frame and was putting a piece of wood that had been freshly cut—I could smell the fibers—between the two sides. The large block of wood that Tyler had lain under the middle of my mattress had been kicked to the side.

"Mom!" I called out. I kept my eyes on Terrence but hollered over my shoulder.

"What?" She showed up a second later, still in her bikini top from earlier but wearing strong perfume. "I'm making tortillas." She'd done them when Lon moved in too—pulled out some of her tricks to show him how good life could be with us. Pretty soon she'd be sleeping 'til one again and asking if Terrence could run to the store to get her Bud and some tampons while she touched up her roots with the Clairol.

"I don't want strangers in my room."

"Aww, well, he's trying to fix your bed."

"Tyler already fixed it."

My mom looked at Terrence, then back at me. "Okay," she said uneasily.

"That's all right," Terrence said. "I'm already done, but I can take it out." He let the mattress fall back on the frame.

"I didn't think it was comfortable with that block under there," my mom said. She was wearing eyeliner.

"What else is he going to do?" I asked.

"Nothing if you don't want him to, sweetie," my mom said. She leaned against the doorframe and lifted her arm over her head with her chin tucked.

"Quit it," I said.

"What?" She stood up straight. "What is it with you, Meg? I swear."

"Can everyone get out of my room, please?" I put my hands on my hips, trying to sound as mad as I was. "Is this my room or isn't it?"

"Sure is, and that attitude's all yours too. You better get a clue, sister." My mother twirled a piece of her short, stick-straight hair around her finger and made chomping noises on her gum. Terrence tried to laugh off the moment, because there he was, flipping my mattress with my mom acting like she was back onstage at Shakers. It dawned on me that here I'd thought I was immature. No one I knew acted a second older than me, even if they didn't paint rocks or have a pet snake.

When they'd both left the room, I reached under the mattress to make sure Tyler's block of wood was still there. Terrance might be replacing Lon for my mom, but he wasn't going to replace Tyler for me.

I went to bed that night feeling a shift change me; one half of my life was over, and the other half would be spread out on a much bigger canvas. The first part had made all the decisions for me. I still had one more day in it, one more day to make the rest of me go thin, like oil to watercolor. Yes, there was still one more day. But sometimes what's done is done.

29

2024

I woke up at four o'clock in the morning with what felt like a hangover but clearly wasn't. I hadn't had even a sip of alcohol, not in what seemed like years. I didn't care too much for it anymore. Having watched Ferrol use it as an excuse for everything from forgetting my birthday to having bad gas, I was kind of done with crutches, generally speaking.

I took a Tylenol and decided to go for a walk. When Nina and I moved to Tuskin, I had resumed my long walks but sometimes had to get creative about where I went. I'd walked almost every day in Atlanta—miles and miles. Everything was paved there; a person could go for days without leaving concrete. It wasn't the same in Tuskin. Two miles in, on the tenth day home, and I got bit by a snake. A Tuskin Rattler, the doctor called it. I said I'd never heard of rattlesnakes in Georgia. He said people always told him that. He also told me the medication he prescribed for the bite was made of

Jolly Ranchers. I heard later he'd retired shortly after, having had a significant mental health decline in his later years.

I was terrified of snakes long before the rattler found me on the side of Lumpkin, where it was lurking in the high grass and I walked, heavily and with crossing steps through the pockets of earth, trying to outsmart the unruly clumps that threatened to trip me. Nina said I looked like I was drunk when I was out walking. "You stumble," she told me.

"There's no sidewalk. I'm literally climbing!" It was true of about 60 percent of my journey.

It was for this reason that I almost always wore boots. Even when I was walking around in my backyard with the hose or polishing the weather vane—an object that served no purpose but that I would also not remove—I wore boots of a different kind, but they were boots just the same. Nina said I looked like a park ranger; she often had a comment about me looking like something she felt was unflattering, a drunk park ranger being but one of her observations.

"I don't want anything to get me," I said of the boots time and time again.

"We live in Tuskin, Georgia," Nina would say back. "What could get you? Death by a thousand mosquitoes?" I'd laugh, but none of it was funny. She would never understand. And yet, now she did.

I'd done all that walking thinking that I was trying to bring my Atlanta life back with me to Tuskin. But it was the other way around. We'd walked all over hell's half acre when I'd been a kid. I could remember going for long stretches barefoot, trailing behind Tyler or alongside him and Larisa. I hadn't cared a bit about snakes then.

I kicked my boots out of the way by the front door and said to hell with it. I was going out like I did when I was young. I really thought I could beat the shit out of a snake right about then with how mad I was at the world for how it has to keep on messing with people. Real life's always there, just when you think you might get away with it.

The night had a blue tint to it, bruised and fleshy. The sky appeared to be leaking; meaning and nonsense both tumbled out of holes in the atmosphere, leaving a trail of lips without breath. Blue lips. Blue lips. Blue lips. I closed my eyes, trying to forgive the sky for all the reminders.

I didn't have much of a destination in mind, and so I walked toward the back entrance to my neighborhood. That direction led to Platts, to the old house, to where Tyler's family had lived. To where Larisa's house sat at a crooked angle on the river. Crooked Street. She told us she'd named it that because she could not only see signs but she could change them. There wasn't a sign on the little path where her aunt's house sat, but because she said there was, I believed it. I believed everything she said, in a time when believing was so easy. Now I wasn't sure if I believed I had ten fingers and ten toes. I could count them, but I didn't know what that meant.

The grass was wet; beads of moisture soaked my feet. They picked up filament from the ground. I was making my own shoes in the moonlight. It was waning crescent. I'd always known the moons; it was something that Ferrol had found so endearing. He asked me every night, until one day he stopped. That was about a year before he filed for divorce. I should have known. If a man loses interest in the moon, he's lost interest in the woman who told him about it. I would sometimes think of calling him when I looked out the window at night, to tell him what the moon was doing, to see if he'd be charmed. To see if we could get it back, but it was only him who'd lost it, and then I knew that he'd never had it at all.

I walked all the way to Pirkle and made a left. It was getting on now, probably nearing to five. There were some cars out, their headlights not as sharp in contrast to the dark air. I knew at this point I wouldn't get home before it was light enough to really notice me, this shredded thread of a woman grinding down the road like a knob, tamper and meat.

I was passing the river on the right and all the land that led to it. The cabin sat there with yellow tape around it on little wooden posts, the kind that are used for paint samples. "Oh, that'll really keep 'em out," I said to myself. I took another step, then stopped. I'd stepped on a gumball from a sweetgum tree, and goddamn, did it hurt—felt like a sponge with spikes, but it wasn't that. I remembered something. The memory had been caught in the bottom of my foot; the prongs of the gumball nudged it out of me. Small secretions of terror at what I had witnessed and what I knew. I pressed my foot harder, but the pain would not repeat itself. *I've told you. Now you know. I will not tell you again. The shame.*

30

1974

Tyler came to pick me up the next morning. He'd called the house and said Larisa was ready. "We're gonna go to her place though."

"I thought the snake had to be at home or something," I said. My mouth twitched as I looked over my shoulder, hoping my mom hadn't heard me, but she was watching TV with her feet up on Terrence's leg. He was very pleased to have a couch and a woman with painted toenails to himself. Lon had never sat on the couch first. Never. He hadn't thought it was his house.

"She says it'll be easier without my parents and Rich around barging in and all that," Tyler said.

Tyler's parents never barged in. They left him alone at the house. I wondered what he would have done if he came in and found Terrence under his mattress. "Okay," I said.

"I'll come get you."

I went to the bathroom to comb my hair and make sure I didn't have any crust in my eyes. I looked fine; my hair wasn't as much like yellow pine straw as it normally was, and I had some color on my cheeks and nose from the good weather.

"I'm taking off," I said.

"Like hell." My mother shot up from her back. "It's Sunday."

"Okay. What's Sunday?"

"Family Day."

"First I've heard of it," I said. "And anyway, I have plans."

"You have plans." My mother laughed and nudged Terrence, showing him how funny we could all be when we were bickering about Family Day.

"I do."

"Well, we were going to clean out the carport and have a nice dinner. Rainy's not working."

"I'll be back for dinner," I said, walking toward the front door. It would take Tyler a few minutes to get over to the house, but I preferred to wait outside. My mom kept talking, giving me instructions about the carport. Most of the stuff out there was my dad's anyway. He was kind of a collector type. There was his junk in every corner. My mom had moved it all there. I guess she was waiting for him to come back.

Tyler rolled in just when it started to sprinkle. The sun was still out, but the sky was softly spilling, overfull and leaden. I wiped a faint layer from my forearm after getting into Tyler's car, then rubbed it into his seat.

The car had the cool, musty feel of one left out overnight and its insides weren't catching up to the temperature outside. I immediately rolled down my window to let different air in. "Ready to have a vision?" I asked.

"I guess." Tyler didn't sound convinced. "I'll have a vision of a Big Mac or something."

"Yeah," I agreed, trying to laugh. "Why're we even doing this?" I was asking the dashboard more than I was asking Tyler.

"I don't know—"

"I just don't want to be normal," I said, interrupting him with what I thought was the right answer.

"Well, Larisa's not normal." He sounded proud.

"Neither am I." My chin dropped while I thought about all the normal around me. "No way."

"Don't worry, Meg. If you're normal now, you won't be after we do this." It was almost like a dare.

Larisa's house sat at the edge of Pirkle and Deer Valley. It was a dark-green house, something that didn't help in trying to distinguish it from all the vegetation on the porch. That was a word my mother used. "There's all that vegetation," she'd say of some overgrown place or another. She'd probably said it of Larisa's house, not knowing a Bagley lived there.

"Weird place for a house," I said. "Just sitting over here by itself."

Tyler turned off the main road. "This is kind of a shortcut."

We went through the field that lay next to the river. Tyler was bulldozing his way over all manner of uncut grass, stalks, and weeds. "Are these crops?" I asked, thinking we were about to get pulled over and arrested before we even got to drink snake venom and have visions.

"Used to be. Larisa's dad's family owned all this land, but they couldn't take care of it. Her dad took off. Nobody looks after it anymore."

"My mom says she's from a bad line."

"Real bad," Tyler said. This was actually the first time we'd really talked about the Bagleys. I'd kept my mom's concerns to myself. Tyler had some thieves and tricksters in his family too. I remembered them celebrating somebody getting out of jail at the New Year's Eve party. "Murderer."

"Her dad?"

"He didn't get killed, but he killed somebody." We were traveling slow over the land. There was a path from Pirkle to the house, but Tyler always liked off-roading when he could. He said he had the right kind of tires for it, even though his car wasn't made for the traction.

"What about the rest of them?" I asked. "Her sister—"

"Don't say anything about her sister in front of Larisa," Tyler said sternly. "Don't say a word."

"Okay," I said. "But what happened to her?"

"She died, and it eats Larisa up. I don't know how it went down, but it makes Larisa sick to think about it. There's always been trouble. That's why Larisa is the way she is." Tyler kind of shrugged while dropping the clutch into second gear. "She's been on her own for a long time, and before that, it was her getting knocked around."

"Where'd she live before she went with her aunt?"

He shook his head. "I don't know. Lotsa places. All bad. Somebody threw her down the stairs. S'why her teeth are all bent up. That happened after her sister died; they all said it was Larisa's fault."

"Does she tell you all this?" It felt good to be talking about her straight. It made her seem less powerful. We'd been mistaking misfortune with wisdom; that was something I'd see a lot of in Tuskin. The harder the story, the more people would listen to the teller.

"Not really. My mom knows about some of it. That's why she lets Larisa stay over all the time and cares about her so much. It's not her fault her family's like that." He was agreeing with himself.

"Nobody picks their family," I said. It was Rainy I was thinking of. She didn't seem to have as good an eye on things as I did. I thought I'd get out of the cycle, but she probably wouldn't. She'd be like Tyler's parents, having so much fun doing the same life over and over again.

Larisa came out onto the front porch, probably having heard the car. We'd popped every twig this side of Alabama with our rumbling. She bowed to us before turning around and going back in.

"She's a real trip, isn't she?" Tyler said. It was the first time I thought he didn't take a lick of what she said or did seriously.

"Dresses like she's colorblind." He laughed again, and I knew it was probably because he thought he could have her. I'd heard men laugh at my mom that way, like she was too stupid to understand that she'd made herself attractive in the wrong way. I crossed my legs; it was another revelation. I never wanted to be laughed at, not like that.

"Come on," Larisa said as she came back out. We were taking our time getting out of the car. "Come on, now."

The house was only two big rooms. Larisa had a bed in the corner. There was a long hall in the back where her aunt's things were. The rest of it was open, with furniture covered in clothes and boxes. It was dark, with only one bare bulb glowing in the back corner. I didn't like it there; I'd felt that way the last time we were over.

"He's in here. I'm calling him Sheridan," Larisa said. "He's piping-hot mad, which means it'll be good."

The terrarium was on Larisa's bed, which was a double mattress lying on the floor, half covered in clothes. She had a pink sheet on the bottom and a fake fur blanket. I was jealous for a half second, which was a real surprise. I couldn't figure out who would want to live like this—a few steps below even my family—but I guess it was me. At least it seemed like they had their house like this on purpose; we were trying to look like somebody up the street with a better house and better furniture and carpet that wasn't sticky.

"Where's your aunt?" I asked.

"Not here." Larisa was waving her hands around Sheridan's cage. "I burned crab apple over him earlier."

"You burned an apple?" I asked. Things were really getting serious, was all I could think.

"It's an herb," Larisa said. "Don't freak out, Meg. Or I won't let you do it."

"I've eaten a crab apple," I said. "It's an apple."

The argument was over, and Larisa was back to her heavy mood. She hummed and made shapes with her hands, saying words I didn't understand under her breath. It didn't sound like another language, just muttering with a melody.

"Creepy," Tyler said, smiling. He winked at me. We were both still standing next to the bed while Larisa knelt and slid around.

"Y'all sit," Larisa said. "You're making him nervous. It'll be bad bile."

Tyler went cross-legged on the floor next to the bed while I knelt with my feet turned in under my butt and pressing. "Crazy." Tyler seemed to have just one word to say. I could hear myself breathe; there was a little whistle in the exhale. The pollen had been heavy and stuffing me up. Larisa turned her head toward me with her lips pursed. I thought she might tell me to be quiet, but she went back to her movements and singing, and that was that.

It sounded like a door opened and closed somewhere in the house. A latch clicked, then a soft slam. No one else seemed to notice it, but my attention had been poked. It was while I was listening closely for more noise that Larisa lifted the bricks off the screen, one by one, before dumping them on the floor next to her bed. They made a crude, crashing sound. I jumped a little, switching the slant of my feet so the left was now turned out and pressing into the floor and my rear more aggressively.

The screen came off next. Larisa laid that on the bed carefully while I leaned back, afraid the snake would jump out at us. But he didn't. He moved his tongue in and out of his mouth, letting his head dart from side to side. He hadn't noticed the freedom.

Larisa reached in and grabbed him very gingerly, like she was applying a bandage to a wound. She whispered to him, calling him Sheridan and assuring him he was going to be okay. I didn't know how we'd get the venom out of his mouth, but she made it sound like he was going to love every minute of it. She held him up to us; his body was squirming, but his head was still. Larisa had a firm grip on it, squeezing with her thumb on top. His tongue kept at it. "He's smelling," she said.

I hadn't noticed the knife before. It was half covered by the pink sheets. Larisa tilted Sheridan toward her knee and pressed down on his bottom half with her leg while grabbing the knife. It was a switchblade—Lon had always carried one and had shown me how to open it with a flick of my wrist—already opened; Larisa wouldn't have to toss her hand to get it to snap. I thought I heard the door again and turned away, trying to figure out where the noise was coming from. While I was looking at the far corner of the house,

Larisa slit the snake's head open and put her mouth right up on top of where she'd made a cut.

"Quick!" she said to both me and Tyler. "Quick."

I jerked my attention back to the bed as Tyler leaned over and sucked on the snake's head. He did it without using his hands. He kind of looked like a snake for a second; we were all agreeing it was better to slither, I suppose. I was scared to the point of shaking but leaned in too. Sheridan had been writhing a bit when Larisa had her mouth on him but had gone slack by the time I got there. I put my lips on the slit in the back of his head but didn't suck. I barely even let myself touch the hole; it was leaking pus and had long skinny bones in it. I could see his eyes out of the corner of mine. I squeezed everything shut, but when I opened up again, I was staring him down.

"You're not getting any," Larisa said to me, pushing Sheridan's body toward my face. "You're not getting nothing."

"It's okay," Tyler said. "Maybe she's good." He coughed and jut his jaw forward a few times. "Jeez. That's freaking disgusting."

"You got it good," Larisa said. "Meg's a chickenshit."

"No, I'm not," I said. "Y'all took it all."

"You didn't even put your mouth on him. He died for nothing where you're concerned. That's bad luck, Meg."

"Quit it," Tyler said. He was still making strange faces, twitching and turning on his bottom. He'd pulled his legs up to his chest and was curled in a ball.

"Are you okay?" I asked him, putting my hand on his shoulder.

"I'm fine," he said quickly.

"He's adjusting to his new self," Larisa said. She was swallowing a lot but otherwise acting like nothing had happened.

Tyler didn't say much for a while; his mood had changed. Larisa was busy with the corpse and still singing to herself. It sounded like the music from *Rosemary's Baby*. My mom and Rainy had watched that three times over Christmas break. I hated it and couldn't understand why anyone would want to even finish it one time, much less three. I'd walked out halfway through and sat in my room. All I could hear was the music. Larisa must have seen it too.

"Is somebody here?" I asked the third time I heard a door.

"No." Larisa was brushing her hair. Tyler still hadn't said much. I figured he was waiting for the visions to come. "Let's go to the water so we can connect." She looked in the mirror, a cracked oval that leaned against the wall, covered in black dots and splotches. It was about as tall as Larisa and made her look even longer and more hollow because of the way it was positioned.

"Okay," Tyler said, clearing his throat loudly. He hadn't moved from the floor.

We walked over to where we'd been the day before. It was bright and very still out. I could hear everything—chimes from a distant house and a lawn mower cranked and running across the road. The branches were still mostly empty or just buds. It was taking forever for the green to come back. The daffodils were out and starting to curl, but the dogwoods were only skinny stems, and the maples had red tufts but no leaves yet. It just hadn't been warm enough. There's nothing like waiting for heat in a place that's hotter than hell most of the year.

"I don't feel right," Tyler said.

"It's the powers," Larisa told him.

I didn't feel a damn thing because I hadn't even touched the snake. Everyone knew it, even though I kept saying that I had touched its eye with my tongue. I didn't want to touch it, but I was also pissed at myself for being chicken. It was just another way I wasn't really with them, always the tagalong, the nuisance they felt forced to include.

"Naw," Tyler said. "I have a bad stomachache."

"Maybe you should puke," I said. He looked like he was going to anyway.

Larisa stopped walking and turned around. She'd been in front of us, with Tyler trailing me as he went slower and slower. It wasn't a long walk to the river but a rough one, over the uneven crop graveyard.

"What used to grow here?" I asked.

"Peanuts." Larisa's voice sounded like it was coming from behind me. I looked over my shoulder, taking in the house again. Larisa was still up front, but sounds were coming from all directions. Tyler was breathing heavy, and I could see movement in one of the windows. I rubbed my eye, still seeing the snake right next to it, and although it went fuzzy from the dust pressing, I swore there was someone watching us.

"Larisa," I said, "where's your aunt?"

"I don't know." She kept going. "Peanuts kill people," she said. "People are allergic. They're like poison too."

"I need to sit down." Tyler stopped. We were right out in the open, halfway between the house and the river. The sun was to our left, banging its rays on the houses' windows. I saw something again, a jerking motion of something dark—perhaps a sleeve. Or hair.

"What?" I asked. Larisa was talking, but I'd been locked in a moment with the window of her house and whoever was behind it.

"Tyler." Larisa had her hand in his hair. She was combing it away from his face, which was very pale. He was sweating by his hairline. "Tyler." She was calm but didn't sound completely like herself. "It's okay, Tyler."

"What's wrong?" I was standing next to him now, my shadow covering his face. "Tyler, what's wrong?"

"I don't know."

"He might be about to have a vision," Larisa said. "I feel the effects. I'm buzzing for real."

"No." Tyler had his hand on his stomach. "No, I'm not buzzing." He leaned over and started gagging.

"Tyler, are you faking?" Larisa asked in a singsong voice. She was looking at the house now too. "What'er you doin'?"

"He's sick," I said.

Larisa looked at the house again. "No, not really." She was paying attention to something else.

"Something's wrong," I told her.

"Naw," she said.

Tyler started to gag again and leaned over. "I gotta go to the hospital. It's the stuff—"

"Tyler," Larisa sounded impatient. "Come on, then—we talked about this."

"I'm… Something's wrong."

"His lips are blue," I said. "He's choking, Larisa. His lips…"

Her face dropped, more in frustration than worry over him. She kept looking back at the house. "I don't know," she said. "I don't know. He had a bad card, Meg."

"What don't you know? Something's wrong." I started waving at the road. There weren't any cars coming past. "Who's at your house, Larisa?"

"Nobody." She clenched her fists at her sides, looking much younger than I remembered her, ever. "No one. It was a bad card. He was going to do something."

Tyler reached for my forearm. "Call somebody." Later I would wonder at that, the way he reached for me.

"His face's blue, Larisa!" I screamed at her. "What are you even talking about?"

"I don't know." She pulled her hair. "Let's go. Come on, Meg. Come on." She grabbed my hand too. "Come on. Now, or we'll get jacked out here. Come on." She yanked me.

"No. Tyler's sick. We gotta call the ambulance."

"We can't." Her mouth twitched under the strands of hair that waved over her face, seeking to cover it. The skin under her eyes was a pale red, almost pink except for its anger. "We gotta go. Come on, Meg."

"No!"

Tyler was doubled over now with his fist in his stomach. There was a stream of white bile coming from his mouth; his lips were open and blue like sapphires. My mom had always wanted sapphires, but no one ever bought them for her.

31

2024

I t's always the throat with these people," I said, hauling ass back to my house. There was some honking, and a couple of people slowed down and asked if I needed a ride.

"You okay?" a woman about my age said as she went by me. "I can stop if you want me to."

"I'm fine," I said, continuing on without looking at her. "Mind yer own." She accelerated away.

"You're bleeding," said a young man who'd also slowed down.

"And you're ugly," I said. I hadn't even looked at him. "Sorry," I said under my breath, because he'd sounded nice enough and I was bleeding. I'd cut my toe—the pinkie, so it wasn't much to worry about, but it was leaving a mess. I knew I wasn't limping; I could walk with a broken ankle.

When I got back to my street, I went straight to the Pollards' and banged on the door. A woman who was a little older than Nina came to the screen. I was surprised upon seeing her, because I was sure that it would be Larisa, living at the end of my street the whole time, watching me and pushing memories down the lane like grocery items on a conveyor belt. It was not Larisa; this woman looked nothing like her.

"I'm Lucy DeWitt's grandmother," I said abruptly as she opened the door. "Are you Melanie's mother?"

"Carrie Pollard," she said, moving away from me, clearly a little taken aback. "How's Lucy doing?"

"Well, that's a stupid question," I said. "She's not doing too good, is she, Carrie Pollard? She's in jail. Where's your daughter? Where's Melanie? Who I've never met, by the way. Y'all living here all this time with the girls coming over, and you never even introduced yourself." I was bobbing my head around aggressively, like I was looking for a fight. I had my hands in fists and was in the process of lifting them to my chin.

I could tell Carrie Pollard was surprised by the way I was acting; she took another step back and drew her brows together. "I don't recall you introducing yourself neither," she said. "I didn't know you lived here. Lucy said she lived off Weston."

"She does, but—"

"No, I never thought I needed to meet her grandmother."

"Yes, her grandmother," I said. "I'm from Tuskin," I added, perhaps trying to explain why I was acting like I wanted to kick her ass. Tuskin women are a real handful.

"Okay." This obviously meant nothing to Carrie Pollard, who probably considered herself a real handful too.

"Have you always lived here?" I was looking at the plants on the porch.

"No. You mean since birth?"

"Who'd you buy this house from?"

She paused, about to give me another empty reply. "Listen, lady, I don't know you. I'm not gonna answer all these questions. I'm worried about the girls too, but you're up here in my business. That Josh kid was a rapist and a bully and all the rest. I'm glad he's dead."

"No," I said, looking at the plants again. I was talking about Tyler. I'd never be glad Tyler was dead, no matter what Larisa said.

"Whaddya mean, 'no'? They all said it. Kid was a psycho. Now, I'm not saying they should've done what they did, but he was doing some bad shit—your granddaughter was one of 'em who got… Well. And anyway, are you okay? You're half naked and your foot's bleeding."

"I know my foot is bleeding, but…the thing is…I just have this feeling…" I trailed off. "There was another boy," I said, more to myself.

"Yeah, Daniel. He was over here all the time too."

"No—I mean who died."

"I don't know nothing about that."

"Did you put all of this here?" I pointed at one of the hanging pots. "The plants and flowers." I'd shaken myself back into the moment.

"It was all here when we bought the place. I've just kept it alive." She softened a little, relieved to be talking about something else or perhaps sensing I was as unwell as I looked.

"It reminds me of someone." I almost said her name, Larisa. I made the first shape with my tongue lifted and my lips open, but no sound emerged.

"The arraignment's today," she said.

"Okay." I hadn't known that. I wondered if there would be a message waiting for me at home. An arraignment—I would have to look it up in my law dictionary.

"It's surreal, isn't it?"

"No." I turned around and walked down her front steps. "It's very real. Did you know the people you bought the house from?" I said, looking back at her. "It reminds me of someone." I saw movement in the window, a sleeve. "Do you have other kids?"

"Yeah, but they're not here. All grown."

I watched the window again. "I don't like this house. I've never liked it."

"Okay then." She huffed in displeasure; she hadn't the faintest idea what I was talking about.

"Sorry," I mumbled under my breath as I walked toward the street. Carrie Pollard remained at the door, watching me. I could see her from the corner of my eye. Someone was always watching me from that house. "But it's not the same house, Meg," I said to myself. I'd spoken aloud this time.

Sure enough, I had a dozen messages and notifications on both phones when I got back inside. Most of them were from Nina, who wanted me to meet her at nine—no, ten; no, nine; how about nine thirty? The other messages were from Deirdre Mansell and Ferrol, both of whom sounded desperate to talk to me.

I called Nina first and agreed we would meet at ten. The arraignment was at noon; she said we could try to stop it. "It's not like that, Nina. We're not going to have a picket line or something."

"I've made signs." She was crying. "I was at Walmart last night and got materials."

"Nina, you're going to make yourself sick. Some of this, we're going to have to just get through. You're going to have to sit back and—"

"They're saying she was raped, Mom!"

A stunned silence passed between us. "I do not need to be reminded of that," I said. "There's a bad vibe," I went on. "These things creep through places, like bad water underground. Poisons everything."

"I always told you I thought this place was a dump," Nina reminded me. "I could never understand why you wanted to move back here. This is the worst place to live. Look what's happened."

"I know." I was resigned. "But, Nina, we don't know if Lucy was—"

"I know it," she interrupted me. "A mother knows. I'll see you in a little bit," she sighed, then hung up.

I showered and mindlessly wiped down several surfaces in my house. I couldn't find Bingo, which was a worry, and I'd tried to call Deirdre Mansell back without success. Her phone was clearly off. I left four messages, one on accident, which consisted entirely of my heavy breathing and saying "Shit" when I realized the line was recording.

The phone rang as I was heading to the door to meet Nina. I'd eaten an apple and peanut butter, tasting nary a bite of it, and had yet to pee despite having had three glasses of water. I barely remembered the night or my walk. It was all fuzzy and sliding around in my head. I thought it was a real shame that I was crossing over into the next life already; they say a person starts to remember being a child again and sees things as they did when they were young. I couldn't get anything straight; it was all overlapping, as I suppose it was bound to do. That's what happens when things are packed up real tight and the zipper breaks.

They said all manner of wildness at the arraignment when I got there. Lies, is what I thought. Lies about Lucy and these girls who they were saying she was friends with. They were wearing jumpsuits; they looked like dental hygienists sitting there with their hands in their laps. Lucy wouldn't look at us. Deirdre Mansell stood up and made some motions or defenses or whatever it is that lawyers do, and then Lucy said, "Not guilty." Nina gasped, like this was the biggest surprise. They all made the same claim.

"But the one did it," Nina said to me. "They're all saying it was the one girl."

"Well, she's not saying she did it."

"Not guilty," Melanie said. I couldn't get a good look at her face. She hadn't turned toward me, her face obscured by her long, brown hair, severely parted down the middle. She was taller than the other girls, sturdier, with broader shoulders and a looming presence. I saw Gracie Bagley with her short, tight ponytail swishing left and right, flopping down in the shape of a teardrop. She could have been Lucy from behind. They were both slightly hunched, humiliated by what had befallen them. Daniel was there too, seated away from them but clearly in the same amount of trouble—for the time being, at least.

"He rolled on 'em," I said under my breath.

"What?" Nina asked.

"Lucy should roll on 'em too."

"What's that mean?"

"Snitch."

"I don't think it's like that," Nina said. "I think Daniel was trying to help Lucy."

I rolled my eyes. "They said there was a witness. That's how all this started—a witness said Lucy was there. I know it was Daniel. I know it."

A woman in front of us turned around. "Shhhh," she said, her mouth locked in an angry clinch. I rolled my eyes again, but Nina apologized.

"Where's Gracie's mother?" I asked.

"I don't know." Nina had done her makeup for court, but it had been done in haste and clearly with a shaky hand. I laughed at how awful she looked, but my giggle turned into a small sob as I bit the knuckle of my right index finger. "This is such an awful place to be. Really. This is awful."

Everyone said their piece. It was a mostly uneventful beleaguered experience, with a lot of reading from paper and Deirdre Mansell acting busy and exhausted while she, too, read from various papers, always tilting her reading glasses down, then up, down, then up; I was motion sick just watching her.

"So she doesn't go home now?" Nina asked. She was pushing around people to get to Deirdre Mansell. "Deedee," she said over and over. "Deedee!"

"She doesn't go by 'Deedee,'" I said. "Why do you keep calling her that?" I reached for Nina's shoulder. "Stop it, Nina."

"They didn't let me talk to Lucy," she said.

"They will." Deirdre Mansell was now standing with us again. "They will, but not here. We're going back to the detention center now so we can talk to her. Just…"

Deirdre turned to me, then to Nina. "Please let me do my job. I understand how you are feeling. You will get to talk to her."

"I—" Nina started again.

"I'll see you at the detention center," Deirdre said very finally. She then walked to one of the other attorneys with her glasses on her head.

"Excuse me," I said to the one woman who I thought had shown interest in Gracie. Carrie Pollard had cried hysterically through the entire proceeding while Andrea Farmer nodded knowingly, standing next to her husband, who looked at the door every few seconds. We all wanted a way out.

"Excuse me," I said again to the woman I hoped might be Gracie Bagley's mother.

"Yes." She turned to face me, unfamiliar and clearly uninterested in talking to me.

"Are you here with Gracie?"

"Who?"

"Never mind," I said to her mottled complexion.

"I work for the county," she explained.

"Thank you."

I got up to leave, following the hordes of people out of the building and through the metal detector. I needed some air, and my stomach had the bloated, hungry feeling I got when sitting for too long in tight pants. I'd never been in a courthouse before, not even for the divorce. We'd done everything in Ferrol's lawyer's office. I'd expected polished wood and patriotic feelings upon seeing a judge behind a bench. Instead, the whole thing reminded me of the DMV.

The day was filmy; we were expecting rain. I took a couple of breaths with my eyes closed. I was bumped on the shoulder by passersby, only some of whom said excuse me.

"Mom!" Nina was behind me, shrill and panting. "You left me!"

"Sorry," I said, trying not to sound annoyed. "I just needed a minute."

Nina started to say something else but was interrupted by Deirdre, who was calling my name. "Ms. Gregory! We can talk to Lucy!" She was hollering over the heads of people going in and out of the courthouse.

"Okay," I said. "Let's go." I grabbed Nina's elbow.

There was a whole maze of secret areas behind what could be seen from the courtroom. We went through several panels of doors before coming to a holding area, where there were other people in prison jumpsuits surrounded by police officers and lawyers. Everyone was serious and hushed, looking at papers and nodding or shaking their head "no"—insisting on something that mattered. And there was Lucy. She looked tired, jumpy. Her head bounced around, taking in her surroundings while her eyes had a faded, watery look. She looked at the people to her right and left, and ran her fingers through her hair a number of times; it was a nervous gesture. Lucy had never been one for nervous gestures.

Nina ran to the bench where Lucy sat and scooted in next to her, wrapping her arm around her shoulders. "Oh my goodness," Nina said over and over. She was petting Lucy like a dog, rubbing her back and putting her hand through her hair, perhaps alleviating Lucy's need to do that for herself.

"So," Deirdre said upon kneeling in front of us. I'd taken a seat next on the other side of Lucy. The room was full of unfamiliar smells, most of them unpleasant, like rancid breath and body odor. Lucy smelled like nothing. I tried not to give that meaning. I couldn't smell her, like she didn't exist.

I coughed to clear my sinuses. "Sorry," I said.

"I think we've made some headway," Deirdre said. "Both Daniel and Gracie are saying that Lucy had nothing to do with the actual murder and that it was Melanie who not only did it but masterminded the whole thing. I'm meeting with her lawyer this afternoon, but at this point, Lucy was only an accessory."

"What does that mean?" Nina asked.

"It means she won't be charged with murder." Deirdre sounded frustrated that she was having to explain everything several times. She'd had this agitated tone with us from the start, like Nina and I were the village idiots, sent to scuttle about under her feet.

"Oh," Nina said. "That's good, right? But I just can't understand how she could be charged if he…hurt…her." Nina looked at Lucy, who continued to stare straight ahead.

"Yes." Deirdre was unequivocal. "It is a good thing."

"Good, then." Nina patted Lucy's back.

I'd yet to hear Lucy say anything about Josh, the murder—any of it. She sat silently when we were around, allowing us to talk over her head as though we were not at all interested in what she might have to say.

"Melanie," Lucy said.

"What?" I leaned in. "What did you say?"

"Leave Melanie alone."

We all went quiet, subdued by worry.

"What's that, now, Lucy?" Nina asked.

"She had to do it," Lucy said.

Deirdre stood up. "Okay, I think that's enough for now. This isn't privileged," she said, mostly to me. "So whatever she's saying… let's wrap up now." Deirdre was looking around the room. No one looked back. We were invisible in a place full of people with problems.

"What are you talking about, Lucy?" I asked, leaning closer. Nina leaned too, her eyes bloodshot and weary.

"No, no more questions." Deirdre lifted her eyebrows. "Thank you both. I'll be in touch later today."

"Can Lucy have lunch with us?" Nina hadn't budged from her spot on the bench. "She's got to be starving."

"No. It's time for you to go."

"Come on, Nina," I said. I, of all people, knew how irritating Nina could be, but I didn't like the way she was—we were both— being dismissed. "Let's go." I kissed the top of Lucy's head while Nina started to cry again, tousling the hair that Lucy had tucked behind her ears.

I offered for Nina to come to my house or for me to go to hers, but she said she was tired and wanted to be alone. I drove home, my usual meandering about on the road causing honking and aggressive tailgating like it always did. When people would roar past me after having to put up with riding behind me at a snail's pace for several miles, they would turn their attention to me with disgust but, upon seeing I was an older woman, would roll their eyes and move on without another raised fist. They felt sorry for me, or they felt sorry for whoever had to deal with me on the regular.

The afternoon was nothingness. I couldn't make myself get up off the chair. I had errands I could run, tasks I could do around the house. I could finally get around to mopping the floor, but I was consumed by misery.

The only thing I could think to do to get past this moment—and these moments came. They weren't waves; that's a lie. They're more like illnesses, something unwanted settling in a vulnerable part of your body, where it festers, depleting you until you feel resentfully compelled to do something about it—which this time was to call my mother. It was not something I took lightly, a conversation with her.

"Hello?" She sounded fit for a fight. Heather Gaines was eighty-six years old, hard of hearing, and living in a care home. At least, I think Gaines was her last name; I couldn't remember if Terrence was the last man she'd married. She had her own room there and was "pretty with it," as Rainy said. Neither of them was in Tuskin anymore. They'd each wandered off, purposelessly and with no particular destination in mind, just somewhere to be. It was mostly fumbling from one thing to the next, like Ferrol and his marriages and me and my tragedies.

"Mom."

"Who's this?"

"Mom, it's Meg."

"Well, whaddya know?"

"My granddaughter's in jail," I said as an introduction. My mother and I were long past meaningless pleasantries.

"Nina? She's too boring to go to jail. They'll have her leave because she's boring everyone to death." My mother's voice was a rake on rocks, craggy and split up. She sputtered her words at me rather than saying them.

"No. Lucy. Nina's daughter."

"All girls," she mused. "Rainy's got girls too."

Rainy had three daughters. I didn't know them at all, having walked away from everything in that life when I went to Atlanta. I'd invited her to the wedding too, but she didn't come. I barely knew what had become of her. I'd spent the better part of twenty years trying not to know what became of people. I'd call now and then or send her a Christmas card with a picture of Lucy, but it wasn't much. She'd tried more a few years back too. Rainy was a nice girl, a nice woman. She was a nice lot of things. It would have been good for me to have her in my life.

"How is Rainy?" I asked.

"Well, she's not in jail."

"No, Mom." I waited, ready to talk to her, really talk to her. I'd been avoiding it for so long—talking to her or to anyone. I allowed Nina and Ferrol because they were mine. I didn't have the right to deny them the way I could with everyone else who'd ever crossed my path. I suppose I could have chopped Ferrol, but he was Nina's father. That's what I kept telling myself when I called him for ridiculous reasons, even this long after we'd split.

"You gonna come see me?"

"Oh. Well. No, I don't think so. I'm kind of tied up here. There are a lot of problems here right now."

"Always problems." I heard movement and talking behind her. I'd actually been surprised she answered. I'd called a couple times the year before when I got spooked or rattled, and only got her answering machine. Me and Heather, the only oncs left with answering machines and phones with cords.

"I'll come see you," I lied.

"Oh, yes." She knew.

"We're dealing with Bagleys again."

"Who's that?"

"Bagleys. You know, from Tuskin."

"I don't know 'em."

"Larisa," I said firmly.

"Oh, hell."

"Do you know what happened to them? To her?"

"You'd know better than I would. I don't even remember, Meg. That was a lifetime ago. Last I heard, she was still in jail. For good."

"How are you, anyway?" I backtracked and tried to start the conversation over. "How are you feeling? You had pneumonia before." That was at least five years ago.

"Right. I'm fine. Listen…"

I waited, knowing what was likely coming. She'd hang up the phone after telling me I never got what I deserved and that luck wasn't saved for good people. That was a favorite line. *Don't think because you got lucky it means you're good. Bad shit happens to good people all the time and the other way around too.* It was usually how it ended.

"I'm not going to tell you what I've told you a hundred times, Meg."

"Thank you," I said, not trying to sound flippant.

"But there is nothing anyone can do about the past, Meg. You've got this hollow leg on you, and every once in a while I get a call and you want me to fill it up, tell you it's okay. You want to pretend that you're all right. I can't tell you that. I mean—I can, but it's not going to do any good. It's not the way I look at you that bothers you so much; it's the way you look at yourself."

"Would you want to live next door to me?" I asked. I'd asked her this before. Once, a long time ago, and I hadn't waited for the answer.

"Yes. But I'm your mother. And I wouldn't want to talk to you. I told you I'd never speak to you again, and I meant it."

"And here we are," I said.

"Well."

We talked for a few more minutes, mostly about nothing—the senior living facility where she lived and the food there. Rainy's daughter, who was getting her master's degree in engineering, though my mom didn't know what kind because "I don't really know what that means—engineering." There were a few other stories, reminiscences. She had kept her wits about her better than I would have expected. Sometimes I felt like I was the one who was lagging and not my mom. She told me the reason she'd held up so good was because she worked.

"You should work. It's good for you. Keeps you young."

It was funny because I could remember her complaining about the toll work was taking on her all my life. She would say she was haggard and it was because of the bar. She'd worked at a community college library when she got older. "From the outhouse to the penthouse," she used to say, because she thought it was cool to be surrounded by college kids.

"Well then, Mom." I was ready to get off the phone, having gotten what I came for—reality and guilt, one and the same most of the time. "I'll try and let it go."

"I don't think you should let a single thing go," she said, correcting me. "I think you should learn to live with it better. It's nobody's problem but your own."

"Just can't figure out why we're dealing with the Bagleys again."

"Oh, cut it. There're a million Bagleys in the world. That's not an excuse anymore."

"But what if it's her?"

"It's not."

We hung up. I'd think of calling her again at least five times the following week and would probably send Rainy an email on my ancient email account. She'd respond, and we'd say we were going to see one another, but we wouldn't. I'd been down this road before. There is no accounting for the past and its incensed determination to penetrate the roots of everything that's planted after it.

32

1974

Larisa pulled me toward the house, her jagged fingernails ripping into my wrist. I tried to get away, but only half-heartedly. I kept turning around, which slowed me down and made her think I was yanking back.

"Come on!" she hissed.

"He's dying!" I was screaming.

"Be quiet, Meg," she seethed.

And he was dying. There would be talk later that if he'd had his stomach pumped, he would have lived. We could have run to the road or even called the police from the house, but we went inside and hid. There was a woman and a man there when we went through the front door. Larisa pushed it open the wrong way—a screen door that was locked from the inside with a little latch and loop. She pulled at first, but it was caught, so she kicked it, tearing the screen away from one corner on the bottom half. Her mouth was twisted up, with her bad teeth and scarred lip pulled to the right.

"Come on, come on," she kept saying. She was talking to herself.

"What?" The woman inside the house looked at us as we came in. She had long, dark hair like Larisa's but was very tall and sturdy, whereas Larisa was small and soft, even with those bad teeth that stuck out like needles from her mouth. "What're you doin'?"

"Just hiding out." Larisa was still whispering in that angry, wheezing way.

"What'd you do?" It was the man. He, too, was tall with dark hair. He towered over us as we pushed our way through the house and to Larisa's pink bed.

"It's the concoction." Larisa looked at me; her eyes were full and red rimmed. "Meg, he had bad cards." She bit her lip.

"What?" I looked around. The house felt full of eyes on me. The man and woman were hovering over us, leaning and bending down. I felt like I was falling through the floor the way I kept getting smaller. "We gotta call the cops." I poked Larisa, who was in front of me. "We gotta call the police."

"Larisa," the woman said, her accent like a sling for words to keep them from falling. "What'd you do?"

"Larisa, we can't leave him out there." Now I was hissing. I got my arm out of her grip; it was covered in scratches and half-moon indentations from her squeezing. I took off toward the front door, looking out to where we'd left Tyler. I couldn't see him. The grass was too high, and the day was taking on a tint because it was going to rain. The air was fusing colors with the ground, making everything a dark green. "Tyler!" I yelled. The sound landed and died on one of the house's walls; it did not reach him. He would have no idea I was calling his name.

"No!" Larisa grabbed for me again. Her hair had gone stringy around the front and was lying in coils on her neck. She was sweating; I hadn't noticed before. She was wet with it, all around her head like she had her neck in a fire. "You can't."

"What'd he take?" It was the man again.

"Nothin." Larisa shook her head and started to pull the sheet over her face.

"What was it?" the woman was barking at us. She looked like a Great Dane lingering over a food bowl the way she was towering over us and yelling. "What'd you give him? Larisa!"

"It was the snake!" I yelled it before Larisa could answer. She had the sheet up to her chin. Her teeth were chattering.

"What snake?" The man kicked something. He had a wide mustache. Lon had worn one like that for a while but shaved it off. I wondered what Lon looked like now that he was in prison—maybe he had the mustache again.

"The snake!" I pulled the sheet away from Larisa; she put her fingers in her mouth. In the drifting, green-tinged light coming from outside, she looked sallow and tired, with bags under her eyes. A ruined child. The thought came to me as quickly as it went away.

"She tried to give us the sights!" I was yelling at Larisa but trying to make myself understood by the adults in the room. It was still a habit to think the grown-ups would help me. "It was the snake!"

Someone started laughing. At first I thought it was the woman, but it was Larisa. She was giggling and crying at the same time.

"Y'all are all crazy." I pushed my way past the man and woman, who weren't really blocking me but, with their size and angles, seemed like hurdles. I ran out the front door, the edge of the screen sliding on my bare leg and leaving a scrape, and into the grass. Tyler was lying in the field face down. I already knew, but I ran as fast as I could anyway. It was raining now, the water heavy enough to make it hard to see. "Tyler! Tyler! Tyler!" I yelled his name a hundred times. People were calling to me from back at the house. It was the man, mostly. His voice was getting drowned out in the rain, which was coming down a lot harder, but I could hear the bottom of it, just the ground of his scream; I was pounding on it with my feet. All the sounds came together as one, lost in the rain.

I knelt there for a long time. No one came at first. I was pulling on Tyler's shoulders, trying to flip him over and slapping the side of his head. I was trying to get to his cheeks but only got as far as his ear. He was too heavy and limp for me to move. "Tyler!" No one answered.

Finally, I felt someone grab me from behind. I remember looking at the road. Pirkle was empty like always, but there was a car parked over by Larisa's house with its lights on. The doors were open. I got pushed over, rolled back, and stepped on. It was the man; now he looked like a Great Dane, a giant dog jumping on me, keeping me off-balance, helpless, and overturned. He might have said he was sorry or told me to get out of the way. I was muddy from lying in the grass. I saw him lift Tyler and put him over his shoulder. He stood up, shaky with the weight, and started heading toward the car. I could see an ashy frond of exhaust coming out the tailpipe; the woman was in the driver's seat. I thought they were taking him to the hospital. That's really what I thought.

33

2024

Lucy was meeting with a psychiatrist. Nina called to tell me. "With a doctor."

"Yes, I know what a psychiatrist is. Are you going there?"

"Yes. Of course. They're at the jail."

"Should I come?"

I'd had trouble sleeping again, after the conversation with my mother. I lay in bed feeling like a child, which I sometimes did when I talked to her. I didn't know my mother as an adult; I'd left too young. I was reminded of the Meg who'd left, or rather the one who became the Meg who left. My sixty-four-year-old body suddenly felt small, soft, vulnerable in a different way than my age had started to make me feel. I could remember trembling and pulling my sheets up to my neck after it happened. I was doing it again. I kept telling myself it was not the same thing. It was Lucy now; I needed to worry about Lucy.

I sat up on the mattress. But why was Lucy having to live through it? I saw their ponytails from behind in the courtroom— lined up like little flowers on the thin stems of their necks. I wondered what I had looked like from behind when I was running away from Tyler in the grass.

I did end up falling asleep around three, slept late, and woke up feeling dazed, like I'd been boozing the night before. "Not a drop," I told the mirror. I had heavy bags under my eyes, filled with perceptions my head hadn't yet let in. They'd wait in pockets on my face, for use at a later date, to startle me when I thought I was doing okay.

"I'm going to find Gracie Bagley's dad," I said. "Fuck the psychiatrist."

"No, it's a woman," Nina said stupidly.

"I want to talk to him—Mr. Bagley."

"Why?" She sounded angry.

"I know that family. I'm about done with the feeling that I'm having. Like they got their claws in Lucy too. They skipped you… I'm pretty sure I know why." I was muttering a little, trying not to be heard while saying what I meant.

"We're not supposed to be talking to the other parents." Nina was officious. "You might say something that gets Lucy in worse trouble."

"She can't be in worse trouble, Nina. I'm going to get to the bottom of this."

I hung up while she was arguing about me coming to meet

the doctor with her. I was Lucy's guardian for the purposes of law enforcement. She had the lingo down—that, and the lecturing tone.

I got myself dressed and headed out the door wearing only one boot and my reading glasses on my head. I hadn't brushed my teeth and had a real bad itch in my ass. I didn't care anymore.

I didn't go to the jail. I decided I'd go to the Lattimers' house. No one had mentioned them at all, and here there was this hideout place on their land. There'd been some back-and-forth about the cabin with Detective Rinaldi during one of the interviews, but Lucy didn't say much. She said she knew where it was. He'd asked if she knew what was inside, and she'd said yes but then wouldn't elaborate. I'd tried getting it out of her too, but it was always this dazed affectedness with Lucy now. I swore to Nina that she was on something.

"It's pills. I'll bet all this happened 'cause she was taking pills," I kept saying. Nina had searched the house up and down and found nothing. I'd gone through the closet in the guest bedroom three times already and didn't see a single thing out of place. I'd run my hand under the mattress in there too, and told Nina to do the same in her house. Nothing.

I drove my usual slow pace, crossing over the double yellow and taking wide turns. I felt alone on the road. Everywhere looked empty and forgotten. My mood was affecting my vision; I wasn't sure I would return to my normal way of seeing things. It had been like this before, and I'd gotten rid of the film on my eyes. Or maybe it was a layer thicker. I wasn't exactly sure when I was seeing more or less clearly.

The Lattimers' place was unchanged. It was about a quarter mile up from where the shack sat, still locked and surrounded by yellow tape. It was a mile or so from where Larisa's house had been.

There were a few mailboxes by the street. I figured maybe somebody was living in the barn now, or the old house was apartments. It was a huge place, with a wraparound porch. It was blue with white woodwork that had faded and chipped. There was a truck parked outside and then a road that went farther back toward the water, where I could see another small house, and then the barn was over to the left. The trees shot out between the buildings, like darts in cork, straight and randomly placed, in the way and hanging heavily overhead.

I went up to the front steps, feeling like I'd knocked on more doors in the last week than I had in the last decade. All this had been here, in Tuskin, alongside me the whole time, and I'd decided not to notice.

No one came at first, so I banged again. A man came around from behind the house in jeans and a T-shirt. He was older but not pushing ninety. It was not Wynn, who'd been my mom's age; I had to guess either his son or someone who'd bought the house. Wynn's son had been in my grade in school, maybe a year younger. He was a bit of an outcast, kind of slow on the uptake and not very good at sports.

"Mr. Lattimer?" I said.

"Yeah." He wasn't unfriendly, and he didn't correct me.

"I'm Meg Gregory."

His face didn't change. I'd not been as significant as I thought, or maybe I couldn't tell. My reading glasses were on top of my head and would have been useless in trying to see far. He did not appear to know who I was.

"My granddaughter's been hanging out over at the shed…or… the shack or whatever it is. Do you know about that?"

"Yeah, we had the police over here the other day. Those kids put a lock on it."

"Yes, there was a murder."

"Yeah." He was uncommitted to the conversation and turned to walk away from me. "I remember you," he said before he had fully changed direction. "I remember what happened."

"Yes, that's why I'm here. I… Do you think the Bagleys had anything to do with this? The girl—Gracie—do you know her?"

"I don't know any Bagleys anymore."

"Right," I said. "I'm just trying to figure out what's going on with Lucy. Did you see her? Was she over here?"

"They weren't over here. They were hanging out at the fishing shed. We didn't let 'em; they just did it. It was that one kid at first. He'd go over there all the time. McGill. The kid who got himself killed."

"Josh was over there?" I watched his face. I couldn't get a good read on the guy. His hair was graying but not all the way gone. He had a droopy midsection from age and lack of effort. I was fighting the same thing tooth and nail.

"Yeah," he said, sounding a little done with the conversation. He'd met mud he thought more of; I knew the look.

"Do you remember Larisa?" I said. My voice sounded like it was a leaf in the water, slithering down to Melbourne like a snake. I shuddered. I could hear the river and feel it pulling me along.

"Oh yeah," the man said. "Hard to forget." He looked down while he put his hand to his mouth. I thought he was going to say something else, but he didn't. He was careful, as I was not to be trusted. A little like Josh, he didn't want to look me in the eye.

"Do you see Larisa?" I could hardly ask it. There was a cottonmouth in my throat, a snake going down to the pit of my stomach to fetch my nerve. I looked at the sky—blistering and white, the clouds had retreated so we could see what a void looked like, in ourselves and up above. "Is she…" I started to say out, but it wouldn't make the jump from my tongue. *Is she out?* I didn't really want to know.

"She never got out," he said. "I would think you knew that." He had a line of sweat on his forehead. It wasn't so hot, only heavy.

"No." The word got caught by the cottonmouth. Water moccasin. People were always so afraid of them. I had one inside me, the creek of my guilt muddy and slow-moving, a trickle.

"She'll never get out." I thought he said "you too," but I was hallucinating sounds again. It had happened before. The sadness will do that.

"Yes," I said. "Of course."

"That kid was bad news," he added.

"Larisa?" I asked.

"No. The McGill kid."

"What'd he do?" My right hand was shaking. I put it in the pocket of my pants, where it trembled more furiously, sweating in the shape of a claw.

"He'd take girls over to the fishing shed and—I don't know. I just don't think he was a nice kid. There were some complaints, is all I know."

"There were?"

"Yeah. That detective was over here asking me about it."

"He was." I exhaled.

"I caught the McGill boy over there a few times. Drinkin' and just…messing with girls."

"Did you ever see Lucy?"

"I don't know. I don't know who the girls were."

I took a large breath, feeling faint and desperate for air. "I'm sorry to have bothered you."

"It's no bother. Was never sure why you moved back here anyway. When I heard you came back, just made me wonder."

"No!" I said emphatically, perhaps challenging his wonder. I was not to be wondered about, or even contemplated.

"Sad thing, but anyway…"

"Too sad," I said. I had nothing more to offer.

When I got back in my car, I pulled the cell phone from my purse. There were all manner of alerts on its screen, none of which I could decipher. I called Nina.

"Hello?" she said, sounding both startled and angry.

"Ryan Lattimer said Josh McGill was roughing girls up. I'm over here now."

"We're about to go in with the doctor."

"I'll come there. I'm on my way."

"Rat bastard," Nina said, sounding forced. She'd never mastered expletives. It always sounded like she was trying too hard.

"Well, he's dead now."

I hung up the phone and turned the car around. As Ryan Lattimer watched me go, I detected a sorrowful resistance on his face. He felt bad for me but didn't want to. I did not garner sympathy well.

34

1974

Larisa showed up at my house that night and tapped on my bedroom window. I had no idea what time it was, late with a low moon; it peered into my room right next to Larisa's head. She was biting her lip; I could see her twisted teeth in the moonlight. They somehow defined her, those teeth on the snake's head and her pulling me away from Tyler with that crooked sneer.

"What?" I said. I'd been lying in bed, crying. I ran home when I saw them put Tyler in the car. It was raining hard and I got lost at one point, missing a turn when I was passing between Platts and Forte Street. I was in someone's backyard; I could see them looking out the back window—an old woman. She looked frightened of me. I was frightened of myself.

When I finally got back to the house, I was crying so hard I was almost hyperventilating. Strange, gulping, gasping sounds were all I could hear, and they were my sounds—angry and unfamiliar.

"Meg!" my mom yelled the second I came through the door, probably because of all the water and mud I was carrying in. "Where's your shoes?!"

"I don't know." I was panting, heaving, clawing for air.

"What're you doing?"

"I don't know! I don't know!" I was shrieking.

My mom got me a towel out of the hall closet. It was frayed on the ends, with the beginnings of a hole in several spots. I wiped my face and my hair. "Meg, you're soaked. Can you go and change?"

I looked at the couch; there was Terrence, acting like he was concerned and that he had some stake in my life. It made me want to spit, it was such nonsense. Tyler had cared about me. No one else did. I could really tell no one else cared. My mom was more worried about me getting the matted carpet wet.

"Why do people have to be living with us all the time?" I said angrily. "Can't we just live on our own?"

"Meg, why are you so upset?" Her face had pulled down at the edges. "What's wrong? Did you get in a fight with your boyfriend?"

"He's not my boyfriend!" Now I was screaming. "That's just so stupid. He's not my boyfriend. He's not like that. All he wanted to do was be an actor in Hollywood."

"Well, I hope he doesn't bet the farm on that." My mom laughed to herself and looked at Terrence. She was wearing a T-shirt. I could tell she thought she looked really cute.

"No." I started shaking my head. "No. No. *No.*" The yelling had developed a low hum. I wasn't sure I'd ever made this sound before. Everything about the day was different, even my voice. It would not come out of me the same again. It was a transformation.

"Meg, what on earth is going on here?" She kept glancing over her shoulder at Terrence. "Stop it." She didn't want him getting freaked out because of how I was acting. She'd done this with Lon a couple of times, too, when I got especially upset about something. Once was when she'd backed over my bike in the driveway and crushed the frame. I had a real fit. She kind of pushed me into the house and into my room, urging me to "be quiet… He's gonna freak if he thinks this happens all the time!" She did get me another bike. Actually, it was Lon who got it. He had a friend whose daughter had outgrown hers.

"Meg, what is going on here?" My mother had shuffled me into my bedroom and shut the door behind her. "What's going on?"

"Mom." I couldn't swallow, so I just kept saying her name. "Mom."

"Meg, what is it?"

"Tyler." I said only his name.

"What about him? Did he hurt you?"

"No! No. Nothing." I wiped my eyes, pulling at the skin, which felt tight and puffy. "Nothing. Just… It's nothing. I want to be alone." I continued wiping, pulling, pressing. My face was inflamed.

"Okay." My mom put her hand on my shoulder. "Okay, Meg." I thought she was going to say something else; I was waiting for it, but she patted my shoulder and turned toward the living room, where Terrence was waiting for her. "Okay." I went to bed without eating, but no one seemed to care. I heard Rainy come in at one point and complain about the weather. My mom told her there was ice cream.

"Come outside." Larisa leaned her head against the windowpane. Her skin went flat and paler where she was pressing. It wasn't raining anymore but still had the feel of it. Water everywhere, just not falling from the sky.

"No," I said quietly as I shook my head. "No."

"Meg." She widened her eyes—I thought maybe to scare me. "Come on, then."

"What?" I hadn't been deeply asleep, more dozing in and out of hopeful, then terrifying, thoughts. I thought maybe Tyler was okay and that they'd taken him home.

"They're lookin' for him," Larisa said. "You gotta not say anything."

The bed sank from underneath me. Quicksand. The place where Tyler had put the block to keep the mattress from sagging was a hole into which I was falling. "What do you mean, 'they're looking for him'?"

"'Cause he didn't go home. No funny business, okay? You can't say nothing to nobody."

I was about to ask if he was at the hospital, but saying it would have only made me more certain of what I had done. What I hadn't done. The shame.

"Go away," I said instead, waving my arm toward the window. My bedroom faced the ridge where we kept the trash cans. It was a small hill that led up to a forest. I'd played there when I was little, but then Rainy told me people went there off the main road to take dumps when they couldn't find a bathroom, so I'd stopped climbing up there, not wanting to find shit. Because my window was next to a hill, we'd never bothered to put up a shade. But the moon was in my eyes on this night. I figured I'd never been awake at this hour to see it watching me while I slept.

"Meg!" Larisa was urgent. "They're callin' around. You gotta keep your mouth shut or there's gonna be bad omens. You're in trouble too, you know. You're in bad trouble too."

I was over on the edge of my bed now. "I didn't do anything," I said. "I didn't do one damn thing, Larisa." I would decide later that this had actually been the most important moment, when I said I didn't do anything—because I hadn't. I'd left him there in the grass. I hadn't done one single thing to help him. This was when I made a promise to the other Meg that I would never see her again, a final goodbye. She went through the sunken center of the mattress, through Tyler's board, right into the floor, and was never seen again, while the new Meg remained in the room and went on living—the Meg who didn't help Tyler.

"Shhhh," she said. "Come outside'r you're gonna wake everybody up."

"I'm not coming out." I scowled, about to tell her that I wished

I'd never met her, that I only ever talked to her because of Tyler and I never wanted to see her again, when I heard the phone ring in the kitchen. I could tell Larisa didn't hear it at first, because she kept shushing me and making a bigger circle with her forehead on the glass, leaning. Then her expression changed. Her eyes went wide, with all the whites showing.

"It's the phone," I said, suddenly sounding like I was with her on something, like we'd hooked up and were going to work together on this. "It's the phone. Is it the police?"

I heard footsteps out in the kitchen and a banging noise. It was probably my mom shutting a cabinet. Rainy had a bad habit of leaving every door and drawer in the kitchen open. We were always banging our shins and arms and sometimes even our heads.

"Yes?" My mom's voice was loud and scratchy.

"Larisa," I said, putting my knuckles in my eyes. "Larisa, go away!"

"Meg!" my mom hollered. I heard heavy feet approaching now.

"Go away!" I snarled at the window. Larisa moved away from the pane and disappeared right as my mother opened the door.

"Where's Tyler?" she asked. "Is he here?" She sounded like that would have been funny, if he'd been there, like she would be proud of me for having him around in the night. It was my mom's whole goal in life to have some guy around in the night.

"I don't know," I said. I was trying not to cry, though I could feel my eyes filling up. I put my knuckles in my mouth and chewed. "I don't know. That's why I was upset," I said. The lie just rolled out of my mouth, a marble off a table. I hadn't meant to, but it went out into the world on its own, and like anything that gets let out like that, it stayed out. It was a prisoner released. "We couldn't find him."

"Well, his dad can't find him neither," my mom said. She turned to walk back to the kitchen. "She doesn't know. She said they couldn't find him before… Yeah…this afternoon. Right. She was crying." She was still talking, but it wasn't to me; the phone remained pressed to her ear.

I got out of bed and ran to my door. "I wasn't crying," I said as though this was the most important detail. "I wasn't. We just couldn't find him when it was raining."

"Mm-hmm," my mom said. "Right. No. She was home by five or so. Mm-hmm. No, I haven't seen him. Right." There was a little more before she hung up. "They can't find Tyler," she called to me before going back into her bedroom and shutting the door.

Larisa didn't come back that night, but I saw a gum wrapper outside my window in the morning when I went to make sure she wasn't there. Larisa loved bubble gum. She always had it and always smelled like it.

The next day I was shaky and distracted at school. It seemed to me all the teachers were whispering and talking behind their hands in front of us, like they knew a war was going to break out and were trying to keep everything calm until the bombs started falling so that we wouldn't miss an assignment.

"You know that boy's missing, right?" It was my friend Claire, who never said much to me. We were friends because of our comfortable silence.

"Is that what everybody's talking about?" I asked.

"No," she said, looking confused. "He's your friend though."

"Yeah." I nodded.

"My mom says they were out looking for him this morning."

"Okay." It was the end of civics class, and our teacher always lost control before the bell. She was still talking and pointing at things in the front of the room, but no one was listening.

"It rained yesterday," Claire said. She was always telling me the most obvious thing. She had her hair cut in a bob. It looked like a football helmet.

"Yeah. Hard."

"I wonder if he fell or something."

The bell rang and that was it. I picked up my things.

"What's wrong?" Claire asked. She was looking at my hands; they were shaking.

"Nothing." I walked as quick as I could to my locker without saying bye.

Claire was the only one to say anything to me about Tyler. He was older, and no one knew about him. He was someone vague in the high school, not like a football player or some guy with a convertible. Just Tyler. That had been enough for me.

Johnna picked me up from school. I hadn't known she was going to be there. I saw her car idling out front. She yelled my name when I came out. At first it was embarrassing because she was pretty loud and waving her arms.

"Yeah," I said when I got close.

"I'm gonna take you."

"Okay." We were both having to holler a little because of the bus engines, which sounded like tanks.

Johnna had her hair slicked back in a tight ponytail. It was her favorite hairstyle and hid her roots better than other styles she sometimes wore. "Get in," she said. She was not smiling.

"What is it?" I put my backpack down on the floorboard.

"The police are at the house. Your mom wanted me to get you and drive you around."

"Why?" I asked.

"Meg."

"What?"

Someone honked behind us. "Meg."

"What is it, Johnna?" I wouldn't look at her. The car started rattling, which it did whenever she sat for too long with it in drive but not moving. I stared at the dashboard. "It's so hot," I said. It was, but that was beside the point.

"Did something happen? His parents are saying he was with you."

"I don't know," I said.

"That's a real interesting dashboard."

The person behind us honked again.

"He just ran off."

"Why did he run off?"

"I don't know. Maybe he was mad or something."

Johnna took her foot off the brake and said something about going to The Rack, which was a store that sold stuff that was left over from better stores.

We drove for a while in silence. We weren't going to The Rack though; I could tell. "Are we going shopping?" I asked after she turned left for the second time when she should have gone right. We stopped at a light and sat quietly, no rattling. I heard wind chimes coming from somebody's porch; they were playing with each other, clanging in unison, then back and forth, like call and response. Johnna had the radio going; it was a song I didn't recognize. She always listened to the country station, I think because she thought of herself like one of the women in the songs. She was sad a lot, with a man who died from sadness and dark weather. Men ran around on their girls with her and drank whiskey when they thought about her. She hummed along before answering me.

"Naw. We gotta go somewhere we can talk."

"Please not Burger Heaven," I said.

"No. I'm done with that place." She was stone cold. "We'll go to the park like we did before. I don't have anything to feed the ducks."

"They're fat anyway," I said, and we both laughed like our lives depended on us forcing it out.

It wasn't near as hot as when we'd gone to the park so she could tell me that Lon robbed the restaurant, but it was bright, and all the benches had bird shit on them. We couldn't find a clean spot anywhere. Finally, Johnna gave up and said we could sit between the white streaks. I hadn't stopped being nervous and couldn't concentrate on bird shit no matter how hard I tried.

"So, Meg."

"Yeah," I said. I was pulling on my hair.

"Is there anything you want to tell me?" Johnna turned toward me and put her hand on her chin. "We've seen a lot, Meg…Heather and I… We've seen a lot. There's not much you can say to us that would shock us or whatever. If something happened, I want you to tell me. I won't even tell your mom, but she said the police are all over the house and…" She stopped talking. Her voice had kind of gone back inside her. It wasn't like my lying, which went out and wouldn't ever come back. She had control over the things she said.

"No," I said. "No. We couldn't find him."

"Meg—they found him."

I inhaled very loudly. I'm not sure what I was going to say or if I was trying to survive, but it was a gasp. Johnna looked surprised. "Where was he?" I asked quickly.

"He's dead, Meg."

I bent over. All I could see was Tyler throwing up in the grass, a foamy bile. I felt it inside me now. The snake's eye was in the blood in my mouth, like I'd swallowed it, but it wouldn't go down.

"How'd he die?" I asked.

"Organ failure." Johnna had a funny accent when she said it. I turned to look at her because the voice didn't sound right. "Did y'all take something, Meg?" She was back to sounding like herself. "A lot of kids try drugs, sweetie. That's normal, but you've gotta tell me if y'all took something."

"What? No." I was crying quietly. "No." I wiped my face, trying to hide it.

"What about that girl, Larisa?"

"She's my friend," I said. "We're friends." A bird came to rest on a branch that hovered over my head. I'd been told all my life that getting shit on by a bird was good luck. The bird fluttered its tail and jumped off, flying in the direction of the parking lot.

"Something bad happened to him." Johnna had her eyes turned toward me.

"I know," I said. "Because he died."

"He didn't die natural, Meg. If you know more about it, you're going to have to tell somebody. You can start with me, and we'll go from there."

I sat very still, thinking about what she was offering me. I could tell her every last word of it, let her have it all, but then what would she do? She'd have to tell the police or a judge or something, and then Larisa would get into a whole heap of trouble. I didn't care about that, but I just kept imagining myself saying that I didn't help him, that I was there and didn't do anything. Surely the judge, or whoever it was, would ask why I left him in the field like that, turning blue and screaming for his life. So then I'd have to say that I ran away scared. "I don't know, Johnna." Once it was outside my head, it was a decision. Normally those are made before someone speaks, but not this kind of choice. This kind is made in the middle of a breath. "I don't know what happened." I said it again, giving it my stamp of approval.

"Okay then." She swung her feet under the bench, only this time she wasn't wearing flip-flops. "Yep," she said. She swung her legs again, looking like a little girl. I'd never felt older.

35

I waited at home. I was hungry as all get-out when I left the Lattimers'. I thought it was a good sign that I had an appetite. Everything I'd eaten as of late tasted like cardboard, and had the same effect on my stomach.

I was in the middle of a bowl of macaroni and cheese made with half-and-half, for a lack of milk—it was delicious, and I planned to eat the entire thing—when the phone rang. At first I ignored it. I wasn't well, is what I kept telling myself. I was unsettled, sick in the head, in shock—whatever vague condition I could give myself to excuse the state I'd been in for the previous week. I suddenly couldn't imagine feeling any differently, like I would spend the rest of my life half there, wondering where the other half of everything—mostly my mind and my time—went.

The phone rang again, so I got up. "Hello?"

"It's Nina. Why aren't you answering your cell phone?"

"I don't even know where it is."

"Mom."

"Yes, Nina."

"Lucy still won't talk. Deedee says she has to admit what happened to her if she wants the judge to consider it, like they can't use it as part of the defense if she doesn't offer it or whatever the word is."

I had a wad of macaroni in the side of my mouth. "Sounds about right," I said. "Typical. Make her face it, make it her problem. She hasn't had it bad enough already."

"But she won't say anything."

"Right." I spit the noodles back into the bowl.

"The other girls are saying that's what happened, but not Lucy."

"Well, what does she say?"

"Nothing. She keeps bringing up the cards or that he was going to do bad stuff, like they prophesied it or something. That's all she'll say. But the neighbor girl up the street says he was known for this kind of thing, known to get rough with girls."

"Then why would Lucy go out with him? What would she have wanted from that guy? I just don't get it."

"The doctor lady is really nice. At least there's that."

"Where is Lucy now?"

"Still at the jail, but they're keeping an eye on her because of suicide watch." Nina sounded very far away, subdued and gentle. It was not how I thought of her.

"Are you home now?"

"No. I'm sitting in my car. I haven't left the center yet."

"I'm on my way," I said.

"No!" she answered emphatically. "I want to be alone. I'm going to call Dad anyway. I need to give him an update."

I tried not to sigh. "Good," I said. "Good."

"Just don't do anything, Mom."

"What would I do?" I asked.

"Don't do anything."

Like hell is what I thought, but I settled myself and sat at the table for what felt like a long time but was probably only a matter of minutes. I got up and walked to the door, unsteady but focused. I could feel every small grain of dirt, debris, kernel of loose matter under my feet. It was neither painful nor pleasurable but instead profound. I tried to get all thoughts to go to my feet so that they could shed into the ground like dead skin. I could remember telling Lucy once, when I took her to the beach, that the sand was a great exfoliator. She didn't know what that meant at the time, but I heard her repeat it to Nina when we got home. "The sand was exfoliated," she said.

I walked very carefully, determined to absorb. I'd put it all in the ground myself. It's where things fall. Tyler too.

I honestly hadn't been sure where I was going, but the car practically started itself and rolled down the driveway without any help. "I want to talk to that doctor," I said to the dashboard as I turned the wheel in the direction of the detention center.

"I'm Meg Gregory," I told the young man sitting at the front desk at Yeldon. "Lucy DeWitt's grandmother."

His face betrayed his confusion. "Oooookaaay," he said.

"I would like to talk to Lucy's doctor."

"I'm afraid—"

"I'm her contact. You can ask the police. Detective Rinaldi." I quietly congratulated myself for nailing his name.

"We have hundreds of inmates," he explained.

"Lucy DeWitt. She's new."

After a superior was called and some disgruntled exchanges were shared with a woman who had to enter something into the computer and swiped her badge at a door leading to the right, another woman walked up to me and said, "I'm Dr. Cheek."

"You talked to Lucy?" I said to her, realizing I was barefoot and not wearing enough deodorant.

"Yes, I'm treating Lucy DeWitt."

"Can I please talk to you?"

"You can, yes. Would you like to come to my office?" She looked down at my feet.

"I'm afraid I've made a habit of entering government buildings without shoes," I said.

"Let's just say it's your form of protest." She smiled gently. Dr. Cheek was very tall and slender, with her dark hair tied back in a low bun. She wore pearl earrings and a red silk blouse. Everything about her appearance and demeanor suggested professionalism, calm and careful consideration, and an inability to be rattled. I knew nothing of these traits and had never been so certain of my societal place than when I was standing in front of her, some useless redneck woman from the sticks who'd never done anything with her life but work a low-paying job and rely on a man so she didn't have to anymore. I almost apologized for my existence.

Dr. Cheek's office was underwhelming, which helped my feelings of inferiority. It was very small, with only a tiny corner window and old filing cabinets, dented and covered with half-removed stickers.

"I'm not a doctor," I told her immediately upon sitting.

"That's fine." She wasn't sure what to say.

"But something is wrong with Lucy."

"Why do you say that?" she asked patiently.

"I think she's brainwashed."

Dr. Cheek sat back in her seat. "What would make you think that?"

"She's hanging out with these bad kids who are getting her into trouble. I had a similar experience with a girl when I was younger, and I know how a kid can get manipulated into thinking all sorts of things, but this isn't her. She had it better than me—a better foundation. She's not like I was, so she wouldn't just go along with this. She's a good kid. This isn't her. I think these girls have it in for her. The one…" I stopped myself, knowing I was heading in the wrong direction. "And…" I took a deep breath because I could feel the onslaught of tears, whimpering, total humiliation. "He hurt her, didn't he?"

Dr. Cheek sat still for a moment before speaking. "She is still not saying exactly what happened between her and Josh McGill. I have not yet determined the extent of that situation. Her change in behavior, however, would be a result of that trauma and not necessarily the influence of these other girls."

"So you're saying he did—"

"I don't know. My impression is that there was the threat of it."

"Yes, you see…" I paused, recalling this threat. It was just a threat, just something she said was going to happen. Prevention. "Does that make what they did okay then?"

"No, I don't think so," Dr. Cheek said. She was used to telling people what they didn't want to hear. She was not going to make me feel better.

"But don't you think Lucy's being fooled by some local girls with a bad reputation?" I tried this angle, hoping for a different response.

"Local girls? Lucy is from here, is she not?"

"Yes. I just meant girls who are…a little rougher." I was digging a hole. "I'm just so scared of what might have happened to her. To make her do something like this." I felt my face fall. I felt all of six years old. "What would make her do something like this?"

"What would make any of us?" Dr. Cheek asked.

"Fear," I said before I had a chance to think. "And loneliness." I added that last bit, not sure where it came from—just a feather in fear's cap, I suppose.

36

They had a funeral for Tyler; it took a while to happen because there was an investigation into his death. Everyone was sad as hell but not really suspicious. I thought it would be the same if it had happened to me. People would think, oh yeah, she was bound to end in tragedy, but let's not dwell on it. The only person who acted like she didn't believe a word of the story about what happened to him was Johnna, but she was careful. She kept looking at me funny but didn't say anything.

Me, Johnna, and my mom went to the service even though I said I wasn't going to go inside. My mother wore a long dress with lace around the wrists. She borrowed it from Johnna, who had worn it for Uncle Ray's funeral. Johnna and my mother were different sizes, so the dress fit funny and looked more like my mom was wearing a black Kleenex box. She and Johnna got out of the car and asked me one more time if I was sure I didn't want to go in.

"It's open casket," I said. I hadn't known what that meant, but Rainy explained it to me.

"You'll be able to see him," Rainy said.

"Okay." I made my decision then. I wasn't going inside.

"All right," my mother said. "I've been to a lotta funerals. I can handle it." She let the door shut; the angle of the hill where we were parked had made it damn-near impossible for her to get the door open in the first place. It was ten times heavier because of the lean. I stayed put, pulling my fingernails over the seats, making faint lines, then erasing them with my palms, then doing it again.

Larisa was not there; I knew she wouldn't be. She told me her family didn't believe in funerals. They said they were for the living and not for the dead, who had already crossed over. "The funeral doesn't matter." She'd come over every day, keeping a close eye on me. I figured that was how she'd been with Tyler, always around, except now she was making sure I didn't say anything to anyone about what happened. There was a lot of confusion in my head about what happened anyway. All Larisa did was talk when she was with me, and I sometimes felt like she was trying to put a spell on me so that I wouldn't remember things right, so if anyone asked, I'd sound crazy or like I hadn't been there at all. No one asked, and I kept my head down. Johnna had been the one to tell me to keep quiet.

"Stay out of it," she said out the corner of her mouth one day while there was still some talk around town about maybe there was foul play and kids don't just die like that. "Just stay out of it. Trust me." She hadn't gone to jail when Lon stole all the money from Burger Heaven. She knew a thing or two.

The word was that they'd done medical examinations on Tyler and found that he had a stomach ulcer and drank some poison. His mother said he'd had trouble with his stomach for his whole life. The medical people said folks were drinking poison all the time; that was why there was a hotline. Everyone just accepted it. He was odd, was the excuse. Odd people are allowed to die for strange reasons; people are tired of trying to make excuses for them anyway.

It was said that he'd killed himself. Even his parents had said he was in a low state of mind lately but that they hadn't known he was that sad. They said they'd missed the cry for help. "Deaf to it," his mother said. Her interview was in the paper.

"You okay?" my mom asked me when she and Johnna got back in the car after the funeral. "We sat in the back."

"Yeah," I said, looking out the window.

"Why'd a good kid like that go and kill himself?" Johnna asked. I thought she threw her voice to the back a little, hoping I would think I needed to answer the question.

"You could tell he was depressed," my mom said as she was trying to get Johnna's dress to lie right under her ass in the seat. "Something was off with him, no doubt."

"No there wasn't," I said, but it didn't seem to matter that I'd spoken. They were continuing on with their conversation without me, saying that when kids don't have direction, they start to wonder why they're alive. "Yeah, like Rainy?" I said, because Rainy was always wondering what she was supposed to be doing with her life and couldn't seem to get herself into a good position where she didn't feel like she was missing out or doing the wrong thing. Even when she and my mom had been so happy together at Shakers, she'd get these looks on her face like she hoped this wasn't the rest of her life. She said things to me all the time about going back to school to be a teacher or anything but the bar. "She's sure stuck," I said. And anyway, if I was honest, I'd say my mom and Johnna were the most down and out. Tyler had been in a better mood than either of them twenty-four hours a day. Neither of them answered me.

"I didn't see the Bagley girl there," my mom was telling me and Johnna on the way home. "They stay away—always have."

"Well, they do and they don't," Johnna said. "They're around when they want to be. Sometimes they're really around, if you know what I mean."

"Right," my mom said. She cracked her window, which meant she was going to light a smoke. They both chuckled a little, remembering something about the Bagleys being really around.

"But I woulda thought that girl would have been there. Somebody from that family." It was Johnna. She was turning toward the back seat again, hoping I was paying attention.

"They don't go to funerals," I said.

"I'm sure they don't," my mom answered, still snorting under her breath. "They've caused a few funerals."

"So sad though." I wasn't sure which one of them said that. Before he was sad, he was a weirdo. Now he was sad.

I didn't say another word, taking a vow of silence from the back seat. I'd had a funny spot in my lung since that afternoon at Larisa's, a place where the air was leaking out. I felt out of breath all the time and like I was making a wheezing sound that no one could hear. It was a faint whistle. That was all I heard the rest of the way home, this little crackling bell coming from my chest. They could talk all they wanted, but they didn't know a thing. No one knew the other part—the part with the snake and us leaving him heaving up his lunch in the grass with a blue face. Running away from him while he was screaming for help, watching Larisa laugh and the Great Dane people snatch him up like a piece of trash in the weeds. I listened to the lies and the whistle in my chest and wished something would change.

Larisa was waiting outside my window when we got home. I could see her elbow as Johnna pulled up to the house, but the bone slid behind the siding when the car got closer. She'd been coming over every day, just showing up and waiting outside my room by the garbage cans. She talked a mile a minute through the glass. I would usually just sit there and listen to her ramble, daydreaming of ways to reverse time or to trade her for Tyler.

I would ask myself after she left why I was letting her hang out.

I could have called my mom back there to tell her to leave, called the police, left my room and gone into the kitchen where she couldn't get to me unless she came to the door. I could have told Johnna—Lord knows she'd asked. There were a hundred things I could have done but didn't. I figured I was under some kind of spell, because I'd just sit there and let Larisa talk to me. I wondered if I did get some snake juice after all or if I thought she was going to be able to convince me of something that would make me feel better. I kept waiting for her to say the one thing that would make it okay, but she didn't. She made it worse.

At first she'd acted like she was cut in half by him dying and that it was the saddest thing in the history of the world, but after a couple of days of that, when it seemed like we weren't going to get in trouble for what happened, she started to tell me a different story. I didn't pick up on it right away; if asked, I would have said she started being cocky about it, not the kind of cocky like a kid at school who got a three-pointer and was pushing everyone around because it was such a swoosh. She got that tone that she had when she thought she could teach me something. It was how she'd talked to me when Tyler was around; since he died she'd been softer, more like a person trying to make friends or at least not bother anyone. She changed though. She had power again. It was a quality I would notice in other people in my life; when someone can hold something over you, they get a little skip in their step or a click to the way they talk, a lift to their chin to make themselves look taller.

But she was still careful. She stayed outside my window, and when she left, she slid away undetected—like smoke from a cigarette. I never followed her, part of me wishing every time she left that she would never come back, that she would fall in the woods back there and die, choking and gasping for her life in a pile of dead leaves. Not grass—she wouldn't get grass like Tyler.

It started with her asking me if Tyler told me what she gave him. She had a song in her voice when she said it, kind of shimmying herself, raising an eyebrow, dancing to music I couldn't hear. "Did he tell you what I gave him?"

"No."

"I did it for you, Meg."

"What?" I wasn't curious. I think sometimes I felt like I was messing with her as much as she was messing with me. I didn't like her anymore. I wasn't even sure if I'd ever liked her; either way, there was a hate inside me. I'd never felt such a hate as I was feeling toward her; it was a hate I had for myself too.

"S'called ricin," she said. It was a Saturday when she first told me. She showed up early and stood at my window. I was lying in bed, which I did more and more. My mom said it was because I was a teenager going through puberty, but it was because I was down, really down. I thought about Uncle Ray and wondered if I would eventually want to off myself—thank God it was summer. Uncle Ray had died in January, in the gloom. "Ricin." Larisa said it again like the word would matter more the second time.

"Okay?" I'd never heard of it. She had a small rock in her hand that she was tapping on the glass. "What's ricin?" I only asked because I couldn't think of anything else to say to her.

"Castor," she said. "You make a paste out of it. Ancient poison." When I didn't really respond, she told me her aunt had the plants all over the house and that the oil had a grime that you could use to kill people. "So much evil out there, you have to be ready. We've always been ready."

"Like with your sister," I said. I wasn't looking at her when I said it, but something in the moment rang true. I'd unlocked the door.

"That's not how she died." She paused. "But Tyler was full of sorrows because of what he did to you, and worse because he couldn't stop. You know he couldn't stop. He was going to do it again and again. I had to end the badness. Some people are called to kill sorrows. I have a hard life because of it, but it's my path."

"He didn't do anything to me." I couldn't figure what she was getting at.

"Meg. He did. I saw him."

"Saw him do what?"

"He was gonna do it again too."

"Oh, so you killed him then?" But I already knew that.

"Meg," she said. "Come outside."

"No." I rolled on my bed, away from her. I could feel the block of wood Tyler put under the mattress pressing into my left hip. It was a familiar feeling, bringing with it a wave of regret. I had a hard time taking a breath; the air stayed in my chest, where it became hot and thick, like a paste. I felt the worst kind of lost, blind and fumbling.

"Meg."

"No." I lay there with my back to her, refusing to move.

I knew she hadn't left; I could still see her hair, but nothing else. The dark strands were floating in the window frame, small slices of her—waving at me. I felt, as I always did when I knew she was there, that same drag of fear's fingertips over my scalp. I wondered if Tyler was also scared but unable to get rid of her. I would meet other people like this, people who came in and wouldn't leave.

After what felt like at least an hour, I got out of bed and walked over to the window—empty at this point—where I pressed my face against the glass. Larisa always leaned in and pushed her forehead, making a large white spot on the pane. I was relieved that she was gone and stood there for a moment, pressing harder. I closed my eyes, trying to catch my breath, which had been too heavy to hold. When I opened my eyes, Larisa's face was right in front of mine. The circles of our flattened skin met on the glass. I flinched, jumping back.

"Don't be afraid of me," she said. Her breath made a foggy cloud. "I killed him for you. I had to. Meg, he hurt you," she said. "Real bad."

"No, he didn't." Now both of our voices met on the glass, battling for the upper hand, each side of the window wet and warm. "I'm not you," I said. "People don't hurt me." I was talking to the gash on her mouth and her broken teeth. "People don't hurt me, Larisa."

"He didn't want to do that to you, Meg. He's happy now because he knows he won't do it again."

"He was my best friend," I said. "He didn't do anything to me."

"Some people have bad streaks," she said. "I got rid of his."

"You're just mad because nobody's ever knocked me in the face. You think everyone's gonna throw you down the stairs. I'll bet you said your sister had sorrows too. I'm not listening to you anymore. Go away, Larisa." It was the first time I said it. *Go away.* I meant it too.

"My sister has nothing to do with this." I could tell I'd struck a nerve, but she was keeping herself together. "You just don't know, Meg. You are so used to surviving that you don't know. You don't let yourself see things the way they are."

"No." I turned around and walked out of my room, shutting the door behind me. I knew she wouldn't come to the front door. That was the way things were too, and I knew it—I did know that.

I could hear my mom talking in the living room. She had this chipper way with Terrence; it was probably because things with him weren't really going the way she'd planned. All Lon did was sleep and then fix things, but Terrence wanted a say in our life in the house. He rearranged stuff and took up a lot of room on the couch. He didn't like some of the groceries my mom bought and complained about the toilet in the hall bathroom because it was always clogging. He said Rainy was doing it on purpose with her tampons. He accused my mother of other stuff too, like sleeping in the middle of the bed and smoking all his cigarettes when she knew he didn't like her brand.

When I went back into my bedroom a while later, after sitting on the couch next to my mom and Terrence, who were necking like it was their job, I saw there was a mark on the window where Larisa always leaned in; the oils from her face left a residue. I don't like to admit it, but I asked God to have her eat some paste too. There was a crack in the glass below the spot that looked like her teeth, busted and twisted behind the scar on her lip.

37

I don't want her to do the plea thing," Nina said as soon as she walked in the door of my house. I hadn't known she was coming over, but as she was my only visitor—ever—if I heard someone at the door, I figured it was her.

"What plea thing?" I had a message from Deirdre Mansell but hadn't called her back yet; I found I was avoiding talking to her in general. Deirdre had such a bossy, dictatorial way about her that made me feel like I was being called a moron under every breath. And I was a moron, but not in the way she thought I was. I wasn't educated the way women like Deirdre Mansell were, and I didn't own pantsuits and an array of blouses in various pale colors, but I still felt like I knew more than she did about a few things.

"I've got a PhD in human nature!" I yelled at her once after we'd hung up the phone. "Human fucking nature!" I could hear the dial tone as I shouted. I doubted she could even fathom some of the bits of my life.

I was uncomfortable and full of effort every time we spoke. I couldn't say anything without second-guessing it or trying to make it sound better by embellishing or making fun of something else, as though belittling Cool Ranch Doritos, which I'd done during our last conversation, was going to make Lucy's situation more bearable.

"Can't they just be called Ranch? What's cool about them? If anything, they're room temperature! And another thing…" She'd stopped me because she was trying to explain that she and the other lawyers were using the joint defense rule so that they could share information without breaking privilege. She spoke to me like one might to a deaf person from an obscure foreign land who was in the way. I'd told Nina that Deirdre talked down to me. Nina had wondered why I cared. She was right.

"She wants Lucy to make a deal to avoid going to trial," Nina said. She might have been talking for longer, but I'd been caught up in my head, busy with internal errands having me rush from one conclusion about myself and the people in my life to another. "She could plead to conspiracy to commit murder."

I'd had the television on and went to the den to turn it off with a dramatic press and flick of the remote. "I don't see why that would be less, or…why would it be better to admit that than make them try to prove it?" I said, walking back toward Nina, who had not moved from the foyer.

"I don't know," Nina said. "I don't understand, but she says the punishment will be less severe."

"What kind of punishment are we talking about?"

"I don't know. She's a minor, so not the same as if she was an adult, but she'll have to serve time. They're not going to charge them as adults, so apparently that was a big win."

"I'm going to have to call this woman. It sounds to me like she's dropping the ball here." I headed for the kitchen. "There's got to be a way to keep Lucy out of jail, for God's sake…"

"I think Lucy wants to go to jail," Nina said quietly.

I scoffed. "That's ridiculous."

"She's scared. She thinks she'll be safe in there."

"Did she tell you this?" I asked. The evening sun was slicing through the window at an oppressive angle. I could see the fine lines forming around Nina's mouth, the skin's inevitable folding and falling.

"Yes," Nina said. "I mean, not in so many words, but she's not defending herself."

I stopped moving, stuck in this addled moment. "What do you mean?"

"She's not saying she didn't do it, Mom."

"If I could just talk to her," I said.

"You should go talk to her!" Nina threw her hands up. "Please, go talk to her! She's not listening to me, and I can't really make sense of what this lawyer lady and the doctor and all the rest of them are telling her to do. She picked you, Mom. You're her contact."

"Right." I looked at the floor. "Right. I know…"

"You can't be scared, Mom. *We* can't be scared. She's a kid. We have to face the music."

"Oh, Nina, believe me, I've faced the music. And anyway, it's those girls," I said. "I know it. She's under the influence. They've messed with her head, and she doesn't know which way is up. I know that family…" I said, allowing my voice to trail off. "She should never have gotten mixed up with that Gracie Bagley girl. I know how that ends. I do." I was looking out the window and talking to myself. "I've seen it all before. I have faced the music, Nina… I've—"

"Mom," Nina said, impatiently interrupting me. "I'm going to tell her to do whatever the lawyer tells her to do."

"Right," I said, pausing. "Right, I'm sorry." I think I was apologizing for yet another meaningless rant or because I hadn't tried to talk to Lucy or because I was making everything about me, or because Nina was right. She was absolutely correct. I'd never faced anything. All I ever did was run away. "I'll call Deirdre back right now. I'm going over there."

"If it's anyone's fault, it's Melanie Pollard's," Nina said, more to herself, appearing to not have heard me say I was going to talk to Lucy. "She's the one who got them all riled up to go after Josh because she had her own run-in with him. She's the one who you should be angry with. I can't figure out for the life of me why Lucy would have palled around with her, but they're saying it's because of Josh, and Melanie told her to stay away from him because she'd dated him too, then—you know…and so Melanie came to the rescue, but I just don't understand it. How could you not know she was going over there, Mom?" Nina snapped herself out of this contemplative state to accuse me.

I looked up. "Oh." I hadn't realized she thought this was my fault. "Oh," I said again. I couldn't tell whether I was surprised or not.

"I just don't understand how she could have been hanging out with that girl and you didn't know."

"Well, they weren't hanging out here." I heard the edge creep into my voice. "I wasn't hosting their meetings, if that's what you think. It sounds to me like she was saying she was going to Josh's and she wasn't. She was meeting those kids over at the Lattimers' shed or whatever it is. She was lying, Nina. It's what teenagers do."

"I never had any secrets," Nina said defiantly. I didn't want to tell her that I knew that. I'd never met anyone with fewer secrets. Nina wouldn't know a scandal if it walked up and hit her in the face; she'd been a bland person, rule oriented and safety focused. She could hardly stand to pay a bill on the due date and not a week early. She kept it all together with an arm-twisting fervor, and then she didn't. And now here she was, angry and officious in my living room, telling me that everything would have been different if I'd been following Lucy around.

"Well, I had secrets, and when they're really bad, they take you away from people. They push you out of rooms, homes, places you love. It's like a wall that goes up, Nina. And you can get behind it forever if you're not careful."

"Well, something real bad must have happened to you," she said, cocking her head to the side a little, just to show me she didn't think I was worth the brine I'd been pickled in. "Something worse than having your parents split when you were fourteen and being moved to the middle of East Bumblefuck to go to high school with the cast of *Deliverance*! Yes, I'm sure it was pretty awful. I'm sure it was terrible."

"Divorce is hard on kids," I said, attempting to be agreeable.

"Okay, so now this is because of the divorce?" She crossed her arms in front of her chest. Her eyes were growing red again. I could see she was trying not to cry. I felt so sorry for her in this moment, this pitiable woman with no armor, who I had created. There was so much more I could have done, and yet I'd made her into what I might have been, another version of me, a half person, hollow and easily hurt because of this lack of substance.

"No," I said. "No. I meant that when your dad and I split, that was very hard on you. And moving back here. I admit it. Moving back here, taking you out of your life, it was hard. It affected you." I dipped my chin in acknowledgment. I thought maybe I should stand too, go over to her. I'd never been able to hold her the way a mother should. I hadn't had the requisite fearlessness; I would have been too shaken if pushed away. I did light pats on the back and some side hugs seasoned with "well then" or "okay now." I had always been that way with Nina.

"I'm going to go home," Nina said. "It's not you. I'm just…very confused."

"I'll call you after I talk to Lucy."

"I doubt it's still visiting hours," she said.

"I'll figure it out." I finally walked fully into the kitchen to grab my purse.

It was the same young man at the front desk of the detention center. He did not appear to recognize me and only told me that visiting hours were over at six.

"What time is it now?" I asked. I had no idea where I was in the day. "Can I still see her?"

"It's five thirty, so yes." He had resumed his condemning impatience, perhaps recalling our last encounter or lumping me in with every other person he'd met at Yeldon who was exactly like me— indignant, demanding, and desperate. He asked to see my ID but otherwise said very little. It was quiet in the lobby of the building; I felt alone there, not unwelcome but like I had been forgotten, some- one continuously overlooked. I thought I might end up locked in for the night with the file folders and Coke machine.

I was told I would have to wait a few minutes before someone came to escort me to where Lucy was waiting. I looked around, hoping I might see Dr. Cheek and be able to ask her if there had been any developments that I should know about.

When a woman did come out from the back, pushing through a large door with a loud buzzing, then clanking, sound to tell me that Lucy was ready, I was so overcome with guilt that I could hardly stand. I pushed myself up from the chair and walked toward her. "I'm sorry I haven't come to talk to her," I said. "I've been..." I was going to say busy, but it wouldn't come off my tongue. "I've been..." I couldn't finish my sentence.

"Is that right?" the woman said. It was the end of her workday. She was weary; her interest in the details of the job were waning. She wore scrubs like we were in a dentist's office. "Right this way. You girls don't have long to chat." She had an accent—local, from Tuskin. I could pick them out of a crowd.

Lucy was at a table in the small room where I'd been directed. It wasn't a bit like the movies, with us reaching for each other through plastic and talking over a filthy phone. She was also wearing what looked like scrubs, similar to what she'd had on in court. Other than the fluorescent lighting giving her skin a pale-green hue, she looked remarkably unchanged; she looked like Lucy. I wasn't sure what could have happened in only a matter of days, but I had anticipated finding her unrecognizable every time I was to see her. It was always her, this small diamond-shaped face full of placid wonder. And now this. The shame. My hands shook, so I put them in my pockets, where I found an errant thread to pull. It was hard to walk and then sit in the cramped space with them in my pockets, but I wouldn't remove them. I found I was struggling to swallow, breathe, blink—do any of the automatic bodily actions. I wanted to think my way through it, but here I'd done too much thinking. Too much thinking at all the wrong times. The thinking should have happened a long time ago.

"Lucy," I said.

"Hi, Tata." She tried to smile, but it was a weak attempt. She reminded me of the worn-down woman who'd escorted me to the room.

"I'm so sorry," I said.

"Why?"

"I haven't come to talk to you."

She dipped her head slightly to the side. "It's okay," she said. "There's not much to talk about."

"Oh, yes there is!" I sounded urgent, unhinged. I closed my eyes and stopped myself. "Is there anything you want to talk about with me? I don't mean to—"

"Tata," Lucy said with deliberation, "do you believe in signs?"

I tried not to roll my eyes or huff when I exhaled. "I do not, Lucy. I mean—I'm not sure what you're talking about, but I don't believe in things like that. They don't lead to anything good, ever."

"But what if they can warn you?"

"But that's the thing, Lucy. How do you know if the warning is real? Or just some cuckoo nonsense by some fear peddler?"

"I don't know what that means." She slumped, probably tired of not knowing what anything meant. I hadn't given much thought to how confused she must be. I couldn't figure out which end was up and didn't understand most of what Deirdre Mansell said to us. It had to be much worse for Lucy. She was fifteen.

"Right." I shifted in the chair. I'd been on the edge, with my butt bones pressed into the slope of the plastic. "It just means I think that people use signs and cards and all of that to manipulate situations. They try to get everyone all riled up so they can do whatever they want."

"Like kill somebody?" Lucy asked.

My skin went cold. It wasn't chills, but a small sliver of death come to say hello. Sometimes when I took a nap, fell into a deep sleep during the day, I would wake with a start, jolting out of unconsciousness as if making sure I was still alive, fearful that I had slipped under for good. I had this same sensation now, that I was barely escaping something but perhaps that Lucy was not. It was following her this time, closely and with fangs bared.

"Well…" I said very deliberately. "Yes, I suppose if a person is convinced of something, they might think killing someone is their only choice. Or if you were hurt very badly." I hadn't meant to switch over to talking specifically about Lucy. "Or anyone, for that matter…was hurt…or…"

She looked to the side, deciding whether to tell me something. Her eyes were caught in the middle distance. I heard doors closing and footsteps in the hallways around us. Lights had gone on and off in rooms that I could see out of the large rectangular window on the door. Everything except the floor, which was a black, gray, and white checkered linoleum, was painted a light blue, an attempt to calm.

"Did he do something to you, Lucy?" I took a breath and tried again. "Did something happen with Josh?"

She did not look at me. Her face began a slow trip to adulthood that commenced right there in that very room. The concerns and realities that escape most of us for at least the first part of our lives were rolling over her like a wave, slow but determined and with a frothy crest she would not be able to avoid. "I think he would have done it again, Tata," Lucy said. "He wouldn't have stopped. We had to. I don't care if I have to stay here forever. Someone had to stop him."

I closed my eyes and tried to swallow. She had not answered my question. I heard movement at the door, figuring they were about to kick me out—closing time. I saw a girl there: long, dark hair; a crooked smile; a forehead pressed against the glass. "No," I said. "She's not here."

"What, Tata?" Lucy asked.

"Nothing."

38

1974

I found a vial in my bedroom. It was stuffed behind some shoes in my closet. They were from Walmart, on sale, but I'd refused to wear them because I thought they were so ugly. My mom said I was ungrateful. I'd actually gone into the closet because I could hear a scratching sound. We'd had mice before. I told my mom there was something in my room, so she sent me to look with a hammer.

I'd only seen vials at the doctor's office or on TV shows. Little curved glasses with corks; it would have been something I would have wanted, touched, maybe even thought of stealing from the store. We didn't buy things like that. No plants or wind chimes or trinkets.

I hit the floor of my closet with the hammer and yelled, "He got away!" Then I sat back on my heels to examine the vial. It had a white glue-like substance in it with little flecks. I immediately shoved it in my pocket. I was wearing shorts that were a couple of sizes too small, so there was a bulge. I pulled my shirt down over it and walked out into the living room. "I'm going outside," I said.

"So you didn't get it?" My mom was making a batter and smoking in the kitchen. Terrence said he liked brownies and why didn't we have brownies more? He was always questioning something about us, like he'd lived in our house his whole life and really had a bone to pick about one thing or another.

"Why are we leaving the front door unlocked?"

"Why can't we fix this window?"

"What's wrong with our vacuum?"

It wasn't his vacuum, as far as I was concerned, but there was my mom, running over to fix it. She suddenly had a screwdriver and said she knew how to use a wrench. Terrence was always grateful, and showed it by reminding my mother that she didn't have to work anymore.

"Bye!" I yelled even louder.

"Did you get the mouse?" my mom yelled back. She had cocoa powder in her hand and was scowling.

"No. He ran off." I pulled my shirt down even more and let the front door slam behind me.

It took me close to an hour to get to Larisa's aunt's house. I had only this hazy picture of the woman in my head, someone I wouldn't have been able to pick out of a crowd. I'd seen her in the rain and in the dark and then when I was running and crying. She had the same straggly way about her as Larisa, even if she was bigger and more hardened. They all looked like they could use a sandwich and some orange juice or something with a lot of vitamins.

The car was in the driveway, the one that had been used for Tyler. I didn't know who it belonged to, but I'd only seen it that one day. Dark blue, a Nova or something. Rainy had bought a car a couple of weeks earlier. She was so excited, but then Tyler died, so she had to pretend she wasn't as happy. I'd hear her turn her music down when she pulled in the driveway because she didn't want to seem like she was enjoying music too much with my best friend dead in a ditch.

I started running toward the house, which sat at a funny angle to the road, turned a few degrees off a straight line. I figured it was there before the road and now they were competing to see who could look right. The front door was open like it had been that day and the other time I was there. For people making poison and murdering and casting spells on everyone, they certainly were carefree.

I stopped running, feeling that I'd been spotted. I was out in the open, so it wasn't a surprise, but I couldn't tell which direction the feeling was coming from. It wasn't necessarily the house. I turned around, looking behind me, toward the river, back at the road. I thought I saw little tremors of movement everywhere, like maybe there was an earthquake in Tuskin, but only a few of the trees were going to topple, them and some blades of grass—handpicked by

God to be knocked down. There was the sound of feet on leaves, but all I could see was a squirrel thrashing around in some brush by the house.

"Larisa?" I said. I couldn't tell how loudly I'd said it. I turned around again to look behind me and thought I saw a white flash, followed by some dark streaks. "Larisa!" I said more forcefully.

I looked at the house again; there was a silhouette in the front door. It was a woman, or maybe a girl. I couldn't see her face. She didn't move like Larisa, but then she did. The hair down to the shoulder blades and the long legs and knobby knees—it all looked like her, but there was something else. I thought I saw a snake slink along its belly on the porch, but I was too far away to tell. I blinked and looked again.

I heard a car on the road and felt some relief, like someone would say they'd seen me there if my body turned up on the side of the road, and then Larisa would have to go to jail or whatever they did with bad kids. I put my hand on my pocket and felt the vial. I pulled it out and threw it in the weeded grass, then turned around and started to walk back home. I thought I felt something hit me on the bottom of my leg, but I didn't check or even reach to touch it. I turned and started to run.

My mom and Terrence were on the couch when I got back. I didn't say anything to them and went into my room. I lay on the ground and ran my hand around under my bed and went into the closet again, turning shoes over and pulling things out of the corners. I didn't see any more vials or anything else that I didn't recognize, but when I sat up from where I was crouched in the door to the closet, I saw Larisa outside my window.

"You came by today," she said, leaning toward the crack in the glass. Her breath left a fuzz of moisture on the pane.

"Yeah." I sat up straight and squeezed every muscle in my body. "What is it?"

I pointed at the closet. "Why'd you do that?"

She frowned. "Maybe it wasn't me. Maybe it was Tyler."

"It wasn't Tyler," I said.

"He's watching." She bit her lip. "Maybe he put it there to punish you because he didn't get to do what he wanted…"

"Why do you keep saying that? He never did one mean thing to me, ever." I'd sat farther back on my heels, torquing my knees real hard. It hurt, but at least I knew where I was.

"Meg!" It was my mom in the kitchen. I squinted, partly from a headache that was growing on the left side and partly because I wanted to go and tell her what was going on. I didn't really think of my mom like that—someone you would run to. I didn't have a lot of memories of her making me feel better about things or trying to right a wrong. Once, when I was still young enough to go door-to-door on the street, knocking and asking if anyone wanted to play, the little boy a few houses down, Jason, told me I was stupid and slammed the door in my face. I hadn't particularly wanted to play with him; he had an older sister who could be fun sometimes when she was in the mood. She had a dollhouse and would let me touch everything in it while telling me stories about where she got this piece or that. Their house was very proper and well kept, a little like Johnna's. It was out of place on our block, if you asked me. Everyone else was like us, in a rental with a lot of problems—leaks and rotted carpet and all that.

I remember thinking Jason was a real jackass and that it was typical of him to yell at me for no reason. He was in my grade at school and just plain didn't like me.

When I got back to our house, having decided not to go see Charlie—the boy who lived at the next house with his grandma and who was nice but a little strange and always talked in a robot voice—I was crying. I told my mom that Jason had pushed me. He didn't, but it sounded better.

"Well, that's just great," she said. "Someone ought to push him." She'd been at the kitchen table doing bills, which always made her edgy, because some things were going to have to wait with late fees and all that.

"If I were you, I'd go over there and kick him in the balls," she said. I was around eight at the time but knew what she meant by "balls," though the only balls we'd had in our house were gone at the moment. This was during the time my dad would come and go. I could never tell how my mom was feeling about him from one day to the next and when he might take off again.

I stuck around the table for a few minutes, playing with the stamps and clicking her pens, fingering the envelopes and smelling their glue before walking back over to Jason's house and knocking on the door. It was his mom who answered this time.

"Hi, Meg," she said.

"Jason said I was stupid," I told her. He'd walked up behind her and stood to the right of her shoulder.

"Jason," she said. "Say you're sorry."

"Sorry," he said. He had hair cut in a straight line across his forehead. I always thought he looked like a pencil, with his hair as the eraser; it had a light-red tint to it.

"Show me your balls," I said.

"What?" He looked up at his mother.

"Okay, Meg. Go on home." She was never very nice to me either. Her name was Debra. Johnna said no one ever thought Deb would marry local, but there she was.

"I wanna kick his balls," I said.

"No kicking." She started to shut the door. "That's enough now." Jason just stared at me like a dumb deer.

When I got back home and told my mom what had happened, she laughed and said that she wasn't serious about kicking him. "Don't ask a boy to see his balls. Come here, Meg." She put both arms around me and said, "You're not stupid. Everyone else is. That's just how it goes." That's my only memory like that. Rainy hugged my mom, but it was Rainy doing the reaching. I just never had the confidence.

"Meg!" my mom called again. I stared at Larisa through the window.

"Yeah?" I said loudly. Larisa cut her eyes and pressed her head even harder on the glass. I heard the crack slide just a hair.

"Can you make me and Terrence some popcorn? He's rubbing my feet!"

She did always have to brag when somebody was being nice to her, especially if it was a guy. "Fine!" I stood up. "Did you put more of that stuff in here?" I asked Larisa in a quieter voice. "I'm gonna find it, so you might as well just tell me."

She didn't answer. She suddenly had a sleepy look to her, like she would pass out right there outside the window. "Don't worry so much, Meg. Sometimes people are okay when they're gone. This is no place for a soul like Tyler."

"I have to go make popcorn," I said. It was no place for a soul like me, then, either.

I was in the kitchen for a long time. I burned the first batch on purpose. It set off the smoke alarm, and Terrence got mad because it was the best part of *Dirty Harry* on TV and he had to come and wave a towel by the smoke detector. My mom said she didn't even know we had a smoke detector. Terrence said he put it in. He was running up a tab at the store. I'd heard my mom say something about going into the Ace and having the guy there tell her she owed him money. It was Terrence. He would go in all the time and say he forgot his billfold.

"That's fancy," my mom said about the beep.

"Sorry. I'll do another."

"Don't waste the oil," Terrence said, like he was the oil police.

After I gave them the popcorn and they complained there was too much salt, I went back to my room, but Larisa was gone. I went outside because it was a fine day, not too hot at all and all the pollen was gone so a person could actually enjoy sitting nowhere without covering their butt in yellow. I had a feeling, so maybe I was becoming more like Larisa, but I went around to where she would come up to my window. She'd put a small baggie of the mashed-up glue stuff there, covered with a couple of leaves and old dark-brown pine straw. I figured it had to be all over the place. I was glad we didn't have a dog. She would have killed it.

39

So part of the problem is that they're admitting they were planning to kill him before he did anything to Lucy." Deirdre had had a peel. Her face was red with streaks and small craters. She'd worn a baseball cap to hide it, pulled low—that, and lipstick. We were meeting at the detention center where Lucy and the others were being held. Andrea Farmer made sure to announce every time we saw her that Daniel was not being charged with murder.

"He's an accessory, but they think that will be dropped," she'd tell anyone who would listen. "He won't be here much longer." She made these decrees whenever we were in the hall or were waiting in a holding area together. "It's ridiculous he's still here." She seemed especially intent on telling me this, very specifically, as though I were personally responsible for him being held.

"Why does that matter?" I asked. Nina was worse for wear on this morning; I could tell she hadn't combed her hair or brushed her teeth, and there was a faint rancid smell coming from her direction every time she let out a heavy breath. I, on the other hand, had tried to look especially smart for this meeting. I hadn't slept well and was attempting to make up for that by using a straightener on my hair, which only served to make it look like a wedge of cheese, and I was in a hot-pink suit. It was something I'd purchased on impulse a few years earlier when I'd made the daring proclamation, to only myself in the bathroom mirror, that I was going to get a job. I didn't have any particular job in mind and virtually no skills to speak of. Before I met Ferrol, I'd worked menial jobs at restaurants and retail counters. I'd been industrious but unambitious.

"You look nice," Nina said in the middle of Deirdre's explanation.

"Oh?" Deirdre said, thinking that Nina had been talking about her.

"I like the pink."

"Yes," I said. "It's very bright." I was glowing in the pale-blue-and-tan waiting area. "Very bright."

"So," Deirdre said. "Sorry, but I want to make sure we have this conversation before we see Lucy. So, obviously the crime was premeditated and intentional—meaning that they intended to kill him; they had the requisite mindset for first degree murder."

Nina's shoulders slumped forward as her head dropped. I put my hand on her back and patted awkwardly. I was briefly reminded of burping her as a child. I'd been so uncomfortable with all those duties; her dependence on me had been confining and intolerable. I had wanted to hold Lucy all the time. And here we were.

"But," Deirdre stressed, "as I've said, I think only the Pollard girl will be charged with that. But I want to talk to Lucy one more time before we meet with the judge to make sure she's got her timeline correct and in line with the other kids."

Deirdre continued to talk while I pretended to listen. I was interested in what she was saying but also distracted by all the kids milling about the building. There were windows into hallways and other rooms. The adults working at the center seemed to think they had a normal job. They were making jokes with one another and drinking coffee or eating bagged snacks from the machine. They showed each other their phones, nodding or chuckling. I could have been one of them, working here day in and day out. I wondered if they even noticed us, the adults who did not work there, the adults accompanying children, teenagers, kids—all of whom were in terrible trouble. I wondered what they thought of us, other than that we'd failed. I looked at Nina and asked myself if I thought she'd failed. I didn't know what I thought. The responsibility was hovering over us in thin cirrus clouds. It would accumulate and darken before it fell. I waited to find out where it would land and if I would be in its zone of condemnation.

I could tell Deirdre was annoyed that my attention was wandering. She spoke loudly and with more emphasis. "Ms. Gregory?" she said as I turned away.

"Yes." I looked back at her and saw over her shoulder the man from the court proceeding, the one I had been convinced was Gracie Bagley's father or uncle or guardian. I stood up, startling Nina, who had all but disintegrated into her chair, a wet towel of a person, heavy and sodden. "I'm sorry," I said, putting my hand on Deirdre's shoulder as I pushed past her and toward the Bagley man. He was with a woman on this day; I did not see Gracie. I figured they were going to find her. All the kids had an appearance before the judge. Lucy was first.

"Sir!" I called. He was making a left around a partition. The waiting area was divided up, but we could all see one another. Its design had clearly not been meant for privacy, only rounding up and separating.

The man turned toward me, stopped briefly, rolled his eyes, and kept moving. I was taken aback and called louder, pushing my way around several chairs—some with people in them—to get closer. "Mr. Bagley?" I said, so certain of myself. He resembled Larisa, the dark cast to his hair and olive skin tone; his eyes were heavy and pulled down at the edges, doe-like, what might have looked sad but was instead hard, warning and bitter.

"Bailey," he said, turning around. "Jon Bailey."

"Oh." I looked down. "Oh, I…" I had to have known. I had the vaguest recollection of being corrected or of someone squinting in indecision. Should they tell me I was saying the girl's name wrong, or should they be kind to this rattled grandmother whose granddaughter was in jail and let it slide? I could hear Nina saying *"No, Mom; that's not her name"* over and over again. I shuffled my feet, feeling very unprepared and disoriented, like I'd stumbled into an important business meeting in a bathing suit. "I must have misunderstood," I said, more to myself.

He stared at me, indignant and exhausted as we all were. "What is it?"

"I'm…I'm Lucy's grandmother."

"Yes." He was clipped and clearly in a hurry.

"I thought you were her—"

"We're meeting Grace right now. I can't…" He didn't finish his thought; the woman with him grabbed his elbow and said something as she pulled him away.

"Are you a Bagley?" I asked the woman.

"What?" She turned to the man. "A bag lady?"

"It's Lucy's aunt or something," the man said. "Gracie's waiting on us."

"Thank you," I said ridiculously. "But I'm her grandmother," I added, as though anyone cared.

"We have to go," the woman said. They both looked at me over their shoulders as they started to move toward another part of the floor. "Lucy was a very nice girl. I'm not sure what happened to her," the woman told me as if this were a warranted update, one I had asked for.

I flinched, thinking I should say something back, a retort,

a defense. "She is a nice girl," I said, sounding unsure of myself. "Nothing has changed. She was hurt. You know that, right? She…" I was pleading. My voice had taken on a tremble and was raised to be heard over the growing distance between us. I suddenly felt taller than both of them, than everyone around me, as though I were standing on something and shouting, not to be heard but understood.

"It was her idea," the woman said sharply as she stopped walking. "Gracie said it was Lucy's idea." She was facing me completely now and scowling.

"No." I shook my head. "No! And I know you." I pointed at the man. "You're one of them. I know what that family looks like. I'd know 'em anywhere." I shook my finger at him as they again turned to go. "I know you. I know you! I'd know you anywhere!" I was yelling and throwing my arm as though I were going to hit him. The only person I'd ever hit in my life was Ferrol, and that hadn't been a punch. I'd slapped him while crying. I'd had red wine and thought he was flirting with the waitress. It was during our anniversary dinner at Kendrick's. It was supposed to be fun, he kept saying. I was not having fun, and the waitress was wearing a black dress. I'd almost worn a black dress. I was angry at Ferrol for telling me to change.

"Even the help is dressed better than I am. You wanted me to wear…this stupid fucking blouse!" I spilled red wine on the table and stormed off to the bathroom with Ferrol following behind me, trying to figure out what the hell was wrong.

"Are you okay?" He'd been genuinely concerned. It was in the small area between the men's and women's rooms where I reared back and smacked him. We ended up going back to the table and finishing dinner. It was strained and uncomfortable, with me pulling at my shirt before realizing that the woman in the black dress was the manager. She'd seen us by the bathrooms and sent over extra bread—on the house. I claimed she wanted me to get fat.

"Are you okay?" Ferrol had asked again. I pushed the bread basket toward him and crossed my arms. He had a large red blossom on his cheek from where I'd popped him.

"Ma'am." It was a police officer. "Ma'am, can you please come with me?" Gracie's parents were several feet away, and I was being mildly restrained.

"What?" I looked behind me. It was a woman holding my elbow. She appeared reluctant with her eyes downcast, so tired of everyone's misery.

"I'm sorry," I said.

"Well, let's get you away from that couple. We can't have people getting into it in the lobby." She had almond eyes, both in shape and color. I stared at her intently for a moment too long.

"They're kids," I said.

"I know it." Her hair was braided in hundreds of rows around her scalp. I thought she was insufferably lovely, and I couldn't reconcile her with this place. "But you need to sit back down and leave those people alone."

Nina hadn't noticed the incident. She was too withdrawn,

festering like an untended wound on her plastic chair. Deirdre watched me, her eyes beady and worried. "Meg," she said.

"Yes. It's Bailey." I looked at Deirdre accusingly. "It's Bailey, not Bagley."

"Yeah, I thought we already talked about that." She sighed impatiently and adjusted her baseball cap and the papers in her lap. "There's no one named Bagley—not sure why that keeps coming up."

"Gracie Bailey," I said, needing more finality. "She's not related to Larisa."

"I'm not sure who Larisa is, but let's stay focused on the hearing today if we can." She adjusted again. "The judge has indicated that she will be giving a lot of weight to the psychiatric evaluations, and so..." She went quiet.

"So, what?" I said.

"I think it will work in Lucy's favor to have her discussions with Dr. Cheek included."

"Okay."

Nina sighed dramatically. I thought for a moment that it was a call for attention; it was that gusty. "When will this be over?" she asked.

"Not for a long time," Deirdre said emphatically. "And you have to be a beacon of calm for Lucy until it's been decided what will happen. No more flying off the handle." She turned to me.

"Isn't it considered rude to wear a baseball hat indoors?" I asked, feeling mildly vindicated.

Deirdre rolled her eyes. "We meet with the judge in a half hour. Please get yourself prepared. No more yelling or sighing." She looked at Nina. "We're the adults."

I sat next to Nina, not knowing how to comfort her. She looked around heavily, as though moving her eyes in their sockets required profound strength. "It will be okay," I said. "This is the hand we're dealt." Johnna had said the same to me. She was talking about Uncle Ray, but for everyone who's looking for a reason, the hand they're dealt is a decent enough answer.

We were called to head back to the courtroom. It was a different setup than where we'd been before. This was less formal, smaller, less intimidating. The judge was still in a robe, but she was not hovering over her surroundings with as much authority as the first judge who'd decided to hold Lucy and the rest of the kids in the detention center. I understood that the nature of the crime had been the reason they were not released.

My attention waxed and waned throughout the hearing. Once again there was so much back-and-forth between the judge and Deirdre, who did remove her hat once inside the room; she refused to look at me after doing so. Her face was glowing red in the overhead lighting, but she appeared unselfconscious about it and spoke confidently, presenting report after report to the judge, who moved her reading glasses up and down her nose with admirable efficiency.

I noticed, after Judge Mason bumped it with her elbow while taking some papers, that she had a framed photo of her cat on her desk. Like so much else in the building, it was incongruous with what was happening there. I could not get past what it must have felt like to see these proceedings every day, then go home and have dinner with your kids and not either die of fear that they would end up in the building with you or die of gratitude that they hadn't.

All I could think about, while sitting and listening, feigning understanding and some sort of "belief" in the system that I did not feel, because what else could I do, was that I should stand up and make an objection, that I should interject and make a case for Lucy that I didn't feel was being properly made by anyone else. I'd read some of the entries in my law dictionary and realized very quickly that I was probably not going to have anything to offer. I couldn't even correctly hug Nina or forge a meaningful connection with my neighbor, Melanie Pollard's mother, so that we could better address this situation. I wasn't a useful person; I'm not sure I'd ever meant to be, but it had never been more apparent to me. I moved forward in my seat, leaning like I was going to get up. Nina looked at me, bleary but alert.

"What are you doing? You can't go to bathroom now," she said.

"I'm not going to the bathroom." I pulled my hand away from her and continued to rise. "Excuse me," I said. "Excuse me."

The judge stopped talking. She had honey-colored hair cut like a teardrop around her face with small, wispy bangs. It seemed many women had this haircut, the turned-under ends on a pert little bob. I reached for my own hair, straightened aggressively, so assertively different, like I cared very deeply. I didn't.

"I just want to say, hasn't enough awful stuff already happened? Are we… What are we doing here? A bunch of terrible stuff has already happened, and now we're having a meeting about it." I pointed at Deirdre. "I don't know what's better or worse. Something terrible happened when I was a kid too, and we didn't have a meeting. There weren't lawyers or people with desks and all of that. It was different here then. We were ignored. Everyone was. I don't even know if they had courts or—" I stopped talking because this was not what I'd really wanted to say. "I don't think that anyone would be better off if she'd gone to a facility or juvenile detention or whatever this is. People will get in trouble if they're going to get in trouble. You can't prevent"—I said the word as though disgusted by the notion of it—"people from facing all that there is to face. He did an awful thing, and so did Larisa. So did I, but nobody got together and said we should talk about it with doctors and whoever else. There are literally two hundred adults in this building, and the kids are all fucked up." There were a couple of grumbling gasps, people feigning shock at hearing an expletive, like it was the first time in their lives being exposed.

"They're totally screwed up, and he was part of the problem. You can't go and take matters into your own hands, but what better do any of us know? We're not any better than—"

"Mom!" Nina's voice shattered my resolve. I supposed she'd been saying my name for some time, but I hadn't heard her. I looked at the judge, who did not appear angry but who was also not amused.

"You're not helping Lucy." It was Deirdre. She'd turned from the desk where she'd been sitting in front of us; she'd sat with her back to us in both proceedings. "You're not helping Lucy," she said again. Lucy had not turned around; her shoulders were slumped in the manner of Nina. My creations—defeated and afraid.

"I just don't understand how we can be sitting here analyzing all that's happened. Where were we a couple of months ago? Where were you?" I pointed at the judge. "We're all just here after the fact."

"That's how it works, Miss…" The judge looked around, perhaps hoping someone would shout out my name. "We're not trying to fix what happened. We're trying to do what's right now."

"Yes, but…" I started to sit down. My knees had taken over, and they were done with this spectacle. "We're making it worse," I said, more to myself.

"It can't get worse," the judge said. "We have a dead teenager. And some very confused kids."

"Right." I sat down very finally. "Right." They didn't feel sorry for Lucy. They didn't feel sorry for me. I suppose that was what I wanted, for these people without ghosts to be sorry that I had them, that Lucy would have them now. I could remember a woman at one of Nina's playgroups—the one thing I had done with her when she was a toddler, mostly because someone Ferrol was trying to impress had suggested it, a client—telling me that when it rained at her wedding, it was the worst thing that had ever happened to her.

"Not the whole time, but we had to cut the cake under an umbrella," she said.

"A girl I knew murdered my best friend when I was in seventh grade" had been my response. "They left him in a ditch."

"Oh," she said, scooting back a little with her son in her lap. Nina and I did not go back to Toddler Tumble Time. We sat in my car with Nina locked in her car seat every Tuesday morning from nine to nine forty-five a.m. just in case Ferrol was paying attention to whether or not we'd left the house.

Now rain at her wedding would not be the worst thing that ever happened to Lucy. Now she had this to haunt her.

It took a moment for the proceedings to begin again. There was more paper shuffling and chairs sliding back and forth under tables. People shifted on the benches, though there were only a few of us. Gone was the crowded, spectacle feeling. Now it was somber and clerical, like going to the dentist's office or picking up a prescription. I thought someone was going to ask me for my insurance card.

I should have been embarrassed, but I wasn't. I certainly felt numb, out of body, extracted in a way, like I'd been the victim of an accidental dissection. Someone was being called to put my spleen back in my body, with apologies.

The proceeding was lengthy at best, interminable. I did find that I knew what was going on and by the end understood that Lucy was going to be released. She would not go to trial, which had been tossed around as a possible consequence.

"So there's no trial?" I asked as the judge formally ended the proceedings.

"No, this is juvenile court," Deirdre said dismissively. "There was never going to be a jury trial, not unless she was charged as an adult."

"Okay, so there was a chance for a jury trial." I dipped my chin, needing to be right for some reason.

"She will be on probation for five years. If she does anything even slightly risky during that time, she can be incarcerated," Deirdre explained to me and a bug-eyed Nina, who appeared to have just woken up and was trying to understand.

"So she can come home?" Nina asked.

"Yes, but she has to report once a week, and there are a lot of restrictions. You'll meet with a probation officer weekly. She'll only be allowed to go to school and to a job or any other approved activity. Does she play sports?" Deirdre asked Nina, her face even more irritated than it had been that morning.

"No. Just church," Nina said. There was a slow peel of embarrassment over us, an outer layer of our sham being removed, or perhaps reattached. Church seemed like such a silly thing to talk about, given the circumstances.

"She's out of the woods," Deirdre said. I think she was looking for gratitude. Nina nodded and mumbled something that sounded like "thank you." I was unable to muster a response.

40

1974

I went to live with Johnna. At first I said it was because of Terrence. He seemed flattered that he'd caused such a ruckus. He was definitely the kind of man who wants to make a nuisance of himself to feel powerful.

My mom was shaken up that I said I wanted to move out. "Why?" She must have asked me twenty-five times. Just "why?" Because I think she was kind of excited to be rid of me. Now it would be all adults in the house, and that was easier. I hadn't been acting right since Tyler anyway. I hid out in my room most of the time, waiting for Larisa to show up but also scared of seeing her outside my window. She was in a bad way too; one day when she came, I could tell she'd been crying. I asked her what was wrong, and she just said she didn't want me to worry about it.

I went from feeling sorry for her one second to hating her the next. Things were mixed up inside me, and everything at school was falling apart. I was set to be done with eighth grade in a few weeks when I told my mom I was going to stay with Johnna for the summer. She argued, but only a little. I was soon to be fourteen.

"Okay then," she said when I didn't give her any real answer. "It's about Tyler," I heard her tell Terrence. "I've got a man here now, and her man is gone."

I was standing on the front steps, having gone outside to check the mail. I waited, listening to my mother, who always thought things had to do with having a man or wanting one.

"She's jealous," Terrence said, like I would hope for someone like him in my life.

"Naw, it's just being left out. If she's with Johnna, she can be the center of the world."

I walked into the house, my shirt catching on the door latch. I heard it stretch, then tear a little, the hem coming loose. "Damn it," I said.

"Was there any mail?" my mom asked. I'd only gone out there for something to do. I didn't think there would be any mail, and I don't think my mom did either. We were always talking without anything to say.

"Nope."

Johnna said she would come get me after school and I could set up at her place. "It's not permanent," she told me. I'd called her a few times, not totally unusual, but she acted surprised when she answered. She was always home if I called in the evening. My mom said something about that being sad, but she and Terrence were always home in the evening too, acting important because they had someone to act important in front of. I could tell Rainy was also getting the itch. She made a joke about going to stay with Johnna, but I set her straight.

"There's only one extra bedroom." I was pretty hard about it. "Only one."

"Don't worry, Meg." She was getting ready for work and doing her hair in the bathroom. Her mouth turned at the sides, and I knew I'd hurt her feelings.

Johnna had a new car when she pulled into the lot. It still had the license plate from the dealership. I could tell she was real proud; she sat up straight and was wearing new sunglasses. I could see where she'd pulled the sticker off and it left a smear.

"This is nice," I said. Once I got in and realized it wasn't a brand-new car, just new to Johnna. The seats had a couple of stains, and it smelled like an old man.

"Yeah. Been saving." She smiled. I had a big duffel bag with me, one Rainy had let me take. It was from when she played soccer in high school. Now she said she couldn't run across a soccer field to save her life, which I guess she thought was funny because she laughed even though I didn't. She'd been good at soccer, with her barrel chest and the way she ran with her fists closed.

"You been carrying that around all day?" Johnna asked.

"Yeah."

"S'not permanent," she said. "Just for summer, okay?" She'd told me that on the phone too. She didn't want me getting ideas. "Just 'til it settles." I guess she was talking about Tyler.

We'd pulled out onto the main road. Tuskin Middle sat on Madden Road, right next to the high school and across from the Marcuses' farm. Kids sometimes hung out next to the road and smoked cigarettes, dropping their butts over the Marcuses' fence. Mr. Marcus was old, but mean and heavy. He'd come out with a shotgun and chase everybody away. Once he even shot the gun up into the air to make a point about whose land that was and who was allowed to smoke on it—only him and brother, it seemed, because Mr. Marcus and his brother were pulling on Camels when he fired off.

The high school let out before the middle school, so we always saw the kids over there. Johnna made a right on Madden, punching it a little to show off the power of her new ride. I looked to my left, to watch Johnna's face because she was really enjoying herself, and there was Larisa, standing on the side of the road like she was a regular high school kid. She glowed pale in the afternoon sun, like nothing could touch her, not even its rays. I watched her closely as we drove past. Johnna didn't seem to notice, or she figured I was looking at her, admiring her new ways.

I turned in my seat, twisted my neck around as we sped past. Larisa wasn't looking at Johnna's car. I figured I was safe; she couldn't even follow me home, because she didn't know where I lived anymore.

I went back to my mom's house every once in a while and just for short visits. My mom came to see me at Johnna's and said Johnna needed to ease up on Pine-Sol. "It smells like a hospital in here—too much cleaner or something."

Johnna would smile and say we all have our own style.

"Just checking on Meg." My mom looked me up and down. "That Bagley girl still shows up all the time looking for you."

"What do you say?" I asked. Johnna had us all sitting on her white couches with the pale flowers. She'd made sweet tea. She was very formal now, not having to spray herself with perfume after her shift so she didn't smell like a fry basket. Her car was a sedan; she kept telling us, because I think she figured it was a good thing to have a sedan, much better than a truck or a station wagon or whatever it was my mom drove.

"I just tell her you moved out. She doesn't come to the door, just goes and stands by the trash cans. S'creepy, but I told her you were gone." My mom didn't seem to think this was very important and went straight to talking about how Terrence got a raise and was going to build an addition to the house.

"Why would he do that?" Johnna asked. "It's not your house."

My mom looked surprised. "I mean…it's just something nice, so it's a bigger place."

"I wouldn't put a penny into somewhere I was renting," Johnna said. She had her pinkie sticking out from her glass. "Not one penny."

"Well, you're all high and mighty now," my mom said. "Now that you're gonna have a mortgage."

I thought maybe they were fighting; it didn't sound too friendly, and the tea had a funny taste, like fake lemon. Johnna was trying her hardest with her ponytails and her scrubbing, but my mom was still in a cutoff shirt and not really buying the whole act. She kept talking about Terrence like he was better than a mortgage. I figured Johnna just didn't want to be like my mom anymore, even if I never thought they were all that much alike. They were more like things that get pushed together but repel; we did science experiments with magnets all the time at school. Every year, they got the big bucket of magnets out and acted like we were supposed to be so excited to learn the exact same thing again. My mom and Johnna were magnets in the bucket; sometimes you're friends with someone because you have to be—you're in the same container.

"Yeah, the police took that girl's aunt in. I'm telling you, you never hang out with a Bagley."

"They did?" I put my tea down and wiped my wet hand across the side of my head to slick my hair back. It was catching some air from the vent and waving like stringy feathers next to my eye.

"Yeah. You can't have that poison stuff in your house. They said she endangered the Cross boy. His parents made a big stink over it. You know they were kind of quiet at first, but I guess a lot doesn't really add up, and now they're mad that the woman was keeping a bunch of poisons in the house for the kids to get into. I guess I'm lucky you didn't end up dead, huh, Meg? But you never went over there, not to a Bagleys' house, no sirree."

Johnna looked at me because she knew that I was still very fragile; she'd said that. She could see that I was "walking on eggshells." She said that was why she let me come and live with her, because I was so "fragile." I hadn't argued with her about it. I did feel like I was about to break, but it was mostly because of Larisa. I couldn't think about Tyler with her around all the time. That was probably the point; she didn't want me having any ideas, even sad ones.

Things got a little more comfortable after we stopped sitting on Johnna's couches drinking the weird tea and went for a walk around her neighborhood. She was going to buy her house from her landlord, so now she was very interested in all the riffraff on the street. She said someone was getting evicted behind her, and good riddance because of his dog and he was probably a real townie. My mom and Johnna talked back and forth, mostly over my head, with my mom saying something about Terrence every chance she could and Johnna nodding and then mentioning having an appointment at the bank to show her finances.

When we got back to Johnna's, which I'd never noticed before was a funny green color with the paint peeling off at every angle, my mom said she would go home. "Okay, Meg." She reached out to hug me. "I'm real sorry about what happened to Tyler."

I looked at her as hard and as straight as I could, because it wasn't anything like her to say his name or to be sad about him. "Okay," I said.

"I can tell you're having a hard time."

"Yeah."

"They come and go," she said. She was still looking at me. She had a small freckle in her left eye. She had hazel eyes, which she always said were better than any other color because of how rare they are. I was getting so much taller that I was looking more at her eyebrows than anywhere else on her face. For most of my life, I'd been looking at her stomach or her neck, both of which were puckered like wet fingers and a dark mustard-brown color that she thought was very good-looking.

"I don't want men always coming and going," I said. I wasn't mad, but I wanted to be understood. It was hell-hole hot with the way the sun was sitting between the trees and glaring at us; one side of my face was getting scorched. I could feel my skin changing from the glare.

"Not just men, Meglet. Everyone." She was trying to be nice by spreading her wisdom, but it just made her seem mean. Maybe in her life, people would come and go because there was nothing to keep them around, but my life was going to be different.

It was a strange thing to do right after being mad that she said people always leave, but that night I told Johnna I was going for a walk, and I went and hitchhiked to Atlanta. I thought if I got molested and killed, then I could just go and hang out with Tyler. It sure would beat listening to my mom and Johnna talk about mort-gages and Terrence.

It was a woman who picked me up. She wasn't drinking a beer and barely talked to me. She was listening to a baseball game on the radio and every once in a while would mutter, "Goddammit" under her breath when the Braves did something bad. Terrence liked to watch baseball on TV. My mom had pretended to be really interested sometimes. I said something to Rainy about it like, "Why is Mom such a poser?" And Rainy said they watched baseball at the bar and that Mom knew a lot about it. I was feeling a little bad about making fun of her when the woman driving the car said, "Stand-up double," with a cheerful clip in her voice. I guessed that was a good thing. The woman told me her name was Carol and to let her know if I needed to go to the bathroom. She was a good bit older than my mom and had a sad, long look to her face and body with the way she slumped down over the steering wheel. I'd walked to the freeway and stood out there for about an hour before she pulled over. She said she was headed to the city. I said that's where I was going too. I hadn't even really thought about it.

I swear, as we were taking the exit that led to the bigger freeway, I saw Larisa standing on the side of the road, like she was waiting for me. Her bare legs hanging out of her dress, worms on a hook. She was just as she had been earlier that day outside of school, her face with its bruised, swollen quality, staring at me sniperlike from behind her hair. I'd shuddered in my seat, checking my neck for bullet holes.

The woman dropped me at a gas station in some nice part of town. "It's fine," she said of where she left me. She had gray hair, which she'd pulled back on her head in a frizzy braid. Her nose was like a beak, everything about her moving forward and down, slowly pecking, almost like she was trying to get one last bite of food before she died right there in the seat.

I had a few dollars with me and some coins, not feeling nervous at all about survival because I'd never thought I was living all that great anyway. I called Johnna's house, having planned to do that for about the last thirty minutes of the drive. Part of me thought I might just go back, see if Johnna could come and get me or ask about the bus. People took the bus sometimes—there was a stop a few miles outside of Tuskin.

"Hello?" Johnna said, sounding tired.

"It's Meg," I said.

"Where'd you go?"

"I'm in Atlanta somewhere."

"Oh, Meg, for crying out loud."

"I don't want to come back."

"I'm sure you don't, but what are you going to do? Did you hitch?"

"Yeah, some old lady."

"I thought you weren't doing that anymore."

"Yeah, but now Tyler's gone." The light above me buzzed. I looked up and saw the moths circling. I caught the faint outline of a bat above where the light faded into the night.

"I can call my brother," Johnna said. "Where are you?"

I stayed with Johnna's brother for a year before I moved in with a girl I'd met at the restaurant where I worked. She was older and thought I was too. I barely remember any of it. It was all I could do to keep breathing, but the breathing was better away from home. That's what kept me going.

41

I took Lucy to see Tyler's grave. He'd been buried in a cemetery off Crockett Road. It was a shaded place where the grass still grew, long and blue-like. There was a chain between two poles up at the end near the road to keep people from driving in there. He didn't have a fancy headstone, just a marker with his name, Tyler Armory Cross, and the dates he lived. That was it, no "beloved son" or other remarks. I'd only been there once before. It was shortly after it happened, when the earth was still roughed up from the digging. There was a small mound over where he lay.

"They accepted it," I told Lucy. "What they were told about him." I was talking about Tyler's parents. "It was different then. We kinda didn't know which way was up here." I suddenly sounded very Tuskin. "Police were scary. When somebody died, it was sad; there just wasn't all the thinking. That's what education will do for you, Lucy. You'll have the right to think." I shook my head slightly, having not planned to lecture her. "What I'm saying is that if this happened now, I would have done something about it."

"Weren't you really young?" Lucy asked.

"Well—yes." I paused. It was true. I had been young, and probably the least likely of anyone to be able to right a wrong. "My mother's friend Johnna never believed any of it. She used to call me sometimes in the middle of the night and tell me that she knew what happened. She didn't, but she knew better than anyone else."

"She died, didn't she?" Lucy asked.

"She did. Too young. She got sick before your mother was born. And that was that."

Lucy was more or less on house arrest, but it wasn't as restrictive as they first made it sound. Melanie Pollard was in juvenile detention, awaiting trial. She was going to be charged as an adult. Her eighteenth birthday was right around the corner. Her mother had come down to talk to me a few times before she put up a For Sale sign in their front yard. People said it would take the house a long time to sell, given everything that had happened.

"Anyway, he was my friend," I told Lucy. "My very best friend, a lot like you and Daniel…I think." I glanced furtively at her, not sure of the nature of any of her relationships, at least less sure of them than I'd been.

The day was unexpectedly crisp, or rather there was a wall of cool air coming from the line of trees that separated the graves from the road. Cedars are God's AC; their branches held hands and created a barrier. I felt we were in a secret grove, when really we were right off Milton—full of potholes and rambling trucks with cigarette butts and people calling each other idiots for slamming on brakes and the rest.

"Tyler," Lucy said. She'd been in counseling three days a week. She was not allowed to communicate with Daniel or Gracie, who were also out and under strict supervision. Melanie Pollard would be gone for a while. There was some insistence that she wanted to do this, that she had been looking for an excuse, that she had told people she hated Josh well before anything happened with Lucy. She was deemed sociopathic, a menace, toxic. Nina had certainly signed on to this theory—all good kids rounded up and infected by a bad one. It was the theory I had ascribed to myself. We had but a single conversation where I asked why the other kids went along with it. Nina stared at me, haughty and stricken. There were no answers, was the answer.

"He was a lot older than me, at that time. Now he and I would be considered the same age. It's funny how that is, with kids. Age differences are everything. When you grow up, you stop paying attention to them." I was rambling.

"What happened?" Lucy asked. I could tell she wasn't all that interested. She wasn't allowed to go anywhere without an approved adult, so the cemetery was going to have to be it. I didn't have any-thing else planned. I was compelled to have "lessons" be a part of everything we did. It was a time of transformation because of how responsible I felt. Nina was in the throes of anger and blame. All I could think was that I should have told Lucy more about my life, that I should have been honest, because then she wouldn't have been alone. I was having a hard time maneuvering between lessons and lectures, but I felt strongly that the effort was worth it—to make this time count, to be of some help to her.

"He was a real gentleman," I said, urged to make that clear. "He was a wonderful person. One of the best. There aren't a lot of people around like Tyler, not anymore. Not then, really, either. Folks my age always say shit like that, like 'things were so much better.' They weren't. Tuskin was a shithole; it's much nicer now." I paused and put my hand on Lucy's back, at the small, so much more tender than the shoulder. "Not everything, of course."

"I don't think he meant to," Lucy said.

"Tyler? No, he didn't. He didn't kill himself—that was the thing. It was what we let everyone think, but that's not what happened. He was just fine. He was." The shame came back. It had been there the whole time, connected to different feathers on the same bird.

"No," Lucy said. "Josh. He did a bad thing, but I don't know if he really got it."

"Well." I frowned. "I don't forgive him, Lucy."

"No," she said distantly. "No." Her hair had grown, and with it the shape of her ponytail had changed. It had gone from a kind of cute, bubblelike thing on the back of her head that made me think she was effervescent or floating to a long rope of hair that went down between her shoulder blades, slicked and severe, like a sword.

"Tyler got killed," I said. "My friend gave him poison, and I never told anyone. Not a soul, until now."

"I told Melanie," Lucy said. I could tell she was going through it too.

"I should have told someone what really happened," I said. I didn't want the moment, but it was slipping from me regardless, my redemption. I don't know what I expected Lucy to do; she couldn't offer absolution, and it would have been slanted and vicious of me to seek it from her. I suppose I wanted to make her feel better, but somehow she was heading in a different direction, turned on a side road I hadn't seen, barreling.

"I shouldn't have told Melanie," Lucy said.

"Okay." I clasped my hands in front of me. I wasn't praying; I didn't know how. "I watched him die. I knew he didn't die in that ditch. I knew they took him and dumped him there to get him off their property. I watched him die in the grass. Larisa gave him something and told him to take it before we kissed the snake's neck, but it was real poison. She knew it would kill him; that's why she didn't tell me." I was vomiting the words, hurling them at Lucy as if, by launching them away from me like cannons, I would somehow make it right or make her understand. I didn't know what she needed to understand either. I was suddenly very selfish. "I could have done something," I said very finally. "But I didn't."

"I didn't either," Lucy said. "But it wasn't grass. Just the seat of his car. There was so much blood. I knew we couldn't take it back, you know?" She hadn't looked at me once. "It was like I didn't know what I'd agreed to. You know?"

I inhaled, the sword of her hair stuck in my throat. I could breathe around it but for the blood from the cuts down my windpipe. "Yes," I said. "Yes, I do know."

"It was like I said okay, but then we were in his car, and I hated him but I didn't want to do that. I don't want to do that." She shook her head like she'd just figured out that she didn't like slitting throats and going to court to explain herself. "I wouldn't have done it."

"Right." I looked at Tyler's grave. "I don't think he thought I was going to save him," I said. "I can remember him looking at me and…he was lost. I wasn't really the person he wanted to see. I was just there. He was so confused."

"Right." Lucy had started crying, but it was timid, hiding from exposure by being silent and slow to trickle to her chin.

"I just wanted to show you that I have regrets too."

"Right." She scratched her chin.

"Things I can hardly live with."

It was quiet for a moment. There were cars passing, but they sounded like they were on a different road from the one we were standing on, hidden and headed in the wrong direction, away from us. Everything was going away from us; even the grass on the ground parted as if blown in multiple directions, a small pock in the middle. I might have thought there was something significant in the center, but it was nothing. Tyler was no more. He'd long disappeared into the earth. They say the dirt in Georgia is red, but it's brown as anything where they bury people. No red clay preserved Tyler or anyone else. It's not that romantic.

"But that's not it, is it, Tata?" Lucy said. She looked at me, our eyes meeting. "That's not it, is it?"

I put my hand at my throat; there was no one to slice it—not Lucy, not me. I didn't have the nerve. "Oh, I don't know," I said. "It's one of those things I feel bad about—but then again, she had it coming, didn't she?"

"Who's 'she'?" Lucy asked.

"Oh." I put my hand to my mouth, surprised at what I'd said. "Never mind that."

I'd run into Detective Adam at the cell phone store the day before. I'd told Nina I was done with the whole thing and that she could return it. She said that's not how it worked and now I was stuck with the phone. I drove up there and told the young kid working behind the counter that I wanted it turned off.

"I'm pretty sure it's broken anyway," I said. He picked the phone up and shrugged. What did he care?

"I can cancel your service, but I can't take the phone back."

"I'll use it for target practice," I told him. Neither of us laughed.

He looked to be about Melanie Pollard's age. I thought I might ask him if he knew her, but Adam Rinaldi walked in the store. I recognized his voice when he said thank you to the kid at the counter who'd told him to let him know if he needed help.

I turned around. Adam was thumbing his way through a stack of phone cases. "Ma'am," the boy said.

"Hold on," I answered. He was a red-faced young man with gelled hair, very clean cut and wiry—the way all young people looked, like their bodies were processing life at ten times the pace mine was. I'd slowed to a screeching halt; the only overactive part of me was my mouth trying to keep up with my mind. "Detective Rinaldi," I said rather loudly.

"Yeah," he looked up. "Oh. Ms. Gregory."

"So what do we do when we run into each other?" I smiled, but he did not. "Are we friendly?"

"Well, that's up to you." He looked at me blankly, as though our trouble had passed and with it any recollection of my significance.

We stood staring at one another over backup batteries and charging cables for quite some time. I felt the urge to avoid blinking but finally closed my eyes in defeat. "I'm so sorry," I said. I might have been willing him to say that to me, but instead it came out of my mouth—a shared sentiment that found the path of least resistance to unfurl between us.

"I am too," he said. "I'm sorry about what happened to your granddaughter."

"Yes. We stopped nothing, didn't we?"

His face dropped slightly. I'm sure he'd been hoping that I would end the conversation with apologies and that we'd leave the cell phone store both feeling lighter and that we'd done all we could.

"I'm not sure what you mean." He reached for a cord and checked the price.

"No one stopped that boy from hurting Lucy, and no one stopped those kids from taking him out."

"Murdering him," Adam Rinaldi said, correcting me.

"Lucy didn't…" I stopped talking. His face was again fading into a shadow of familiarity. If he held his chin a certain angle, he appeared to be mocking me—that, or urging himself to tolerate me for just a little bit longer. "I'm sure I know you," I said instead. "I'm certain of it."

"You do know me," he said, and I felt a twinge of hope. "We know each other now." It was a disappointing answer. I heard the ding of the doorbell but didn't take my eyes off Adam. Not immediately. He looked over my shoulder and allowed his face to slide into a lazy grin. "Hey, Dad," he said. I felt the warm air from outside leak through the now-closing door, slivers of it finding their way to the backs of my arms. I was suddenly hot and a little dizzy. I took a step back and turned toward the door, which was now sealed shut, the air no longer mixing, the outside trapped at the handle, helpless to pull. It was the Great Dane man from Larisa's house. He gave Detective Rinaldi a hug. I stood very still, only my right hand shaking. It had been the hand that answered the phone when they called about Larisa. It was the one that had turned the knob on my apartment door and driven to Tuskin to seal her fate. It was reminding me of the power that I held. My uselessness gone in an instant. All I had to do was say that I saw her there. And that's what I'd done.

My mother had called me one day when I was living in Atlanta. It was before I met Ferrol and was working with Janine at the third of five restaurants I would work at in the city; then it was Macy's, and then it was Ferrol. We didn't talk much; I kind of felt like I did my mom a favor by leaving, and she never really dispelled me of that notion. She was grateful to have gotten rid of the responsibilities that were weighing her down. In the end I don't think she thought she was doing me any good anyway. She couldn't be convinced that she was of any use to me. I didn't want to work at Shakers like Rainy did, and that was kind of all she had to offer.

"That Bagley girl's in trouble," she said. I could tell my mom had something on her mind the whole first part of the conversation. She kept clicking her tongue and saying "Mm-hmm" to my every response. Finally, during a long-enough break in whatever we were talking about—probably boxed hair dyes or the vacation Terrence was going to take them on; he overpromised and made bold proclamations about going off to exotic locales and then ended up taking her to Macon to stay at the Ramada—she said, "Oh yeah. Big trouble this time." Her aunt had been released shortly after being picked up. The stuff about her keeping poison in the house didn't land her in jail for very long. Tyler's family had been devastated when she got out and had even started saying they didn't think he was a bit depressed and that the aunt should get charged with murder. It was Rainy who would usually give me updates; most of the time she didn't sound like she really understood what she was hearing. Eventually, though, the Crosses moved to Tennessee or Alabama or wherever they were from. They left Tyler in Tuskin, his grave a reminder of what happened there and why they didn't stay.

I shared an apartment with Janine and another girl, Hailey, at this time. Hailey was ahead of us in every way. Even on a strict budget like we all were, she'd find a way to dress to the nines and reuse old stuff to make her bedroom look like a magazine. We lived in that apartment for two years. I found out later that Hailey got married and had a whole bunch of kids and was living in Texas.

No one was home when my mom called, just me. Janine was dating a guy at the time who did deliveries around the city, and she liked to ride with him for whatever reason. They'd get Cokes and go from place to place. She said she loved the air-conditioning in his truck and the radio. Janine didn't have cares, just interests. I could never tell if I was interested in something or cared about it and figured that I was mostly nerves and worry. I was too nervous to be interested in anything that wasn't making my stomach clench.

"They pulled a body out of that house."

"Oh." I swallowed.

"Yeah, it was some woman the aunt knew. Vicky something. I guess she was over at the house all the time. Anyway, Kim Bagley said Larisa killed her."

"Oh."

"Yeah, it's a big stink."

"I'm sure," I said.

"Police everywhere, even though it's an old body. Been there a while, like years. Somebody came to the house to read the meter or something and saw bones in the crawl space. Can you even believe it." It was a not a question.

"How'd she die?" I was sitting on my bed in my room. Hailey was home but quiet. She'd been in the kitchen earlier, making something that required soaking beans and cutting onions. The apartment had a funny, briny smell because of it.

"Throat slit, I guess, but I don't know how they can tell now—somebody said there was a chip on the neck bone, cut so deep there was a chip."

"Yeah." I pulled my legs up to my chest. I took special care of my feet since I only had jobs where I had to stand. I always thought of Johnna when I wore flops to let my toes wiggle. The one place had let me wear sandals, but then one of the bus boys dropped a glass on his foot and got shards stuck at every angle, so they said close-toed after that. "Yeah," I said again.

"Just bones, I guess, but there was a knife cut on one of the bones—neck bone, like almost clear off. So they figured out it was this Vicky woman who went missing a long time ago, and they did the thing where they examine it, and sure enough."

"Oh, wow." I didn't want to hear about the neck bone anymore; I couldn't figure out why she kept talking about it.

"They're saying it was around when that buddy of yours died. It was that long ago."

"Tyler." I said his name but it sounded like breathing, no shape or anything from the throat. The air came up from my lungs and went out of my mouth.

"Yeah, so the aunt's, like, turned her in or something. Larisa."

I heard Hailey. She was near the front door. "I'm going to Ace!" she said. "There's still roaches in the cabinets."

"Yeah!" I was in agreement about the roaches. We'd find them everywhere. When you went to get a dish out of the cupboard or opened the cabinet in the bathroom, there'd be a handful of them squirming and darting. It made me sick to my stomach. So much about life was this way; I felt almost constantly sick, either from the bugs or the news.

"What's that?" my mom asked.

"Roaches all over the place."

"It's the weather," my mom said. "Hot and wet."

We'd all talked about moving, but Hailey was thinking of going off on her own, and Janine and I could only afford the place split three ways. We'd rented a studio for a while, the two of us, but that was hard. We were on each other's nerves, edgy and always blaming the other for things we couldn't find.

"Well, so somebody might try and talk to you," my mom said, finally getting to her point. "The police were over here."

"Oh, they were?" I could now hear my voice coming from another part of the room. I was hiding in the closet. It was just like when I was at home and Larisa would show up at my window, which was in the same corner as my small closet in my mom's house. If there'd been a closet door, it would have covered the window when open. I had no way to block her out. And here she was again. I was fifty miles away, and here she was again. Our apartment was on the ground floor; she could have walked up to my room just like she used to. I'd see shadows sometimes at night, people moving through the complex. It always made me shift in my bed. She couldn't have found me, I'd tell myself.

"Yeah, so I thought I'd let you know. I had to give them your address and all that."

"Oh."

"You know Tyler's family is long gone. They left awhile back. Over in Alabama now or something."

"Tennessee," I said, because I was pretty sure that was where they were from. Or maybe it was Alabama. I should have known.

"Maybe. Anyway, the officer fella didn't ask me about that, but he said that somebody told him you used to run around with Larisa then and that you might know. I wasn't sure what to say, so I just told him where you were." There was an odd pleasure in her voice in telling me this, like the association with these terrible things made us important, or it made my mother important to have news to share. "And anyway, Rainy's moved. She's in Macon now. I told her how nice it was when we were there at the Ramada, so she got a job at this preschool place, or day care, whatever. Her friend's working there too."

"Oh, that's great."

"So I'm on my own in Tuskin now. My girls are all gone."

"Right." I looked outside. It had rained all night but was now glowing sunny. Everything looked as though it had been painted in slippery acrylic. We talked for a little longer, but I wasn't paying attention to anything either of us said. I remember hanging up and thinking that I would say she did it. I would tell them Larisa did it.

42

1980

Y es." I said the word forty-six times. I counted in my head. Yes, I saw her. Yes, I would testify. Yes, she hid the body. Yes, I saw her do it. Yes, I will say it in court. Yes, it happened right after Tyler Cross died. Yes. Yes. Yes.

They called me at first, I suppose trying to decide if it was a good idea to come to Atlanta to talk to me.

"There's a message from the police," Janine said when I got home from work. "From Tuskin."

"Oh." I tried to act surprised. I waited until both Janine and Hailey were securely in their bedrooms before calling the number back. The phone was in the kitchen. I died on that hill— that the phone should always be in the kitchen. It was where all the important calls of my life had taken place, in various kitchens, in homes I rented. When Ferrol and I moved in together, I was still a renter. It was his house, and there was a phone in the kitchen. My mother told me she never wanted to speak to me again on it.

I muttered my responses into the receiver. This was not the conversation with forty-six *yes*es. This was when I agreed to go to Tuskin and say yes to everything they wanted to know. I would put the nail in the coffin. Larisa never got out. She got sick in prison and died there. It was not long after Lucy's ordeal that I heard that. It was something said in passing. Larisa Bagley died. She had some sort of decline. It was her blood; in the end it poisoned her. I could have told them that was going to happen.

I agreed to come to the station the following day. They had Larisa in custody. "How old is she?" I asked before I hung up with the officer, a man named Chet. I didn't know whether Chet was his first or last name. "Larisa."

"What's that now?" Chet and I had had a hard time under-standing one another. Even when I said "Yes," he would ask me to repeat myself. "What's that now?" he kept saying.

"I just wondered how old she is."

"Ahhh, she's… Let's see. Twenty-three."

"Okay," I said. Tyler would have been twenty-three. The fact that she had an age made her real; everything else about her had been almost and barely, like some person caught between worlds. I had often wondered if I'd imagined her.

"Yep, twenty-three in January," he said, perhaps guessing that I needed further confirmation.

When I got to the station the following day, Detective Chet told me that Larisa had confessed.

"About—" I stopped myself, knowing that I shouldn't. "She did?"

"Yes. She signed a confession about twenty minutes before you got here, so I'm afraid it was a fool's errand. I still want to take your statement though. It's important for us to have that on record."

"Oh." I went pale. "No," I said. "No, I think I'd rather not."

"Well, she confessed because we told her you were coming." He was a tall man, built like a brick, with sharp shoulders and a pouty mouth. He was imposing but gentle, the kind of person my mother would have called "a gentle giant." She'd always wanted to be with a gentle giant, someone who could ward off the men with their grabby hands and catcalling, tugging on her clothes and trying to get her to let them touch her. Rainy said that. I wasn't sure why seeing Detective Chet made me think of it; maybe it was that he would never like someone like my mom. She'd been lucky to get Lon and even Terrence. Most guys didn't want to date the girl from Shakers, especially not the one who was too old to dance on the tables anymore.

"Can my statement be anonymous?" I asked.

"Well, no. We can't do that. You'll have to sign it. And she already knows who said it, if that's what you're worried about." He had been sitting behind his desk; the way we were talking was informal, like he was asking me about my summer plans. I didn't have any. It was July and felt like it was too late to have plans. It wasn't like when I was a kid and school was out, and I could look forward to it and think of ways to pass the time that didn't have anything to do with school. But now, time just passed on its own, without me even knowing it was moving forward. There were no blocks or breaks, just long stretches and me thinking that I would never have to go back. And here I was. In Tuskin.

"I have to go to the bathroom," I said, standing up and bumping my knee on the front of his desk. It was made of metal filing-cabinet material like everything else in the room. "I'll be right back." I walked out of the police station and to my car. Janine and I had Toyotas. We joked it had been a two-for-one; it wasn't, but they were both beat to shit and junkers. I was so happy to have my own car though. I'd had to take my driving test three times before I passed. I couldn't get the turns right and kept hitting curbs and bushes along the road. I'd even sideswiped another person taking their test.

When I got back to the apartment in Atlanta, I went to my room and sat with the door shut and shades pulled for three hours. When it was time to go to work at Paradise Bar and Grill, where Janine and I worked, I called the restaurant and said I was sick. "I threw up," I told John, the manager.

"I hope you're not pregnant," he said, laughing. He'd put his hands on Janine's waist a few times since we started working there. I figured it was his dream that someone should worry they were pregnant after a night with him.

"I'm not," I said. "I ate something bad."

Later, when I should have been at work, the phone rang in the kitchen. Hailey was home but doing her toenails. I jumped up at the sound but then walked very slowly toward the kitchen. I'd been sitting on the couch with Hailey with a blanket pulled up around me, claiming to have a chill even though I was sweating. I don't know why I thought it mattered; Hailey didn't pay that much attention to me and Janine anyway, and thought Paradise was a dump. She was always telling us to quit. She worked at the Ritz and did gangbusters, a lot more money in less nights.

"Hello?" I said. I'd waited long enough that I thought it would stop ringing. I let it go at least eight times. Hailey said I was gonna miss it, but she was stuck with her foot up because of the polish.

"Were you here?" It was my mom.

"Where?" I asked. I put my fingers in my mouth and started gnawing. I only chewed my nails once in a while. Something had to get underneath my skin pretty bad for me to start that up.

"Here!" she said. "I heard Larisa Bagley's going to jail for a hundred years and that you were here."

"Who is it?" Hailey asked.

"Nobody," I said.

"What?" my mother asked.

"Nothing, Mom. Yeah, I went there."

"Did you tell the police something about that woman whose body they found?"

I didn't answer.

"Meg."

"What?"

Hailey had turned around to look at me over the back of the couch. She had the polish brush in her hand.

"Meg, did you tell the police that she killed that woman?"

"I don't know."

"You don't know if you told the police that?"

"They asked me some questions."

"Meg. Did you see that Bagley girl murder someone?" Her voice was scratchy and low. There was no background noise. I didn't even hear the television. "Meg?"

"I just told them that I remember some stuff."

"Meg—you're saying that you saw her kill someone and you just went on with things?"

"I didn't go on with things," I said, feeling like I was about to lay it all on the line. Like I could tell her something, finally. There'd been mountains inside me, clogging all airways, making it hard for me to see, hear, talk. "I just haven't been myself," I said, as if that mattered.

"I'm trying to understand how you saw somebody get murdered and then came home and watched TV with me and my husband and never said a word about it." She called Terrence her husband now. They were married, and boy, did she insist that everyone know it. "My husband," she'd say as though someone was arguing with her about it.

"Or," she said more like an accusation, "you lied to the police because you don't like that girl."

Somehow she'd figured both things out with me seventy miles away, hidden from view all these years. I'd left thinking I extinguished it. I'd put it out, but there were still embers. Things like this don't go away; they flicker on and off, before clinging to a sleeve and burning a small hole. Something ruined. Again.

"They're bad people," I said. It was a direct quote.

"Right. And I told you that. I told you to stay away from them. I told you I didn't want her at the house."

"Mom, that was a hundred years ago."

"Meg, what happened?"

"Nothing. I just told them what I knew."

"Meg, I swear to God, if you are lying to me or lying to the police"—she stopped to take a breath, such was her dismay—"I swear I will never speak to you again. Never. And you could go to jail yourself. You know that, right? You can't lie to the police. I swear to God I'll never breathe your name, Meg. I swear to God."

"I didn't lie," I said, lying through my teeth. She couldn't understand that this was the only way I could get Larisa back without having to say I left Tyler in the field. She would never be able to grasp how hard it was for me to live with him lying in the grass, turning blue while I was running the other way.

That was the first and not the last time my mother promised to never speak to me again; they were empty threats, but they did move us further and further apart. You can't tell someone they're dead to you and then call up the next day to discuss pancake batter. "I'll never speak to you again!" It was what she said when she wasn't sure she ever wanted to. She'd said it to the news of my pregnancy with Nina. She did not think I would make a good mother, given my past and what I had done. It was another thing Larisa had ruined for me, my mother's good opinion of the kind of mother I would be. In the end, though, she was right.

43

Nina and I had lunch in town. We left Lucy at the house, which we were not supposed to do. "I think she's fine," Nina said. "She's in her room all the time anyway, doing her art therapy or whatever it is." She wasn't being snide; art therapy was Lucy's favorite of all the therapies. She'd made dozens of watercolors; some of them were excellent, all of them mildly disturbing. I'd told Nina she didn't fee lovable. It was what I gathered from her work, or perhaps I associated that with myself and chose to see it in her paintings. I did make everything about myself, it seemed. Nina's therapist had been right. I had but a single lens—my fractured one.

"Nina," I said as though we hadn't already been talking over clam chowder and saltine crackers for half an hour.

"Yeah." She drew shapes on the side of her glass, finding good use for the condensation.

"I do talk to my mother sometimes," I said.

"Okay?" Her forehead collapsed in the middle, where the disquiet goes.

"We had a falling out… Well, more than one, but she didn't keep her word to never speak to me again."

"I know." She was relieved, as this was not as serious as I'd originally made it sound. "I've heard you talking to her."

"You have?"

"I don't know, Mom." She took her hand off the glass and waved it at me. "I don't know. I don't know Grandma, so…whatever." There was more waving and dismissing.

"I—" I stopped myself. "I just didn't want you to think I was that awful a daughter." This was not what I had planned to say, but I felt very suddenly and very certainly that I was not going to tell Nina. I had told Lucy, some of it—my unburdening had been on her. Nina had already bore the brunt of the way I felt about myself. She'd endured the marriage to Ferrol, and the end of it, and all my recovering from the letdown that I had not, in fact, recovered from anything. I would spare her the rest.

"I don't," Nina said. She was uninvested.

"I should have done better by you." This popped out of my mouth like bulge over a pants waist—one day it's there and you can't put it back.

"I think that's what every mom thinks," Nina said.

"Somehow this is all my fault though."

She sighed. "Please don't make everything about yourself again."

"Okay." I put the tips of my fingers on my lips, willing myself to silence. I would have to live with it. "The thing is, someone told me that someone was going to hurt me, as an excuse for him dying. It's such a strange parallel, don't you think?"

Nina looked up at me sleepily; I understood she was using medication to curb the panic. It had been noticeable in certain settings. "I don't know," she said. "He did do something bad to Lucy."

"Lucy has never said that," I argued. It was true. She'd never told anyone what happened between her and Josh. Even Dr. Cheek had commented that her refusal to admit it was troubling.

"It's as though she's been told it was going to happen," Dr. Cheek had told both me and Nina during a conference regarding Lucy's progress. "That's the way she talks about it, in a future tense." I remember asking Nina about that on the way home; Lucy had stayed behind to do one of several therapies.

"No, no, she had an exam with the doctor." Nina was effusive. "They proved it. It was part of her evidence." Nina was resolute each and every time. There was nothing else to discuss.

"I don't think anyone is saying she's lying, Nina," I'd said. Nina was driving her purple car, sliding about the road like she was drunk or racing home in a hurry to get that way as fast as possible. "I think she's got the experience locked up, like she's dealing with it that way. It's something that was going to happen. That's why they did what they did—I'm worried about the way she's—"

"Mom! She was attacked!" Nina slammed her hands on the steering wheel. I understood the conversation was over.

And we'd never been told of any incontrovertible evidence. I'd been told that Melanie Pollard's story about what happened to Lucy had been confirmed by the other kids. It was too long after the fact for there to be anything medically. We were kind of glad for that detail; anything else would have implied a severity we were not eager to imagine.

"I'm just wondering if there is a coping issue here. She still isn't saying what's happened to her."

"Why are you doing this?" Nina looked at the ceiling, hoping to find God so she could ask him to strike me down. Her spoon fell from the edge of her bowl and landed on the table in a fuzzy mound of cooling soup. "Why are you making this worse? This is what you do."

"No, no…I've misspoken. I'm just very worried that she's keeping this inside. I want her to—" I didn't continue. I didn't know what I wanted her to do. I placed my spoon neatly next to my bowl. I wasn't trying to make a point. I was very weary of making points. "It's just that I had something similar happen, Nina."

"Oh." She was mildly interested, in an appropriately solemn way. "I'm sorry, Mom."

"Well, it wasn't that, but I never told you about my friend Tyler who died. And my friend who did it, she said he was going to hurt me." There. I'd said it.

"Your friend did what?"

"She killed him."

"Where is this friend now?" Nina asked. Her face had a shade of disbelief, like a caul over her expression, as though she'd gone flat. She was collapsed, a crushed can, nothing inside anymore.

"She died—fairly recently, from what I understand." I pushed myself back from the table to stand.

We left the restaurant after agreeing that soup was the best lunch even in warm weather. It felt wonderful to have a conversation about something meaningless. Soup. I'd mentioned needing to get some weed killer from the store and that the bunion on my left big toe was finally going away from the patches Nina had suggested. I could have gone on like that for days. Lucy's face flashed in my mind between comments about the busted flag on my mailbox and why was the coupon section in the weekend paper so small now? They were complaints, but I was happy to have them.

I hugged Nina before we left. It was a most natural moment, languorous and easy like nothing I ever did, especially not with Nina. "You're so thin," I said. She was always thin, but not like this. This was thin from sadness, not rage. "Sorry," I said. I didn't want to complain about her. I only wanted to be helpful. I was tired of making points and tired of having some quip to make. Quippy old women are a dime a dozen. I smiled. "That was nice," I said. She hadn't responded about being thin. She'd probably thought it was a compliment.

"Yes," Nina said distantly. "I'm going to go home and check on Lucy."

"Bye then, Nina."

About halfway home, at the intersection of Dunedin and Wages, I stopped the car in the middle of the road. Something bad was in my throat—a sword, the shame, some moment. Tyler on top of me in the bed with his hand over my mouth and me crying. Someone honked from behind me, but I didn't even know what it meant; this violent noise had no meaning.

"What did you do?" I said to the steering wheel, seeing Larisa's face in the window of my bedroom, her mouth in a twisted knot with broken teeth and a slivered lip. "What did you do to us?" She was watching.

No funny business.

Reading Group Guide

1. Meg is a very complex character, both as a young girl and as an older woman. How would you describe her? What would you say are some of the differences and similarities between her younger and older self?

2. When she first hears about Josh's murder, Meg is adamant that Lucy could not have done it. Do you suspect Lucy? Do you have any of your own theories as to what could have happened?

3. Meg and Nina approach Lucy's situation in very different ways, causing friction in their relationship. What is your first impression of Nina? How is she different from Meg? Why do you think the two of them are so dissimilar?

4. In the present day, Meg often complains about the effects of aging on her body and her mind. Why might she be frustrated with aging? Have you ever felt something similar? Why might it be hard to accept our bodies changing?

5. Despite how tumultuous her relationship with Nina is, Meg approaches her and Lucy's relationship very differently. Why do you think Meg is able to be better for Lucy than Nina? How did her own relationship with her mother influence her?

6. How reliable do you find Meg as a narrator? Discuss.

7. Johnna and Meg's mother both act as maternal figures in her life, but they both act and treat Meg very differently. How do you think this impacts her in the long term?

8. Whether it's Lon, Tyler, or Ferrol, Meg's view of the men in her life is complicated at best. Discuss the different relationships she has with these men and what they might indicate about her perspective.

9. So much of how Meg defines herself is built on where she's from. How do you feel that the places we grow up shape us? Define us? How did your childhood town shape you, if it all?

10. Throughout the book, Meg struggles with her own self confidence. She's very hard on herself, even as a child. How do you feel this shapes her decisions?

11. Tuskin is such a crucial part of the story, and the land underscores so many of Meg's experiences. How does the setting add to the narrative?

12. Do you think Meg should have shared her past with Lucy? Would it have changed anything? Discuss.

A Conversation with the Author

Your books often have a Southern setting, and this one is no exception! What about the South inspires you? Do you feel like it lends itself to mystery?

I tend to embrace sadness in my work, and although I am happy as a clam living in the South, I find it has its own unique brand of sad that I could write about for a hundred years and never tire of exploring. Whereas the bleak winter months in a place like Ohio or the Dakotas would lend itself to a certain type of storytelling, the relentless, draping growth and broiling heat of Southern settings is perfect for secrets and hidden tragedies, sordid relationships, and repressed memories. Georgia is a rolling, overgrown tangle of trees and hills—you can't see straight here, which makes it an ideal place for a mystery. One never really knows what is right in front of them.

Meg is such a complex, layered, and complicated character, both as a child and as an adult woman. What was it like to write the same character at two very different stages in life?

I tried to capture Meg's rawness in both stages of her life. She never had a chance to refine herself, so her survival mechanisms as a child remained in her adult life. She seems to face everything with a helpless anger. When the problems are Lucy's, she has to find a way for these feelings of impotent rage to help her rather than make her more impulsive. People do change and grow and mature and learn, but I think most wisdom comes from knowing who we are and learning to make the best of it.

The relationships between mothers, daughters, and granddaughters are an undercurrent of this story. What motivated you to write about these kinds of relationships?

Unconditional love and unbreakable tethers are endlessly interesting to me. When we don't feel we have a choice but are compelled to act in certain ways, great, if tragic, stories are made. Even though Meg doesn't have the strongest relationship with her daughter or her own mother, these are people she cannot abandon. She acts for their benefit or with them in mind, whether she wants to or not. With Lucy, her bond is super charged by a desire to protect what was not protected for her and to change the course of her family.

The Sins of Summer Daughters **is your fourth book. Has your writing process changed over time?**

Definitely. I work much more efficiently but have lost the wind-in-my-hair devil-may-care attitude toward it, which is sometimes a good thing and sometimes makes me feel a little too serious. I still allow myself a lot of room to breathe when I am writing, but I can tell when something isn't working much earlier than I used to be able to. This is useful but also like finding out the Santa at the mall isn't the real Santa—I am forced to be more realistic with myself and my work. I am a far more grounded writer now, which is probably a positive.

This book has such an amazing twist! When you started writing, did you have that in mind, or did it come to you the more you wrote?

My characters tell me what happens, so the more I get to know them, the more I am certain of what will become of their story. I knew Meg was holding onto something even heavier than her dysfunctional childhood and bad marriage, but I wasn't exactly sure what it was until I delved deeper into her confusion and despair over what happened to Tyler. It was a twist for me too. I was shaken upon realizing how it would all come together and after fully understanding how much Meg had suffered.

What do you hope readers take away from this book?

As always, I hope readers think deeply about something they might have only peripherally explored before reading it. I never seek to change anyone's mind about anything but rather hope to make them examine how they *really* feel or what they *really* think. I love to be made uncomfortable with ideas that I haven't fully engaged with before or even better when I react to something differently than I thought I would. I am always hoping a reader closes my book (at the end please!) with the sensation that they have been nudged. The biggest compliment a person can give me about my writing is that they couldn't stop thinking about it.

Acknowledgments

I would like to thank the phenomenal team at Sourcebooks, who has treated me with such kindness and sincere consideration in every facet of my career, especially MJ Johnston, who dove right in and helped me keep doing my thing. My tirelessly reasonable agent, Alyssa Jennette, who has consistently provided me with a safe place to land and the best advice an author can ask for. And of course my family, who has never wavered in their belief that I could do this—you are everything to me. A thank-you to all the readers who have given my work a chance…to everyone who ever picked up and read one of my books, invited me to a book club, had me at their store or at a community event. I am so grateful and humbled by the enthusiastic and devoted literary community who has been so welcoming to me. You gave this dreamer a chance; I hope I have been able to properly convey both my gratitude and my respect.

About the Author

© Megan Dougherty

Lo Patrick's first novel, *The Floating Girls*, was a finalist for the Townsend Prize for Fiction and a *Reader's Digest* Editors' Pick. She lives in Georgia with her husband and two children.